Carol Wensby-Scott  Sussex. Before beco antiquarian booksho was published in 197 trilogy about the Perc̲ at the same time moving to Northumberland, the home of the Percys.

By Carol Wensby-Scott

The Percy Trilogy
LION OF ALNWICK
LION DORMANT
LION INVINCIBLE

*

PROUD CONQUEST
COAL BARON

CAROL WENSBY-SCOTT

Lion Invincible

Futura

To the memory of Richard Plantagenet,
King of England:
neither saint nor devil but merely human

A Futura Book

Copyright © Karel Wensby-Scott 1984

First published in Great Britain in 1984
by Michael Joseph Ltd

This edition published in 1985
by Futura Publications, a Division of
Macdonald & Co (Publishers) Ltd
London & Sydney
Reprinted 1988

ISBN 0 7088 2562 1

Printed and bound in Great Britain by
Collins, Glasgow

Futura Publications
A Division of
Macdonald & Co (Publishers) Ltd
66–73 Shoe Lane
London EC4P 4AB

A member of Pergamon MCC Publishing Corporation plc

PERCY, NEVILLE AND MORTIMER.

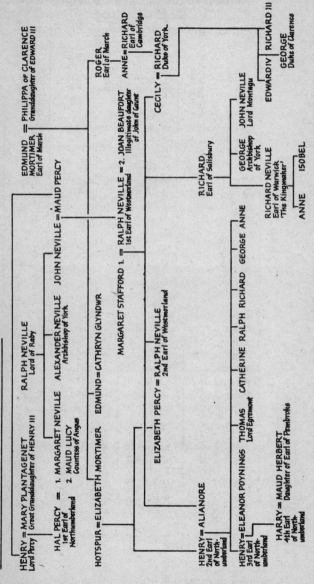

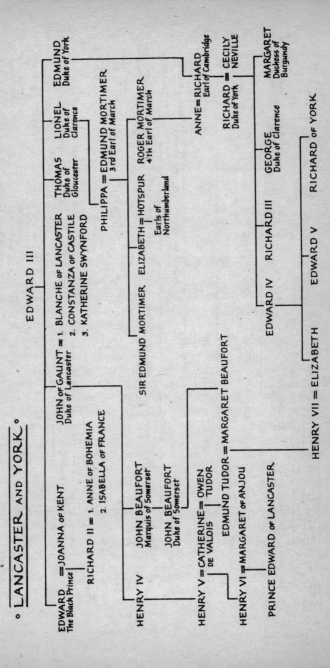

° LANCASTER AND YORK °

EDWARD III

1469—1475

> The Charioteer of York will soothe the
> people. He will throw his master down
> and climb up into the chariot he is driving.
> He will draw his sword and fill with blood
> the ruts made by his wheels.
>
> Prophecy of Merlin

The old priest wept openly as he read the office for the dead and his tired voice tolled like a mourning bell in the overwhelming silence of the room. Occasionally, his eyes would lift from the illuminated psalter between his hands and dwell resentfully upon the woman who knelt outside the perimeter of the candles' glow. Then they would stray to the frail shrouded creature that lay between them and fill once more with hot angry tears.

He blew his nose loudly on the sleeve of his gown. 'Of your charity, pray for the soul of the lady Alianore Percy. May God in his mercy grant her peace.' He had laid a subtle emphasis upon the word *charity* and again he raised reproachful eyes to the woman's face. He doubted though that her conscience would be troubled. Thick-skinned these Yorkists were, at least this one was — Cecily Neville, Duchess of York and mother to the King of England, yet she could see her own sister die in want. And then to come now, when all was past help, flaunting herself in furs and jewels when they'd been hard put to find a decent gown in which to bury her own close kin. Ill-gotten gains they were too, he thought bitterly. The profits of murder and mayhem, the hoard of the Pharisees. His gentle soul writhed in outrage and once more he lowered his weeping eyes to the cold dead face of his lady.

1

He had loved her for all of his long and simple life, ever since she had come to Leconfield as Northumberland's young and unwanted Neville bride. He had been a sickly child, not up to the fourteen hours a day in his father's field and it was she who had taken him and set him to the easier life of clerking at Beverley and brought him back five years later to serve the manor as its priest. How long ago now? For longer than the span of his confused and uncertain memory. Time lost its perspective when you were very old. A year could pass as swiftly as a day, an hour could stretch to infinity. He was not even sure of how old he was himself. He knew he had been born the year King Henry Bolingbroke had died. Usurper Bolingbroke he was called then, before his son Harry of Monmouth had dazzled their eyes and closed their mouths with his hard-won victories in France. After that, men discreetly forgot how the father had acquired the crown that his son so ably wore. They said that King Harry had been a good king and his simple mind had never questioned it. You did not question the deeds of kings any more than you did those of God. A king was God's anointed, the chosen of his people. It was only when kings were set up and plucked down with such frequency that it occurred to him that either man or God had erred. He had a less exalted opinion of kings now. He'd seen three come and go in his time and never one that had put a morsel more bread in the bellies of his hungry parish. But in those days the doings of kings and princes had not touched him. The years had passed in peace and contentment. He had worked and laboured among his parish and seen them birthed and wed and buried. Sometimes he had become vaguely aware of events outside his small and sheltered world. King Henry the Fifth of Agincourt had died and left a babe and two jealous uncles to rule them, but the echoes of their quarrels had not touched his secure and predictable life. The babe had grown into a man and become as saintly and pious a king as ever God could have made. His uncles had died and their ambitions with them. There'd been a new bell made for the chapel that year, and in the summer King Henry, the sixth of that name, had taken himself a French wife. He sighed, remembering. Who could have known then that her dowry was to be all of England's peace? Looking back, he was glad that the knowledge of what was to

2

come had not touched him. There had been time enough since for fear and speculation. He remembered the last Christmas that his lady had kept at Leconfield, when the cold wind of premonition had chilled even him. That had been the year Hagg Dyke had flooded and Thorpe the reeve had drowned in the mud, the year his leg had stiffened with the cold and never thawed out since; the last peace, the last happiness, the last and final disillusionment. Even then he had not felt the full import of it all, for by calling and temperament he was not a man who could ever understand such an overwhelming ambition. So Richard of York thought he should be king! He had often thought he should be Archbishop of York, but it had never made him so.

He shifted his weight as the stones grew hard beneath his knees, accustomed as he was to kneel. He edged forward till they rested on the worn and faded rug, long moulded to the floor with damp. Then he looked up and surveyed his small and illustrious audience once more. Hatred briefly contorted his mild and abstracted face. His lady had died in poverty and neglect because this woman's husband had wanted to be king. Well, he hadn't been but her son was, at the cost of tens of thousands of dead and broken lives. His timid and sensitive soul still shrank within him at the horror of it. Brother against brother, father against son and for what real purpose his mind had not yet been able to conceive. He had been sure once that there was one, some divine and mysterious purpose that he had been unworthy to know. God's ways were infinite and there was surely some greater reason for all the suffering than the mere raising of one man above another. Then as the carnage had grown, so had his uncertainty. His safe and comfortable world had crumbled around him and blown away as dust. He had seen the gentle and saintly king that he had revered for half of his life manhandled like a felon and called usurper. He had seen his beloved Leconfield raped and plundered by men who had once sat as honoured guests beneath its roof. He had seen the family that his own had loyally served for four generations swept away as if they had never been. Northumberland himself had been the first to fall, struck down by his wife's Neville kin at St Albans. Then all of their sons: Thomas, slain by Earl Warwick at Northampton; Richard and Harry had both fallen at Towton;

3

and Ralph was piteously slaughtered at Hedgeley Moor. His lady had been spared, as had Alianore and her eldest son's widow and their son, another Harry, who was as good as dead. He had been King Edward's prisoner ever since Towton; nine years come this Easter.

He remembered quite clearly the day she had come back. The two women, broken and destitute, riding in a cart not fit for pigs. Oh, what anguish it had been to see her so; what joy to serve and care for her. It had been shameful, the pleasure her need of him had brought. There had been no one else. All had fled or been driven out long ago when the victorious Yorkists had come. All except him. He had been of no account, a senile old priest huddled in a corner of his church whilst the Earl of Warwick's men had borne away his chalice and plate and anything else of value they could lay their hands on. For a year afterwards he had lived in empty desolate silence, listening to his own breath as loud as the wind rushing through the uninhabited rooms, hearing nothing but the rats feasting on the glut of rotten wood, the steady drip of rain through the leaking roof. He had prayed continuously, as the rivers seeped through the crumbling dykes and flooded the once lush and verdant fields, as his body had shrunk and diminished with hunger, as his eyes had cried with the bitter cold. He had prayed for death, for release from that useless and purposeless life. And in his mercy God had heard him and sent him not death but purpose. He had been like a young boy again; mending, patching, setting fires to roar in the great stone hearths. He'd begged and, God forgive him, sometimes stolen what he could not come by honestly. Every week he'd walked the four miles to Beverley and whined in the market place for alms, coming home at night, gleeful as a schoolboy with a capon or a cheese beneath his gown. Later there had been gifts, discreetly bestowed by men who remembered who her lord had been and in whose cause he had fallen.

His eyes focused bitterly on the Duchess of York's smooth face. But from this one there had been nothing. Not one scrap or crumb of meat or comfort, when the pearls at her throat could have fed them for a year. Silently he cursed her. May God damn you. May God damn you and your sons and their sons . . . Then his

4

shoulders sagged and he flinched from the ancient pain in his leg. He was old, though he had never really been aware of it till now. There was nothing of worth left in him, not even any real hatred or lust for revenge as there was in that other one.

He was sure it was only pure spleen that kept the blood running in Eleanor Percy's veins. The first time he had laid eyes on her he had disliked her; clinging to Alianore's hand in the back of that filthy cart, the taint of the Devil and madness in her eyes. And then there was that matter into which his calling forbade that he enquire too closely. Some unsavoury scandal that had put her behind the convent walls at Holystone for five years. They said she had fornicated with her husband's brother Thomas. They said . . . He closed his mind to such unseemly thoughts.

Whatever Eleanor's sin, it could be no greater than that of this woman who now rose from her knees and advanced majestically toward him. He stared down at the jewelled shoe placed close to the hem of his gown. He thought, 'Thief. Murderer. Hypocrite.'

Cecily Neville stared down at her sister's dead face. The hair was white, the bleached stark whiteness of grief and shock and her face so fallen away to bone that the hollows of eye and cheek stood out like bruises on the waxen skin. A tall woman once, hunger and poverty had diminished her and twisted the long proud limbs into a dwarfish stance. Yet there was still a dignity and a sad fragile beauty about her. In death she looked almost young again, her brow smooth and untroubled as it had never been in life. Was death so kind? Cecily thought. It could not have been crueller than life to poor Alianore.

She moved away and her gown rustled obscenely in the silence and screamed reproach. She glanced guiltily round the darkened room. There was nothing of ornament, nothing of beauty or comfort. All was bare and worn and reeking of poverty. She gnawed uneasily at her full lower lip. She could have done more, not so very much more in the beginning, for then it had taken all of her influence to persuade Edward to free Alianore at all let alone grant her the least of her manors. But since, she could have done more since. If only Alianore had asked, if only she had told her of her need. But Alianore would never have asked. She had still been that much of a Neville. Nevilles might cheat and steal but they never asked. Again she glanced toward the thin, still figure so jealously guarded by the priest. She thought sadly how strangely fate had dealt with them. Alianore's grief had always been her own joy; Alianore's defeat, her triumph. They had never been close. There were fifteen years between them. She had still been in leading strings when Alianore had wed Northumberland. What had bound them in later years had not been love, but more an understanding of each other's grief and loss. She too had suffered: her husband Richard, Duke of York; Salisbury, her brother and Alianore's. Her son Rutland had been only fifteen when he had been killed. Of the eight children she had borne, only three had survived. She supposed that there had been some consolation in being on the winning side, the sweetness of victory to set against the bitterness of loss. Edward was king; her younger sons, George and Richard, were royal dukes. It seemed small recompense for ten years of mourning, but it was more than Alianore had had. She felt her eyes burn with sudden tears, for Alianore, for herself, especially for herself. Even now she never felt truly safe. So Alianore had been once: rich, powerful, protected by years of rank and privilege, a mirror image of herself. But neither wealth nor position had saved Alianore, and at least she had fallen in a noble and princely cause. If she herself fell it would be through Edward's base and uncontrollable lust. Rage momentarily contorted her handsome face. Had she bred him for this? Had she suffered and sacrificed everything so smilingly for him to put all in jeopardy for that Woodville bitch? Even now, five years on, her mind still reeled in disbelief. Edward, her Edward, *King* Edward, married to a nobody, a widow who had already birthed two sons — and Lancastrians at that. To put all at risk just to get that creature into his bed when he could have had any woman in Christendom. Any woman except Elizabeth Woodville; childishly, she still baulked at naming her queen. They had lost her nephew Warwick over it, faithful dedicated Warwick who had adored Edward and had never had anything but York in his heart. And she couldn't blame him, for Edward had not even had the courage to come out into the open with it. For six months he lied and prevaricated,

6

allowing Warwick to press on foolishly with negotiations for a marriage with Bona of Savoy. And then, when he could put it off no longer, Edward had calmly announced that he was married already, to Elizabeth Woodville — and her four brothers and five sisters whom he had dowered outrageously and married off to every available heir and heiress in the land, even to the outrage and obscenity of foisting the twenty-year-old John Woodville onto her own sister Katherine who was eighty if she was a day. Warwick had had enough, and Edward had been too bewitched to recognise his loss. The house of York had much to be grateful to Richard Neville for. He was called *le conduiseur du royaume* and rightly. Did it ever occur to Edward that if he could make one king, he could make another? That there was one, half-wit though he might be, ready and waiting in the Tower?

Warwick's sulky retirement to his estates hadn't lasted. Within six months he had been out and about, quietly stirring up rebellion, aided and abetted, to her utter horror, by her second son George who had put himself even further beyond the pale by marrying Warwick's daughter Isobel, expressly against Edward's wishes. All this she had predicted and warned him against but Edward was too used to being loved. He thought that he could talk and smile his way out of any impasse. Well, his illusions were well and truly shattered now. The discontent fostered by Warwick and George had erupted into open rebellion. There had been a show of arms in the north that even Edward could not ignore. In July the worst had happened. William Herbert, Earl of Pembroke, had clashed with Warwick at Edgecote and been heavily defeated. Pembroke and his younger brother had lost their heads, the queen's father and one of her brothers also. Not that she counted *that* any loss, except that it had placed Edward in the position where he must retaliate. He had, and unbelievably he had bungled it. He had been captured and taken prisoner by Warwick's brother, the Archbishop of York. His imprisonment had lasted barely a month, for Warwick was realist enough to know that he could not keep control without a king for long. Strangely, his own aspirations did not run so high, though she could not say the same for Clarence. Warwick had meant to do nothing more than flex his political muscles and bring Edward to heel. He was content to rule through Edward as he had always done, happy to be second but never third.

A feeling of sheer panic swept over her. If anything were to befall Edward . . . The panic grew and beaded her lip with sweat. All had been so very nearly lost. It only needed a spark for all to begin again. Daft Harry was still very much alive in the Tower, his French queen and her whelp lurking in France under that troublemaker King Louis' protection. She ground her teeth together in irritation. Edward was a fool to have kept King Henry alive this long. If she'd had her way, he'd have been under six feet of good earth long since. A holy idiot he might be, but he was still enough of a king to point the finger of usurper at York and be a rallying point for Lancaster. Let Edward argue that his death was pointless while his son Edward was alive but it would have been one less obstacle to the total supremacy without which they were always at risk. And now there was this foolishness of setting Harry Percy free. Madness, sheer madness and nothing could have been more certain to inflame Warwick against them. She could see Edward's muddled strategy in this. With almost a third of England under his sway, Warwick was too powerful to be brought down single-handed. Edward thought to break his dominance of the north by setting Harry Percy up against him. All well and good, but there would be consequences of which Edward had not taken full account. It would mean depriving Warwick's brother of Northumberland, and Warwick himself of some of his lands. Warwick would never stomach that without a fight. Did Edward really think he could be so easily put down?

She pressed a silk kerchief against her trembling mouth. Dear God. What foolishness was this? She must control herself. She was Cecily Neville, Duchess of York, the mother of kings and princes. She had come through far worse than this. There was an answer, there was always an answer, if the question were desperate enough. They must pacify Warwick and bring him back to the unity that had once made them inviolate. Surely, now, Edward would see that. But that was the flaw in the whole perfect plan. Edward never saw anything but his own pleasure.

She sank down wearily upon the window seat and watched the beetles crawling busily in the rotting wood. Like the Woodvilles, she thought viciously, insidious and legion, destroying the very foundations of her house though she could easily have crushed a dozen beneath her foot. Could the Woodvilles be so easily crushed now, even if Edward was brought to admit his folly? Like some dread disease they infested every noble house in England: Buckingham, Arundel, Bourchier and Kent and the Queen's son Thomas Grey had the heiress of Exeter. They had bred and multiplied. There were children of some of those marriages now, sons and daughters whose rights could not be put aside without strife. Both she and Warwick would have to make concessions. She passed a hand wearily over her eyes. She had thought all the striving and sacrifice done, yet here she was, past fifty, with all the old anguish and uncertainty back. Stiffly she rose and went once more to look upon her sister's face. Oh, Alianore, she thought. You're well out of it. I envy you your peace.

She said, more to break the oppressive silence than from any desire to know, 'When is the lady Alianore to be buried?'

'Tomorrow, your Grace.' The old man's eyes did not waver from her face. 'The Dowager Countess of Northumberland is to be buried tomorrow in Beverley Minster.'

Cecily's mouth thinned at the use of the empty title, for all knew John Neville had Northumberland now. They didn't give up, she thought viciously. Reduced to rags and pig-swill but they didn't give up. It was still there, burning at the back of their insolent eyes. She would have liked Edward to see this old man's eyes. Let him believe that Lancaster was dead then.

Abruptly she fumbled in the jewelled pouch at her waist and withdrew a handful of gold coins. 'I wish a mass to be said for my sister's soul and a candle lit daily in the Minster for a year.'

The priest made no move to take the money and after a moment she laid it awkwardly on the bed. How ridiculous to feel shamed by this grubby old man, yet she could feel the hot colour flooding her cheeks. Harshly she said, 'If there is anything else I can do . . .'

'No, your Grace,' he said, his voice as offensive as his placid nature could make it. 'She is past all help but God's now.'

His eyes swept contemptuously from the hem of her robe to the peaks of her high horned cap. They came to rest in final and damning judgement on the rope of pearls that encircled her neck and felt like a hangman's noose. 'Madame,' he said, with the sudden perception that sometimes comes to the very young and the very old. 'Madame. If you had been kinder, God might have spared you the grief that's to come.'

From the window of the long upper room, Eleanor Percy observed the plume of dust that marked the Duchess of York's departure moving slowly along the road to York. Memory hung sickeningly about her and seared her throat like an old sour perfume. The last time she had seen Cecily Neville had been nearly nine years ago at York; the last time she had ever been truly alive, the last time she had ever looked and felt a woman instead of the dreadful hag she was now. Yorkist bitch, she thought savagely. May God rot you, fair dame, as he has me.

Abruptly, she turned back into the room. At the far end of the solar a boy and a young girl sat on either side of the cavernous hearth: the girl quietly mending a gown even shabbier than the one she wore; the boy fondling a skinny dog that whined perpetually to be free. They were hungry as always, her daughter Elizabeth's face pinched and thin, the boy . . . She turned her head to look at her nephew, Thomas's bastard, the child he had unknowingly fathered on one of his drunken forays. The mother was dead now and it had been the old grandfather who had brought him and given him almost forcibly into their care.

She called to him softly and watched with open pleasure as he came toward her. It could have been Thomas at that age. The soft black unruly curls were the same, the vivid blue eyes were his. Only when he came close was the illusion dispelled. The eyes lacked the fierce intelligence of his father and his mouth was small and weak. There had been nothing of weakness about Thomas unless it had been his disastrous passion for her.

She held out her hands toward him. Once she had wished passionately that he had been her own child. She had lain with his father often enough, yet in one short night he had sired this boy on a woman he hardly knew. That had made it easier. The unknown roused no jealousies. He was her own now. He was part of Thomas, all that was left of him. It was enough.

She smiled the tender smile that she kept only for him. 'Well, John. What did you think of our visitor, then?'

John licked his lips and opened and shut his mouth in his usual preamble to speech. Eleanor swallowed her irritation for though she loved him she strongly resented the base blood that marred his physical perfection. Even allowing for the fact that he was only ten years old, there was a slowness about him that she found painful. It was such a contrast to Thomas.

At last he said, 'She is a great lady, is she not?'

Eleanor's smile sharpened jealously. 'She thinks so, John. She is the Duchess of York. Your great-aunt on your father's side. The lady Alianore was her sister.'

The boy's eyes rounded in awe. He was always impressed by this seemingly bottomless pit of illustrious kin. It was a trait that Eleanor strove hard to banish, along with picking his teeth and consorting with the scum that optimistically came to scrounge for dole at the gates.

'Did you think her handsome then, John?' she asked.

The boy glanced at her cautiously, sensing the need to choose his words. Instinct shaped his answer. 'No. Not really. I thought she was rather fat.'

Eleanor laughed. 'Yes, John. The fruits of good living,' she said. 'Such as we're never likely to suffer from.'

John laughed with her, pleased with his small success. He was learning fast and though he knew that sometimes he seemed dull of speech and manner it was only because all this was so alien to him. There was nothing wrong with his wits and if he was slow to comply it was because in his heart he did not want to. There were aspects of this new life that he found frightening: the rigid insistence on correctness; the erection of a sudden and uncomfortable barrier between himself and all he had been happy and familiar with; most frightening of all, this strange and fanatical woman who seemed to think herself his mother. He remembered his own with sadness but he did not cry for her now. He did not even speak of her now, for he knew in a confused and childlike way that he should feel ashamed both of her and of the grandfather who had brought him to this better life. The 'better life' was yet to be revealed to him, for ironically he had never been so hungry or

11

poorly clad as he was here. He'd had a few glimpses of it, though, like today when the Duchess of York had come, enough to whet his appetite and make him cleave to this woman who seemingly held the key to the magical door. The world beyond it beckoned with shining promise, his father's world of land and wealth and power. Then he forgot the warm smoky hovel where he had been born and the laughing pretty woman who had raised him. Then he saw himself as Eleanor saw him, a small and perfect replica of the man she had loved. That his father had been a great lord he had known from birth, a faceless anonymous being hinted at by his mother and by Eleanor brought vividly to life. Faceless he was still but now he had a name: Thomas, Lord Egremont, who had been slain the year after his birth fighting for King Henry at Northampton. That was why he was here. That was why the lady Eleanor loved him. There were still confusions. He was astute enough to know that being Thomas Percy's son was not quite enough, that there was some faint and indefinable line that he could never cross merely by right. He was Thomas's bastard rather than Thomas's son and he knew that it made a difference, except, it seemed, to Eleanor.

She clasped his small and brutal hands. Her eyes were bright and feverish, her voice pitched to the staccato sharpness he found so frightening. She said, 'I was once like her, John, rich and powerful, a great lady.' Her eyes swept round the barren walls. Two kings and a queen had dined here once; when Arras silk had graced the walls and fine Turkey rugs the floor, when she had worn blue velvet and twined sapphires in her hair, when she had been young. She turned to look at him and said bitterly, 'Would you believe, John, that I was very beautiful once?'

He strained away from her famished stare. He saw a woman, tall and thin, a face sharp and spiteful, the flesh pared to a hair's breadth of the starting bones; a stranger's face, an old woman's face that filled him with a strange repugnance. 'Madame,' he said fearfully, pulling himself from her grasp, 'may I go to Hagg Dyke and wait for Brother Ignatious?'

She stared at him blankly, still dazzled by the glitter and brilliance of the past. 'Brother Ignatious?' Then she remembered. This was the day that the monk came with the gift of alms from

Beverley: meat, flour, a keg of ale and as much news and gossip as could be stored in his long pointed head. It was the highlight of each dreary month, the day for which they all waited — the children for food, she for the news that never came. Her eyes grew hard and bitter again. Would it ever come? She dare not think that it would not. It was all that kept her sane, all that kept her from complete despair, the hope that one day her son Harry would be freed. The hope grew fainter with each passing year. It was a long time now, nearly nine years in all since Harry had been taken prisoner. The last time she had seen him had been in the great hall at York . . . Her eyes grew blank and void as glass. She saw herself and Alianore kneeling on the stones at York. Harry had not knelt, not even when the great, golden, victorious Edward had commanded him to kneel before his king. She heard Harry's voice, so soft, yet every man in the hall had heard it. *'I see no king.'* She had cursed him silently. What in heaven's name had he thought that show of bravado could gain them? Her lip curled. He hadn't been so brave when they had dragged him away and flung him in the dungeons beneath York. Then had followed a year in the Fleet, five years in the Tower; these last two he had been confined in the Earl of Pembroke's fortress at Raglan. Her flat bosom heaved in an agony of frustration. She might have known better than to put her faith in Harry. When had he not disappointed her? He would be a man now, but all her mind could ever conjure up was the dark swarthy child she had loathed almost as much as she had his father. She glanced malevolently at her daughter Elizabeth named for another Elizabeth, long dead. Her lip curled. What a travesty to compare this timid insipid creature with Elizabeth Mortimer. Lovely, cunning, evil Elizabeth who had taught her all the secrets of life and death and more than anything had taught her how to hate. She looked away. The sight of that pinched, milk-white face served only to enrage her further. All her children had been a disappointment to her. She had two other daughters, comfortably but insignificantly married. They never came by or near. She could have been dead for all that Eleanor and Margaret knew or cared. Not that she blamed them. Ever since Towton, being a Percy was not something a sane person bragged about. It meant persecution and pain, it meant being hounded and humiliated . . . She rose, trembling. It distressed her to think too deeply of the past. The good memories were far distant and long forgotten. There were others, cruel ugly thoughts hidden away in the dark corner of her mind into which she rarely looked. Alianore had said that she must not dwell on what was gone, she must forget, she must forgive . . . She swayed unsteadily, a milky froth slicked her quivering lips. Forgive Warwick? Warwick, who had murdered Thomas, who had hounded and persecuted two helpless women almost to their deaths and reduced them to less than nothing? Forget that it was Warwick who had placed York on the throne in the first place and so begun all of their grief? A harsh animal noise arose in her throat. She looked down in terror as a hand closed around her arm. Elizabeth stared at her anxiously. 'Madame, are you well?'

Slowly the blank abstracted look faded from Eleanor's face. She shook off the tender supporting hand. 'Yes,' she said faintly. 'I am well.' She chafed at her arms to ease the awful chill of her flesh. 'Yes. I am very well.'

Brother Ignatious stamped the dust from his sandalled feet, for he had walked the four miles from Beverley dragging the old broken-winded mule unwillingly in his wake. He beamed with Christian charity on the faces assembled to greet him and allowed himself to be ushered in like royalty and divested of his pack. The old priest embraced him tearfully and the little maid Elizabeth stared at him as if he were God. John prodded voraciously at the sack from which a chicken's leg protruded. The monk patted his head kindly. Mother of God, he thought. He looks hungry enough to eat it raw.

Then Eleanor swept regally into the room and his smile became a little fixed. She cuffed back the old priest as if he were a hungry dog. On him she bestowed a brief chilly greeting, then proceeded to unfasten the sack. She surveyed the contents with customary disdain, as if it were some unwanted gift: a hunk of stinking meat, two skinny fowl, and a skin of wine besides the usual flour and cheese. She raised her brows suspiciously and prodded the fowl with an elegant finger. She was distrustful of kindness, of any deviation from the abuse and humiliation she had come to

14

expect. And for that old skinflint to have sent more than he need? She would have been less surprised if he had sent his right leg.

'Your abbot is unusually generous,' she said whilst seeing all safely under lock and key, for there were some who would not think twice about filching what they thought would not be missed. As if any crumb would not be missed in this household. She could remember a time when she had eyed a rat with savour.

She motioned for him to be served his usual draught of ale. The bread and cheese she served him herself. Elizabeth was inclined to be over-generous and last time the monk had taken away in his belly almost as much as he had brought.

She sat and faced him. 'To what, then, do we owe this surprising largesse?'

The monk drank deeply, not eking it out in his usual way, savouring his moment of revelation as he normally did the ale. He smiled. 'It seems, madame, that once again your credit is good. The abbot deems it honour for you to call upon our house.'

Eleanor's eyes narrowed. She didn't believe that stone was stone till she'd felt the weight of it in her hand. 'My credit?' she demanded suspiciously. 'Who stands my banker, then?'

Brother Ignatious drained his cup and glanced triumphantly at their astounded faces. 'Your son, my lady, and soon our most gracious lord. He is free, my lady, or virtually so. King Edward has summoned him to Westminster.' He repeated himself, seeing her face so stony and hard that he could not believe that she had heard him. He had expected some show of joy at least.

Eleanor lowered her eyes to the rough pitted surface of the table. 'And what of the Earl of Warwick?' she asked softly. 'Has this his warranty? His brother John Neville is Earl of Northumberland now. How will Warwick sanction the release of one who could only oust his brother?'

The monk looked pointedly at his empty cup and saw it speedily refilled. 'I was coming to that,' he said. 'Warwick's sanction is no longer of account. Warwick is fallen, my lady. Out of grace and favour. The council has named him traitor and rebel.'

Now she smiled, such a brilliant and depraved smile that momentarily he averted his eyes. 'You are sure?' she said urgently. 'You have this on good authority?'

'The best. From the King himself. I was there at York when he gave the order for your son to be brought out of Wales. He said, "What better medicine for an overmighty Neville than to loose a Percy against him?"'

Eleanor rose unsteadily to her feet and stood for a moment, swaying. Then without a word she left them, stumbling along the dark unlit passage, feeling her way blindly to the foot of the stairs. Outside Alianore's chamber she paused and leant her face against the wall. It was over. Sweet Jesu Mary, it was over.

Then she opened the door and crossed the darkened room to stand by the bed. 'Alianore?' She waited, almost as if she expected an answer. 'Alianore.' She bent close and her avid breath stirred a tendril of the dead white hair. 'It's come at last, Nel,' she whispered. 'We're to be saved after all. Harry is coming home.'

She smoothed the cold marble brow with her hand. Poor Nel. Poor sweet gentle Nel. She wished now that she had loved her more. She owed her so much, the fact that she was even alive at all. Alianore had been the strong one in the beginning, dragging her back from the edge of madness, coaxing and bullying her into some semblance of life and sanity and keeping her there these past dreadful years. How cruel that deliverance had come too late for Nel. Her full mouth trembled for an instant then hardened into a smile. But not too late for her. Thank God, it was not too late for her. She thought again, less viciously, of Cecily Neville. They were of a like age, no longer young but not too old to enjoy wealth and power. She looked round at the damp and crumbling walls. All this was ending, all this filth and poverty and humiliation. Soon she would be gone from here — to Alnwick or Warkworth, Prudhoe or Langley, any one of the hundred rich and profitable manors of which they had been dispossessed. There would be no more empty bellies, no more scrimping and patching and mending. She would have a gown of sapphire blue velvet, a dozen pairs of cordovan shoes. John could have the fine horse that he yearned for — and so much more if she had her way. The wild impossible thought flitted through her mind: after Harry, John was the Percy heir.

Suddenly her mood of elation faded. How much could she

16

hope for from the son she had once so blatantly neglected. Neither affection nor love, for those she had forfeited a long time since. But duty — Harry would be concious of his duty. Whatever his inner feelings, she was still his mother and his closest blood kin. And surely he would feel pity for all she had suffered? She frowned. Pity and duty? Not all she could have hoped for and certainly not enough to serve her high ambitions. There would have to be more, yet how much more she would not know until she had seen and judged him. Again she wondered about him, sifting through her meagre recollection of the boy in an effort to glimpse the man. Was he still so silent? Would he have lost that dark and sinister look that had so appalled her and been in such contrast to her own and his father's fairness. Strangely, it was his voice that she most vividly remembered, that deceptively soft and exquisite sound. Like music it touched all of the senses and as other men used their bodies to charm and caress and wound and kill, so Harry used his voice. She bit her lips uncertainly. Would she find him even more alien and unlovable than before? What if she did? she thought bitterly. All her life she had pleased others in order to please herself, feigning love where there was none, stifling it where there was. It was what Harry thought and felt that mattered now. For the moment he was the star that guided her destiny. It was his needs and desires that counted. She wished she knew more of those needs. Was he still so hungry for the love that she had once denied him? Could she feed that hunger and make him pliant? But slowly, she must lead him slowly. It was tempting to a starving man to gorge and sicken himself. Just a morsel at a time till she had won his confidence, till he trusted her better than he trusted himself. She smiled. Oh yes. She must love and cherish her dear son Harry. He was all of her salvation now.

Wales
Gwilym Ddu, the bard, struck a dramatic note from his harp, a note of perfect pitch and resonance that grew and burgeoned in the hollow of the roof, echoing sweetly in the mouths of the leaning angels before it slowly diffused into silence. The bard regarded his audience sternly: the strangers and the men like him

17

who had served Black William Herbert for all of their lives. The lord's friends and his kinsmen, his widow, the Englishwoman Anne Devereaux; the ten children that she had stoically borne in as many years. When they were all silent, he said in his lilting Welsh voice, 'I will sing an elegy, composed in memory of our beloved lord so cruelly slain by the traitor Warwick.' Then he flung back his head and threw his voice to the rafters. The long drear notes coiled like a winding sheet round the cavernous hall. 'Our cup is empty. Our board is bare. Our proud lord fallen . . .'

In the far corner, away from the throng, a man and a boy played quietly at chess; the boy with the utmost concentration, his tawny head bent low, his long chin thrust deep into the collar of his gown. The man was distracted and toyed idly with a rook recently captured from his opponent's ranks. A young man, not quite into his twentieth year. It was only his eyes which gave the impression of experience and age, clouded with years of suspicion and regret, like fire beneath green smoke. He glanced up at the leaded window above his head. Dull red light patterned the wall and the hall was heavy with shadows. Almost another day gone, the seven hundredth and twenty-third he had spent within these walls.

Then Henry Tudor said to him, 'Have you left us already, Harry? If so, I fear you have left your king in great jeopardy. I think my bishop has him by the throat.'

Harry looked down at the board and smiled briefly. 'Then I concede, Henry. On this one occasion at least, I will grant you to be the better man. I am afraid my thoughts are elsewhere.'

Henry returned the smile, pleased with the victory no matter how it came. 'You know, Harry,' he said as he reset the chessmen with meticulous care, 'I shall truly miss you. This place will seem even emptier when you are gone.'

Harry looked away. But I shan't miss you, Henry, he thought grimly. Not Henry Tudor nor any one of the faces that had intruded on his life these past two years. Impassively his eyes swept over them. They sat enraptured as the bard's strong voice eulogised their loss: the Welsh knights, Rhys ap Thomas and Richard Griffith, the Countess Anne, plump and bewildered as

18

her brood of infant sons and daughters whined and fidgeted and tugged at her skirts; her eldest son, silly William and his equally silly Woodville wife. And one he did not think grieved so very much, Margaret Beaufort, Countess of Richmond.

Harry's eyes dwelt thoughtfully on the face of Henry Tudor's mother. A young woman still, Margaret Beaufort had been thirteen years old when she had married the Welshman Edmund Tudor. She had been fourteen and already his widow when she had borne his son, only eighteen when the Yorkists had captured Pembroke and herself and her four-year-old son and bestowed all upon William Herbert. If she had ever felt resentment at the rights of herself and Henry being thus usurped, she had never shown it. She accepted it as she accepted every reverse and misfortune of her life, with patience and smiling resignation that accorded neither with her blood nor her ambition. She was, as she was often heard to declare, the daughter of John Beaufort, Duke of Somerset, and through him the great-grand-daughter of King Edward the Third. She forebore to mention that all the Beauforts were descended from the illicit liaison between John of Gaunt and his mistress, Katherine Swynford. Deliberately, she cultivated her air of quiet regality and clung determinedly to her first husband's country. Though she had been swiftly married off again to Henry Stafford, it seemed it was a marriage in name only. She had preferred to remain in Wales, close to her son. All knew it was where her love and ambition lay. Then suddenly the small devious eyes met his. The sharp clever face creased into a tacit smile.

Harry inclined his head in acknowledgement and looked quickly away. Across the hall the bard thrummed ecstatically, the shrill discords of war. Visions flew from his fingers, the drum of hoofbeats, the scream of steel and for an instant Black William's bloody and headless corpse took shape in the shadows of the room. At the bard's feet a young girl sat listening with rapt and shining face: Black William's eldest daughter, the lady Maud, the joyous happy child who was to marry Henry Tudor. Now there was a travesty, Harry thought cynically; all that youth and laughter shackled to Henry. He looked at the boy's long face, almost with dislike.

19

'You'll not miss me for long, Henry,' he said. 'You'll soon be wed. You'll not lack for company then.'

.Henry smiled his sad and wistful smile and his sallow cheeks coloured with pleasure. Yes, he thought. Soon he would have Maud to love him. He looked for her tenderly across the room and then as an afterthought, threw an anxious glance at his mother. She wasn't best pleased with the match. She had hoped for something better for him than the daughter of a Yorkist upstart, especially one who had blatantly usurped his uncle Jasper's title and lands. Moreover, the Herberts' antecedents were somewhat dubious: minor Welsh lords sprung from a long line of minor Welsh lords till Edward had raised William Herbert up and created him Earl of Pembroke. They came from good Welsh fighting stock. Black William's father had been Margoah Glas; his grandfather, David ap Llewellyn ap Hywel, was the Davy Gam who had fought so valiantly for King Henry the Fifth and had been slain in his service at Agincourt. Nothing of course, to set against his own illustrious lineage. Henry's Welsh ancestors were mighty and legion, stretching far into the realms of fantasy and legend. Through his grandfather, Owen Tudor, the paramour of Queen Katherine of Valois, he could trace his descent as far back as Noah. On his mother's side his ancestors were equally regal. He never forgot, his mother never let him forget, that he was the great-great-grandson of King Edward the Third.

He said, frowning, as if he considered some weighty problem. 'Even so, Harry. I shall still miss you.'

Harry looked into the boy's face that had nothing boyish about it. It was already an old face, long and learned, the brow furrowed with constant thought, the mouth thinned with mistrust. An unhealthy face, grey and moist, like his eyes; in the spring, Henry suffered badly with the tertian fever. But then perpetual captivity was not compatible with youth and health: running, hiding, being dragged from one grim fortress to another in the wake of that tyrant, Jasper Tudor. For the past ten years he had been William Herbert's prisoner. They had been prisoners together for the last two of them. Except that for him it might be at an end. In a few days he would know the best or the worst of it, whether he had merely exchanged one prison for another or if

King Edward's surprising summons to Westminster meant freedom. *Freedom*. The very word turned him sick with longing and he felt a deep and sudden compassion for Henry whose longing must be as great. It was one thing they had very much in common — a desperate and overwhelming need to be free, no matter how kindly they were kept. And what else? he wondered, looking again at that pale repressed face. Captivity must lay an indelible stamp upon a man. The years of enforced subservience must surely show. Was he himself so introspective and dull, so eternally patient and humble?

He looked down at his long well-shaped hands. No. He was scarred in a different way, impregnable behind a wall of real indifference that Henry still struggled to climb. There were few emotions that came readily to him now. Nothing touched him in his isolation of pride. He gave nothing and received nothing, for neither loving nor being loved gave him his only freedom. Sometimes he felt pity, a strange perverse compassion for all hurt and wounded things. He could weep for the death of an injured bird, yet see a man hanged unmoved. Love and faith were alien and unknown. He had discovered long before he had ever lost his freedom that his fellow man was to be despised.

Then Henry said in his thin puerile voice so at odds with his old man's eyes, 'So you leave tomorrow for Westminster?' He could not keep the envy from his voice. All he knew of the world was Wales and he was truly saddened by the loss of the man he counted his only flesh-and-blood friend. Most of Henry's friends lived between the pages of his books: poets and philosophers, men of science and art. Boethius, Tacitus, Sallust, all these men he knew intimately. They too had been lonely and persecuted in their time. But suddenly these old friends had lost their appeal. Boethius never listened. Harry Percy did.

He said, wistfully, 'And you think Edward will release you and restore you to your lands?'

'He might,' Harry answered. 'If it suits him.'

Henry linked his bony fingers together and leant his chin upon his knuckles. 'And it might well do, Harry. If Edward truly has a mind to break with the Earl of Warwick.' He paused and plucked thoughtfully at a loose thread upon his sleeve. 'And no doubt

Edward will expect to find you grateful.'

'Shouldn't I be?'

Henry pushed his mouth in and out in the nervous way he had. 'I myself would have my doubts about cleaving too closely to the man who was responsible for the death of my entire family.'

'And you see that man as Edward of York?'

Henry looked startled. 'Do you not?'

The amber eyes burned up suddenly into flame. 'No, Henry. I do not.'

'Who then?' Henry tilted his head on one side. 'Warwick? But what was Earl Warwick but Edward's minion? Warwick. Edward. They are all of a piece. False and perjured traitors. Oh, I know,' he said quickly as he saw Harry's warning look. He laid a long finger against his lips. 'I know. Accept what you must, but remember that the true king lies in the Tower. Bide your time. Lancaster will come again.'

Harry groaned. 'Oh, I hope not, Henry. I devoutly hope not.'

Henry looked shocked. Himself as an object of derision he had come to expect, but not Lancaster. Lancaster was sacred, the hallowed vessel that held the spilt blood of two whole generations. 'How can you speak so, Harry?' he said in an outraged whisper. 'Does the sacrifice of your family mean nothing?'

'More to me than it ever will to you,' Harry answered him coldly. 'That is why I can question it. For what, exactly, did they die?'

Henry stared at him blankly. In terms of blood, perhaps, his own sacrifice had not been so great, but still he had suffered. His father had fallen to the Yorkists at Carmarthen, his grandfather Owen Tudor at Mortimer's Cross. His uncle Jasper had been hounded into exile. He himself was attainted and dispossessed. But he had never questioned it. One did not question destiny. 'They died for their king,' he said at last. 'They died for love of their king.'

'Edward of York is the king now.'

'The true king,' Henry persisted. 'The king your father and grandfather died for.'

'A sick old man not capable of tying his own shoes, let alone ruling a kingdom. That is what they died for.'

'Oh treason, treason,' whispered Henry. 'I never thought to hear this from you, Harry. After myself, I thought you the truest in our cause. Your very blood is Lancaster.'

'My blood is my own and I prefer to keep it running in my veins than draining out on some battlefield.'

'And what of honour?' Henry demanded archly. 'Or did you surrender that to Edward of York along with your liberty?'

Harry shrugged. 'Honour is different things to different men, Henry. I do not think it honourable to leave what remains of my family in poverty for lack of a little humility on my part. I do not consider it any dishonour to give my loyalty to Edward of York if he is worthy of it. The only dishonour would be if he was not. Henry of Lancaster is not worthy of it and whatever love you bear for the man himself, you know in your heart that he's not fit to be king. He's been kept in the Tower for four years and not kept too cleanly or tenderly either. How will his reason have stood up to that? How could he be anything more than he was before — the tool of the Frenchwoman, Queen Margaret? For God's sake, Henry. It's against all reason and logic.'

'Loyalty does not conceive of logic,' Henry said stiffly. 'Besides, there is Prince Edward, his son.'

'If it is his son. There are some who still believe that he is Somerset's bastard. Can you believe that King Henry was capable even of fathering a lustful thought, let alone a flesh-and-blood child?'

'So then,' Henry looked at him with scorn, 'you are content to serve Edward of York, despite the fact that he is usurper and murderer, despite the fact that he has taken nine years of your life and now only thinks of setting you free because it suits his purpose.'

'Henry,' Harry said wearily, 'you have missed the point. Lancaster or York, I care not which. A man's loyalty should not be for an idea, for a blood line, for one side or another, but for England as a whole.'

'And you think that Edward of York serves England's interests best?'

'Better than a madman and a sixteen-year-old boy who can speak hardly a word of the English language.'

23

Henry had ceased to look outraged. He worked his mouth agitatedly till a froth of spittle filmed his lips. 'Has it ever occurred to you, Harry, that there could be another choice?'

'There always is,' Harry said mildly. 'Which one did you have in mind?'

Henry hesitated, years of caution binding his tongue. The secret of his ambition weighed heavily upon him. He longed for approval and support other than his mother's. He longed for encouragement beyond his uncle Jasper's harsh bullying. Most of all he longed for recognition, an open acknowledgement that the vision he had of himself was more than in his own mind. The words came slowly, laboriously, as if he gouged each one from steel. 'You are aware of my lineage, Harry.' He attempted a haughty smile. 'After King Henry and Prince Edward, I am the next male heir of the house of Lancaster.'

Harry listened in disbelief. He had to suppress the urge to laugh. It *was* laughable, this youth of fourteen, all arms and legs and scrawny skin with his bonnet awry on his head, speaking so earnestly of kingship. Yet the laughter died in him as he looked into Henry's avid face and saw the naked ambition that had eaten away at all of his blood since his great-grandfather John of Gaunt had first set his eye upon a crown, the same ambition that had brought his own house to ruin by making it a reality.

Henry plunged on. Emotion, so rarely felt, welled up inside him and overcame the dam of his reserve. He spoke of omens and auguries, portents seen in stars and smoke. He recalled the words of Taliesin, the bard magician, the prophecy of Merddin before Gwrtheyrn, the angelic voice that in a peal of thunder had spoken to Cadwallader, all these foretold that out of Wales would come a king . . . Then he looked up into Harry's face and saw the incredulous amusement that would become the open laughter of other men. He saw the mild derision that would become their contempt and scorn. Worst of all he saw pity, as if he were some wretched cripple that presumptuously aspired to walk. He knew then that he had blundered, that he had mistaken a mild liking for friendship, a shared experience for a shared cause. Henry clutched his long outmoded gown closer about him. He saw himself as Harry saw him, a drab gangling foolish youth, everything

24

about him puny and stilted as if God had grudged his very making. *Annwyl Crist*. If only they knew how his heart longed for greatness, how his spirit longed for dominance and release. They all thought him so humble and biddable, and he was; but only out of need. There were other qualities kept hidden at his mother's bidding: craft and cunning, an iron will, a determination to succeed that had survived greater onslaughts on his pride than this. He looked wildly for his mother across the hall, summoning up the opiate of her strong voice that echoed the distant approval of his ancestors. Their names dripped soothingly through his mind: Maredudd and Hywell; Gruffyd and Llewelyn; Uther Pendragon and Arthur himself. His was the blood of the dragon Cadwallader, of the great Brutus from whom all of Albany was sprung; not angels and magicians but princes and kings who had believed, as he did, that the hour of Wales would come again.

He looked up into Harry's closed and impassive face and the hot words of vindication died in him, a slow, cruel, silent death. He knew he would never speak of his dreams again. And into the silence that fell between them came Gwilym Ddu's silver voice extolling his glorious dead. Other names rose in Harry Percy's mind: his father, his father's brothers, his father's father — all gloriously dead because they had meddled too deeply in the affairs of kings. He would not make the same mistake himself.

There was still enough light left to hold the shape of the mountains: Waun Fach, Pen y Fan, the weird riven crag of Mynydd y Dduw, and westward, into Carmarthen, the sun hung low between the twin peaks of the Brecheiniog like a jewel between a woman's breasts. In the east, night had already darkened the meadows by the Severn, and beyond, dwarfed by distance, all that Harry could see of England, the faint shadow of the Cotswold hills. It was enough, and for the first time in years he allowed his thoughts to go beyond the walls of his prison. He thought of Northumberland, smiling now in her summer green with the sunlight warming the bleakness from the moors. He thought of the pitiful shattered remnants of his family: his grandmother, his mother, the three sisters whose faces he couldn't even recall and, calling him home more surely than all of them, Richard Neville, Earl of Warwick. His heart turned sickeningly within him, beating in thick heavy strokes. He had forgotten that emotion was such a treacherous thing. He breathed deeply. He would not indulge himself in the passion of hatred any more than he would that of love. Both weakened and crippled the spirit, both made a man intensely vulnerable. He saw his vengeance only as the honourable payment of a debt, as one would repay a cheat at cards or a merchant who gave short measure. There was a colder, more practical view, as there was in all of his thoughts. Richard Neville and his brother stood in the way of his ambition: therefore they must be removed. Reluctantly he pushed the thought to the back of his mind. There was no profit or purpose in speculation yet. He had schooled himself never to think beyond the moment, never to dwell on what was past or what was to come. Only thus had he kept himself from utter despair, only thus had he kept his sanity.

He turned as a light footfall sounded in the doorway. Maud stood watching him, one hand smoothing the folds of her loose dark robe, the other raised hesitantly to the latch.

'I came to say goodbye,' she said. 'I thought I might not see you again. Rhys ap Thomas says you are leaving at dawn.'

Harry frowned at her bare feet. 'You should be in your bed,' he said. 'You'll catch cold.'

'I won't. It's hot. Too hot, my lady mother says. She thinks the well might even dry up.' She advanced into the room. Her hair was loosed from its ugly braids. It spilled to her waist, a crimson flood, so startling in its colour that the chaplain had bade her keep it covered in hall lest it stir the lusts of men.

'Have you upset Henry again?' she asked innocently. 'I saw him marching from the hall with his mouth twitching the way it does when he is angry.'

Harry smiled wryly. 'Yes. I'm afraid I have upset Henry again. I think I hurt his pride.'

'Oh, I shouldn't think so.' Maud curled herself on the window seat and tucked her feet beneath her robe. 'Henry hasn't got any pride. He says it's a luxury only free men can afford.'

'Would you like some wine?' Harry asked, smiling.

26

'Oh, yes. But only a little though, otherwise Ysbaddaden will smell it on my breath.'

'And who,' asked Harry, 'is Ysbaddaden?'

'She's my nurse. But William and I call her Ysbaddaden after the giant, because she has a waist as thick as the boles of twelve trees like he has.' She held out her hand for the wine and Harry caught it and turned the small soft palm towards him. The ends of her fingers were torn and had bled.

'I practised too hard on my harp yesterday,' she explained. 'It hurts at first till your hands get used to it. But Gwilym Ddu says that pain is inspiring.'

Harry loosed her hand. 'Foolish child. You shouldn't believe everything that old cretin says.'

'Gwilym Ddu is not a cretin,' she said defensively. 'He is very wise and a great *penceredd*. He played before Prince Owain Glendwr when he was a boy and the prince gave him a beryl and emerald clasp, he was so moved by his voice. And anyway,' she added haughtily, 'I'm not a child. I shall be twelve at Michaelmas. Henry's mother was only thirteen when she married Edmund Tudor.'

Harry looked down at her. He had not realised she was so old. She said, 'Will you sit down please, Harry? I feel very small when you are standing up.'

He smiled. 'You are very small,' he said mockingly.

'Now you're laughing at me.' She looked at him reproachfully and the hurt in her voice was real.

'No,' Harry said gently. 'I'm not.'

'But you do sometimes. At all of us. Not out in the open, but inside you.'

Harry lowered himself onto the seat beside her. 'Do I? I'm sorry. I never meant to.' He was silent for a moment, looking down into her upturned face. He thought, she'll be quite lovely when she's grown, too lovely for Henry with his colds and his agues and his old man's eyes. He said, almost harshly, 'Maud. Are you . . . are you fond of Henry?'

'I think so.' She frowned. 'Yes. I am fond of him, although sometimes I don't like him very much when he sniffs all the time and when he tries to make me learn Greek. But he's really very

27

kind. Besides, it was my father's wish that I marry Henry and I am duty-bound to honour it.' Her soft mouth trembled. Every night she prayed for the repose of her father's soul and wished the pain of hell upon that of his murderer. Even now she could not think of him as less than whole. She could not think of him as cold and dead, his fine body violated by the headsman's axe. He was always as he had been the last time she had seen him: the fierce dark face bronzed by the sun, the torque of yellow gold that he always wore glittering ferociously as he laughed — like Harry Percy's eyes. The torque had always reminded her of Harry's eyes. And now he was leaving, though perhaps it wouldn't be for good.

She said thoughtlessly. 'Rhys ap Thomas says that it's not certain that King Edward will restore you. Will you come back if he does not?'

Harry's mouth tightened as she put into words the unspeakable thought. 'You'd better ask Rhys ap Thomas,' he said shortly. 'He seems to know everything else.'

Maud sighed. 'Now you are angry with me.'

'I am not.'

'You are. I know you are. You look like King Arawn when you are angry.'

Harry laughed in spite of himself. 'King who?'

'Arawn, King of the Otherworld. When a wicked man dies, Arawn hunts his soul with his pack of white red-eared hounds. He is very fearsome. Gwilym Ddu has a carving of him slaying the great boar Ysgithyrwyn. She looked at him in amazement. 'Have you never heard the Dogs of Arawn baying for their prey?'

'No I have not,' he answered scornfully. 'Who fills your head with all this heathen nonsense?'

'It isn't nonsense,' she cried hotly. 'It's the White Book of Rhydderch. You're like all the English, sneering at everything Welsh.'

'Now you are angry with me.'

She laughed and as always the warm delicious sound filled him with pleasure. It was such a free, uninhibited sound, so alien to himself who rarely laughed. Then suddenly her mouth drooped.

28

'It's wrong to laugh with Father so soon dead. Brother Hugh told me I was irreverent.'

'Then Brother Hugh is a fool and so are you for believing him. Your father would have thought so too.'

She smiled at him gratefully. 'Do you think so, Harry?'

'Yes, I do. Now drink your wine and get back to your bed. I don't want Ysbaddaden in here breathing fire.'

Maud giggled and obediently sipped the dark fiery liquid that was not unlike the colour of her hair. 'Harry.' She regarded him gravely over the rim of the cup. 'Is it wicked to hate someone?'

'Ask Brother Hugh,' Harry said with mild exasperation. 'He would know more about it than I do.'

Maud pulled a face. 'Brother Hugh thinks everything is sinful, even the colour of my hair. Judas hair he calls it.' Absently she twined a lock of it round her finger. 'Do you think it is sinful, Harry?'

He stared at her. 'No,' he said softly. 'I think it is very beautiful.'

She looked up at him, startled. 'No, I meant . . .' She laughed and blushed furiously. 'No. I meant, did you think that hatred was sinful? I think it must be,' she went on without giving him time to answer. 'But when I think of Earl Warwick and what he did to my father, I can't help it. I know it's wrong, though, because it makes me weep and I cannot play or sing or do any of the things I love. I think it must be God's way of punishing me for being . . .' Then suddenly she flung herself into Harry's arms and began to cry.

Startled, he held her. Her body was soft and cool through the thin robe and she smelt of honey and flowers.

'I can't help it, Harry,' she whispered against his throat. 'I don't care if it's wicked. I hate Earl Warwick. He killed my father.'

Harry stroked her hair. 'Yes, I know,' he said. 'He killed mine too.'

The royal barge slipped silently from its moorings below Westminster and nosed its way downstream. At the prow the Sun in Splendour blazed with fearful brilliance; astern, the Falcon of York skimmed the water with gilded wings and beneath an awning of damask silk, Edward Plantagenet, King of England, sprawled his gigantic length. He bit hungrily into a sugared plum and parted the curtain a hand's width. By the Wool Market a dozen Flemish scuts rode low in the water piled high with English fleece. He smiled acquisitively, thinking of the revenues that were his due. Thank God he had cleaved to Burgundy instead of France as Warwick had wished him to. Louis would have had England licking his boots by now and Edward's mercenary soul cringed at the thought of the exactions the French king would have squeezed from him if he'd turned his back on Burgundian trade. Besides, he owed a loyalty to Burgundy beyond mere policy; past favours, past unities, past and present dread of French domination, all had combined to make Burgundy his choice. Let the Earl of Warwick pander to Louis if he would, but not in the King of England's name. It was all signed and sealed now beyond redress. His sister Mary was wed to Burgundy's son Charles and he had treaties with both Flanders and Brittany. What need had he of Louis now? What need had he of any man, especially the Earl of Warwick?

He yawned and leant back among the piled silk cushions. The late September sun probed the shadows at his head and kindled his yellow hair to flame. The barge heaved gently beneath him like a woman in a love embrace and he thought of Elizabeth, his Queen, great with child again for the fourth time. His long body twitched in irritation at the thought of further abstinence from her bed. Not that he was without comfort. He had mistresses and whores enough: lately his steward's haughty but obliging wife, and in Southwark there was a Spanish harlot with breasts big enough to fill his two cupped hands. But none could rouse him as Elizabeth did, that pale cold sepulchre of Beauty in which he buried himself nightly and emerged like the dead himself. Even now, with her body swollen and distorted with child he still desired her. He sank his white teeth savagely into a peach and licked the spurting juice from his wrist. God grant that this time she bore him a son to stop his mother's tongue. Five years wed and still no heir, though he'd kept her belly full every year. If any man needed a son, he did; especially now, with Warwick plotting so determinedly against him and dangling crowns before his brother Clarence's eyes. George's perpetually flushed and discontented face rose before him. George was always the first to see a slight, always the last to see reason. Warwick could have found no more willing tool and no better time to use it. Clarence had been ripe and ready for mischief, already incensed by Edward's refusal to sanction his marriage to Isobel Neville, more than ever piqued by the Woodvilles' swift and steady rise. Edward pursed his full, sensual mouth. Yes, he should have seen that. He should have made more of Clarence and less for once of the clamorous ambitious tribe who had so admirably suited his purpose in alienating Warwick. He shrugged his broad velvet-clad shoulders. Too late now. What was done was done and though he'd vastly underestimated the extent of Warwick's spleen he'd found warmth enough in Elizabeth's arms to compensate for all of Warwick's disapproval. It had been more than time for pupil and master to go their own ways. He'd learnt his lessons well enough and eternal gratitude was such a wearying thing unless it was Elizabeth's. He closed his eyes, seeing in his mind's eye her pale white body beneath him, her hair spread like moonlight across the bed, her red lips parted to receive his kiss. Elizabeth douce, Elizabeth loving, Elizabeth . . . Then the memory of his mother's harsh complaining voice scattered his thoughts. '*Edward, my son. For this woman you have thrown all away.*'

He sat up abruptly, the stab of fear pricking at his mind but never quite reaching his heart. Nothing ever truly penetrated the aura of optimistic well-being which surrounded him. He had talked and charmed his way from worse impasses than this. Warwick would come round when he realised that he would not be ruled and that there was nothing to be gained by holding out. And George was more than halfway his again. Like wine, optimism flooded through his veins and warmed him. He thrust his head from the awning and the wind ruffled his hair to an improbable halo of light. The tide was ebbing swiftly now, leaving the tiny boats marooned like upturned shells on the stretch of glistening mud. The barge gathered speed, swept along by the impetus of the tide, past the Savoy, past the lush gardens and gilded roofs of the Temple. He smiled reminiscently as he saw the spire of St Paul's thrust like an accusing finger over the iniquitous city.

There had been a mercer's daughter in Thames Street who had inflamed his passion once. Her name escaped him now. Their names always did. It was only their bodies he remembered. Only one name was engraved indelibly on his mind and would not be forgotten; the one foolishness, the one paramount folly of his life. The name came unbidden into his mind, shrieked by the gulls that scavenged over Queenhithe, whispered insidiously by the grey chilly waves. Eleanor Butler, old Shrewsbury's daughter . . . He flung himself back into the shadows. The name pounded deafeningly in his ears. If Elizabeth ever knew, if Warwick knew . . . He drew a long shuddering breath. But only he knew, he and the young pliant priest who had bound them. He closed his eyes. Jesu. What a high price to pay for possession of that young and lovely body. She had been chaste, virginal, and would have him no other way. A long time ago now. Nearly nine years. Before he was king. He opened his startlingly blue eyes. But he was king now and so he intended to remain. There was nothing to fear. Eleanor Butler was dead; the priest, Robert Stillington, silenced with the Bishopric of Bath and Wells. Suddenly he laughed aloud, a high joyous sound that held all of his youth and strength. The past was past, like the turbulent muddy water that churned in his wake. It would soon settle and none would even know of his passing. Today and tomorrow held problems enough. He frowned in concentration and gave his mind to the privy matter that had brought him to the Tower. It was John Neville who was the stumbling block here. Warwick's brother he might be but his loyalty to Edward and the house of York could not be faulted. How then could he strip him of the earldom of Northumberland without recompense? What could he offer him that would suffice to soothe him and yet not touch his own pocket too deeply? A marquisate perhaps? And there were always the forfeited Courtney lands in Devon that he had not yet disposed of. And as an added sweetener, the betrothal of his little daughter Bess to Neville's infant son. He nodded and smiled. Yes. That quite appealed to him. Nothing binding there. Bess was still in leading strings and Neville's son even younger. It would be years before he would have to commit himself further. But first he must see what manner of man this Percy was, whether captivity had mellowed the filthy insolent youth he had last encountered at York. His mouth twisted wryly in remembrance. Strange how that small defiance had irked him. From a grown man he might have taken it but not from a chit of a boy who could hardly keep on his feet through weariness. Edward's eyes grew suddenly cold. Well, he would kneel to him now. At least, he would if he wanted Northumberland back.

The barge slackened speed and he felt the shudder of the oars being shipped. He leant from the awning as they nosed beneath the Water Gate and were plunged into the sudden dark. The hull scraped the landing place with a noise like a cannon's roar. Black oily water swirled and sucked at the keel. Then came silence, an intense overwhelming silence that shrieked the pain and despair of countless men. Edward shivered and called sharply for a cresset to light the flight of green slimed stairs. Halfway up he paused and glanced toward the great square keep. A light burned dimly in the chapel. Daft Harry at his prayers again. Praying for what? Edward thought scornfully. Release from his earthly travail? Well, they all prayed for that, for every breath that Henry of Lancaster drew was an affront to Edward's kingship. A thousand times he had been tempted to quench that breath for ever. What was one more life? Who would know or even care? Then he looked away and smiled his greeting at Constable Dudley who waited to greet him. Edward took his arm and together they spoke of the man he had come to meet.

From the small mullioned slit of the Lantern Tower, Harry watched him. Like a shaft of sunlight Edward lit the walls and his warm carefree laugh came as a summer's breeze dispelling a winter's cold. Harry smiled with grudging admiration. He had no illusions about Edward of York. Beneath the glitter and the affable charm he knew that there was a man as ruthless as death. Edward meant to use him as he had used countless others before him. And why not? thought Harry philosophically. Was not the manipulation of lesser men the perogative of kings?

He turned back into the small square room that was so achingly familiar. Nothing had changed. The walls were still scarred with the scratched prayers and curses of the men who had been confined within them. His own mark was still there: the fetterlock enclosed within the horns of a Percy crescent and the neat incisions where he had kept a tally of the passing days before time had lost all meaning. The stain of the warden's blood on the cornerstone was still there and the iron ring where they had kept him fettered for a month for striking the blow that caused it. It was only himself that had changed. He was master now of his confinement.

He wondered idly how long Edward meant to keep him waiting. It was a month in all since he had left Wales. He knew this strategy — the waiting, the watching, the killing uncertainty, calculated to tear a man's nerves to shreds. But he was used to waiting and over the years he had acquired a deathly patience that could keep mind and body still no matter what threatened. And at least Edward was here. But not necessarily to see him. This might only be another turn of the screw. He breathed deeply to still the sudden thundering of his heart. It could be that Edward had changed his mind. He had no certain news save that Warwick still went free and unhindered in the north and it seemed that Edward had no thought of direct retribution for his treason. What if they were reconciled? What hope had he of freedom if Warwick was returned to power? Then he smiled his bitter empty smile. Perhaps Edward was more of a strategist than he had thought. The waiting was beginning to tell, even upon him.

He sank down wearily upon the planks of his bed. The moment was past and he had no real doubt that Edward was here to size him up before he committed himself irrevocably. And how far would he go to meet him? Once he had believed that if his freedom depended on abasing himself then he would never be free, that if Northumberland depended on the loss of his pride and dignity then it would never be his. That had been a long time ago. Captivity and solitude had taught him hard lessons since. There was not much now that Edward could demand of him that he was not prepared to give. Henry Tudor had at least been right in that. Pride was the luxury of free men.

Then he lifted his head. He heard the slow grating of the key in the lock. The door opened and Edward Plantagenet stooped to enter.

34

The King took a stance in the centre of the room and considered Harry in thoughtful silence. He was taller than Edward remembered and manhood had intensified that faintly sinister look that had been incongruous and ugly upon the boy but was not so upon the man. His hair was a dull and smoky black. His mouth was long and hard and turned in an oblique half smile that never quite reached his eyes. It was his eyes that were the most disturbing: calm yet full of a deep secret rage; mocking yet infinitely sad; indifferent yet burning in their depths with a passionate conviction; the eyes of an old man, long dead, who had looked unflinchingly at kings more dread than Edward and not been quelled.

Edward said in his amiable voice, 'So, cousin. Do we begin where we left off . . . or anew?'

Harry looked steadfastly into the fair handsome face. 'I am willing, your Grace.'

Edward frowned. *He* was willing? As if it were the captor not the captive who was to make the concessions. 'Willing for what, sir?' he snapped. 'Willing to admit that I am your lawful and anointed king? Willing to admit that Henry of Lancaster is madman and usurper and that the Frenchwoman's brat is bastard?'

Harry drew a long deep breath. They were come to it more quickly than he had thought, more quickly than he liked and he knew from the look on Edward's face that he expected an easy kill.

'If it is necessary,' he said evenly. 'I am not a fool, your Grace.'

Edward's eyes narrowed. 'Then what are you? Friend or foe? Rebel or loyalist? Lancaster or York?'

'I would have thought I was a man totally suited to your purpose, sire. Without ambition, save that of regaining what I consider to be my due. Without loyalty except to the man that deserves it . . .'

'Without hatreds, Harry?' Edward interrupted him quietly.

'No. Not without hatreds. If you thought that you would not have brought me here.'

Edward inclined his head. 'So we understand one another then?'

'I think we do, your Grace.'

'You are aware that if I restore you to your father's earldom, it

35

will mean dispossessing the Earl of Warwick's brother and Earl Warwick himself in some instances.'

'I am aware of it, your Grace,' Harry said softly.

In three long langourous strides Edward covered the distance to the window. He stood with his back against the light. 'Warwick is not an adversary to be taken lightly,' he said. 'He is still a very great power in the north. It will take a certain kind of man to stand against him. It had crossed my mind to wonder if you are that kind of man.'

Harry turned toward him so that the light fell full on his face. 'And do you still wonder, your Grace?'

Edward met the cold dead eyes. No. Not any more he didn't. 'And what guarantee do I have that if I restore you to power, you will not use it against me?'

'None, sire. Except my word.'

The King smiled mockingly. 'Not very much in exchange for the richest earldom in England.'

'But all that I have, I fear, sire. You yourself have seen to that.'

Edward grinned. 'A fair point, Harry. I asked for that.' He moved toward him, bright and vibrant in the gathering dark. 'So you are prepared to swear fealty to the House of York? Unconditionally? I must know that you mean to act for me, not merely against the Earl of Warwick.' He smiled mockingly. 'It's not quite the same thing, you know.'

'I am prepared to swear it to you, sire.'

Edward stiffened. 'Why the evasion, Harry? I must know your mind. I must know where your loyalty lies.'

'With England, your Grace. And if you are good and true to England, then it must lie with you.'

Edward listened to the soft persuasive voice and almost against his will was persuaded. Above all he was intrigued and more than a little aware that somehow he had been outmanoeuvred. Not once had he been able to draw this man out, not once had Harry committed himself other than vaguely. Now here, he thought, is a man I can use, especially against Warwick.

'Well, then,' he said, 'with that I can see I shall have to be content.' He moved unhurriedly toward the door, half expecting to be called back; for as Harry Percy had not committed himself,

36

neither, come to that, had he. He paused with his elegant jewelled hand upon the latch. 'Goodnight, cousin,' he said mockingly. 'Sleep well.'

The heavy iron-bound door closed behind him and Harry waited for the familiar grinding of the key. It never came and after a while he crossed to the door and opened it. The cold damp air struck him like a blow. He knew then that he was free.

York

He stood, lost and purposeless amid the throng which moved with such ease and licence around the King. The laughter and music deafened him, the blaze of jewels seared his eyes and his throat was closed and dry with the cloying scent of exquisitely gowned and painted women. For almost half a year now he had bowed and smiled and attempted the gaiety that seemed compulsory. He had eaten rich and fanciful foods until his gorge rose, he had hunted, he had hawked, he had danced and paid court to the bold women who seemed to think him something of a novelty. And he supposed that in Edward's licentious and pleasure-seeking court he was. Like a beggar at a feast. He stepped back a pace as a page staggered past laden with wine. Five months of freedom and still his heart hung in chains. Edward still kept him well to heel and Northumberland seemed as distant as ever though John Neville had been bought off handsomely long ago. He was still plain Harry Percy. He was still very much on trial.

Disdainfully he surveyed the men who clustered around the King. Richard of Gloucester, the King's youngest brother, who had escorted him from Wales. He was dark and thin with a pale melancholy face, a startling contrast to his two elder brothers. Beside him lounged William, Lord Hastings, the King's chamberlain and fellow lecher. And then the little Woodville clique: Richard and Thomas Grey, the Queen's sons by her first marriage, and Anthony, Earl Rivers, her brother. John Neville was there, Marquis of Montagu now though his discontent was obvious. And beside the King himself, John Tiptoft, Earl of Worcester, with his cruel Machiavellian face, patron of the arts and sadist who regaled them now with his latest subtlety.

'I hang them and draw them in the usual way, your Grace. Then I sever the head.' He drew an uneaten fowl toward him and brutally jerked the legs apart. 'Then I insert the stake, so.' The thin chased dagger slid through bone and its needle point emerged between the fowl's spread legs. He smiled his depraved butcher's smile and placed an apple upon the point. 'Then I impale the head thus.'

Harry turned his face away and met Richard of Gloucester's disgusted eyes, red-rimmed and over-bright they looked as if he had been weeping. Over Clarence? Harry wondered, for this last week had seen an end to his brother's aspirations. Both he and his mentor Warwick were fallen. It was the culmination of months of subterfuge on Edward's part. Since Christmas he and Warwick had played out their soft deadly game. Edward, smiling, had penned douce and courteous letters to Warwick requesting his presence at court. And Warwick, smiling the harder, had replied with equal courtesy: that his health forbade such a lengthy journey; that his wife was sick; that his daughter Isobel was with child and near her time . . . With angelic patience Edward had waited, through January and February into early March. Then at the beginning of the month Clarence had come, fair vacillating Clarence who seemingly had abandoned Warwick with the ease he had once abandoned his brother. Edward had welcomed him with open arms and he had not demurred when before the month was out Clarence asked for leave again. He had let him go and three days later heard that his brother had ridden north to rejoin his father-in-law Warwick at Coventry. Then abruptly Edward's patience had come to an end. He had called his army together and within a week they were moving north, ostensibly to quell a rebellion in Lincolnshire. But all knew that they were out for bigger game, the great Earl Warwick himself.

During that time Harry learnt much of policy and deviousness. Edward's strategy was not unknown, that of allowing a man enough rope to hang himself, and by the second week in March Warwick's neck was securely in the noose. At Huntingdon, the rebels' plans became clearer when Lord Welles fell into Edward's hands. He revealed, under what pressure was not known, that

Warwick and Clarence were moving north on a parallel course and were to muster with the rebel force at Leicester. Still Edward made no aggressive move, save to deprive Lord Welles of his head. At Stamford he received letters from the earl assuring the King of his loyal intent and promising to join him at Leicester. Edward replied in his own rounded hand 'that the lord Warwick would be heartily welcome.' That same night he received word that a rebel force under Lord Welles's son was a bare five miles ahead of him. Within an hour they were on the road in full battle array. Surprise, the ultimate strategy, won them the day. The fighting was brief, the rebels fleeing before half the royal army was in the field and shedding their armour at such a pace that the encounter had been dubbed Losecote Field. The King pressed on, resting for the night at Pontefract where the captured Sir Robert Welles freely sang the song of Warwick's perfidy. There Edward dictated a last and not so loving letter, commanding Warwick and Clarence to disarm immediately and present themselves at York. It was his first mistake. Warwick was too old a hand to fall into such a trap and by the time Edward and his army had reached York, Warwick and Clarence were headed south for Portsmouth and hence to France. It was the impasse that Edward had dreaded. In France lay Margaret of Anjou and scheming Louis. In France lay the last hope of the Lancastrian house.

Edward said as much now and John Tiptoft gave a derisive laugh. 'Warwick and Lancaster! God's eyes! I'd like to see the day.'

John Neville was flushed and trembling with rage. 'Your Grace, for all that's between you, my brother would never consort with the Frenchwoman.'

Edward picked idly at a marchpane swan, one eye on Neville, the other on the swelling bosom of the woman who knelt at his feet. 'Would he not?' he murmured. 'Desperate needs call for desperate measures.' He swung round suddenly and beckoned Harry. 'Come, my lord,' he said in his soft drunken voice. 'Will Warwick embrace Lancaster as you have done York? Tell us, Harry. What makes a man turn his coat?'

Harry met the mocking blue eyes steadily. He was used to Edward goading him, for no better reason than to see what he was made of. It had become something of a sport with him, like baiting a bull to see how he could be broken. As yet he had not been broken. He took all with smiling unruffled calm and nine times out of ten gave as good as he got. He knew these men better than they would ever know him: men like Hastings and Rivers who would have patronised him till they met his eyes, and those who were openly hostile like John Neville. There were a few like Richard of Gloucester who sensed the man beneath the passive veneer and treated him with respect.

'Usually necessity, your Grace,' he said equably. 'Sometimes greed — for were not all the Nevilles true Lancastrians once, before your lady mother wed the Duke of York?'

Edward's eyes narrowed fractionally and he held up his hand to still John Neville's growl of protest. 'But at the heart, Harry,' he persisted. 'At the heart of him does a man really change?'

'I doubt if Earl Warwick has such, your Grace.'

Edward's eyes clouded. 'He did have once,' he said morosely, remembering when he and Warwick had been as one, one heart, one love, one loyalty. He drank deeply from his gilded cup. 'And you, Harry? Do you have a heart? What moves you, my lord? What pleases you?' Edward glared at him malevolently. 'Nothing, I think, that has been offered you here, for I've seen you picking at table as if it were carrion on your plate and sipping your wine like a maid. *This* is how a man drinks, Harry.' He raised the goblet in a blaze of light and downed the contents noisily. 'There. So that it warms you. So that your belly glows.'

He laughed uproariously and flung a velvet-clad arm round Hastings's neck. 'We will have to school him. I'll swear he's the only virgin in this hall.'

His eyes rested with smiling malice on Harry's face. 'Have you no appetite for that either? Shame on you, Harry. Nine years in hold and not one woman here to take your eye?'

Tom Grey sniggered. 'God's eyes. I would have laid the first wench I clapped eyes on.'

The King nodded. 'Then why not you, Harry? It's not for want of offers, is it?' He prodded Harry in the chest. 'I've seen a dozen or more eyeing you up. And why shouldn't they? Do you see how fine I have made him, my lords? New velvet and silken hose and

40

gold and topaz at his throat. And all seemingly wasted.'

Harry waited till the gusty laughter had died down. 'I thank you, your Grace,' he said in a quiet amiable voice that was more chilling than if he had screamed aloud. 'I had not meant to seem ungrateful, either for your lavish hospitality or the new velvet with which I am truly pleased. It is a long time since I had anything new. Usually my possessions have been very well worn — like the fair ladies you so thoughtfully put at my disposal.' He looked smilingly round the circle of lascivious faces. 'I had a fancy for something a little less well used.'

Edward stared at him and then suddenly dissolved into helpless laughter. 'Oh, Harry. You'll do. I really think you'll do.'

Then Tom Grey clapped him heartily on the back, Hastings saluted him mockingly. Only John Neville remained unsmiling and aloof as if, seeing Harry with Edward's arm around his neck, he suddenly realised his danger.

The next day Harry walked toward the King across the very stones on which he had once so steadfastly refused to kneel and the gesture so long witheld sealed the wordless compact between them. He placed his long hands between the King's and in his beautiful voice swore the oath of fealty that bound him irrevocably to Edward and York. When he rose he was Northumberland and the first face he looked for was John Neville's. It was the twenty-fifth of March 1470, nine years all but four days since Towton.

Harry came down from High Cheviot at noon, down the long winding drovers' road that plunged headlong to the valley floor and rose again, a thin nebulous thread among the peat hags and heather of Comb Fell. He rode alone except for a gangling wolf-hound pup that pounded happily at his heels. Grey horned sheep scattered wildly from his path, hares and conies bolted for cover and once, recklessly, he chased a boar till he lost it in the elder woods below Cushat Law.

He fell laughing and exhausted from his horse as the beast crashed away into the undergrowth and called back the undisciplined young dog when he would have followed. He was tired

41

and dirty and unutterably content. It was the seventh day of August. Today he was twenty-one years old.

He closed his eyes against the sun's ruthless glare. He had been riding since early dawn, before the sun had fired the torches of yellow broom upon the moor and only white stars of hawthorn lit the hills. From the summit of Cheviot he had watched the sun rise. The sharp white light had pierced the hills like a spear, waking green and gold from the bleached summer grasses, climbing the bland open face of Scald Hill, flushing out the hollows of Hedgehope and the Schill before it had burst smilingly upon the summit.

He had lain for hours in the warm scented grass. He had watched an eagle circling lazily above him; black as it rose against the sun, glittering with golden malice as it plunged to view this intruder. He had looked down into Scotland and seen a mirror image of dark hills and forests and deep impenetrable glens, passive now under perpetual truce for the English had been too busy fighting each other, and the Scots had wet-nursed a boy king. Not so much of a boy now, though. James the Third of Scotland would be at least seventeen; effeminate, so they said, devoted to books and music and art. Harry had wondered why it made a man less of a man because he preferred beauty to warfare. And no doubt James was well sated with the possession of Berwick, the strategic jewel that Queen Margaret had bartered away in exchange for twenty thousand Scots and French mercenaries. It was one of the few offices that Edward had not been able to restore to him, that and the wardenship of the West March which he had strategically withheld as a safeguard against Harry's complete dominance of the north. The East and Middle Marches had been surrendered to him in June by a furious John Neville, pushed to the limits of his forbearance and loyalty by the added grievance of having to yield the Percy lordship of Wressell which had been granted him only the year before. Harry had pushed him a little further and made no secret of his triumph. Deliberately and wantonly he had made John Neville his open and deadly enemy.

He had made others since; dishonest clerks and pilfering stewards who had thought him an easy touch. Making friends

42

had been more difficult though there were plenty ready and willing to name themselves such; among them his two elder sisters and their impoverished Lancastrian lords, total strangers to him now for there was nothing in those two hard and grasping women to recall the little girls he had loved. And they had only been the first in a long and wearisome procession of scroungers come to pay duty and homage to their lord. In his heart he hadn't really blamed them. Times had been hard for all Lancastrians, particularly in the north where a change of master was not undertaken lightly. Old loyalties died hard, especially Lancastrian ones, and there he knew he was bound to disappoint them. They expected far more than he was either able or willing to provide. Did they really think he would deliver them from the Yorkist toils? Many did, old stalwarts whose families had served his for generations; sons who had lost fathers at Towton and St Albans, fathers who had lost sons and were seemingly prepared to lose more to restore Lancaster to the throne. It was the nearest he ever came to open anger, to see them all in their patched and mended doublets, living hand to mouth on a pittance of alms yet speaking so reverently of the 'cause' and the holy imbecile who inspired it.

His own desires were not so exalted. Northumberland was his only steadfast belief, his one love, his one loyalty and all of his creed. He had his inheritance but not whole and intact as it had been in the first earl's day. Seventy years of attainder and confiscation had eaten away at the Percys' once vast lands. He knew of at least a score of rich manors lost or swallowed up by the crown: part of his mother's great Poynings inheritance had never been restored, and there were the Durham lands, the four lordships in Kent . . . He laughed aloud, a smooth soft sound, quickly broken off as if the timbre of it surprised him. And he had thought he was not ambitious!

He rode slowly home through the summer dusk, reluctant to relinquish the passing day. There was nothing at Alnwick to call him back and he'd had his fill of stone walls and shuttered rooms. Only Eleanor would be waiting, playing the matriarch and trying desperately to overcome the antipathy between them. He smiled grimly to himself. Did she really think he cared? Did she think he didn't know that this charade of concern for him was only to

43

advance the boy John? He supposed he should have been angered by that, to see his own mother so jealous and defensive of this stranger's rights, but Eleanor had long ago lost the power to rouse anything in him but a vague irritation and distaste. Towards the boy himself he bore no malice. It was only his actual physical presence that he found disturbing and offensive. To meet those vivid and unforgettable blue eyes, to see that dark head bent close to Eleanor's. Seemingly it had never occurred to his mother that Thomas Percy's face would be the last that he wished to see.

Eleanor stared broodingly at St Sebastian's agonised face. Pearls of sweat glistened upon his brow, diamond tears upon his cheek. Gilded arrows pierced his silken flesh, his wounds wept founts of ruby blood; sixty-four pearls, twelve diamonds and fourteen rubies impaled upon arras silk besides thirty pounds of goldsmiths' work. It was her most treasured possession, yet today even St Sebastian palled.

She glanced toward the window. The rain had ceased, a brief summer storm that had set every blade and leaf quivering in a wanton dance. A sad reminiscent smile curved her mouth. Once she had loved to dance, her body swaying in the stiff sensual rhythm of a virelay, whirling in a mad rondeau . . . Once. When she had been young . . . The smile hardened and grew bitter. Youth had gone and though she painted it on her face daily, age seeped through like the damp on a wall. Men looked at her now with pity instead of desire. She had heard one say with cruel compassion. '*I hear she was very beautiful once.*' Once, a long time ago . . .

She glanced down at her youngest daughter who sat at her feet. Elizabeth was plain and thin, but enviably young. She leaned forward and pinched the girl's arm viciously.

'Smile, child, for pity's sake,' she whispered. 'You are to be wed. Are you not overjoyed, daughter?' You ought to be, she thought with disdain. At least you'll be spared the pain of childbirth for a while. Elizabeth's prospective husband, the son of Lord Scrope, was a babe of less than two years old.

Her other two daughters she regarded with more interest. It hadn't taken them long to come with their begging bowls.

Eleanor, she noticed with satisfaction, had grown coarse and fat. Margaret was more like herself, sharp and devious, anxious to please and openly ambitious for the stolid knight Gascoigne to whom she had been reluctantly married. Yes, she thought. She would keep Margaret by her. She would have need of such to serve her.

She smoothed her gown of faultless samite. She fingered the jewels that jostled for brilliance at her throat. Her restless insatiable eyes darted from face to face; and as she watched them she saw how they, in their turn, watched Harry. She saw the awe and speculation on their faces. They were wary still of this silent, smiling and derisive man, uncertain yet of how far they could overstep the bounds of privilege before they were called to account. He was still an unknown quantity whose strength and weakness had yet to be proved. So far he had shown them all a smooth impenetrable front backed by an understated ruthlessness that was impressive and had drawn more men to him than it had driven away. Quietly he had dazzled them, with his soft mellifluous voice, his wordless arrogance, his swift and confident assumption of power so that whether his air of omnipotence was assumed or real, no man dared question it.

She chewed fretfully at her lip. So much for her hopes of manipulating him, for none of her carefully wrought schemes had gained ground. It was not that he stinted her. She had had jewels and gowns and counted that a victory till she had realised that he had a like taste for magnificence himself and that the sumptuous tapestries and furnishings were more to please himself than her. Oh yes, he allowed her her woman's pleasures well enough but of himself and his thoughts he gave her nothing.

She frowned, thinking of some way to reach him. Did he ever laugh or weep? Was there anything at all beneath that deadly calm? Love and hate she knew how to combat but indifference completely defeated her. Yet there must be something, some small weakness, some flaw in that immaculate self-control. She wondered if he had ever felt passion or lust and decided that he had not. There was something virgin and untouched about him. He rarely looked at women but when he did it was without knowledge or experience. Her eyes hardened. And so it would remain if she had her way. She had no mind for him to marry and get sons yet. Not while John was unprovided for.

She came to him in his chamber at dusk when she knew that he would be alone. The first time she spoke his name he did not acknowledge her and only as she came towards him did he reluctantly look up.

Harry watched his mother approach, jewelled and painted like a pagan queen. Cochineal lips smiled at him from a lead-white face. Her flat scrawny bosom heaved beneath a weight of gems.

'Harry,' Eleanor smiled her douce and submissive smile and laid a diamond-studded claw upon his sleeve.

He looked up at her coldly, mildly irritated that she should think him so easily deceived. Even as a boy he had known all the faces of Eleanor. He had seen her wildly drunk and frighteningly sober, he had seen her at the height of her joy and in the depths of her grief. He had seen her spiteful, tender, devious, sly but he had never seen Eleanor content.

'I have been thinking,' she said, giving him a vague and unworldly look. 'Could not we do something more for John?'

'What more?' Harry laid down his quill. 'He has a tutor, horses, hounds, the hawk that seemingly he could not live without. Plumpton schools him to arms. What more then?'

'Oh, I don't know.' She shrugged elaborately. 'He has no definite prospects yet although he knows, of course, that one day Egremont will be his, but . . .'

He stopped her harshly. 'You are presumptuous, madame. Who says that Egremont will be his?'

She turned wide innocent eyes upon him. 'Well, of course it will be his. It was his father's.'

'And is mine now,' Harry said stonily. 'So I intend it shall remain.'

'You would disinherit him, then?'

Harry smiled faintly and grimly. He said, 'I know of no precedent in law which gives a bastard such inalienable rights.'

'I do not speak of law.' Her voice grew shrill. 'I speak of moral right.'

'*Moral* right! I am surprised that you have the effrontery to use that word to me.' His eyes dwelt unpleasantly upon her face. 'Are you even aware of its meaning?'

Beneath the painted mask Eleanor flushed, though the insult barely touched her. She had endured far worse for the father's sake. She could do no less for the son.

'Well, then,' Harry said pleasantly as he rose from the desk, 'what more can we do for our little waif, this catalyst of the martyr Thomas's blood?' He poured wine into a cup and held it out toward her. 'Is this to be the new sacrament, then? Drink this, for this is my blood. Do this in rememberance of me.' He came and stood over her. 'But if you live upon your memories, madame, then so do I upon mine. I remember how you destroyed my father, you and Thomas. Inch by inch. Day by day. I remember the look upon your face as you watched him die. I heard all that passed between you then. How he asked you if I were truly his son. Were you tempted to lie? To take even that last comfort from him?'

Eleanor's face paled with apprehension and shock. It was the first time he had ever spoken of his father. She cried defensively, 'I told him the truth. I did not lie.'

'No. I know you did not. I heard you. You said that Thomas would never have sired such a weak and puling thing. But how long had he lived with the doubt before you so charitably put him from his misery? You could not bear to see him loved even by me, could you? You had to put that between us.'

Eleanor shook her head blindly. She felt sick and weak. She could feel her mind growing numb and blank. She must say something, she must defend herself. She shook her head again to clear the mist from her eyes. 'Harry,' she whispered. 'You did not know him . . .'

'I know that at the heart of him he was honest and courageous and gentle and whatever else he was, only you and Thomas made him.'

'And I know other things.' Rage gathered at last in her bony breast. 'He was weak. He was bestial . . .'

'And so you climbed into his brother's bed. My God, madame. Are you sure it was he who was weak and bestial?'

He wrenched his eyes away from her but not before she had

47

seen the dreadful agony in them. So this was the weakness, this was the flaw, and ironically it was one that she dared not exploit without danger to herself. Desperately she tried to soothe him. 'Harry,' she said gently. 'Harry, my son. We must not quarrel. What's past is past. It cannot be undone. And God knows I have suffered for it and repented it often enough. If your father himself forgave me, can you do any less?'

He turned and looked at her. 'Go and wash your face, madame. You look like a painted whore.'

Outside in the bailey the object of their quarrel fought doggedly with Robert Plumpton, the son of his tutor and master at arms. The elder boy's opinion of both his opponent's breeding and skill showed quite plainly on his face and in the contemptuous flick of his blunted sword. John lunged back and forth, clumsily parrying the lightning thrusts. The ring of avid and watchful faces moved with him, marking his every blundering step with covert sneers, his miscast strokes with derisive laughter. He knew that there was not one amongst them who would not delight in seeing him thrashed for they made no secret of how they despised him. And he despised them, for their smug arrogance, for their rights and privileges that they wore as unconsciously as their clothes, for their birth and heritage that was so unquestionable that it never had to be asserted. He felt the disparity so strongly that it had soured his dealings with the few that had treated him fairly. Somehow he could never strike the right balance. Those that were kind to him he patronised and bullied. Those that were not he courted for favour and made himself the more despised. Most treated him with a vague condescending indifference that seemed infinitely worse than either. For all his fine clothes and the trappings of high birth they neither envied nor acknowledged him. He was not one of them nor ever would he be and they made quite certain that he knew it.

The thought put strength into his flagging arm and he almost penetrated Plumpton's guard. But he had lunged too soon and too hard and the slighter boy danced nimbly from his path and sent him headlong into the crowd.

With howls of fiendish laughter they sent him back. His head pounded like a beaten drum. Sweat ran blindingly into his eyes. He blinked Plumpton's narrow haughty features into focus. He fought bareheaded and his long fair curls were hardly disturbed. He looked so cool, almost bored as he effortlessly prodded and weaved around him. John knew that he was playing with him. He could have struck the blade from his hand a dozen times in the last half hour and made an honest end to it. That, perhaps, he could have borne, but this, to be made a spectacle of . . . That it was all of his own making did not make it easier. He had goaded Plumpton unmercifully, all but challenging him to the combat. And not for the first time. This was only the culmination of weeks and months of provocation on his part and he, so secure in his own conceit of himself and the Countess Eleanor's overweening protection, had at last pushed his credit to the limit. None had been more surprised than himself when at last Plumpton had chosen to retaliate.

Then the boy's long arm reached out and swung hard and fast at his head. Too late he parried and his sword was born effortlessly down. He retreated under a sudden flurry of blows that struck sparks from his stricken blade. The next would have knocked it clean from his grasp but it never came. He was left stabbing foolishly at the air. Plumpton had turned away.

'Enough.' It was Harry's voice and coming so quietly through the tumult he wondered how they had heard it. But heard it they had and Plumpton obediently put up his sword. The spectators fell uneasily silent.

'Enough,' Harry's voice was sharp now with criticism and inwardly John smiled. 'Are there no combatants of your own age, Robert, that you need to match yourself with the boy?'

Plumpton's pale eyes rested disparagingly upon John. '*He* issued the challenge, my lord. Repeatedly. I have witnesses. I was honour bound to meet him.' The arrogant mouth curved in a sneer. 'Perhaps, my lord, he did not understand that. He seems to think himself immune from any form of retribution.'

John's head came up fiercely. He saw the youth leaning nonchalantly on his sword. He saw the company close and fast at his back. Their eyes mocked and excluded him. *You see, upstart? You are none of us.*

49

Enough, Harry had said. For them perhaps, as they had made him look as foolish as they had meant. But not for him. Oh, no. Not by a long way was it enough for him.

Suddenly he lunged with all his strength and swung a murderous blow at Plumpton's head. The flat of his blade cracked satisfyingly on bone. Blood flamed darkly beneath the pale skin. He watched him fall, clean felled as an oak, blood bursting now through the ruptured skin and spattering the dazed and astounded crowd. The sight of it inflamed him more and he would have struck again had not an iron hand jerked him off his feet and flung him face down in the dust.

'Take him.' He heard Harry's voice, fire sheathed in ice. 'Shut him up in the Ravine Tower. And see that he is chained.'

It was fully dark when Harry at last came to him. Three hours, John reckoned, since they had flung him unceremoniously into this dingy and fetid cell. He had not gone easily. He had fought and kicked, and screamed such gutter filth that even the hard-bitten guards had blanched. He still trembled with the satisfaction of it; the release of all that pent-up rage and frustration, to see the shock and horror on their foolish faces . . .

He smiled happily to himself and dropped his legs over the edge of the narrow bed as he heard the guards approach. He could move quite freely, for though they had shackled him, the manacles had been made for men not boys and he had managed to slip them easily.

He stood quite still, facing the door. The footsteps had halted and he heard the brief murmur of voices. Then the footsteps again, one man alone who paused outside the door as if he were listening.

He tilted his head, listening as hard. What, he wondered, did Harry hope to hear? For he knew instinctively that it was him. Perhaps the sound of him weeping, cold and contrite in the darkness? Did they really think he was afraid of the dark? He, who had once crawled nightly on his belly through dark woods to snare his next day's supper? But then what did any of them really know about him? Each saw only the part of him that they wanted to see. Plumpton saw only his base and peasant blood. Eleanor saw only his father. But nobody actually saw *him* — except Harry perhaps. He thought that Harry knew and understood him. It made life a little easier. He didn't have to pretend so much with Harry.

And what now was he pondering so long and hard outside the door? What subtle punishment was Harry devising? He knew it would be nothing obvious or crude; not the short hard lesson he would have preferred. He jutted his chin defiantly to cover his fear. Let Harry do what he liked. He didn't feel even the slightest remorse. He only wished now that he had struck harder.

When the door finally opened he was ready for him, his head held high, his eyes blinking in the sudden light of the flare in Harry's hand. He did not enter immediately. The flame drifted disembodied in the darkness and lit the dark sardonic face. His eyes held and intensified the flame, burning up the space of shadow between them, so that it seemed for a moment that the light emanated from the man himself rather than the flame in his hand. Then Harry smiled and stepped lightly into the room, his brilliance dimming only a little as he placed the torch in its high iron sconce.

'Well, John.' Harry seated himself on the edge of the bed so that their eyes were on a level. 'I must say that I had thought to find you more repentant — outwardly at least. That is one of the first rules here, John. A man of honour owns to his fault and tries to mend it if he can.' He stared hard into the boy's belligerent face. 'Do you find our lessons so hard to learn, John? Or is it we who are poor tutors?'

The boy remained silent and Harry frowned. He had often wondered how a boy of twelve could build up such a fund of dislike. He knew now, the long and sorry tale told by a hundred willing tongues: the bullying and petty cruelties to boys half his age and size, the lies, the taletelling and, besides all that, the calmer testimony of his elders and betters whose authority he had flouted quite blatantly, secure in the knowledge of Eleanor's patronage. And there was the crux of it — Eleanor with her sick and morbid passion for a dead man. This defiant and unhappy little creature was wholly her creation.

'John,' he said gently. Answer me. Did you lose your tongue

51

along with your wits when you struck Robert Plumpton down? You have not even asked how he does.'

John shuffled his feet uneasily. The voice was kind, unbearably kind. It would have been so easy to loose the flood of tears that pressed insistently against his eyes — if Harry had not been the enemy, if Eleanor had not prepared him so well to resist the onslaught of that voice. 'I don't care how he does,' he burst out. 'Why should I? I hope he dies.'

'As he may very well have done if you had struck him again as you had meant. What then, John? Will the Countess Eleanor protect you then, when they came to hang you? For hang you they would. Even within these walls you are not above the law.'

He waited, the crooked smile turning his mouth and saw the fear creep slowly into the boy's eyes. 'And whilst we are about it,' he said casually, 'what was young Plumpton's crime that you all but knocked his brains out? Over what were you fighting in the first place?'

John stared sullenly at his feet. 'He called me a bastard,' he said.

Harry looked at him with contempt. 'Is that all? And for that you almost killed him? Does it touch you so deeply, then? A name, a word? Christ, boy. You'll have to learn to take worse than that before you're older.'

'There is no worse,' John cried hotly.

'Is there not? Bastard was the least of the slurs I heard laid against your name today.'

'And you believed them all, I suppose. Their word against mine and theirs taken because they are the sons of knights and earls and I am only Egremont's bastard.'

'No. Theirs taken because you are a liar and a bully and a coward though it might well be that you are all of these things because you are Egremont's bastard.' Harry smiled malevolently. 'Like father, like son.'

John's head came up. 'My father was a brave and honourable knight,' he shouted. 'Don't you dare malign him.'

'He was also a drunkard and a lecher who pleasured himself on any woman who was willing, especially upon my lady mother who was more than willing.' Harry lunged suddenly to his feet. 'Has it ever occurred to you, John, that it is by the grace of God that we are only cousins instead of brothers?'

The boy shook his head blindly and could not make an answer. Tears burned in his eyes but remained unshed. He saw Harry come toward him, a shimmering corruscation of black and gold. He took him gently by the shoulders.

'So there you have your parentage, John. Not so very much worse than mine. You must learn to live with it yet be apart from it. You must accept it for what it is and remember that if there is any shame or dishonour in your birth, it belongs not to you but to the man that sired you without thought or care for what he did.' He reached out a hand and turned the stubbornly averted face toward him. 'You can be other things besides Egremont's bastard, John. You could be plain John Percy and what comes to you then will be from your own worth and not just the leavings of a dead man.'

Still the boy remained silent and in the end Harry turned away. 'Tomorrow,' he said heavily, 'you will be sent to join Lord Scrope's household at Bolton in Westmorland. You will serve in his household for two years as a page and you'll be given neither preference nor favour as you have been here. I'm afraid you must learn, John, that despite what the lady Eleanor tells you, there is no quick and easy way in the world.'

He left him then, as stubborn and unrepentant as he had found him, while he himself went filled with an obscure inner despair that came and fastened on him from nowhere.

He halted in the dark doorway and leant his cheek against the stone. For a moment, remembering the boy's stricken face, he was tempted to go back. It would be a hard and bitter lesson that he would learn at Bolton. More strangers; more rules and prejudices for him to overcome. He sighed. But learn it he must if they were ever to make anything of him. He would be a better man for it in the end. Harry lifted his head and looked out into the darkness. Now there was Eleanor to face.

'Where is he?' The door of his chamber crashed resoundingly against the wall and admitted a wild and furious Eleanor. Her hair was loose, her face streaked and blotched with tears. She wore only a loose robe, stained and stinking with wine.

Harry eyed her with revulsion. 'If you refer to that murderous little protégé of yours, he is still in the Ravine Tower.'

'I demand to see him.'

'Demand then.' Harry turned his back on her and seated himself in a chair by the hearth.

Eleanor advanced toward him with an elaborately steady gait. 'You cannot keep him locked up forever.'

'I do not intend to. Tomorrow he leaves for Westmorland. John Scrope is going to teach him some manners.'

'No.' Instantly she was contrite and tearful. 'No, Harry. I beg you, let him stay. I know he was foolish today but . . .'

'*Foolish!*' Harry stared at her in disbelief. 'My God, madame. Where are your wits that you can describe what happened today as foolish? He almost killed young Robert and would have if he had struck harder and higher. For his own protection John is better elsewhere. I can assure you that there's not a man here who is not itching to get his hands on the boy and teach him a sharp lesson. Plumpton's father is almost beside himself with rage . . .'

'Plumpton's nobody,' she shouted. 'Since when has Northumberland been dictated to by his servants?'

'He may not be anybody to you, but he is to me. Will Plumpton has faithfully served this house for the last fifty years.' He smiled at her tauntingly. 'Unlike you, madame. Fidelity and constancy I hold dear.'

He looked away from her white furious face. 'Besides which, I think you have harmed him enough.'

'Harmed him? How have I harmed him? I took him from some filthy hovel . . .'

'And did him the greatest disservice of his life by thrusting him among strangers and teaching him that he is greater than he is.' He turned his head and froze her with his chilling gaze. 'Leave him be, madame. If you have any love for the boy, then let him alone.'

'So that's it. That's your revenge.' Eleanor came threateningly toward him, a hand outstretched to claw at his face. 'You're trying to take John from me, to turn him against me.' She stumbled on the hem of her robe and fell heavily against his chair and he recoiled at the smell of the sweet wine upon her breath and the hot

54

unwashed scent of her body.

She saw his eyes, dark with revulsion, as if some awful foulness had touched him. She was suddenly aware of her wild, dishevelled hair, her naked face, the soiled gown hanging open to reveal her sagging breasts.

She began to laugh shrilly. His father had always looked at her like that. She said, sneering, 'Oh, poor Harry. Do I truly offend you so much.'

'Yes,' he answered her gravely, almost sadly. 'Yes. You do. You offend me very much.'

The laughter diminished to a faint and bitter smile. His reply did not anger her. She felt only an intense relief that the pretence between them was over. She clutched her gown closer about her and put up a hand to smooth her hair. Then she turned away, her shoulders sagging with pretended defeat. Let him think for now that he had won. There would be another time, she promised herself. The battle was only just begun.

At the door she paused. Would he be magnanimous enough to grant one last concession? She said, pleadingly. 'Harry. May I see John for a moment before he leaves?'

He did not even look at her. 'No,' he said. 'You may not.'

The streets of York were full of men, armed men, who came and went seemingly without destination or purpose; the Duke of Gloucester's men, flamboyant in sable livery with the white boar upon their sleeves.

From the upper room of his house in Walmgate, Harry watched them. Two men-at-arms rolled dice on the corner, another passed his door for the fifteenth time. They had been there all morning, since he had ridden in from Bolton, where two days ago he had lodged a still sulky and defiant John. Only at the actual moment of parting had the boy weakened and come anywhere near repenting. But it was too late then. He had been committed. John would stay at Bolton for at least a year. He would think upon it then.

He glanced along the wide cobbled street that ran eastward down to Hull. Pale autumn sun fell in chevrons of yellow light between the pointed roofs of the gabled houses. Harry's eyes lingered briefly on the square broken tower of the church of St Denys. His father had bled to death there the day after Towton. He was buried beneath the altar on which he had died.

Then he leant closer to the lattice as a curtained litter rumbled past and turned at speed into Fossgate. The painted doors bore the badge of York. He raised his brows in mild speculation. Cecily Neville, Duchess of York, and an hour before, her son, Richard of Gloucester. Both in haste, both heading for the great stone fortress ringed by the Foss and the Ouse. And below him, Gloucester's men still maintained their casual presence.

His brother-in-law, Will Gascoigne, came and stood at his back. 'Still there then,' he observed thoughtfully.

Harry nodded. 'And like to be, I think, while I am.'

'What's Gloucester about, I wonder?'

Harry turned to face him. 'I think it is time we found out.'

Richard of Gloucester received him alone and with the air of anxious aggression which coloured all his dealings with his fellow men. Nervously he watched Northumberland approach. A tall man. They were always tall men, unconsciously pointing the finger at his own lack of height, emphasising by comparison the spare limbs and narrow shoulders that were so deceptive of his strength.

He said in his strong but quiet voice. 'You are welcome, my lord.' He added, half-heartedly, 'Cousin.'

Harry straightened from his formal bow and looked full into the sad dark eyes.

'I thought that perhaps I should come before I was sent for, your Grace,' he said amiably. 'Besides, I was as tired of watching your men as they were of watching me.'

Gloucester flushed but he did not rise to the bait. Briefly and with veiled curiosity his eyes dwelt on Harry Percy's face. They must have met at least a score of times since he had brought him out of Wales. Yet he knew him no better than he had done then. He remained aloof, an enigma, uncommitted to any one cause except the pursuance of his own private ambitions. Watch him, Edward had said, for every Lancastrian was suspect now, particularly one like Northumberland who had a long and grievous score to settle. Again he searched the dark impassive face and unflinchingly Northumberland returned his look, without impatience or rancour, without expression at all except for a mild amused contempt that filled him with sudden anger at the thought that it might be for him.

Harshly he said, 'And what makes you think that you would be sent for, my lord? What have you done that your conscience troubles you?'

'Not conscience, your Grace. Merely hard common sense. Surely every man's loyalty must be called into question now' — Harry smiled obliquely — 'now that Warwick has made compact with Louis of France and Queen Margaret and has wed his daughter to her son. I hear that he has declared utterly for Lancaster and sworn to restore King Henry to the throne. They say he has gathered a mighty fleet and only awaits a fair wind.'

Richard grew pale. To hear it all said out loud brought the pain agonisingly close to the surface: Warwick, whom he had loved as a father; his daughter Anne, whom he would have loved as his wife. All gone, smashed and broken like images of brittle glass. Except that for him it wasn't as easy as that. He still loved Warwick, he still loved Anne. All that saved him was that he loved his brother Edward more.

He said stiffly, aware of Northumberland's mocking glance upon his face. 'You are well informed, my lord.'

'I would have thought it common knowledge by now, your Grace. I had it a week ago from my steward at Wressell. He had it from Lord Dacre's man who said he had it from John Neville himself.' Harry paused, then added with smiling malice, 'I wonder who John Neville had it from? His brother Warwick, perhaps?'

The insinuation was clear and Richard cried hotly, 'That's a vile and utterly contemptible thing to say. Montagu is completely loyal.'

'So was the Earl of Warwick once,' Harry observed. 'Men change, your Grace. As do the seasons.'

'You say so, my lord, but I know different. John Neville would not betray my brother Edward.' It was said with more confidence than Richard actually felt. He had always judged it an error to deprive Neville of Northumberland and the March. He was still sulky and aggrieved, and rightly so, for Edward's grudging reparation for the loss of his lands had fallen far short of what he thought he deserved. And he could not put it from his mind that it was one of Montagu's men who had stirred the men of Lincolnshire to another of the sporadic and mysterious risings that had always melted away at Edward's approach. He had his own ideas on that. It would be typical of Warwick's cunning strategy to let Edward run himself ragged in the north whilst he made a leisurely landing in the south.

'I hope you are right, my lord,' Northumberland said, breaking into his thoughts. 'I understand you have given him commission of array in the Midlands.'

'Meaning?'

'Meaning that you have given Neville command of a vast army of men which, should they be turned against you . . .' Harry shrugged and let the implication settle uneasily in Gloucester's mind. Then he probed ruthlessly at another sore spot. 'And his grace of Clarence, your brother? Is he concerned in this?'

Gloucester chewed agitatedly at his lip. George was still with Warwick in France. In his heart of hearts he still clung to the wild hope that his brother would return to his senses. Surely Warwick's move to embrace Lancaster would show him clearly where he stood? False and ambitious Clarence might be but he was Yorkist through and through. Then his vague irritation flamed into sudden anger as he again became aware that Northumberland was watching him. Who was Northumberland to question him? And moreover, he disliked this blunt and open approach. He was used to men who chose their words with care and spoke them with a like constraint.

'Since you are so concerned with loyalties, my lord,' he said, equally bluntly, 'perhaps we could speak of yours. Where exactly, I wonder, do you yourself stand?'

'Do you mean, shall I bring the north out for Lancaster if Warwick invades?'

Gloucester pursed his lips. Again that direct and seemingly open approach; this habit of answering one question with another that still left the answer lacking.

58

'Yes,' he said. 'That is exactly what I mean.'

'Let it suffice to say that I shall not fight for the Earl of Warwick.'

'That is not what I asked you,' Gloucester persisted. 'I asked if you would declare for Lancaster.'

'Then, no. I shall not,' Harry answered him quietly. 'But neither shall I for York.'

Gloucester blanched. 'Are you aware that what you are saying is tantamount to treason?'

'Yes, I am aware of it.' Harry looked hard into the younger man's face, a sensitive, intelligent and likeable face once the stiff self-conscious manner was set aside. 'Can we speak honestly, my lord?' he said.

'I know of no other way.'

'Then you must know that at its heart the north still champions Henry of Lancaster. Towton was not so long ago that men have fogotten. There is still a great deal of bitterness against York.'

Richard nodded. This he knew from his own dealings here — how precarious the Yorkist hold was.

'The north will not fight willingly against Henry of Lancaster. I could not guarantee that even if I put them in the field at the last minute they might not go over to Henry.'

'What can you guarantee then?'

'Not very much. To keep them still. To make sure that if they will not fight for York, neither shall they for Lancaster.'

Richard smiled bleakly. 'As you say, my lord, not very much.' Even so, it was better than nothing. The north had always been their weakness and they had kept their tentative hold on the peace only by virtue of Warwick's Neville following. But Warwick was for Lancaster now and the men they could once have relied on to hold the balance for York now tipped the scales in Lancaster's favour. His heart turned within him. To think that Warwick was the enemy now and his beloved Anne the wife of another man. He thought of Middleham where he had spent his boyhood years, the quiet joyous days that had so abruptly ended. He felt the betrayal far more than Edward. Loyalty and friendship were just bargaining counters to him, won and lost on a throw of the dice. To Richard they were more, so very much more and once given they could never be retracted. He knew that it made him intensely vulnerable. Edward had said that he would always be disappointed because he expected too much from men. But was it too much? Loyalty and honour, the keeping of a man's faith and his word? It seemed that it was for some. No man was to be relied on. Even John Neville was suspect now. He glanced up, his eyes narrowed with suspicion. No man was to be trusted, yet here he was, on the verge of trusting to the word of a man who by blood and heritage was his mortal foe.

'Why?' he demanded. 'Why this sudden favour to York?'

'No favour, sudden or otherwise. My concern is wholly for the north.' Harry's eyes were suddenly bright and hostile. 'Do you not think that we have suffered enough? Thirty years of warfare and the brunt of it borne by the north?'

Richard flushed. 'You cannot lay all at York's door,' he protested. 'Lancaster must take part blame for that.'

'Does it matter whose is the fault?' Harry said scathingly. 'Do you think a man cares whether it was Lancaster or York who burnt the roof from over his head? Do you ever spare a thought for the men who fight your wars? The men who risk life and limb for a shilling a day? Could you hold your life so cheaply, my lord? A shilling a day fighting for some lord who probably doesn't even know your name. What does the outcome really mean to him? Henry of Lancaster or Edward of York — do you honestly think he cares?'

'Do *you* care?'

'No. Not very much. I don't believe there's a great deal to choose between you. You've all lost sight of England in your squabble for a crown. Between you you've reduced her to poverty and need. None of you have ever had thought or care . . .'

'No. That isn't true,' Richard cried passionately. 'I care, my lord. I care for England very much.'

Silence fell suddenly between them, soft and fine as a gossamer thread that bound them without restraint or tension. Harry turned his head to meet the dark intense eyes. The strange thing was, he believed him.

60

Wide-eyed and staring, Eleanor lay in the dark cave of her bed. The familiar sounds of daylight came to her faintly: the silly feminine laughter of her women from the next room, a rush of light young feet upon the stairs. In the bailey they were raising the portcullis gate with a high-pitched rattling whine.

Slowly she turned her head. Where the bed curtains met, a knife edge of light whittled determinedly at the gloom. It was past noon but she rarely rose from her bed till then. What was there to entice her from this warm dark place? There was no John with his tender lovesome smile, there was no purpose to the empty days. Only here was she safe, only here was she protected. Outside these walls all was governed by Harry, every creature subject to his will. She had to guard even her innermost thoughts. She knew he watched her. His spies were legion. Even her women were suborned. Her eyes narrowed viciously. That ingrate, Joan Eure, she knew quite well, was Harry's minion, tittle-tattling her every word back to her lord who would then pass it on to Harry. Thus, subtly, he kept her prisoner, bound with chains of mistrust. But if she was kept from the world she made sure the world kept nothing from her. She too had her spies: her daughter Margaret; her clerk and physician William Rilston, the knight Henry Thwaites. No messenger came but that she was not among the first to know. No happening ever went unreported. Harry might wall her up in this premature tomb but he could not cage her mind or close her ears. With the rest of them she had heard the incredible news that whilst Edward still chased shadows in the north, Earl Warwick had made a landing. More unbelievable still, Lancaster's name was to be heard again, but the voice that cried it was Warwick's.

Her head dropped back onto the high pillows. Warwick! She could not think of him now without the ugly shadows crowding her mind.

'Warwick!' She spoke his name aloud, the word spurting from her lips like vomit.

And he would surely be crushed. She was certain of that. Even now Edward amassed a mighty army. She shivered pleasurably, envisaging Warwick's head upon York gate, his black heart drawn screaming from his body. She would be avenged.

Thomas would be avenged . . .

She closed her long heavy-lidded eyes. Thus easily could she withdraw into that other world where the dead moved with vibrant and unquenchable life, where she lay nightly with Thomas and felt his cruel and ardent kiss. Last night Elizabeth had come and blessed their union with her smile. Her eyes flew open, distended with unease . . . Elizabeth! Who always presaged death or grief . . .

Then she heard a scream. Was it her own? The door of her chamber burst suddenly open. The room was filled with a babble of terrified voices. She saw Joan Widdrington's coifed head appear through the hangings.

'Oh God. Oh Jesu,' her voice tailed away into a little yelping cry.

Eleanor flung herself from the bed and stumbled to the window. Then she stood quite still, staring down. Scarlet livery savaged her eyes. Like blood from a ruptured vein they flowed across the drawbridge and into Alnwick. She swayed against the wall in disbelief. They were the Earl of Warwick's men.

Richard Neville, Earl of Warwick, paced the hall with his measured and acquisitive tread. The very sight of him was like a blow to the heart and Eleanor leant, sick and breathless, against the gallery rail as he strutted the floor below her.

He paused and surveyed St Sebastian smilingly, brushing an elegant hand against its sheen. He moved on and then halted again, this time to examine tenderly a goblet made from rose-coloured glass.

Sickness rose and clogged her throat. So, once before, had she seen him strip Alnwick to the bones, not wantonly, but at his leisure, with cruel and expert appreciation of its worth. He had lost none of his arrogance, then. In fact, he had hardly changed at all. The thick hair had darkened to an iron grey and his face was less well-fleshed. But he still moved with the same regal grace, his bearing was still majestic. Yet there was something missing, something was gone from him, for she knew every nuance of that imperious voice. She had the strangest feeling of having been cheated, as if carrion crows had already picked him over and left her only the bones.

Then in his loud and arrogant voice he stripped Harry of the March, one of many changes, he promised them. Triumphantly he told them, his voice tinged with the same wild disbelief he saw upon their faces: Edward of York was fled to Holland, his Woodville queen to sanctuary. The old regime was restored again. Henry of Lancaster was king.

He spared them no details of his amazing coup. At times he could hardly credit it himself. During those bleak months of exile he had almost believed his power spent; months of placating Louis, of grovelling to that she-wolf of Anjou. The best part of an hour she had kept him on his knees whilst he had cozened and soothed and begged and bribed his way to the only alliance that was left to him. It was still gall in his mouth, for Margaret had taken the full measure of her revenge. She'd made him pay in blood and sweat for every insult he'd uttered against her. He'd had to repeat them word for word but this time levelled against York. Thus she had stripped him of his pride and honour and the heart of him had died.

But not now. Now the blood pounded wildly in his veins. This was *his* triumph, without Edward to steal his glory, without Queen Margaret who still cowered in port at Harfleur. She had sent him on ahead to pave the way and instead he had blazed a trail of glory — from Dartmouth, where he and Clarence had landed and the Earl of Shrewsbury and Stanley had joined him, on to Coventry; and from there he had dispatched word to the rebels, especially to his brother Montagu, moving on an unsuspecting Edward at Doncaster. He had been twenty thousand strong by that time, twenty thousand loyal men who came neither for Lancaster or York but came because of him. In the event he had not needed them. It had not even come to a fight. Edward had fled like a thief in the night at the news that Montagu had deserted him. Then at his leisure he had moved on London and had been admitted unopposed. From the Tower he had released the grubby lice-ridden old man who had once been Henry the King. He'd had him washed and clad in a clean velvet robe and had lodged him in the bishop's palace by St Paul's. The next day he had led him out. By barge they had gone to West-minster. Personally he had sat Henry on his throne. So, his eyes told them, did Richard Neville make kings.

It was then that Eleanor began to laugh, a harsh cracked sound from high above his head. He jerked his head up but saw nothing. The foolish thought occurred to him — the laughter of the gods?

Then he saw her, a ghostly retribution, her greying hair float-ing wide, her mouth open and laughing. She advanced upon him. He stared at her for a long time without recognition. Then at the foot of the stairs she paused.

'Eleanor?' he said faintly.

She acknowledged him with only a slight bitter smile. Her eyes fastened accusingly upon his face, the silent advocate of the grisly unseen corpses he imagined at her back. 'Eleanor,' he said again.

She answered him then. 'Oh my lord,' she whispered. 'If you did not cleave so well to Lancaster you could be all of my heart's desire.' That was all she said, the same trite phrase that he had uttered to her once long years ago in the gardens at York. It meant nothing to those watching and they murmured to see him stagger as if from a blow. Suddenly he saw himself reflected in the woman's eyes; grovelling on his knees before Margaret of Anjou, going cap in hand to Louis. He saw himself leading Daft Harry from the Tower where he had once so triumphantly placed him. He saw himself riding through the London streets crying Lancaster as he had once cried York.

Eleanor watched the quivering haughty face avert itself from her stare and her whole body shuddered and ached with the glorious revelation of his pain. And when at last he turned to look at her again, she had her sweet and silent revenge. He knew himself to be perjured and dishonoured and the knowledge broke his heart.

'So! You intend to sit still like a maid and do nothing?' Eleanor said scathingly.

Harry looked up. How he hated that voice; sharp, critical, on the edge of a sneer. 'I do,' he said mildly. 'Until there is definite word from Edward, there is nothing to be done.'

'By which time Warwick will be even more firmly entrenched,'

Eleanor cried. 'It has been five months now. How long before Edward stirs himself?'

Harry sent her a quelling look, reminding her that she was only here under sufferance. He turned to the lawyer Thomas Middleton who had ridden in from York that morning.

'You say, Thomas, that Warwick and Clarence have quarrelled?'

The lawyer nodded. 'Not openly, my lord. But the signs are there to be read. The venture, it seems, has not brought his Grace of Clarence all that he had hoped for. When he first allied himself with Warwick it was in the expectation of the crown for himself. Now Warwick is committed to upholding Lancaster and although he has pushed a bill through Parliament naming Clarence as heir after King Henry and Prince Edward, it falls far short of his original hopes. I think it is fast dawning on Clarence that he is not much better off than he was under his brother Edward.'

Harry frowned. 'Earl Warwick has complete control then, if he can pass his own legislation?'

Middleton spread his hands in an indeterminate gesture. 'Yes and no, my lord. We have here an unique situation. Men are linked with a double chain. On the one hand we have Earl Warwick's immediate following: die-hard Yorkists for the most part, men who have been taught to revile Henry of Lancaster as both weakling and usurper and yet who are now suddenly expected to honour him as king. On the other, we have the Lancastrians themselves, men who have suffered greatly in King Henry's cause and who now find that their saviour is Warwick, the man who inflicted that suffering. It is not a happy compromise, my lord. There is much suspicion, much mistrust. Even Queen Margaret herself hesitates to commit herself irrevocably. For Warwick to maintain his effective control it is imperative that he has Queen Margaret's backing. Yet still her fleet hovers distrustfully at Harfleur whilst the advantage slips slowly from them. So far, all has been bloodlessly and quietly done but now men are beginning to stir. I have had reports of many slipping away to join Edward. The Duke of Norfolk, Essex and Lord Mountjoy have been placed under close house arrest to prevent their collusion with rebels. The city too grows uneasy. Whosoever touches the merchants' pockets least, also touches their hearts. It is known, my lord, that Warwick grows desperately short of funds and, besides which, his proposed mercantile alliance with France is far from popular as it would mean turning their backs on established Burgundian trade. Mark me well, my lord. These are the men who hold the balance of power, not the lords. If the merchants, especially the London guilds, declare for Edward . . .'

'But will they?' Harry demanded shortly. 'There seem to be a great many "ifs" and "buts".'

Middleton shrugged. 'At the moment they are waiting to see which way the wind of advantage blows. To my mind, it is more a question of good timing than good fortune. Edward has had nigh on five months to recoup, besides a handsome loan from Burgundy. If he can effect a landing before Queen Margaret, then his chances are good. If he cannot, then he will have a fight on his hands, for once Margaret and her son land in England, all the Lancastrians who have been holding back out of mistrust of Warwick will flock unfailingly to her cause.'

'And if Edward did land, tomorrow, say, how in the south would he be received?'

'Not with any great joy, I fear, my lord. The commons are apathetic. It matters little to the small man who wears the crown and it could be that the apathy that let Earl Warwick in would also keep Edward out. If he was foolhardy enough to contemplate a landing in the north, I would say his chances of victory were nil. I do not have to tell you, my lord, that for the most part, the north is set dead against him. The city of York, I know, would give him no room. Warwick himself is held in no high esteem but Edward's name is virtually anathema.'

Harry nodded. The lawyer's grim words he knew to be true. He had seen the apathy and disaffection at first hand. It had been no hardship to hold the north off from Lancaster while Warwick held sway. Only John Scrope had openly supported him. The rest had waited and watched, albeit uneasily, and he wondered how much longer he could hold them impartial. How deep did their fear and loyalty go?

He rose slowly to his feet. 'Continue to keep me informed, Thomas,' he said thoughtfully. 'I intend to remove to York at the end of the week.' He took the lawyer's arm and moved toward the door. 'Your letters will find me there, Thomas. Send to me the minute there is word of Edward's landing.'

Eleanor watched their departure smilingly. She paced the floor gowned in rose silk. Her step was light, youthful almost. Her blood, warmed with wine and powerful herbs, pounded hotly in her veins.

She laughed soundlessly, anticipating Warwick's fall with the glee of a spiteful child. The knowledge of his inner torment had not yet palled. She thought, exultantly, his day was done. He was nothing, less than nothing. He had set his foot on the downward path the minute he had abandoned York. He had sold his soul to buy a continuance of his power, but power would not be enough to sustain that mighty heart now that honour and pride were gone. She saw again his stricken face: shamed and broken, dishonoured and spurned . . . But still alive, a nagging inner voice reminded her. The heart of the man might be vanquished but the man himself was not. He still lived. He still breathed, tormenting her with his vibrant and seemingly unquenchable life.

The long firm step faltered. Middleton's words had been less than comforting. If Edward did not make a decisive move soon; if Margaret got there before him . . .

She halted and looked up, tears of rage and frustration suddenly filling her eyes. She caught her breath. Harry stood watching her and she felt the ridiculous urge to cross herself at the nameless thing she saw in his eyes.

'Be still, madame,' he said in his deceptively sweet and honeyed voice. 'You shall have him. If I promise you nothing else in this life, I promise you that.'

February dragged uneventfully into March and the north waited out the chill empty days in futile speculation. Rumours stirred them briefly but nothing ever came of them. Warwick still sent his frantic commands and his brother Montagu tried to implement them but though one or two chafed under Harry's restraint, none would break away. They sat in their manors and looked to him. Whilst Northumberland made no move neither would they.

Then in the second week of March the rumours hardened into cold fact. From Thomas Middleton, Harry received the news that Edward had made an abortive landing on the Norfolk coast and had been driven off by the Earl of Oxford. Three days later he heard from the Mayor of York that Edward had landed on the fourteenth at Ravenspur and was now outside the gates of York asking for admittance.

In the Guildhall beneath the shimmering splendour of banners, the mayor and the council of twenty-four rose uneasily to greet him.

The mayor surged forward in a flurry of green velvet and starched Holland cloth. 'My lord. Welcome, my lord. Welcome.' He led Harry to the chair of estate normally reserved for the king. 'It was good of you to come, my lord. I knew I could rely on your good lordship.'

He beamed upon Harry, then chewed at his lip. 'The fact is, my lord, we are in somewhat of a quandary and unable to decide for the best. The King, the late King, that is, the Duke of York, is without the gates asking admittance. Should we yield, my lord, or no?'

'No.' The fat little goldmith Eli Casse rose belligerently to his feet. 'Hull refused him and shut the gates in his face. So should we.'

'But then,' said another, remembering that Edward still owed him for three tuns of Rhenish, 'he says that he comes only as Duke of York. Can we refuse him admittance to his duchy?'

'Hah. That's what Henry Bolingbroke said seventy years ago and look what happened then.'

The mayor shouted them down and looked appealingly at Harry. 'You see, my lord, how opinion is divided. And also, my lord, there is a letter to be given only to you. It bears the Duke of Gloucester's signet.'

Harry took the sealed roll and broke it open carefully. The message was brief, written in Gloucester's own small rounded hand. 'My lord Northumberland and well beloved cousin. I greet you well and say no more than to remind you of the last time we

68

met. If you love England as you said you did then, I beg you, open the gates of York.' It was signed, Richard Gloucester.

Harry laid the letter down and it sprung closed of its own accord. He glanced up and saw their hard suspicious eyes upon him. 'Gentlemen,' he said, and his voice immediately soothed them. He thrust the letter across the table. 'It is no secret what Gloucester says. Read it if you will.' None was so bold as to pick it up but the gesture won their confidence.

The mayor leant forward. 'My lord, the position is this. I sent the recorder Thomas Conyers to warn Edward off as I cannot vouch for the mood of the city. Feelings are still running high against the Yorkists. Towton is only a bare five miles away. There are many within these walls with long memories and short tempers . . .'

'Aye, that's right enough. We've not forgotten,' shouted a man with an empty sleeve. 'I left a son and a good right arm at Towton.'

'And you think *I* have forgotten?' Harry said and his voice was like the soft weeping of tears. 'You must all of you know that there is more of my heart on Towton Field than there is left in the whole of my body.'

He had them then, caught and held by the sheer beauty of his voice so that even the most voluble amongst them fell silent.

'So.' He spoke softly into the rapt and breathless hush. 'You boast of long memories, do you, *messires*? But if they are long they are also grievously at fault if you lay the blame for Towton solely upon Edward Plantagenet's shoulders.'

His lordly glance swept hotly over their faces. 'Have you forgotten that there was another with him? A man who thought to order the affairs of kings before Edward was ever born, a man who had the death and ruin of hundreds of good men to his credit before Edward had years enough even to lift a sword. This man . . . this man, who was his general and chief advisor at Towton, and even when it was done and the toll paid in full, could not rest till he had harried and pillaged every corner of the north. Who was it who pounded Bamburgh with his guns? Who starved out Alnwick and Warkworth? Who was it who laid your fair city waste, burning and raping and looting?' His voice, abrasive and stinging as salt, opened up all the old wounds. He reminded them again of Towton, of outrages long before and since. He filled their nostrils with the stench of blood, their ears with the sound of pitiful screams. Like a whetstone his voice sharpened the dulled and blunted edge of their rage. He saw it shining in their eyes, hard and bright as burnished steel. With exquisite precision he turned its deadly point and plunged it into his enemy's heart.

'So,' he said, 'has the Earl of Warwick loved all of you. And this is the man you uphold against Edward of York?'

'No. No, my lord. It is not so,' the mayor protested, wiping tears from his quivering cheeks. 'Not Warwick, my lord. It is Henry of Lancaster that we uphold.'

'Then show me Lancaster. Or shall I show him to you? A sick and broken old man once cruelly abused by Warwick himself and only cossetted now as a means to Warwick's salvation. What else is King Henry but Warwick's tool? You are not fools, *messires*. You know full well that though Henry of Lancaster may wear the crown it is Richard Neville who rules.'

'My lord.' The goldsmith Eli Casse lumbered uncertainly to his feet. 'My lord, with respect. I hold no brief for the Earl of Warwick, nor for any of them, come to that. The plain truth of it is that we're weary of the fighting. We're tired of mourning and counting the cost.' The harsh seamed features quivered for an instant. 'And a bitter toll it is too, my lord. Three sons I've lost myself and the eldest barely twenty-one. I tell you straight out, my lord, I'd pay homage to Butcher Wrangwish here, if I thought it would bring us peace.'

There were murmurs, then shouts of agreement. Tom Conyers shouted above the rest, 'Then for pity's sake, if it's peace you're after, we must not let the Yorkists in.'

'*Messires!*' Harry spoke into the confusion, a small sharp sound that set their teeth on edge. 'Do you think to gain peace merely by keeping Edward Plantagenet out?' He dropped his voice to a gently persuasive note. 'You are all men of business here, are you not? You know the better buy when you see it. Then choose your king as you would a piece of merchandise for when all's stripped of its fine feathers, it comes down to that. Would you buy a side of beef, old and tough and crawling with worm or would you choose young meat, firm and healthy? Ask yourselves what you can expect if Lancaster remains in power. Debts of gratitude will have to be paid. Louis of France has kept Queen Margaret for years. It is French gold that has equipped her fleet. What then, in payment, will Louis demand? War with Burgundy whose duchy he covets — Burgundy, your best customer! Where is your peace and prosperity then? And Warwick? What use will the Queen have for him when she lands, bringing loyal Exeter with her? Will Exeter have forgotten that Earl Warwick had all of his household slaughtered to a man, down to the meanest scullion? Do you foresee peace and amity when these two meet? No doubt Warwick will feel himself slighted as he did when Edward was king. Did England fare so badly then? Was trade ever better? Were your purses fuller? Ask yourselves who began all this. Was it Edward, for marrying the woman of his choice, a dispossessed *Lancastrian* widow? Or was it Warwick because he had other plans, because he could not bear to be crossed, who threw England and her peace to the dogs rather than be overborne? Ask yourselves, *messires*, and give me the only answer that you can.'

It broke from their throats in a howl of pure fury. Eli Casse turned a face purple with rage toward him. 'Warwick,' he cried thickly. 'God damn his soul. Death to the traitor Warwick.'

Harry lowered his eyes and smiled. 'Then let Edward of York come in.'

Edward smiled genially at his host and allowed his cup to be replenished. 'So, Harry, my instinct did not fail me. I knew I was right to set you free.'

Harry smiled. 'Your Grace was ever a good judge of men,' he murmured with heavy sarcasm.

Edward laughed, more from the sheer relief of still being able to than out of any amusement. He thought, too, that Northumberland was doing his own share of laughing. When he had come out to meet them on Walmgate Stray there had been the suspicion of a smile around his mouth, a secret and intensely private smile that had reminded Edward uncomfortably of the sport he had made of him once. He supposed he could see the wry humour of it; himself

71

and Richard, unshaven for a week and in filthy rags, Northumberland attired and accoutred like a prince, leading them like beggars into York.

Irritation thinned his full sensual mouth. But there had been nothing humourous about the welcome he had received. He recalled the implacable hatred on the faces of the citizens; himself, falsely sporting an ostrich plume, and the few men that had been allowed to accompany him crying stonily at his back for Lancaster; then lying prettily that he came only for his duchy of York, smiling as they patronised and demeaned him. Then he had been only too thankful to be on dry land again to care. He shivered. That nightmare journey was with him still. Three days and nights trapped in the bowels of that leaking hulk, lashed by rain and a howling gale that had scattered his fleet and flung him up at last on the Yorkshire coast, unhurt but terrifyingly alone. He had thought it the end then, all of his ships lost, his brother Gloucester with them. He had prayed as he had never prayed before, invoking every saint and martyr that he'd heard of. He'd even sworn an oath to abjure the flesh if only God would grant his prayer. And then, as if in answer, the sun had come out. Like balm it had soothed the angry sea and melted away the sulky cloud. Within the hour he had sighted the rest of his fleet limping brokenly toward the land. Then had followed the humiliation at Hull where the gates had been shut in his face. York had been his last remaining hope — York and the enigma of Harry Percy.

Over the rim of his cup he observed the faintly smiling and sardonic face. Not a face that one would instinctively trust, yet there was no gainsaying that Northumberland had saved them. If they had been turned away from York they would have been finished. As it was they had breathing space now, time to think and plan and consider the next step. And what was the next step? A long one from the north, for he was well disillusioned of any support here. John Neville lay with a force at Pontefract. The Lancastrian Oxford approached from Newark. Again he surveyed that sharp clever face. It was a brilliant strategy and had served him better than a half-hearted and potentially treacherous army. Only a Percy could bring out the north, only a Percy could keep it still and whilst he did, it gave him safe conduct toward the south.

If he could reach Leicester unopposed . . . It was in the Midlands that his chief support lay. Hastings wielded great influence there and Norfolk and Essex were solidly his men. For a while it might pay him to stick to his story of claiming only his dukedom of York. He smiled, thinking of how the wheel had come full circle. Seventy-two years ago, the usurper Bolingbroke had landed at Ravenspur telling the self-same tale. The smile broadened into open laughter. It had been a Percy who had let him in then.

He yawned happily, as optimistic now as he had been cast down. His belly was full of claret wine and a good feather bed awaited him — a solitary bed. He thought of Elizabeth and his little maids still braving the rigours of sanctuary. There, in November, his longed-for son had been born and named Edward after him. Fortune was cruel, he thought, just like a woman. Now he had his heir, all he lacked was the crown for him to inherit.

Then he rose to his feet and raised his cup. He cried hoarsely, 'I give you my son, Prince Edward.'

'The Prince of Wales,' Hastings echoed drunkenly. 'And in God's good time, our king.'

Richard of Gloucester reached out and touched the rim of his hanap to his brother's. 'May God grant him a long and happy life,' he said in his quiet and passionate voice.

He lingered, long after Hastings and Edward had gone to their beds. Gloucester looked at Harry and shyly smiled.

'I have not thanked you yet, my lord,' he said.

'There is no need,' Harry flung a last log on the fire.

'I think there is,' Richard said fervently. 'I asked a favour and you granted it. Why is there no need to offer thanks?'

Because it was not done for you, Harry thought, but he did not say it. He prodded absently at the smouldering log. 'What will you do now?' he said, changing the subject. 'Head south for Leicester or Nottingham?'

Richard nodded. 'Edward thinks perhaps to go via Wakefield and our own town of Sandal. We might gather support there before pressing on.'

'John Neville lies at Pontefract,' Harry remarked casually. 'Less than seven miles away.'

Richard flushed. 'Was that said to remind me of my foolish belief the last time we met?'

Harry turned to look at him. 'No. It was said to remind you that Sandal is seven miles from Pontefract. Are you always so touchy?'

Richard glared at him for a moment, then smiled ruefully. 'Usually,' he admitted. 'It's a habit. I have got used to being on the defensive.'

'Against what attack?'

'I don't really know.' Richard sat and stared wistfully into the fire. 'Because I am different, I suppose — the runt of the litter, as my lady mother so lovingly calls me. I spoil the Plantagenet image, you see. I am not like my brothers, George and Edward.'

'That, possibly, is to your credit,' Harry remarked drily. 'The Plantagenet traits are not always admirable.'

Richard stiffened, sensing criticism. 'You have your own share of Plantagenet blood, if I remember rightly.'

'I do not boast of it, though. I find that it shortens a man's life rather than prolongs it. It is not the asset it once was.'

'No. That's true.' Was anything the way it once was? Richard thought bleakly and swallowed hard on the choking misery that suddenly rose in his throat. He had no heart for a fight against those that he loved: Clarence, false, treacherous Clarence but still his brother, still loved; and Warwick . . . He glanced hesitantly at Harry. 'Is there . . .' He broke off and chewed anxiously upon his lip. 'Do you have news of the Earl of Warwick?'

'Only that he lies at Coventry, your Grace.' Harry's eyes rested thoughtfully on Richard's pale and wretched face. 'Does it grieve you so much, even now?'

'Yes. Yes, it does.' Richard stared down at the toes of his scuffed boots. 'I loved Earl Warwick well.'

And still love him, Harry thought, hearing the anguish in his voice. He said carefully, 'Your Grace, Earl Warwick is a proven traitor. Would it not be better to put him from your mind?'

'I cannot,' Richard answered him stonily. 'The affection of a lifetime is not so easily put aside.'

'Warwick has put it aside. He embraces Lancaster now.'

'On the surface perhaps. But that is pretence. At the heart of him he is for York, as is my brother Clarence. Edward knows this also. He will be merciful. When he sees that Warwick is tamed of his rebellious notions, he will be merciful.'

'You think then, that if God grants you the victory, King Edward will spare Earl Warwick?'

'He will spare our brother Clarence. How can he not Earl Warwick?'

Harry stared into the fire and the diminishing flames leapt to light his face and kindle dark fires in his eyes.

'Do not think of it now, my lord,' he said gently. 'You have need of sleep. Tomorrow will be a long and arduous day.'

Richard smiled at him gratefully. 'You are kind,' he said. 'I pray that my brother Edward will be as kind to Earl Warwick.'

The next day Harry escorted Edward as far as York's southerly gate. It was a discreet and orderly procession with armour concealed beneath heavy winter cloaks and the accoutrements of war well hidden.

Edward smiled grimly as he rode through the silent crowds. Yesterday, he had been too numbed to be fully aware of the extent of the bitterness against him. He was aware of it now, though, aware, too, that if it had not been for the man riding beside him, he would never have got out alive.

Once outside the gates he breathed more easily and smilingly surveyed his men. Refreshed with victuals and an untroubled night's sleep they were drawn up ready to meet him; his own Yorkist retainers headed the column, the Flemish gunners brought up the rear. Then his smile froze into a grimace of fear. There were other men, on either side of the road ahead. He glanced frantically at the banner above their heads and knew them — Lancastrians all and men whose blood debt against him was heavy.

He swung round, knowing himself trapped. 'What treachery is this?' he cried.

Northumberland's voice fell soft and sweet in his ear. 'No treachery, your Grace. You may proceed. They will not hinder you. They are here at my command.' He added almost as an afterthought, 'One thing more, your Grace.' He smiled his cold and ruthless smile. 'Your magnanimity to the enemy is well known, my liege, and if God should grant you the victory in this . . .' He looked past Edward's set face toward the fluttering banners. 'The Earl of Warwick — there is no question of his being spared?'

Briefly the King held the cold blank gaze. Then he inclined his head in perfect understanding. 'No, my lord,' he said. 'No question at all.'

The running man emerged from the mist. His armour had a ghostly sheen and clanked with a skeletal rattle. He stumbled and fell, his long jewelled hands clawing deep into the mud as he struggled wearily to raise himself. He ran on, pursued by the rolling white cloud that had death and dishonour at its heart. He fell again, borne down by a weight of armour and grief and this time he did not attempt to rise. Like a shroud the mist enveloped him, filling his bursting lungs with its chilling vapour, blinding his streaming eyes. He heard the rasp of his own tortured breath, loud as the roar of the battle he had fled . . . and another's, soft and even and measured, like sand falling through a glass. He turned on his back. He could see nothing, yet he knew he was not alone. Then out of the mist a hand appeared. A sword reached lovingly for his throat. Blood spurted from the great throbbing vein in his neck; it filled his mouth and drowned his frantic cry; it choked and smothered the high womanly scream . . . Eleanor's eyes flew open. The whole chamber was filled with the shrill piercing noise, so loud, so close . . . Then she clapped a hand over her own mouth. It was her voice. It was she who was screaming — not Warwick, as she had thought.

She lay for a moment, trying to recapture the dream. It was not unfamiliar, for she had imagined his death a thousand times, impaled upon the knives of her revenge, his head severed by the sword of retribution. But never so vividly, never so clearly and always, before, she had been there to mock and gloat and witness his painful and ignominious end.

She crept shivering from the bed and thrust her bare arms into a robe. It was still night. Darkness and shadow filled the room and she felt her way to the long low chest where she knew there was a pitcher of wine.

She drank deeply, half emptying the cup. Thomas had taught her how to drink: rich dark claret spiced with honey and ginger; sweet malmsey floating with cloves . . . She stared down into the wine's dark ruby depths and thought of Warwick's blood spurting redly from his mouth. She sank down wearily upon the floor. The ultimate triumph eluded her still, though Edward had gone from strength to strength since his furtive departure from York. At Leicester he had been joined by three thousand men, and Clarence, true to form, had performed yet another *volte face* and brought him another four thousand. Warwick's back was against the wall but he was very far from being vanquished. Queen Margaret was expected to land any day. Could Edward withstand such an army as she would bring? And even if he could, it did not guarantee Warwick's elimination. Edward was always eager to forgive and forget. If he could forgive Clarence . . . She bit her lip in savage fury. Jesu, was she never to be rid of this fiend? Were his death and dishonour to be seen only in dreams?

She rose and went to the window, flinging back the shutters. It was almost light. The familiar walls of Alnwick emerged slowly from a uniform grey, taking on shape and proportion in the advancing light. Below the soaring turrets, the town seemed ghostly and distant, the sharply angled roofs blunted by a clinging white mist that vividly recalled the dream. Again she saw Warwick's stricken face, the sword reaching for his throat . . . She stiffened. She remembered now the hand that had held it had been Harry's.

She found him sitting by a long-dead fire as if he had been there all night. Across his knees a parchment was spread, weighted down by his strong slender hand. He turned his head slightly when she entered but did not look round. It was as if he were expecting her, as if she had done no more than answer his call. Not until she stood before him did he acknowledge her fully and then he only smiled; that oblique and sinister turning of his mouth that always made her a little afraid. It was his eyes that were the revelation: yellow as marsh fire, blazing and triumphant as a summer sun.

Whatever it was that the letter contained, it pleased him more than well.

Eleanor seated herself in the small chair that faced him. Their eyes met and held, mother and son joined for once by something more than blood. No word needed to be passed between them. She sighed with deep and sure contentment. 'He is dead, then?'

'Yes. Both Warwick and his brother Montagu.'

Eleanor looked away into the cold dead hearth. 'Tell me,' she said faintly.

He passed her the letter that lay on his lap. 'Read it for yourself. It will tell you better than I.'

She snatched it from him eagerly. It was undated, written in a clerkly and uniform hand.

'My Lord and most honoured and well beloved master,' wrote the lawyer Thomas Middleton from Westminster. 'I now expand upon the brief message I sent by word of mouth a week since. On April the eleventh, King Edward was admitted to London. I later discovered under the insistent pressure of the city guilds and not a little from their wives. Warwick's brother, the Archbishop of York, put up only a token resistance and submitted with alacrity in true Neville fashion. He had in fact but little choice as the Dukes of Exeter and Somerset had left him high and dry, gone to await Queen Margaret's landing in the west. And there, I think, you have the nub of it all and the Earl of Warwick's great weakness. Neither Exeter or Somerset nor any true Lancastrian would have any truck with Warwick. Conversely, Warwick's men, born and bred Yorkists at heart, could raise only half-hearted support for Lancaster.

'However, I digress. King Edward's first action when London was secure was to thrust King Henry once more into the Tower. Canterbury had hardly touched the crown to his head again before he marched out of London to confront Earl Warwick who was camped at Barnet, where the road forks for St Albans and Hatfield. This was on Good Friday eve and the bishops had much to say, I can tell you, about warfaring over Eastertide. Howbeit, during the night the two armies drew up, in such a fog that no man could see his fellow. At dawn on the Saturday, Warwick attacked, firing blind into the murk. That was his first advantage lost for though he had the heavier guns, their target could not be seen. I have no other certain details of the actual fray save that it was long and grievous as there was much at stake. The turning point seems to have been when Montagu's men fell upon their own flank, in the uncertain light, mistaking Oxford's banner of a star with streamers for the sun of Edward of York's. There was confusion and talk of treason. Oxford's men fled and before Warwick could rally his line, King Edward was upon them. John Neville, the Marquis of Montagu, was slain; I have heard it said, by his own men because they thought his attack on Oxford was deliberate. What followed I can make neither head nor tail of except to say with certainty that Earl Warwick fled into Wrotham Wood and was there slain, his throat pierced by a sword. By what man or men seems to be unknown and it is said the King is much displeased for, on the pleading of his brother of Gloucester, he had given an order for Warwick's life to be spared, but given too late, it would appear, to save the earl. The losses on both sides are said to be very great, a thousand or more on each. Of the Yorkists, the Lords Saye and Cromwell, Sir Humphrey Bourchier and William Blunt are known for certain to have been slain.

'Given this fifteenth day of April at Westminster. Your humble and most devoted servant: Thomas Middleton.

'This last given in haste at the courier's departure. On the very day of Barnet, whilst the battle raged, Queen Margaret made a landing at Weymouth. It is thought that she progresses north to make a junction with Jasper Tudor out of Wales. King Edward left London an hour ago at the head of a mighty force.'

Slowly Eleanor laid the letter down. No dream then, but a vision, a glorious reality. Except that Harry had certainly not slain Warwick. Harry was here.

She glanced up at him. But he'd had a hand in it somewhere. That glow in his eyes was from a personal triumph and though his hands might not have struck the final blow, in some unknown way, it had guided the one that had. She smiled ruefully. No wonder he was jubilant. Warwick and his brother John Neville dead, the third brother George, Archbishop of York, an old and broken man. All of the Nevilles. All that generations of Percys had striven for, accomplished in one short day. And he had never even raised his hand. Oh, how she had underestimated him. She had always thought him a weak and spineless thing.

Then Harry said in his soft and exquisite voice. 'Are you content now, madame?'

She dropped her gaze. She should have been. Warwick was dead. The man who had murdered Thomas with his own hand was dead. What more could she ask? What more was there? Then why did she feel so empty and bereft, as if it was she instead of Warwick that was slain? She looked blankly into the ashen heart of the fire, cold and dead, burnt out to dust as hers was. The chilling thought occurred to her: she was now deprived even of her hatred.

It was an hour past curfew but still the long hot summer's day struggled fiercely against the darkness and tinged the twilight with an amber glow. The city swam in a hazy dusk, the streets silent save for the calling of the Watch. The revelling was done, the wine casks empty, the victory garlands crushed by a thousand ecstatic dancing feet. The gay banners hung anonymous and dark. London slept, drunk and happy. The war was over and Edward of York had won.

In the royal apartments of the Tower, the shadows were black and still. Richard of Gloucester raised his dark intense eyes to the King's face and basked in the warm approval of his voice. Across the table Clarence mocked him, leaning close to whisper the malicious reminder that praise was something Edward could afford to be lavish with — it cost him naught. But still Richard smiled and was content. Tonight his mood was happily mellow and even Clarence could not offend.

He slid a little further into his chair. He had drunk more than he was used to, a victory cup Edward had called it, and had seen to it that Richard drained it dry. They all had much to celebrate. The French bitch was utterly vanquished; the soft bewitched day of Barnet as nothing now besides Tewkesbury's fierce and bloody victory. It all seemed so effortless now, the blunders and near disasters forgotten in the triumph. But he had not forgotten. Each error of judgement he had clearly marked and learned from: the first, he knew, had been their slow and leisurely progress up the

80

Thames valley whilst they waited for Queen Margaret to make her opening move. His thin mouth twitched in remembered rage. Jesu, but that woman had led them a dance, drawing them so cunningly away from their line of retreat with first one feint and then another. Edward had followed her — south toward Bath only to find she had swung left down the Avon and captured Bristol. Then she had marched out of Bristol as if to meet them head on, only to strike north for Gloucester, leaving them standing like fools in full battle array. They'd been well and truly outmanoeuvred there and the tale might have had a different end if the Lancastrians had gained the city of Gloucester. Sweet Jesu preserve Richard Beachaump, the governer of the town, who had refused Margaret and her army admittance and forced them to march on and attempt a crossing of the Severn at Tewkesbury. It had been their last chance to prevent Margaret joining forces with Jasper Tudor in Wales. In a desperate all-out march along the high road of the Cotswold ridge, they'd outstripped the Lancastrians struggling through woodland and narrow lanes below them. By nightfall they had been a bare three miles off the enemy, and Margaret with the Severn before her and Edward at her back had had no choice but to stand and fight.

Richard shuddered and closed his eyes. And such a fight it had been: the heat, the dust, the roaring of Severn at its high spring tide, the screams of men and horses dying — the scream of one man in particular, no older than himself, as Clarence and his henchmen cut him down though he had begged in tears for his life. Abruptly Richard opened his eyes. So had Edward of Lancaster died. Edward, Prince of Wales, Anne's husband, and though he'd had no hand in his death, he felt the guilt as strongly, for he had wanted him dead above all things. Was the thought as dishonourable as the deed? There were other dishonours, small but unbearable stains on Edward's perfection. He thought of Somerset and the other Lancastrian lords that Edward had dragged from Tewkesbury Sanctuary to the block. Traitors, traitors all, he reminded himself fiercely, yet his conscience shouted him down. The law of sanctuary was inviolate, even unto kings.

He took another sip of wine, but the sweet pungent liquid turned him sick. Unsteadily he rose to his feet and muttered a need for air. He heard Clarence's sniggering laugh cut short by their mother's sharp rebuke. He smiled faintly as he widened the shutters and breathed the dark still air. Clarence was undoubtedly spoiling for a fight over Richard's desire to marry Anne Neville. Not that Clarence grudged him a wife but he did grudge him the half of the Warwick estates that he would have to part with if Richard had his way. And he would have it, he thought grimly, both Anne and her share of the Warwick estates. His melancholy deepened. He still could not bear to think of Warwick. He lay now in St Paul's, past all treachery and betrayal. Yet the stench of his heinous deeds lingered still. He recalled the hurt and bewildered look in Anne's eyes when he had told her that her father was dead. Dear God, but he had done his level best to save him. If only Edward had not prevaricated, evading the issue until it was too late, almost as if . . . as if he had wanted Warwick dead, but the blame for it laid at another door.

He turned and quelled the dreadful thought with a sight of his brother's face. Ruthless and self-centred Edward might be, but he had never known him to be devious. Tonight he seemed quiet and thoughtful, very much aware of the presence of their mother. Then Cecily raised her cup and her eyes dwelt proudly upon them.

'Well, my sons? Are we supreme again or are we not? Can we truly say at last that Lancaster is fallen? Barnet and Tewkesbury are fought and won. London is ours despite the attempt of Warwick's kinsman Fauconberg and his rabble of Kentishmen to storm it. Edward of Lancaster is dead, the Frenchwoman our prisoner within these very walls. Who then is there to gainsay us now?' Suddenly her eyes fastened fiercely upon Edward's face. 'Only one man, my son. Only one crazed and feeble half-witted old man.' She laid her goblet softly upon the boards. 'It is time, Edward. Let us be rid of him once and for all.'

Edward slowly raised his head. 'You make him sound harmless enough to be of small concern.'

'As a man he would be, but as a king he is not.' Cecily laid her hand persuasively on his sleeve. 'For God's sake, Edward. Have we learnt nothing this past year?'

'I agree,' Clarence opened bleary eyes. 'Send Holy Harry to his

Maker. It's where he wants to be.'

'You have no choice, Edward,' Cecily urged. 'One man's life for the thousands that could be saved. Believe me, my son, the killing will go on whilst King Henry lives. He will be a perpetual focus for anarchy. Why hold back now? His son is dead. There are none to follow on.'

Edward stared down into his empty hanap. How foolish to hesitate, for he knew his mother spoke the truth. Yet he did hesitate. For all the deaths that could be laid at his door, never once had he killed in cold blood. And to murder a crowned and anointed king, especially such an innocent as Henry. Such deeds often brought dire retribution. They said that Bolingbroke had never known a moment's peace for the slaying of King Richard.

He called to his brother standing stiff and silent by the wall, 'What say you, Dickon? Shall we put poor Harry from his pain?'

Richard licked suddenly dry lips, yet surprisingly he felt no qualm. It was as their mother had said, one life in exchange for thousands and he thought it just if it was for England's weal. Aught was just if it was for peace. He nodded his head. 'Yes,' he said quietly. 'Make an end.'

Edward sighed. 'So be it, then. Have Dudley fetched. If it is to be done, let it be done tonight.'

Richard looked out again into the dark and silent night. In the squat round tower that adjoined the hall, a small flame burned with a strong steady light. Was Henry still at his constant prayers? Did he sleep? Richard hoped that he did. Let him remain innocent until the end. At his back he heard the rustle of his mother's heavy skirts, the gurgling sound of Clarence pouring more wine. The Constable Dudley came and went, marked only by the furtive whispering of voices and the dull rattling of his keys. Then Edward's loud and over-hearty laugh rang out, echoed by Clarence's nervous giggle. His mother came and touched his arm. He breathed the heavy rose scent impregnating her flesh.

'Come,' she said blithely. 'We will sup together at Barnard's Castle. I have had your favourite dishes prepared: goose patty, syllabub . . .'

Richard stared at her blankly. *Goose patty, syllabub . . . Poor*

Daft Harry's head upon a platter!

She led the way with sure purposeful steps. Richard followed, lagging behind his brother's roistering progress, aware that behind him men moved as surely and as purposefully to snuff out an old man's life. He glanced behind him. The altar flame still burned.

They emerged into the outer ward and onto the steps of the Watergate. Edward's barge rode the faint swell like a graceful bird. He stared at the blazons that embellished the prow: the falcon and the fetterlock, the grim insignia of York; the three lions passant for England. He swallowed down his sudden fear. Yes. Yes. It was right, it was just, for York, for England . . . He looked once more over his shoulder before he set his foot on the heaving deck. He saw that the little flame was extinguished.

'They say he died of pure melancholy and displeasure,' the Lady Margaret Beaufort said. Her shrewd black eyes fastened knowingly on Harry's face. 'But we know better, do we not, my lord?'

Harry acknowledged the remark with a slight inclination of his head. All the world knew, if there was truth in the tale, that King Henry's corpse had dripped blood onto the stones of St Paul's. It was year-old news now, displaced by the miracles that occurred daily at his tomb: a woman of Kent cured of scrofula; a blind man given eyes; and a month ago on St Agnes's Day a devil cast out from a boy of ten before his mother's very eyes. Every day now, pilgrims trampled and chipped relics from his tomb. Even in death the saintly king could find no peace.

He said, in an effort to turn the countess from her dangerous talk, 'Is Queen Margaret still held in the tower?'

'She is — God help her in her terrible grief. I asked leave to visit her once but my request was denied.' The countess shivered and crossed herself devoutly. 'I pray for her daily. It must be a dreadful thing, to lose husband, son and kingdom all. It would have been kinder to have murdered her as they did her husband the king.'

Harry ignored the potentially treasonous remark and watched the dancers who leapt and cavorted in nervous delight beneath the Queen's censorious eyes. She sat, enthroned beneath a cloth of estate, a stiff glittering figure but beautiful still, though she was now well into her thirty-sixth year and at Christmas had borne her seventh child — another daughter, much to the King's disappointment. Behind her chair her mother the ageing Jacquetta of Bedford knelt; a sister, Buckingham's duchess, crouched at her feet; the Woodville satellites maintaining their protective orbit, for her brother Earl Rivers would not be too far away and another now approached her chair. Lionel, Bishop of Salisbury knelt and waited submissively till his sister bade him rise. None were exempt from this elaborate show of respect and even the dancers paused before the Queen to make low and careful obeisance.

'Is she always so tender of her dignity?'

'Always, my lord,' the countess replied. 'Her Grace needs to be constantly reminded of the greatness of her estate.'

Harry merely raised his brows and continued to watch the Queen. He had seen Elizabeth Woodville no more than half a dozen times — the first time when he had been a boy, at York. She had been the wife of the Lancastrian John Grey then, a softer, gentler Elizabeth, untouched by avarice. The wide blue eyes were hard and anxious now, the exquisite mouth thinned by greed.

'A pity,' murmured Harry regretfully. 'I must admit I preferred her as plain Dame Grey.'

The countess smiled. 'I should warn you, my lord, her Grace has very sharp ears. A word out of place and you could be a fallen man. Oh yes.' Her smile widened at his look of mild disbelief. 'I can name you a score or more: Earl Desmond and his two innocent sons; Sir Thomas Cooke and Chief Justice Markham; Earl Warwick himself — all poor men now or dead, my lord, because they displeased the Queen in some way.' She nodded her dark, neatly coifed head. 'Take heed, my lord. The Queen is a dangerous woman to cross while she has the King enthralled.'

'All women are dangerous if they feel themselves slighted,' said Harry. 'Accordingly I treat them all with suspicion and caution.'

The countess impaled him again with her piercing stare. 'Yes, you do, don't you?' she said thoughtfully. 'But there are women and women, you know. Do you believe us all to be shallow and contemptible creatures?'

Harry returned her measuring glance and in spite of himself could not help but admire her. She had changed very little from the last time he had seen her; still handsome in a pale aesthetic way. She was dressed in a drab self-effacing gown, her only ornament a heavy gold reliquary that contained a lock of Edmund Tudor's hair. Her eyes were her finest feature, dark and quiet and full of the fierce intelligence and learning that was so wildly at odds with the discreet and almost humble stance which he knew quite well to be assumed. It was a guise adopted by quite a few Lancastrians in this now exclusively Yorkist regime. On the surface they accepted defeat with equanimity and paid Edward the lip service that was his due. So they should, thought Harry. Few had lost by it and many had gained as a result of Edward's customary leniency. The countess herself had suffered less than she deserved. Edward, magnanimously, had left her the bulk of her estates and rather more foolishly, her freedom. Harry thought that in her way she was far more dangerous than the vain preening creature upon the dais.

'No,' he said and meant it. 'I have never believed it of you, my lady.'

The countess smiled at the compliment, a sad wistful smile that reminded Harry very much of her son. He said, remembering their unhappy parting, 'And how does your son, the Lord Henry?'

Her eyes softened with unimaginable tenderness. 'He is well. Well and safe in Brittany in the care of his Uncle Jasper.' Her lips curved in a dry little smile. 'It was thought politic to send him abroad when Kind Edward regained the throne — for the sake of his health, you understand.' She did not add that it was only by the skin of his teeth that Henry had escaped. She thought grimly of his headlong and terrified flight after the calamitous news of Tewkesbury. Her sharp teeth caught hungrily at her lower lip. Nightly she wept and prayed for him and shared his agony of heart. More running, more hiding, another long exile and not in safe pro-Lancastrian France as they had planned but in Brittany where foul weather and pure chance had blown him. Now both he and his Uncle Jasper were held under close but honourable restraint, Henry at Vannes, Jasper in remote Finisterre. Duke Francis had not been slow to realise Henry's worth, doubled now since the death of Edward of Lancaster. Henry *was* Lancaster now and for Brittany, a useful weapon to wield in his quarrel with Louis of France in which he hoped for England's backing, even more useful as the bait with which to tempt Edward into such an alliance. For the moment it was stalemate, for though both Edward and Louis had sent envoys to offer tempting sums, Brittany held out for more than a monetary gain. Eager as Edward was to have custody of her son he could not as yet afford an open affront to France. So Henry was safe while Brittany's quarrel held; Henry, the precious pawn, moved hither and thither across the board at the pleasure of unscrupulous men. So had the pattern of all his life run. But not for ever. Margaret roused herself from her bleak thoughts. Already destiny shaped events to an end. King Henry and his son Prince Edward were dead, leaving her own son as the focus of Lancastrian hopes. Soon he would be a man and able to act for himself. Meanwhile the Yorkist canker would work upon itself, consuming the heart from within. The disease was well advanced, nurtured here in the bosom of the court. The Queen was the pivot on which all spun: Elizabeth with her insatiable greed and monumental insecurity who thought of nothing but the advancement of her own Woodville kin. All were loathed as parvenus and upstarts, especially by George of Clarence, malignant treacherous Clarence who all but outstripped the Queen in ambition and greed. He was not sated yet despite Edward's generous partition of the Warwick estates that had yielded him the lion's share. He had also been appointed to the lucrative office of Lord Chamberlain. That was bound to rankle with his brother Gloucester who had recently wed Anne Neville. The marriage had not been achieved without discord. Clarence had driven a ruthless bargain and all Richard had gained, apart from a wife, were the Neville lands in Yorkshire and Westmorland, and those only while Montagu's son lived and bore heirs to maintain his father's attainder. If young George of Bedford died before he had issue, the Neville lands reverted to the heirs of

George Neville, Lord Latimer.

Gloucester had retired north, seemingly content. As yet he was untouched by the court's avarice, still stiff with honour and principle. He would succumb in the end if only out of self-defence. The Queen loathed him because he could not be bought; Clarence she loathed more because he could, but not at any price by her. Edward himself grew fat and complacent, given more and more to worldly pleasure. There were mistresses already, discreetly kept from the Queen's eyes. But Elizabeth knew. There was little that she did not know and she would know that this would be viewed by the court as visible proof that her hold on the King was weakening.

The countess's glance slid covertly across the tiled and patterned floor. Hard-eyed, she surveyed the Woodville clique: Elizabeth's head was bent to peruse a parchment roll. Her two elder brothers flanked her throne — like chessmen on a gigantic board in defence of a vulnerable queen. Margaret smiled, pleased with the simile, for chess was something at which she excelled; Elizabeth, the white queen, Lionel her bishop and Anthony her knight, masters for the moment. No doubt they thought the game played and won, as theoretically it was. The red queen was vanquished, the king displaced, their pawns scattered and swept from the board. But while Henry lived, play could be resumed. She had men enough still, like de Vere, Earl of Oxford, albeit in exile as was her brother-in-law Jasper. Here in England there were two on whom she could completely rely: her receiver and steward Reginald Bray, a man possessed of a devious wit and the greatest cunning; and John Morton, that able priest, an avid and die-hard Lancastrian who had spent nine years in exile with Margaret of Anjou and had accompanied her disastrous return. He and the countess were old friends and like her, after Tewkesbury, he had submitted and received Edward's generous pardon. Also like her, he merely bided his time. That Edward now cherished him was for his fine legal mind and at the request of his old patron Archbishop Bourchier. Already he was well entrenched in the Yorkist camp, Master of the Rolls and deep in the King's confidence. There was no doubt that Morton was destined to rise no matter who the master he served. And there would be others in time, she thought with confidence, men who would flow in on the tide of changing fortune. The Stanleys perhaps, and of young Buckingham she had hopes. Then, of course, there was Northumberland.

Her shrewd eyes flickered over his dark lean face as he smiled a greeting to John Paston. Nothing to be read there beyond a faint air of boredom. But how much of his detachment was real, how much was assumed? It could be that he merely held his hand till he was approached by the highest bidder. John Morton thought he was worth cultivating, and there was no doubt that his adherence would be a triumph for their cause.

She laid her small cold hand upon Harry's sleeve. 'My lord,' she murmered in her meekest voice, 'you must forgive my long and distracted silence. I was thinking of my son.' She sighed. 'I fear his lot could be happier.' Her eyes rested on him with sudden warmth. 'But of course, I need not tell you, my lord. Were the two of you not friends long enough in Wales? None could know better than you the emptiness of exile.' She went on in a light casual voice, 'I shall be writing to him this very day. Shall I send him your greeting, my lord? It would comfort him greatly to know that he was remembered by his friends.'

'By all means,' said Harry kindly for he could not help but feel compassion. Henry's must be a wretched life. He said, thinking back to the old days at Raglan, 'Did he ever marry that delightful child, Black William's daughter, the Lady Maud?'

The countess gave him a mildly irritated look. 'No,' she said slowly. 'The marriage did not take place after all. It seemed better in the circumstances that Henry remain free. Both I and his Uncle Jasper thought a young wife an unnecessary complication. I thought perhaps you would have heard from Anne Herbert on that account. She had hoped that a place might be found for the Lady Maud with your mother, in the dowager countess's household.'

Harry thought fleetingly of the child whose laughter had been such a joy. 'Gladly,' he said. 'Anything I can do to be of service.'

He looked away from the countess's narrow black eyes, suddenly tiring of her presence. The dancing had ceased, though the minstrels still scraped and plucked a frenzied tune. The courtiers had drifted into little groups, the new men and place-seekers keeping close to the Queen, whilst the old nobility sought the King.

'Shall you remain at court, my lord, or do you return to the north?' The countess broke off and craned to view a commotion by the door. George of Clarence entered, heralded by his short braying laugh and supporting a drunken Hastings.

Clarence paused before the Queen and bowed ridiculously low, then prodded his companion to his knees. 'Lower, my lord,' he said in a whisper meant to be heard. 'That will never serve for the Queen.' He looked up and fixed Elizabeth with his bright conceited eyes. 'Your Grace,' he enquired mildly, 'will that suffice or do our noses actually have to touch the floor?'

All heard the Queen's hissing intake of breath and saw her face blanch. She made a movement as if to rise from her chair but Clarence was gone thrusting noisily through the amused and gratified crowd to join his brother the King.

'His Grace of Clarence grows over-bold,' murmured Margaret Beaufort happily. 'That little slight will cost him dear.'

Harry said nothing, having lapsed into a brooding and irritable silence. Jesu, he thought, how vain and petty they all are. He wished now that he had gone north with Gloucester. The duke had pressed openly for his company. He frowned, thinking of that strange young man who for some reason was courting his favour. Instinctively he had recoiled from Gloucester's overtures of friendship, not from any dislike of Gloucester but from dislike of so open a commitment. Like Gloucester himself he did not make friends easily.

He turned to the countess, about to murmur an excuse to depart when they were approached by a hungry-looking priest.

John Morton bowed over the countess's hand and raised his pale clever face to Harry. His eyes, deep set in caves of furrowed skin, were hard and colourless as glass. He smiled and showed a row of small yellow teeth. 'My Lord Northumberland. I am gratified to make your aquaintance at last. I knew your father well.'

Harry inclined his head. He knew John Morton only by repute — a subtle and ambitious man who quite openly courted a mitre.

'A brave man,' Morton said. 'He gave his life in a splendid cause.'

Harry looked at him coldly, disliking him on sight. 'I have no doubt that he thought so,' he said.

Morton raised heavy brows. 'And you, I take it, do not?'

'No. Since you ask, I do not.'

Morton's eyes flickered but he sustained the rebuff and clung to his worldly smile. He would have turned away but for the countess's insistent eyes. He knew instinctively that this was neither the time nor the place to sound out a man as cautious as Northumberland. But who knew when a better opportunity would occur? And besides, it went against the grain to approach the matter in so direct way. He would have preferred a little more time to draw the man out, at least to let him make some of the running. Not that he felt any great risk to himself. Like every good lawyer he had a defence well prepared. Was he not King Edward's good and faithful hound, unleashed to sniff out heresy and sedition? But still he misliked the look in the younger man's eyes and it was against his better judgement that he persisted.

'You think it was a worthless death to die fighting against tyranny and evil?'

'A tyranny and evil that you now seem quite happy to embrace yourself,' Harry remarked. 'Are you not King Edward's true and loyal man?'

'So I am, my lord, so I am.' Morton smiled his rapacious smile, 'For a season mayhap, till the wind blows warmer from another quarter.' He paused, then added meaningfully, 'From Brittany, perhaps.'

Harry looked steadily into Morton's hyaline eyes. 'I fear you favour me with too much of your confidence.'

'Too much or not enough,' Morton countered. 'I have heard, my lord, that you are a cautious man. How sure do you have to be?'

Then Margaret Beaufort's gentle voice intervened as she saw Morton lose the advantage. 'My lord, you must forgive us if we seem to presume. But it has been said that if it had not been for the Earl of Warwick you would have declared wholeheartedly for Lancaster.'

'Many things are said, my lady. I doubt if the half of them are true.'

'But you took no part, either for Lancaster or for York. Surely when a man refuses to commit himself openly then there must be doubt, in his own mind as well as in the minds of others.' She smiled a smile of feminine persuasion that sat oddly upon her face. 'We cannot be blamed for wondering where your true inclinations lie. After all, all of us have our privy allegiance beyond that of duty and fealty. There is no harm in showing one's true colours in quarters where they do not offend. That way a man is not misunderstood.'

'How am I misunderstood, my lady?' Harry enquired mildly. 'What gives you cause to think that because I am not openly enamoured of York, I must be so of Lancaster?' He bowed stiffly and courteously over Margaret's hand. 'Forgive me, my lady. I have more to concern me than whether my king is descended from John of Gaunt or Lionel, Duke of Clarence.'

Morton pursed his fleshy lips as he watched Northumberland depart. 'And there, Countess, you have the art of speaking but of saying nothing.' He smiled ruefully. 'He would have made a fine lawyer.'

'So we are no further forward then?'

'Oh, I would not say that. He's not as indifferent as he pretends to be. Such men on the whole are extremely rare; even wolves need to live in packs.' His eyes narrowed thoughtfully. 'At the bottom of him he's a man capable of deep conscience and loyalty. He pays lip service to Edward as we all do but his heart is not there. As yet he has not found his true allegiance but when he does it will be to one man rather than any particular cause.'

'Then we must make sure his favour falls upon Henry, my son,' said the countess.

Morton nodded. 'Yes. We must make sure,' he said slowly. 'For I think there will be no second chance. Once he has made his mind up only death will turn him from it.'

It was August, the end of a month of long hot days that slowed life to a dreaming pace. The heat of the room lay on him like a soft heavy cloud and Harry leant his elbows on the narrow sill to watch the passing of the day. The cluttered roofs of York were blurred in the summer dusk, the narrow streets filled with stillness and shadow. He watched a drift of fiery cloud tip the Minster spires, streaming westward like the flame from a beacon. Another sunset, tomorrow another dawn with only darkness in between, like the darkness that filled his heart and blinded him to life, that kept him trapped in this unfeeling limbo, afraid to go forward or back. All his life he had felt a sense of being alone, as if all the world were enclosed in an orb of glass and only he was shut out, seeing all but feeling nothing, always looking on but never taking part.

He thought without pleasure of the days ahead: from York to Newcastle to meet the Scottish conservators of the truce; then to Warkworth; then to Alnwick to see what manner of mischief Eleanor had been brewing. She'd grown stranger still since Warwick's death, silent and introverted, almost as if she mourned him. In a way he could understand that. Hatred was such a sustaining thing, it must leave an emptiness when it was gone. He only wished he'd had the same respite. His own hatred, for he knew now that despite his vigilance that was the thing that had driven him, still gnawed at his heart with nothing but ghosts to feed upon. Hatred did not die with the perpetrator of the deed; the pain and the outrage lived on, corrosive, destructive, needful of another living creature to fasten upon else it would consume its host. He should have been satisfied. Richard Neville was dead and he had no successor — or so he had thought until now.

He moved back into the dimly-lit room. On the table by his bed lay a small richly-bound book emblazoned with his arms and the Brabant lion, the gift of Richard of Gloucester. A cynical smile twisted his long mouth. *Beware of princes bearing gifts.* He had wondered why Gloucester courted his favour. He thought that perhaps now he knew.

He sat and took the book in his hands. His mind drifted back over the evening's events. He had dined with Gloucester in the house of the Augustinian Friars, a surprisingly lavish and extravagant feast. Even so, the company had been restrained and discreet in their talk. These were the vanquished Earl of Warwick's men, still resentful and wary of their new lord and for the moment loyal only because he had wed their master's daughter.

Harry had met Anne Neville only once before, on the day she had married Gloucester. Even then he had thought her a frail sickly thing. She possessed none of her father's lust for life, none of his overwhelming arrogance; quiet, devout, unnervingly thin, she was a travesty of her lordly sire. She was the kind of woman that he rather depised; the sort one spoke to only of pleasant and trivial things and always in a tender voice. Yet there was no doubt that Richard of Gloucester adored her. His happiness was almost a physical thing that reached out and touched every man in the hall and filled Harry with a vague feeling of irritation that he did not recognise then as envy. He had watched them with his faintly mocking smile. So this was love? He had never viewed it before at such close quarters and in his narrow and arrogant way he had seen it as almost an undignified thing. He would never make himself so obviously vulnerable.

After they had eaten and watched a small devout masque contrived by his duchess, Richard drew him aside into a private room.

In silence he poured wine for them both. His movements were tense and jerky and as he handed Harry an overfull goblet a little wine spilled on his hand. He wiped it self-consciously on his sleeve, then said, abruptly and without preamble, 'My lord. Did you know that the King has appointed me to the Wardenship of the West March?' He spoke stiffly and defensively, almost as if he expected a rebuff.

'No, your Grace. I did not know,' Harry answered him softly. He wasn't surprised though. It was common policy to counter the overall power of a single lord by setting up another against him. Usually it was a Neville. No doubt Edward thought his brother the next best thing.

He added with a hypocritical little smile, seeing that it was expected. 'Nevertheless I am pleased to hear it now, your Grace.'

'Are you, my lord?' Richard's sombre face lit for a moment. 'I thought perhaps — well, you know, the Percys have always had charge of the Border. I thought, or rather I feared . . .'

'You thought I might be jealous?'

94

'Well, not exactly,' Richard shrugged. 'But something like that.'

'Why should I be? How does it interfere in my own province?'

'It doesn't,' Richard said quickly. 'Not in any way. The East and Middle Marches remain exclusively your preserve. But as the King's brother, naturally . . .'

'Naturally you outrank me.'

Richard stiffened. 'I wish you would let me speak for myself instead of always putting words into my mouth. What I was about to say was that I was afraid of a conflict of interests.'

'How could that be?' Harry turned his head and Richard saw that his eyes were cold. 'The terms of my office are quite explicit, the boundaries of my lands and influence even more so. I can see no possible reason for conflict providing you trespass upon neither.'

Richard coloured hotly at the obvious snub but he kept his voice and eyes steady. 'I had hoped for more than that, my lord. I had hoped that we might work together.'

'As I am sure we can, your Grace,' Harry said smoothly. 'As I said, providing we both respect the limitations of our power.'

Richard stared at him, pale with suppressed anger. 'That won't work,' he said bluntly. 'We're just going back to the old ways then; every man for himself and God damn England. There must be trust, there must be a certain loyalty . . .'

Harry threw him a malicious little smile. 'I would have thought you would have been wary of such. They have not served you so well in the past.'

'Yes. I am wary,' Richard flung back at him. 'But I am not afraid of them as you are.'

'Fear doesn't come into it,' Harry said coldly. 'I learn, your Grace, from past follies. It seems that you do not. Did you not tell me once that you loved Earl Warwick as a father? Were you not raised in his household at Middleham? All those happy years spent together, whispering your boyhood secrets in his paternal ear. Did it ever occur to you then, my lord, that in a few years he would be your mortal enemy?'

'Stop it. For God's sake, stop it,' Richard said through tight pale lips. 'Must you always sneer? Must you always destroy?

95

What pleasure do you get from it?' He turned away, staring blankly at the wall before of him.

Harry said, addressing Gloucester's rigid back. 'Your Grace, have I your permission to retire?'

'No, you have not.' Gloucester turned to face him, wondering why he persisted, why he even wanted this man's trust and friendship at all. Partly because he needed it, for he knew he could not rule the north without him. Northumberland's power was too great to be overlooked: Warden of the East and Middle Marches, justice of the forests north of Trent, Constable of Bamburgh and Dunstanburgh, Newcastle and Knaresborough, lord of countless manors scattered the length and breadth of England. There was no corner of the north where he did not have influence, no place that he could not have Gloucester ousted from if he tried. And he would try, he could see that from his face, cold and closed against him. His own took on a stubborn look. He would not give up. He had a right to a place here, for he loved the north better than he had ever loved woman or man. He had found an affinity here, in the dark secret hills, in the bleak wind-swept moors that were an echo of himself. He glanced again at Northumberland's harsh and uncompromising profile etched darkly against the pallid light. Beyond he could see the shimmering spire of York Minster, the tall leaning gables of rich merchants' houses. He thought bleakly of the day he and Edward had ridden like fugitives through the streets; he could still see those stony faces, the cold wordless hatred in their eyes. He had promised himself then: one day those eyes would look eagerly for his coming. He would win their hearts if it took him the rest of his life.

He said quietly and without malice, 'My lord, I will not quarrel with you because, to be honest, I cannot afford to. Believe, my lord, I am not trying to encroach on your privileges or challenge your authority. I would have thought that you of all men would have known how much there is to be done. It was you yourself who once pleaded the north's condition to me but it seems that you do not set her plight above your own ambitions and interests.'

Harry moved away from him and the one step might have been

a hundred miles for all that Gloucester could reach him. He had said again with the note of bored impatience in his voice that most men found so quelling, 'Have I your leave to retire, your Grace? It has been a long and wearying day.'

'Yes, my lord,' Richard had said stonily. 'You have my leave.'

Harry's eyes narrowed. The recollection was even worse than the actual event. Seen with hindsight, Gloucester's motives were without doubt suspect. He had thought that Warwick had left no sons to avenge him. But Richard of Gloucester was as good as a son. Warwick had raised him, nurtured him, shaped his mind in accord with his own, taught him that perhaps the north was always better in Neville hands. Gloucester's mother was a Neville and so was his wife, he ruled the old Neville lordships . . .

With infinite care he laid the book down, then deliberately and wantonly, with all his strength, he tore the soft parchment across.

Soft as a folding of a night-bird's wings, the last poignant note of the song ebbed away on the merest whisper of sound. Reluctantly Eleanor opened her eyes. How sweetly the child sang. But then all the Welsh did. It was one of the few things they did well. She sighed fretfully as Maud Herbert laid aside the gilded harp and went to prepare her nightly posset. The room was hot and hazy beneath a ceiling of drifting smoke and the fire banked against the November chill threw heavy shadows across her face. She had grown fat and coarse these last few months. The fine aggressive jaw had melted away into a collar of fat and beneath the fur robe her legs, swollen like wine skins, throbbed with the precision and regularity of a beaten drum, though she had swallowed powdered corocynth till it turned her sick, and her physician bled her daily. The little Welsh girl's voice was the best physic, the shower of bright notes falling like summer rain into the burning tumult of her mind, the weird haunting melodies that could draw her pain and leave only a dull nagging ache. The songs themselves she did not care for so much, tales of the past as all Welsh songs were: eulogies to dead men with unintelligible names, the sparring of giants and dragons, all interwoven with the mystical prophecy that the glory of Wales would come again. Eleanor

97

preferred the French chansonettes with their theme of love and courtesy. She remembered vaguely that she had a book of Vidal somewhere . . .

Her eyes roamed the cluttered wealth it had taken twelve strong men the best part of a week to haul up the tortuous stairs: arras from the loom of Dordin, frail goblets of rosy Venetian glass, a chalice of gold and amethysts reputed to have belonged to Charlemagne. She smiled grimly. She lacked nothing except her freedom. Some days like today, she could not even move from her bed, let alone negotiate the narrow stairs. Once a week two hefty men-at-arms would carry her down and she would remind them who was mistress. For the rest of the time this was her sole domain, these four walls and her wondrous cave of riches.

She glanced up as Maud laid a silver cup beside her, carefully covered by a white linen square. She had grown almost fond of the girl in the month she had been here, and this, for Eleanor, was rare. It was one of the few pleasures that she still enjoyed, the abuse of the women who served her. So far the little Welsh girl had escaped her spleen; like her sweet singing, everything about her was soothing. She didn't whine for a privilege as her daughter Margaret did nor cast covetous eyes on her best gowns. She was enviably young, too young for it really to rankle. Unremarkable, too, except for that flaming hair. Her dress was unassuming and quiet, all of which Eleanor greatly approved. Fat and past fifty she might well be but she still did not care to be outshone. Even so, the girl was not unattractive or dowdy which would have infuriated Eleanor the more. Her quick and agile mind could well keep pace with her own and her good humour seemed unquench-able. She had spirit, though, a strong, stubborn and uncom-promising streak that could have proved irksome had it not been tempered with a warm compassion that inevitably allowed Eleanor her own way.

Appreciatively, she sipped of the warming brew. Just the right amount of cinnamon and cloves, enough to mask the bitter taste of the more powerful herbs with which she induced sleep and a magical euphoria. Her plump ringed hand reached into a dish of sugared wafers and she ate three in quick succession. She mused happily on the day's events, especially the news brought to her by

Henry Thwaites. The tidings had both elated and depressed her; her beloved John was coming home but so too was her son Harry.

A frown gathered between her invisible brows. It was six months since she had seen Harry. Would court life have mellowed him? She'd heard that he was much in the company of the King. She'd heard too that Edward's court was iniquitous. She smiled mirthlessly, imagining Harry drunk and debauched. She could have more readily imagined it of the archangel himself.

She turned her mind to pleasanter things and thought joyously of John's return. She recalled the one hesitant and carefully penned letter that she'd had in reply to a dozen of her own. He had assured her of his love and service, proof, surely, that his need of her had not lessened. She smirked. Harry had whisked him off like a zealous priest, thinking to remove him from her influence. Did he really think that distance could sever their bond, that her hold on him could be measured in miles. For a few days last Christmas he'd been allowed home. No word had needed to be passed between them. John had known her mind, known that at all costs Harry's confidence must be won and only he could do it. Her face assumed a cunning look. Sly, clever John, trotting at Harry's heels more obedient than his Irish hound and doing it so well and convincingly that even she had been quietly enraged though all was done at her bidding. She frowned. Yet despite this show of exemplary behaviour, Harry had not been drawn. She saw now that they would have to look further afield. She bit savagely into a fourth wafer. A good marriage, perhaps? It was not the first time the thought had occurred to her, though even here, his field was limited. John was landless, and worse, a dead man's bastard albeit of a noble house. But still, if they did not aim too high, a modest dowry and good connections . . .

Eleanor cast a speculative eye on the girl moving with quiet grace about her chamber. Not so very much to look at though she would be comlier if she gained a little flesh. Her hair was a dull dusky red, her small face marred by that wide humorous mouth. Good teeth, though, which was something these days. Oh yes, Eleanor thought, warming to the idea, John could certainly do a lot worse. There'd not be much of a dowry, though; she still had three unmarried sisters all in ward. But on the credit side, her brother was Earl of Pembroke and, more important, his countess was sister to the Queen. And the girl would probably be glad of an offer after being left in the lurch by Henry Tudor. Nothing to grieve over there, she thought, remembering Margaret of Beaufort's skinny brat. A penniless exile now by all accounts and there was a bastard taint there as well. In the circumstances, marriage to John would not be too much of a climb-down. After all, he was Northumberland's cousin and at the moment his only blood heir. All they needed was Harry's consent and the thing was as good as done.

In a kindly voice she called the girl to her. 'Maud, my dear. Will you not come and sit awhile?'

She covered the girl's small hand with her own and drew her down beside her. 'You look pale, child. Do I overwork you so much? You could have Joan Eure to help you, you know.' She sighed mournfully. 'It's just that I find her so clumsy and slow — and that dreadful rash upon her chin. My daughter Margaret swears that she shaves.'

Maud laughed softly and sat obediently upon the bed. Now that was better, Eleanor thought. Why, the child was quite lovely when she laughed. She said in the kindly patronising voice that she kept for priests and children, 'And how old are you, Maud?'

'I was fifteen in September, my lady.'

'And not yet wed?' Eleanor's pale eyes invited confidences. 'Not even betrothed?'

Maud flushed. 'No. Though I was until recently — to Henry Tudor, Earl of Richmond.'

Earl of nothing, thought Eleanor, but she said sympathetically, 'An unhappy affair. But perhaps for the best. I would not care to have any daughter of mine shackled to a young man of such dubious fortune.' She patted the girl's hand. 'I dare say you're not grieved over much.'

Maud looked away from the Countess's probing stare. No. She wasn't grieved. She only felt sad for Henry. She knew now that she hadn't ever loved him. She pitied him, but it wasn't the same thing. She'd known Henry for nearly all of her life; he had been part of the safe predictable pattern. She'd known him as a small frightened boy and sometimes she had glimpsed the Henry that

100

might have been if life had not used him so cruelly. That Henry
perhaps she could have loved, the shy gentle boy who had nursed
a lame starling in his breast and wept for a day when it died. That
Henry had vanished a long time ago and she had not cared so
much for the one who had taken his place.

'Well then,' Eleanor smiled brightly, 'we must remedy that and
set to finding you a husband.' Her eyes dropped critically to the
girl's small breasts even further diminished by the straining
bodice. 'And a new gown, mayhap,' she added generously. 'We
must have you fine for my lord's homecoming.'

Maud lifted her face. 'Harry? Is Harry coming home?'

Eleanor saw the soft rich colour flood the girl's pale cheeks. Her
eyes narrowed. 'Yes,' she said slowly, suddenly filled with
suspicion and unease. 'But of course, you know Harry well. He
was in care of your family in Wales.'

'Yes.' The glow clung shamefully to her face. 'Yes. He and my
brother were friends.'

Eleanor smiled acutely. 'A sad time for all of us, especially for
poor Harry.' She moved her hands in a frail poignant gesture,
eying the girl from beneath carefully lowered lids. 'Perhaps that
accounts for all he has become, so cruel and hard, especially
towards me. Perhaps it is because he has known so little happiness himself that he grudges it in others.' She smiled wanly.
'Oh, it's not for myself that I care so much but it grieves me the
way he treats John. My nephew John,' she added in answer to the
girl's blank look. 'The natural son of my husband's brother,
Thomas the Lord Egremont.' She repeated his name just for the
love of hearing it spoken aloud. 'Thomas, Lord Egremont. He
was slain at the battle of Northampton twelve years ago.' She
went on, her voice quickening to keep pace with the flood of
emotion that his name had aroused. All the humiliations and
diappointments she had suffered at Harry's hands came spilling
out, every harboured spite and grudge. She glanced down and
saw the play of emotion on the girl's eloquent face. Surprise
paling to disbelief and shock, sadness warming to compassion. It
was a long time since she had had such a willing and sympathetic
ear. 'Harry has never forgiven me for taking John in and raising
him as my own son. Yet what else, in all charity, could I do? He

101

was a child. I could not turn him away.' The vindication, so well rehearsed, sounded convincing even in her own ears. It was with genuine emotion that her voice broke, her eyes wept real tears as if she had pleaded her cause so often to herself that now she truly believed it.

'If there's any fault in this it is mine,' she cried. 'It breaks my heart that John should have to pay for it.'

'Oh my lady.' The girl's hands reached out to her tenderly and for a moment Eleanor saw herself mirrored in the wide and shining eyes: a frail woman cruelly persecuted, the oppressed instead of the oppressor. She smiled inwardly. Oh truly, the child was a treasure.

Maud stayed by her long after she slept, till the fire burnt low and the windows darkened with frost and her limbs grew stiff with cold. She thought longingly of Wales, of Raglan in the shadow of the mountains of Gwent, of Pembroke, a dark jewel in its ring of bright water, a place of grim shadows and incredible brightness never to be seen again.

She rose stiffly and went swiftly to her own bed beneath the far window. It was colder here in the maelstrom of draughts but she preferred to be near the light and air.

She knelt on the skimpy covering of furs and looked out through the mullioned panes. The night seemed without colour or shape and the crowding turrets filled all of her vision, tall, glittering, rimed in frost, like a spun sugar subtlety set out for some lordly feast. She stared with wide unblinking eyes, holding her breath as if to contain the deep hurt that Eleanor's words had inflicted. Added to the pain was a dull confused misery, as if she had reached out to caress a favourite hound and it had savagely bitten her hand. Gwilym Ddu had warned her not to trust the *Lloegyr*. They were devious and sly, treacherous as snakes.

But Harry had been different; Harry had been shining perfection, an untarnished image she had carried in her heart for the last three years. She loved him with a child's stubborn and determined fervour. He was her fate, her destiny — *tyhghedfen* — inescapable as death. He was remembered warmth and kindness; a strong soft hand stroking her hair; a voice — she closed her eyes, thinking of his voice — like clear water running over smooth mossed stones, like a deep muted chord, where the vibration was felt long after the music had died away.

At last she let out her breath in a harsh gasping sigh. The wound bled and she wept silently.

Eleanor watched the first nebulous flakes of snow star the thick horned panes. It would not lie before nightfall, she thought. The ground still harboured a vestige of warmth and was pooled by a night's torrential rain. By dusk the pools would be skinned with ice, the earth iron-hard with frost. She was familiar with this prelude to winter: days of wind and driving rain, nights of treacherous black ice. Then the snow would come, sometimes soft and deceptive as a woman's smile, drifting listlessly on the glittering air, fall upon fall until the drifts climbed to a man's full height against the curtain wall. More often it was borne on a shrieking wind; a gale of whirling white flakes that choked and blinded and suffocated.

Eleanor shivered and turned her face to the fire. At least Harry would not have the advantage on her then — they would be prisoners here together.

Bitterly she cursed her useless limbs, more painful and swollen than usual. Two whole days Harry had been back and not one word to her though she had demanded his presence daily. That was the cruellest torture of all, to be ignored as if she were of no account. She knew that was how they saw her now, a useless and decaying old woman. She had noticed that even her women were becoming lax and stood less in awe of her. She glanced suspiciously across the room to where her daughter Margaret sat stitching placidly. Even Margaret was not to be wholly trusted now. Lately she spent a great deal of time with her sister, Elizabeth, Lady Scrope, who all knew was high in Harry's favour. That was a sure sign that her power was failing. Margaret instinctively gravitated towards the source of wealth and influence.

She slopped wine viciously into a gilded hanap, one of a pair pawned by Margaret of Anjou. Its fellow stood half full as John had left it. She scowled with discontent. Did he think she hadn't known his impatience to be gone? Blatantly fidgeting, his eyes on the door, mumbling excuses that Harry was waiting. Damn

Harry, she thought. Damn Harry and his inexhaustable health and strength that was gradually weaning John from her. He had her well and truly beaten there; hunting, hawking, playing at war, all the things John's heart would delight in. The dreadful thought occurred to her: had his cleaving to Harry not been the pretence she had thought?

Eleanor drank greedily, the thick sweet wine of Gascony that soothed both mind and body. Optimism returned with the wine's euphoric glow. She knew better than that. John hadn't the courage to venture out alone. She must get him wed, out of Harry's thrall. She had set her heart on Maud Herbert.

Again anxiety and frustration gnawed at her. She had never thought to be thwarted by John himself but she could not help but recall the mulish look upon his face. She savaged her lip with sharp discoloured teeth. No doubt he thought the girl timid and plain. Eleanor smiled faintly. He took after his father there. Thomas had liked his women full of laughter and fire, women with warm and willing bodies with which to blunt his lust. But only she had ever been able to quench his need, only he had ever satisfied hers.

A faint animal noise arose in her throat as a spasm of cramp impaled her.

Her daughter Margaret laid her stitchwork down. 'Madame,' she said, 'is aught amiss?'

Numbly Eleanor shook her head and refilled her empty goblet.

'My lady?' Margaret knelt and lifted her cunning face. 'What is it? Are you in pain?'

'Only the pain of being surrounded by fools,' Eleanor gasped. 'Fetch me the Lady Maud.'

Margaret's face grew sullen. 'Must it always be Maud Herbert?' she demanded coldly. 'Will I not serve this once?'

Eleanor clamped her teeth on a rising scream. 'No,' she hissed. 'No. You will not.'

Margaret hovered infuriatingly. 'Madame. Are you sure? Is there aught I can do?'

Eleanor glared at her. 'Only get yourself gone,' she said between rigid lips. 'Do you hear?' she screamed as Margaret still hesitated. 'Get out and take that foolish simpering face away with you.'

Margaret went without a word or a backward glance. The door rattled shut behind her.

Eleanor gave a shrill sniggering laugh. Margaret's rages were easily soothed, usually with a new gown or a jewel. Then she clamped her teeth hard together as pain lanced through her belly. This pain she knew as she knew its cause. The demon was hungry again, the growing ravenous serpent of longing that lived inside her and had begun to devour her inch by inch. She had given birth to him unawares. What had been the harm in the very beginning? A simple draught taken for easement! Without it she could never have survived all those empty years when sleep had been her only comfort. Three months ago she had tried to cast him out and then had begun the dreadful days of longing. She had drowned him in a sea of wine, she had placated him with feasts of sweets and comfits. But he would not be weaned, he would not be fobbed off, only with one thing could he be sated. For him she brewed the dried root of mandragora seethed in wine, the pounded seeds of the white poppy. Four drops only she allowed him each day, barely enough to keep him quiescent. He was always there, coiled in his dark corner and only by the sheer force of her will could she keep him at bay. Today he seemed bolder, slithering out of his corner to lie openly at her feet.

Unflinchingly she stared him down. The creature was of no particular shape or size, sometimes small enough to lie curled in the bottom of her cup, sometimes large enough to fill the entire room. Eleanor moaned as her muscles contracted and knotted. Soon would begin the dreadful shivering. Sweat broke out on her upper lip. She closed her eyes. A sickly pattern of vermilion and gold pressed against her lids, spinning itself into a fiery orb. She heard a quick rustling step and opened her eyes. Maud's tender face leaned close.

'Sing for me, child,' she commanded. 'A song of love.'

Her eyelids drooped at the pure sweet sound. The voice was love and kindness and innocence, like the painted smile on the Virgin's face in the niche above her *prie-dieu*; the song was of chivalry and romance, of Arthur and Guinevere and Lancelot the Shining One — surely, an echo of her own tale, two men and a

woman destroyed by love. But her tale was not ended yet . . .
Her eyelids flickered uneasily. Was there anything left worth the
telling?

She felt the creature stir restlessly at her feet and opened her
eyes to ward him off. It raised its long pointed head and looked at
her — the cold yellow eyes were Harry's.

Half a league away Harry slashed and hacked his way through
thicket and glade. Thorns raked his cheek and tangled in his hair,
his lips dried and cracked with the cold. Ahead of him the roe
deer surged, a pale tantalising streak that had eluded him all
morning. For two hours now it had led them a dance, through
oak and beech grove, through bog and marsh, across open
moorland sheened with snow, turning at last into Aydon forest
for a last desperate hiding. Now, cunningly, it headed for water
in an attempt to throw of the pursuit. And it seemed that it had
succeeded. Harry was first into the clearing and found it empty
and still. The earth steamed beneath a blanket of wet sodden
leaves and walled him in with fog.

He reined in his horse and listened. Distantly he heard the bleat
of the horn rallying the scattered men and dogs, and closer at
hand, the deep bellow of his brother-in-law Gascoigne as he
laboured in a ditch. Of the deer there was no sign.

He edged his mount a little way forward. Stiff dormant grasses
fringed a shallow stream. On the other side the trees grew thick
and dense, tall straight leafless oaks that soared heavenward like
the pillars of a church and roofed the wood in deep shadow. The
fog, drifting eerily between the high arched boughs, reminded
him of incense. He felt the urge to cross himself as if this were an
evil place.

He wheeled his horse as John crashed into the clearing, his cap
festooned with berries. Gascoigne followed leading a lamed
horse and old Will Plumpton brought up the rear.

'By St Paul, Harry,' Gascoigne said, 'we'll have to do better
than this. That fool Cartington is past it, you know. He's out
there serenading those dogs as if they were his own children. He's
turned them soft. They could have had the beast down an hour
since if they'd been taught their proper business.'

John said grimly, 'We've lost her then?'

Harry shook his head. 'No. I'll swear she's here somewhere.' Three times his eyes raked the thicket of sapling trees and even then he almost missed it, a patch of fawn like a scrap of torn velvet.

'There,' he shouted as horsemen and hounds poured into the clearing in a terrifying babble of noise.

The deer broke like an arrow, clearing the stream in a single leap. Harry was only moments behind, but vital all-important moments that allowed their quarry to gain twenty feet of ground whilst they still floundered through the stream.

A horseman pounded close at Harry's heels. He flung a look over his shoulder and saw John's grim determined face. A long way back, Gascoigne, scarlet and top-heavy on a borrowed horse, led the rest of the pursuit. He did not look back again. Now he had eyes only for the deer. Its pale hide gleamed, luminous with sweat as it twisted and doubled through the trees, one minute almost close enough to touch, the next, dim and spectral in the flying mist, as far out of his reach as ever. It was past exhaustion, past cunning, only pure animal terror drove it on.

Dimly he was aware of John not far behind him and even more distantly, the frantic baying of the hounds, echoed by the huntsmen's shrill barbaric cry. '*Sa, sa, cy avaunt. Sa, sa, mon amys.*'

He urged his flagging horse on with muttered endearments. 'A little more, *ma mie*. On, on, *doucette*.' Incredibly the beast was outstripping them. Once or twice it stumbled and he made up a little ground. But the gap was widening again, the path growing more tortuous and he saw the deer, distant as ever, heading for the dark haven of undergrowth that grew so close that neither man nor horse could have passed between.

'Sweet Christ,' he muttered in agony. To lose her now.

Abruptly he reined in his horse, tearing so hard on the bit that she screamed aloud. Again he saw the deer stumble and swerve, its wild flight checked for instant. Harry's numb fingers stumbled for his bow and fitted the shaft to the string. 'Now,' he breathed. 'Now!'

The point nosed blindly upwards then dropped to the lunging

107

flanks . . . But he never loosed it. From out of the shadows at his back a second arrow came, passing so close to him that it seared his cheek. It struck and sang — but not him. The hart had dropped like a weighted sack. Not ten yards from him its body lay, the dark rolling eye already glazed with death. Impaled in its throat, whining still with an angry sound, was a long goose-quilled arrow.

He jerked round and stood staring, his reaction slowed by shock. He saw John's face, fierce with pride, suddenly paling to the greyness of fear.

Harry put up a hand and touched the burning rawness of his cheek. 'Should I congratulate you on the sureness of your aim, John?' He smiled dryly. 'Or not?'

John was slow to catch the insinuation. 'My lord?' he said in confusion. Then his face flooded with burning colour. 'I never meant — dear God — it was the beast I was aiming for. I didn't see you in the mist, my lord.'

'Yet you saw the beast, a good ten feet further on?'

John glared at him. 'I was only looking for the beast.'

Harry stared for a long time into the clear blue eyes and believed him. He'd seen the look of joy and pride that had transformed his face, and besides, John could feign a good many emotions but outraged honesty was not one of them.

Then Gascoigne came lumbering up, cursing his useless mount. His face brightened as he saw the slain deer. 'Your kill, my lord?' he said.

'No,' said Harry, his eyes still on John's face. 'It was John that brought him down.'

Gascoigne looked openly disappointed. He muttered grudgingly, 'Well done, lad.' Then he saw Harry's skinned and bleeding face. 'You're hurt, my Lord?'

'No.' Harry turned his horse abruptly. 'A graze. Nothing more.'

He moved away and rode slowly back the way he had come. The fog crawled apace with him, coiling damply around him as if to hold him back. An evil place indeed, he thought grimly. If the shaft had been another inch to the left, it could well have been his grave.

It was a long ride back. Flurries of snow had begun to fall, soft and weightless between gleams of watery sun. Harry rode in the lead, alone. The men at his back were in nosiy high spirits; Gascoigne loudly and openly boastful, Plumpton complaining of his bruises, good-humouredly shouting down the jeers of the men who had witnessed his fall.

John rode a little way apart, uncertain as always of his place. Nothing had changed in that respect. Even men of no account viewed him with suspicion, being blood kin to their lord. The impenetrable hierarchy of rank and privilege still shut him out and even those who struggled for place took their lead from those able to bestow it. And still he had not lived down the disgrace that had resulted in his banishment. The Plumptons would never forgive him and he knew that they still spoke of it, that every newcomer was regaled with the tale. Nothing was ever said to his face but it was still said, behind hands, in whispers, sniggered over in hall.

He glanced jealously at the intimate company: knights, squires, pages, the ambitious younger sons of knightly families who would have been his fellows if they had not thought themselves so much above him. He knew that if he approached them, the inevitable chilling silence would fall. And Harry? Well, no one approached Harry uninvited.

He looked in undisguised longing at his cousin's arrogant back. He envied Harry more than any man on earth, and not just for his position and wealth. He envied his confidence and absolute self-possession, that splendid and distant isolation that he maintained no matter how many thousands crowded his hall. Nothing disturbed him, nothing provoked him. Harry fought with words where words would serve him and was silent where they would not. Splendour, too, he used as a formidable weapon; a single priceless jewel where other men wore twenty of lesser worth, his habitual tawny browns and golds, like the muted colours of a young eagle that made other men seem like gaudy peacocks. Only the best would ever do, cloth of gold and Damascus, Flemish brocades, the exquisite figured velvet of Genoa, chosen not because of their incredible worth but because of their flawless beauty. And yet strangely, beneath all that steely glittering façade, John sensed that there was warmth and kindness. Harry never patronised or sneered at him. He was always scupulously just and unbiased and had never demanded more of him than he had of any other. Perhaps that was what was so galling — to be treated so equally, without fear or favour. He wanted favour. He needed favour if he was ever to thumb his nose at Gascoigne and his crew. And what was more, he deserved it. For nigh on two years now he had kept his nose clean. St Peter himself could not have faulted his demeanour. Old Scrope had had his money's worth from him. He had cleaned out stables, polished brass. He'd scoured harness till his fingers bled. After a year he had been elevated to a position in the hall. He'd held the basin for my lord to dip his greasy fingers in; he'd handed him the fine linen square on which to dry them. He'd been taught to carve and serve, to pour the wine, to cut and square the trencher loaves. For some reason he had found these tasks the most demeaning though he'd worked alongside the sons of knights and earls. All in all he'd learnt very few of their so-called courtly skills of which, privately, he had a low opinion. Their laws and standards would never be his. These men grovelled harder for favour than the meanest churl. Bowing, scraping and not just any old how: the right knee must be crooked to an exact degree, the left extended behind, then down to the floor where the eyes should be. He sneered inwardly. If only they had known how he had despised them. His face grew morose and sullen. Only one skill had he truly acquired: to keep his tongue still and his eyes steady no matter what the provocation. He'd only had one small lapse in all that time and had been punished for it by three days on gruel and water. Had they but known it, he'd rather have had a good beating. He was always hungry, a relic of the days when food was the staple of his life, a comfort that filled more than his belly. When there was food in plenty he ate till he was sick, when there was not he chewed his nails. The thought made him glance hungrily towards the deer swinging lustily upon its pole — *his* deer, though all seemed to have forgotten that. He imagined the rich succulent taste of its flesh, not stewed and smothered in sickly pungent sauces, but clean honest roasted meat, cooked over a smoking fire, the juice spurting and running down his chin

110

to be mopped by a slab of warm bread. The vision was so entrancing that at first he did not hear Harry call him. He looked up, blushing, as Gascoigne bellowed his name. Harry had paused and so, perforce, had the whole cavalcade. Only he still trotted foolishly on.

Harry moved off again as he drew abreast. 'I'm sorry, my lord,' John said stiffly. 'I did not hear you call. I was thinking.'

'Of what, John?' Harry enquired. 'Of how you slew the deer or of how you nearly slew me?' John said nothing but his face turned an angry red.

'I'm sorry, John,' Harry said and threw him a rueful little smile. 'That was unfair. But then life very often is, don't you think?' He did not seem to require an answer and for a while they rode in silence.

Once or twice Harry glanced at John's face. Thank God, the boy looked less like Thomas now. He would not be as tall as his father had been and his shoulders had a squat and powerful set. His face too had lost its fine-boned look: heavier, fleshier with a fresh round peasant look that was certainly not unpleasing. The resentment was still there, glimpsed now and then in the vivid blue eyes, but not often. His time at Bolton had done him no harm if he could keep it so well concealed. He said, 'And how did you like life at Bolton. Do you fancy the life of a lord?'

John stared unblinkingly between his horse's ears. 'You can't make silk out of sheep's wool.'

'No. Perhaps not,' Harry conceded. 'But you can make a fine wool that is as highly prized. There is no need to settle for coarse homespun.'

John looked at him with a flicker of gratitude in his eyes. Harry always made him feel less of a clod.

Harry changed the subject for one he knew would appeal. 'What do you think, then, of the horse that Ralph Greystoke is trying to sell me? Is it a bargain, do you think, or no?'

'Only if he is giving it away,' John answered bluntly. 'It's too shallow in the chest to hold its wind and it moves as if its feet are tied together.'

Harry smiled. He had thought the same thing but not quite so

111

colourfully. He said casually, 'Curwen thinks it is a sound buy at the price.'

John said nothing. Dangerous ground here — criticism of his elders and betters, though if he had known it, his opinion of Harry's Master of Horse was written quite clearly upon his face.

'You disagree then?' Harry said.

'It's not my place to agree or disagree,' John replied.

'But if it were?' Harry persisted. 'If it were your place?'

John still hesitated, torn between caution and the urge to express his passionately-held views. Caution lost. 'If it were,' he said hotly, 'you'd not have a horse left above a score for pulling carts. Curwen is breeding for clumsiness and weight instead of agility and strength. You need new blood, lighter bone, an Arab strain to offset the Flemish heaviness.'

Harry looked at him with respect and pleasure. It was the first time he had ever heard confidence in the boy's voice, the first time he had known him not wholly conscious of himself. This was the thing that Harry had suspected he could do well. John knew his horses and was one of the few that could match him in the saddle.

'Yes,' he said. 'You have a point. Curwen is old and set in his ways. He knows how to breed warhorses and hacks but nothing in between.' He paused. The boy was young, too young perhaps, but he needed something to give him a sense of identity. 'As I said,' he went on, 'Curwen is old. In six months, I think, he'll be seeking his ease. I shall be looking for a new Master then, John.' He looked away from the avid blue eyes that still reminded him uncomfortably of Thomas. 'Would you care for the office, John? When Curwen retires? It's yours if you want it.'

He was unprepared for the rapturous look that flamed in the hungry young face. John stared at him in disbelief. 'You mean it, my lord?' He shook his head and laughed wildly. Wasn't this all he had longed for, respect, position, but not so exalted a one that he would fall short through lack of knowledge or wit. In this field he knew no man could fault him.

Harry nodded, convinced that John was up to the task by the shining certainty of his eyes. 'Then I offer the position to you when Curwen leaves. In the meantime you will work alongside him. Learn what you can from him, John. He was a good man in

112

his time. And remember that for the moment he is still Master. If you would not have your own authority flouted when you take his place, do not flout his. I daresay he'll provoke you when he can.'

'Oh my lord,' John's eyes shone with rare content. 'Be assured. I shall not fail you.'

'So. He has put you among the animals where no doubt he thinks you belong.' Eleanor's sharp sneering voice drove the light from the boy's face as surely as if she had slapped him. 'And are you content with that?'

'Yes, I am content,' John shouted. 'What more did you expect?'

'More than that. Jesu, you'll only be one step up from a common herdsman.'

'That's not true. Master of Horse is an honourable office. Curwen is a knight and has two manors in York.'

'As much as that?' Eleanor sneered. 'Well, if thats all you aspire to, I can see why you're so well content.'

John looked away from her bitter scornful eyes. He could have wept with rage and disappointment. He had been so proud, so full of himself, so impatient to bring her his wonderful news that he had come to her the moment they had returned. When he had entered the room he had felt he was somebody. Now he was just some village clod, flaking dried mud onto her best Turkey rug.

'My God,' Eleanor went on in a furious voice. 'I did not think you were so easily pleased, John. So easily fobbed off with nothing.'

John stared down at his cracked muddy boots and let her ramble on: sneering, carping, tearing his new-found confidence to shreds. Then would come the vague unfulfillable promises, the hints of a destiny impossible to achieve, even if he had wanted it. And he didn't want it, could her imagined influence have managed it. He had the full measure of her now: the power and influence she talked so much about existed only in her mind. They were just words, empty words that deceived herself only a little less than they did him. He was no longer fooled by her clinging affection. If she cared for him at all it was only because he was Thomas Percy's son. He knew all of her sordid and shameful

113

story now. She had been no more than his father's whore, no better than the tavern slut with whom the men-at-arms took their pleasure.

He glanced at her slyly out of the corner of his eye. Would his father have lusted for her now? This shrivelled decaying hulk of flesh whose hand was never out of the comfit dish unless it was clamped round a cup of wine — a hogshead a week made its way up these stairs, or so the vintner's page had informed him — all in discreet jugs and ewers, of course. Even in that she maintained a pretence.

'John!' Her voice came sharp and sudden into his thoughts. She was smiling now. Having flayed him to the bone, it was time to apply a little salve. 'John,' she said again, softly this time. 'Listen to me. Have I ever offered you false council? Do as I say and marry Maud Herbert. Her brother is Earl of Pembroke and no more than a boy himself. He's not even out of tutelage yet. He'll be looking for friends, men to advance. You'd be first in line as his brother-in-law. Brother-in-law to the Queen also. Have you thought of that? You'd be independent, your own man; no need to court Harry for every favour.'

Her strong glittering hand reached out toward him. 'John,' she said plaintively now as she saw him weakening. 'After all I have done for you. After all I have suffered in your defence, is it too much to ask that you please me in this? After all, what will you get if you stick by Harry? A knighthood mayhap and a manor in York? Your father would have laughed in his face. Would you demean his memory so?'

John swallowed down his sudden choking rage. How dare she speak of his father when she had done nothing herself but accomplish his ruin. He looked away from her bloated face and the hard narrow eyes swamped in flesh. The heat of the room suddenly turned him sick, his throat rasped with its strange and heavy scents — dry herbs, sweet spices, the sour pungent odour of wine. He glanced wildly around the crowded and sumptuous apartment as if seeking some means of escape. Never before had he wanted so desperately to be free of her, yet the past bound him with unbreakable chains, he had lived in her shadow too long.

He said feebly as a last defence. 'I had no mind yet to take a

114

wife, especially one like the Lady Maud.'

Eleanor smiled thinly. 'A man does not choose a wife for her physical charms. It's all a matter of policy. He does not marry to please himself but to please his own interests. Advancement and wealth keep him content, not empty sensual pleasures.'

'They didn't keep you content though, did they?' It was out before he could stop it, the hot wounding vengeful words he had longed for the last hour to say. 'You weren't content until you had lured my father into your bed. You weren't content till you had destroyed him.'

Her face did not change but she grew pale with shock.

'Who told you that?' she snarled. 'Harry?'

'No, not Harry,' he flung back hotly. 'You can have the tale from any here, especially from grooms and kitchen scullions.'

Suddenly Eleanor looked old and ill. She covered her ravaged face with a trembling hand.

'Oh, Sweet Jesu,' she whispered. 'How much longer must I pay for that one year of happiness? One sweet short year, that's all it really was. Not so much out of a life time.' She raised anguished eyes to his unhappy face. 'And he was happy too, you know, John. Whatever the price he paid in the end he thought that it was worth it.'

John stared at her wretchedly, torn between love and hate and remorse. 'Madame,' he said. 'forgive me.' He fell on his knees beside her and she cradled his head against her breast as she done his father's so long ago. Her fingers twined in his soft black curls clutching at the distant illusion *Thomas. Thomas.* She would not let him go. Her fingers tightened until the boy stiffened in pain. Especially this one tangible part of him she would not loose.

She said softly, knowing his burst of defiance spent, 'Will you do as I say then, John?'

He nodded numbly. 'If it please you, my lady.'

Eleanor smiled and kissed him. 'It does, John. It pleases me very much.'

From his warm corner beside the cavernous hearth, John waited impatiently for his supper. He watched as the long narrow tables were set up. Damask cloths floated out like angels' wings and

115

masked the scarred oak trestles. From the open door that led to the buttery, a stream of pages bore in the plate. Meticulously, the steward marked off each item in his book; the twelve silver apostle cups, the set of gilded platters from Cologne, the earl's own plate etched with the lion statant, three bowls of ivory tusk rimmed with gold.

John chewed distractedly at a fingernail. Christ, but he could have eaten an ox raw. It would be at least another hour till they supped. Gloomily he looked down the hall to where three men-at-arms played at dice. He noticed resentfully that they hadn't asked him to join them. Not that he wanted to. In his opinion they played for paltry stakes, an exchange of duties rather than hard cash. Besides, he did not feel in a winning mood. So far the day had been a complete disaster. He'd holed his one and only pair of decent boots and all day his right foot had oozed and squelched in a sodden bag of melted snow. He held it out to the fire and watched the ruined leather wrinkle and steam. And that was only the least of it. He'd worked alongside that devil Curwen in the first stages of his so-called apprenticeship. His visions of a lofty and knowledgeable exchange of views had soon been dispelled. Curwen had set him to work with a vengeance — every filthy and menial task, far worse than he'd been put to at Bolton. And as for airing his opinions even on a minor point, Curwen wasn't having any of that. There was only one voice heard and that was his, loud, arrogant, so set in his ways, that he thought the rowel spur the devil's invention. And as for the beasts he took such an inordinate pride in — warhorses he called them, carthorses, more like — great brutes with clumsy feathered feet and rumps that would have put a rhinoceros to shame.

John hawked and spat into the roaring flames — a perfect hit, smack in the middle of the andiron's brass head. He watched as the gobbet of phlegm hissed and sizzled before it was consumed by the heat. That was his opinion of Sir Christopher Curwen — at the moment, his opinion of life in general.

Still, taking all in all, he'd survived it well. He'd sulked and scowled but he'd kept his head which was all that Harry had asked. In fact there was a strange perverse satisfaction in taking orders knowing that soon he would be giving them. How long, he

116

wondered, would he have to wait? Forever if Eleanor had her way and married him off to Maud Herbert. He sighed heavily. It was not so much the thought of Maud that irked him. He could even find her comely if he thought about it. He hadn't reckoned on being tied down so soon. He'd be shackled with two women then instead of one, for married or no he could not see Eleanor yielding place as his mentor. And then what? Being nice to Maud so that she would use her influence with her brother who in turn might use it with the Queen? More grovelling and favour seeking, dancing attendance on some pimply youth? At least Harry was his own blood kin. He had a right to expect something from Harry.

Voraciously he attacked another nail and chewed it down to the quick. The hall was beginning to fill with men, the known despised faces seeking their places below the dais. He surveyed them all with open disdain. God's Blood, what did Pickering think of himself in that ridiculous feathered cap? And look at Haggerston, the skinny runt, displaying all in satin hose. They thought themselves so much the courtiers, in their piked shoes and padded doublets — padded hose too, some of them. He'd seen more than one blatantly stuffing his codpiece.

He glanced down at his own rough and calloused hands, the nails bitten down until they had bled. It was strange, but disliking them for disliking him never made him feel any better. At the heart of him he wanted so desperately to belong. Perhaps by marrying Maud he would at least achieve that. They could not ignore him so easily then, he would be brother-in-law to the Earl of Pembroke, kin by marriage to the Queen. It could give him a status that his vague and almost shameful relationship to Harry never had. But even that was like wearing a borrowed shirt, the recognition would still not be for himself. He picked dejectedly at a callous of horny skin. Sometimes the urge in him to run was strong, just to mount his horse and ride away. He thought of the deer that he had recently slain. A good death, quick and clean, the end of a glorious life of freedom. Again he glanced with veiled antagonism at the men who filled the hall. He saw how jealous they were of place and privilege; he saw how great and unbridgeable was the gulf between them. Their concept of freedom differed so greatly from his. They all thought themselves their own masters, they all thought themselves free yet they were hedged about by petty customs and restrictions, fettered by inflexible codes of honour and chivalry. None of them knew what true freedom was: riding alone, coming from nowhere, going nowhere except where the road and destiny led them. Once it had been the only life he had known. Once it had been enough and he had looked for nothing more; he had not even known that there was more. But he knew now. He knew that there was wealth and power and good living to be had, if a man had his wits about him. The knowledge kept him chained to this life as surely as it did them. It kept him obedient and subservient, it kept him wretched and uncertain for he knew now that there was no turning back. Even if he had had the courage to break free he could never have survived. He remembered he had found a fox cub once, and kept it for nigh on a year. He had tamed it so well that it had eaten from his hand, but still it had pined for its freedom. He had let it go but it had not lived a day. Its instincts were blunted, its senses confused; it had lost its natural ability to survive. So it would be with him. He was neither wild nor tamed. He belonged nowhere and to no one.

He looked up belligerently as a hand touched his arm. 'Master John. Am I disturbing you?' Maud asked shyly.

'No. No.' John was flushed with pleasure at the thought that she had sought him out. Very few ever looked for his company.

Swiftly he remembered his manners and stumbled to his feet tugging self-conciously at his jerkin. He bowed and offered her his arm in the way he had been taught. 'May I find you a place?' he asked eagerly.

Jubilantly he threaded his way through the maze of tables, pleasurably aware of the speculative eyes upon his back. He seated Maud at one not too far from the dais and squeezed himself onto the end of the bench.

'You do not mind if I keep you company?' he added as an after-thought. He did not want her to think him presumptuous.

She smiled at him prettily. 'I rather hoped you would, John. I, too, still feel something of a stranger.'

John nodded understandingly and felt suddenly drawn to her.

At least they had that in common. They had little else, as he had discovered over the last few days when in his clumsy way he had attempted to court her. He had admired gowns that to him looked like skimpy colourless rags, he had praised the dirge-like songs that Eleanor favoured. Their conversation was painfully limited. He knew nothing about music or books and she knew nothing about horseflesh. Whether or not she favoured him he had no real idea. She was pleasant and kind but no more to him than to others. She neither encouraged nor discouraged his clumsy advances and he had thought it all a pointless and meaningless ritual.

Beside him, Maud glanced round the crowded and opulent hall. Lattens like cartwheels blazed above their heads and illumined a sea of unknown faces: knights and their ladies, esquires and clerks, pages and servitors who scurried between the tables laden with steaming dishes. Rich tapestries billowed out from the walls: silver knights wrestling with gilded dragons; an army of improbable rosy-cheeked Greeks besieging the walls of Troy. On the far wall, the martyred St Sebastian spouted fountains of vivid gore.

She sighed happily. It was a relief in itself to escape from the countess's closed and fetid apartments and the company of the woman whose moods swung from an almost hysterical joy to abject and bitter despair. The countess had been grievously ill these past three days and would have none but Maud by her. This was the first time in a week she had been down to the hall and it was only because she had begun to look so pale and sickly herself that Joan Eure had been persuaded to take her duties. Her glimpses of Harry had been rare and at a distance, for still he had not visited his mother's apartments, though he had sent a curt note offering the services of his physician, a stern old man whose sovereign remedy seemed to be to bleed his patients to death. The countess had said with grim and malicious humour, that Harry had sent him to kill her.

Then she rose in unison with the rest of the hall. Harry had entered without announcement or ceremony, the aged Abbot of Hulne leaning upon his arm. She craned eagerly for a glimpse of Harry's face. She knew that at the sight of him all her doubts and uncertainties would vanish. Eleanor's words, like hard-flung pebbles, had ruffled and disturbed the surface of her mind but once she had seen him . . .

She watched as he seated the abbot with solicitous care. He did not seem so changed; a little more formidable perhaps, his face a little sterner — yet she saw a coldness and hardness in him that had not been there before.

She stared down at the food that John had heaped upon her plate, more than she could have eaten in a week: a brace of tiny fowl roasted in honey, pike in harblet, a fillet of bream shivering in cold cinnamon glaze. She nibbled at a sliver of pheasant breast and stole another glance at Harry. Somehow, she had expected him to come towards her, his hands outstretched . . . She laid down the half-eaten scrap of meat and a knight whose name she did not know pushed a dish of sweet cakes towards her.

'Here, lass,' he said. 'Try one of these. You look as though the whole dish would do you no harm.'

Maud smiled. His eyes were kind as her father's had been and obligingly she bit into the warm crisp pastry.

The knight beamed. 'There, that's better, isn't it, lass? I swear you look plumper already.'

Maud laughed out loud, a rich warm vibrant sound clearly heard above the desultory hum. And once begun she could not stop. The wild happy laughter surged out across the hall. Heads turned: some smiled indulgently; others were shocked at such unseemly display. She saw Lady Scrope, rigid with horror, as if Maud had publically voided wind. She laughed the more seeing their foolish censorious faces, then suddenly the laughter died to a dry breathless sob. A hand clutched at her viciously. She turned and looked into the sharp face of Margaret Gascoigne.

'Come quickly,' Margaret whispered urgently. 'I fear my mother the countess is dying.'

Fearfully Eleanor searched the dark hangings above her head for it was there that the demon lay. She could see him twined in the dusty folds, watching, waiting . . . She dared not sleep, she dared not even close her eyes. It would be then that he would pounce, slithering out of his corner, down towards the bed. She knew the exact manner in which he would enter her body. He would force his way into her mouth — the entrance to her soul, sliding insidiously down her throat to the warm dark cave of her belly. And there he would remain, growing ever larger, his appetite more insatiable till he had devoured her, body and soul.

Four whole days she had starved him. Nothing but water had passed her lips, to swill down Master Benedict's foul innocuous remedies. Now the creature was ravenous and crazed with need. With every passing hour he grew harder to control. It seemed he sensed that she was weakening.

She shivered. Her body felt as if it were wrapped in ice though in reality it streamed with sweat. Vicious cramps assailed her limbs; her bowels were liquid fire.

She retched and a spurt of burning liquid filled her mouth. Lady Eure rushed upon her with a silver bowl and heaved her up onto the pillows. The room spun, shimmering, distorted, as if she saw all through mullioned glass. She spat, and Lady Eure held a scented cloth to her lips. Her kindly face loomed close, filling Eleanor's vision: fretful brows peaked over a long pointed nose from which a droplet of moisture was suspended. The pores of her skin were pitted with grime and there was a large mole upon her chin that sprouted twin black hairs like the antennae of some bristling insect. She sniffed and the droplet was sucked into a large and cavernous nostril. The antennae quivered and her foolish mouth opened in a yelp of fear as Eleanor struck the bowl from her hands and sent it ringing across the room.

She fell back against the pillows. In the velvet darkness the creature stirred and she raised her eyes to ward him off. Yes. There he was, his yellow eyes glittering in the gloom. She must keep him where she could see him. Her swollen lids drooped over eyes that burned for sleep. She could feel her resolve slipping away. She looked down at her arms blotched with crescent bruises where the physician had feasted his leechs. Not the remedy for what ailed her. She knew where that lay well enough. She thrashed her starved and painful limbs. She should have known. Elizabeth had warned her, Elizabeth who knew all the secrets of life and death. She remembered a day, walking in Elizabeth's garden. Her fallen mouth quivered sadly. She had loved Elizabeth's garden: stiff rods of foxgloves belled like a jester's wand, and fragrant clouds of jessamine, sharp-toothed agrimony, roses of hellebore, deadly henbane with its sunny face . . . Elizabeth's black gown sweeping the path, her dry autumnal voice: *'Learn their secrets, revere them and they will serve you well.'* Tears glistened on her sparse lashes. Even that gift she had abused. Now it was she who served them.

She whimpered quietly. She longed for sleep; oblivion, the draining away of all conscious thought, plunging fathoms deep into blissful darkness. Her hands plucked fretfully at the bed covers. She glanced longingly towards the sandalwood chest where she kept a little vial of the potion. What harm would there be in just a few drops, just enough for a few hours' sleep? Then she would be strong, able to renew the fight. If she could just still the creature's gnawing for a while . . . She screamed aloud. 'Oh Jesu Mary!'

Then a small cool hand laid itself upon her brow. 'My lady. Oh, my lady. Be still.'

'Maud!' Eleanor's hands reached out convulsively. 'Send Eure away,' she gasped. 'I would have none but you by me.' She struggled to sit up. She whispered furtively, 'In the chest. The vial beneath the powdered sage.'

Maud stared at her uncertainly. 'My lady . . .'

'For pity's sake,' Eleanor spoke through chattering teeth. Her fingers bit deep into the girl's slender arm. 'For pity's sake, child. If you love me, fetch me the vial or must I crawl myself to get it?'

Wordlessly Maud went to do the old woman's frantic bidding. Eleanor closed her eyes, listening eagerly to the creak of the lid being raised, the trickle of wine into a cup. In one needful gulp she swallowed it down, shuddering as it dried her throat, sighing as the blissful warmth engulfed her. The world shimmered and became distant. Maud was a speck of light at the end of a long dark tunnel. She raised her eyes to the shadows above her head and saw that the creature was gone.

Maud stared down at the countess's sleeping face. A faint bloom of colour had crept into the withered cheeks. She looked so old and frail in repose that all Maud's youth and strength rose up in defence of this poor unhappy creature.

She moved away from the bed and picked her way through the chamber's glittering squalour. In a corner, bolts of silk and brocade gathered dust; unworn gowns bulged from a carved oak press. So much wealth, so little love, as if life were measured in mere possessions. She smoothed the crimson velvet of her high-waisted gown — a gift from the Countess Eleanor as was the collar of pearls. Not since her father's death had she been so richly dressed. At Pembroke, with nine growing brothers and sisters to provide for, there had been no money to spare for finery. For the last three years she and her sisters had made do with each other's castoffs — let out, taken up, as occasion demanded. But what they had lacked in wealth they had made up for in love; their father at least had bequeathed them that. Her eyes softened as she thought of him, his heart so great that he had love to spare for two captive boys that were none of his own. Would Harry deal so generously and lovingly with her now that it was she who was the stranger? She recalled his cold and distant face with trepidation. Would he look, even at her, so unfeelingly?

She went and curled herself on the wide window seat. The thick panes were patterned with whorls of frost; beyond there was only darkness. Sounds ascended on the freezing air, the scrape of a spade clearing a path in the snow, faint laughter from the hall. She heard a door bang, then footsteps, voices. Joan Eure's coifed head slid round the door. She threw a nervous glance toward the bed before she entered.

'My lady,' the bewhiskered mole quivered speculatively. 'The earl commands your presence.'

In the outer chamber a page stood yawning. He eyed her impatiently as she smoothed her hair, anxious to get back to the game of dice from which the earl's summons had called him.

Maud followed him silently down the twisting stairs and across the courtyard sheened with snow. From the hall came the strident wail of a cremorne but it was not there that he led her. He disappeared into the cavernous gateway between the great octagonal towers. It was here that Harry had his private apartments.

The page paused outside the dark oak door and knocked. 'Will my lady enter?'

Harry was standing with his back to the fire. A massive grey hound lept up snarling and subsided meekly as Harry touched its collar. Two pairs of glittering amber eyes watched her approach. Then Harry loosed the dog, who padded amiably to sniff at her skirts.

'Don't be afraid,' Harry said softly. 'Neill will not harm you.'

He stared down into her upturned face which barely reached his shoulder. 'You've grown,' he observed gravely. 'But not very much.'

She smiled. 'No, not very much. William says I am destined to be one of nature's dwarves.'

Harry returned the smile and took her hands. He kissed her formally. She still smelt of honey and spring-time and lilies.

He let her go and moved away. 'You must forgive me for not greeting you sooner,' he said. 'I have been much occupied. And to tell you the truth,' he added with a rueful little smile, 'I had forgotten that you were coming.'

'What reminded you, then?' Maud watched his hands as he poured wine for them both, remembering their gentle strength. He turned to look at her and she saw that his eyes still held that fierce and dangerous glitter that was so at odds with his passive mien.

'I heard you laugh,' he said, 'and for a moment I was back at Raglan watching Gwilym Ddu struggling to free himself from the strings of his harp to which your brother William had tied his beard whilst he was asleep.' He handed her a goblet of pale malmsey. 'Do you remember?'

'Yes,' she said softly. 'I remember.' It had been a long time before the old man had forgiven her for her laughter. He had never forgiven William for the deed.

They smiled at each other, the warm conspiratorial smile of children. 'And how is William?' Harry said. 'And Phillip and Walter and George and all those sisters whose names I fear I cannot remember?'

Yet he had remembered hers! She felt the hot revealing colour flood her cheeks. Her whole body tingled with an almost painful warmth as if she had come in from the cold. 'They are well,' she answered him softly. 'William is quite grown now and Isabel is to be wed to Sir Thomas Cokesay.'

'I am happy for Isabel,' Harry said. He paused, remembering that Maud would have been married herself by now if fate had not decreed otherwise.

He said carefully, 'I was sorry to hear that you and Henry Tudor were not to be wed after all.'

'Yes,' Maud said absently and stroked the great dog who had come to lay his head in her lap.

'Do you ever hear from him?'

'No. I had a letter from him once — a long time ago. A rather sad letter really. He seemed very bitter.' She looked down at the dog, regarding her with its intent golden stare. 'A fearsome beast,' she said to change the subject. She did not want to talk of Henry Tudor tonight.

'Fearsome only to his enemies,' Harry said. 'To those he loves he is gentleness itself.'

Maud smiled. 'Rather like you, Harry,' she said. She looked up at him and her heart quickened to see his eyes upon her. It was a strange look; angry, resentful, as if she had trespassed upon some sacred ground. She averted her own in confusion. Perhaps she should not have called him Harry, perhaps he thought she presumed too much on past acquaintance.

She said quickly to cover her confusion, 'You call him Neill. Is it an Irish name?'

'Yes,' he answered her almost abruptly. He rose to his feet and went to stand by the fire. He averted his face, as if from the heat, staring down at nothing. It was almost a gesture of dismissal.

'My lord . . .' Maud stared at him uncertainly.

He looked at her then and could not look away. Her hair hung unbound down to her waist, the sleek, rippling banner of her virginity. Against the crimson gown her skin was white and smooth as Paris wax. Her mouth was still a child's mouth, faintly coloured, innocent and sweet. Desire lept in him, so alien to his body that it was almost a physical pain. He wanted to touch her, to hold her — he remembered he had held her once before. He remembered the softness of her body and its light flowery scent, her mouth trembling against his throat.

He wrenched his head away, staring down into the fire's heart and after a moment the habitual coldness possessed him. His voice, with its faint undertone of bored disdain asked her if she was happy at Alnwick. 'Does my mother, the countess, treat you well?'

'Yes, my lord. Very well,' said Maud in a small bewildered voice. She added rashly, suddenly incensed by his coolness, 'She is much grieved that you have not been to see her, even though she asks for you every day.'

'Does she now?' he said, mocking and cold. 'She did well enough without sight of me for nine years. How suddenly am I so dear to her?'

'My lord!' Maud pushed the dog's head from her lap and stood. 'I would have thought it natural enough for a mother to want to see her only son. Where else should she look for comfort when she is old and ill?' She took a step toward him and lowered her voice to a note of entreaty. 'Harry, my lord. Whatever there has been between you in the past, I swear there is no harm in her now.'

'Is that what she told you to say?'

'No. It is not.' Maud cried infuriated. 'She does not even know that I am here and even if she did, she is too sick and weak to care. She has been bled and purged beyond endurance these past three days.'

'Yes. So Master Benedict told me,' Harry smiled maliciously. 'He also told me that to indulge herself less on sweetmeats and wine would be a more certain cure.'

'My lord,' she said in a stricken whisper, 'that is a despicable thing for you to say.'

'You think so?' He looked at her pityingly. 'How long exactly have you known my lady mother?'

'Not long, I admit to that.'

'Then allow me to be the better judge. I fear my acquaintance has been the longer.' He looked at her with a deep intense hatred that she knew was not just for her but was for all the world. 'I should tell you,' he went on, 'for your own protection. My mother is a practised and an accomplished liar. She is without scruple or conscience, without affection except for a passing fondness for any who can further her colossal vanity. No doubt she has regaled you with tales of my long neglect? Yes. I can see that she has. I do not deny it. I do not pass my time with hypocrites and liars.'

She stared at him in disbelief. Such bitterness was totally alien to her, such hatred for one's own flesh and blood. 'You are wrong, my lord,' she said, arguing with all the passionate conviction of youth. 'So you may have thought her once. But people change; life makes them change.' She moved closer to him and looked up into his face with grave appeal. 'I beg you, Harry, to think more kindly of her. She is nothing but an old and lonely woman.'

He stared down into her innocent face, glowing with passion and righteousness. He was intensely aware of her, of her mouth so close to his, the sweet fragrance of her hair. He moved away, trembling with fury and longing. What better advocate could Eleanor have sent? he thought savagely. Eleanor, Eleanor, the cloud that always blotted out the sun.

'I wonder why you care,' he said harshly. 'What is my mother to you that you spring so passionately to her defence? What has she offered you that could buy such loyalty on so short an acquaintance?'

Maud regarded him steadily. 'You know full well I have no thought of gain, my lord,' she said quietly. 'If I defend the countess it is out of pure human compassion.'

'Yes, I can believe that. I remember you always had more than your fair share of that; lame dogs, birds with broken wings, orphans and waifs — no doubt you even felt pity for me once, didn't you?'

'Yes.' She looked at him sadly and with sudden perception. There was a kind of savage inhumanity about him that was pitiful, like some wounded beast who snarled and fought out of sheer terror and pain. He was afraid of life though he had never lived it, he was afraid of love though he had never loved. She said calmly and without emotion, 'Yes, I did pity you, Harry. I still do. You're cruel and bitter, and worse than that, you're empty — empty and cowardly. Do you think it brave to persecute widows and children, my lord? Can you find no better adversary than a sick and lonely old woman?'

She turned and went slowly and quietly from the room. Tears

of anger and misery blinded her. He was wrong, so very wrong. People did change she thought bitterly. Harry himself was proof of that.

'I'm not saying that Gloucester isn't confident, you understand. 'Laurence Booth, Bishop of Durham and Harry's enforced guest this past week since the road south had become impassable, eased himself a little closer to the fire. 'I merely consider it is a bad thing for a man to be so inflexible in his judgements. He's not taking account of what's gone before.'

'In what way?' Harry enquired politely.

'In every way.' The bishop's pale eyes bulged indignantly. 'Custom and usage; tradition passed down from father to son — that's always been the way in the north. And the bishopric of Durham, as you know, has a Palatine status. It has special privileges, special concessions that are none of my lord of Gloucester's business. Now here he is, poking his nose into what doesn't concern him, demanding chits for this, accounts for that. How many knights' fees have I granted this year, and then looking down his long nose because it doesn't tally exactly with the lists of my liveried retainers.'

'I think that is the Duke of Gloucester's point,' Harry observed mildly. 'Those of your men who have not received fees should not be wearing your livery.'

'Well, we all know that,' said the Bishop testily. 'But who has ever enforced it before? And he himself is recruiting men hand over fist. If you ask me, it's Gloucester's way of outdoing us all. As the King's brother he can afford to burden his estates with unlimited fees. I told him to his face, you know. His province is the West March and his own Yorkshire estate. He should stick to them instead of tempting men from their customary lordship with fat fees and promises of royal patronage. Four good men I lost last month, all from families that have served the Bishops of Durham since the first King Edward's time. And then there is all this fuss about my fishgarths — illegal, his grace of Gloucester has been pleased to call them. When all know that the Bishops of Durham have had nets and traps in the Ouse and Humber since

128

time immemorial. He actually had the gall to tell me to remove them . . .

Harry sighed inaudibly and let the bishop ramble on. It was not the first complaint he'd heard. Gloucester, eager to prove himself capable, was treading on not a few toes. Laurence Booth was only one of many to whine about the loss of illegal privileges accumulated during the years of war. This pathetic defence of 'custom and usage' Gloucester had rightly dismissed out of hand. It merely meant that because their predecessors had been allowed to abuse the law without retribution, then so too should they.

He stirred restlessly in the constriction of his chair and stared balefully at the tall windows shuttered against the killing east wind. The daylight showed grudgingly through the narrow slits and patterned the floor like the bars of a cage. He thought of the high room in London's Tower that he had known so well. It was three years since King Edward had let him out but in his heart he was still a prisoner. Invisible chains still held him off from life and fettered his heart, and the bitter irony of it was that it was he himself who was his own jailor.

He turned his head as the bishop's voice rose to stress a point. He nodded and made sympathetic noises in his throat — yes, he quite agreed that six shillings for a bushel of wheat was exorbitant, and, of course, something would have to be done about the extortionate tax on the exports of hides that threatened to make poor men of them all. A perverse laughter suddenly surged and bubbled inside him. He wondered what old Bishop Booth would have said if he had known that behind his earnest and polite replies ran wild thoughts of bedding a woman.

The silent laughter faded into grim and bitter amusement. He still resented this subtle undermining of his self-control and struggled against it. The habit of always being alone was hard to lose and though his body yearned for her, his mind clung stubbornly to the familiar, to the cold precise pattern of thought that always led to the safe unbiased judgements from which he could never be swayed. Black was black, white was white and he had lived so long in the grey between them that he instinctively rebelled against committing himself. But now the grey was pierced by sharp bright colours: the flaming crimson of a young girl's hair, the soft cloudless blue of her eyes. The whole world was suddenly filled with warmth and sunlight and he'd felt it almost with a sense of physical shock. The brightness was only a little dimmed by the thought of Eleanor. That enraged him more than anything. To be thought unfair, unjust. Ruthless he was, but never without cause. He was unforgiving only because some things were unforgivable: the betrayal of trust; the wanton destruction of a human life for no better purpose than self-gratification; and worse, the slow and cruel annihilation of a man's soul out of vanity and amusement. Eleanor was guilty of all these, yet that small calm voice persisted. Could he be wrong? Could he have judged too harshly?

Then Bishop Booth's clarion voice penetrated his uneasy thoughts. Having aired his grievances he was taking his leave and Harry rose, bowing courteously over the extended velvet paw before he ushered him thankfully towards the door. Silence settled over the room like a fine, blown dust. He glanced wearily about him. In every corner rare ornaments gleamed; but nothing of him, nothing to say that he lived and breathed within these walls.

He turned and opened the door, beckoning to the page who stood without. 'Send to my mother, the dowager countess,' he said. 'Ask her if she will receive me.'

Eleanor was ready for him, her face as carefully arranged as the folds of her gown. Deliberately she had worn black and the rich dark velvet soothed her high colour and gave her an air of sadness and frailty — indeed, she looked almost holy with her hair drawn back under a douce little cap and the meek and pious expression she had put on simultaneously with the gown. Pain and suffering exuded from every pore and hung in the air, pungent as sweat. She wore no jewels and her only concession to vanity were the twin arcs of her finely plucked brows.

Her voice when she spoke was faint and tremulous. 'Forgive me for not rising to greet you, Harry. I fear my limbs are still a little weak — though once on my feet I manage well enough.' (As he would have seen for himself if he had come a half-hour earlier

130

and found her striding about the solar chivvying her women with mops and pails.)

Now the chamber was airy and sweet. Vinegar and rue had cleansed it of its sick-bed stench and bunches of pungent thyme smouldered among the logs.

Hesitantly she offered him wine but took only a small measure herself. Her hand trembled visibly as she raised the cup to her mouth. Harry watched the performance with wry amusement but he was not altogether displeased. He had not really expected anything less. She had kept him waiting a full hour or more, sending Lady Eure with the excuse that she was sleeping. He hadn't believed that any more than he believed this obvious charade. It was merely a symptom of her lifelong disease — the inability to face reality.

Yet there were some things that even Eleanor could not feign. That dreadful mottled colour was real, as if the blood boiled thickly beneath her skin. Fever had thinned her face to the point of starvation and the skin at her throat hung in trembling grey wattles that danced grotesquely when she spoke.

He said with an effort, 'Master Dominic tells me you are much recovered.'

Eleanor lowered her eyes. No thanks to that old cretin, she thought, but she smiled weakly. 'Yes. As much recovered as my years allow.' She looked at him with impossible candour. 'I never thought I would have the courage to admit it, but I am getting old, Harry.'

She sipped at the grudging measure of wine that she could have swallowed in one gulp and never noticed. 'It's a dreadful thing, you know. To have found peace at last then find there is no life left to live. To have so much to make up for and not have the time . . .' She broke off tearfully and moved her hands in a helpless little gesture. His very silence told her that he was genuinely moved. Pity struggled visibly against his inherent disbelief. He wanted to believe that she had changed, as indeed she had, though not in the way he would like to think. Her motives were still the same but her manner of achieving them was not. She had found that meekness served her better than her old hauteur had ever done.

Then she glanced at him warily. The silence had gone on too long. She said quickly, 'Is his grace the Bishop of Durham still with us?'

'Yes. And complaining loudly. At the moment his grievance is Richard of Gloucester. It seems that the duke is questioning a few of the more dubious sources of the bishop's income.'

'Yes,' she said airily. 'I heard that Gloucester was the new power in the north. Does that not irk you, Harry?'

'No. Why should it?' he said, concealing his irritation and knowing that she knew that it did.

'Because the north has always been our preserve. The Percys have always ruled the Border.'

'So we have liked to think. But in reality we have always shared power to some degree, usually with the Nevilles. It has been sound royal policy to balance one against the other. That way we are too busy fighting amongst ourselves to pose any threat to the king.' It was said more to convince himself than her. The spark of enmity and suspicion against Gloucester still smouldered and once or twice had come close to erupting as he had heard of his high-handed dealings.

Eleanor stared at him, sensing that something had stirred beneath the surface of his calm. 'It has not *always* been so,' she said softly, unable to resist the temptation to provoke. 'Once the Percys were supreme.'

He interrupted her coldly. 'Only God is supreme, madame. We mortals have to make do with second place.'

Eleanor lowered her eyes, warned by his voice. A noble philosophy, she thought scathingly — his father's philosophy, forever content to be second-best.

Silence fell between them, but not uncomfortably. Covertly Eleanor studied his face and saw how the summer had burned the sallow skin to a deep and burnished gold. Beneath long heavy lids the covered fire of his eyes glowed the same tawny colour. He is almost handsome, she thought, in a dark and dangerous way. Yes, she thought warily. Dangerous was a word that described him well for even if she could not love him she was beginning to respect him as an adversary.

She said brightly. 'John tells me that you have promised him the position of Master of Horse.' She smiled at him fondly as if he had offered to set the crown of England upon John's head. 'He talks of nothing else.' She sighed. 'It seems you were right to send him to Bolton. It certainly has made a man of him. Too much of a man, perhaps.' She drew a long deep silent breath. 'Did you know that he wishes to marry?'

Harry jerked his head up and stared at her incredulously.

'Yes, I know.' She smiled grimly. 'I must admit I was taken aback myself. But then thinking on it, perhaps it would be no bad thing.' She stole a sly glance at him and was surprised to see him smiling. So far so good, she thought happily. The worst hurdle was surmounted. She added in a low and poignant voice. 'I think, for all our sakes, it is time I let him go.'

Harry raised his eyes and she gave him a look of such appalling innocence that the hair lifted on his scalp. There was more, he thought, there was bound to be more. Eleanor did not gamble for pennies. He said slowly, 'To whom does he wish to be married?'

Eleanor laughed, reading his mind. 'It's all right, Harry. He's not set his sights too high. It is no one more illustrious than one of my own attendants. The little Welsh girl, Maud Herbert.'

She should have been warned by the very stillness of him but she went on complacently, 'Of course, I realise that until her brother comes of age her marriage is in the King's gift. But if the match has your approval, Harry, I can't see that Edward would object. It's not as if there is a great dower involved. She's hardly an heiress with four brothers and five sisters and only two of the girls wed as yet. I thought perhaps . . .'

'No.' The one word, but said so finally that it stilled her tongue as sharply as if he had slapped her. She stared at him. His face was white, even his lips were white, drawn down to a thin bloodless line.

'Why not?' she demanded. 'I should have thought you'd be pleased to be rid of him.'

He avoided the distended and feverish eyes. He could not speak. His throat was constricted with pain and rage. He could have killed her. His hand ached to fasten round her scrawny throat and to squeeze and shake the life from her, to still that abominable tongue forever. It was as if she had known, as if she had sensed the softness and warmth in him and had wantonly set out to destroy it. He drew a long deep shuddering breath. Slowly the blood flushed beneath his skin again. 'No,' he said hoarsely. 'Not Maud Herbert.'

'Why not Maud Herbert?' Eleanor said, fury rising. 'John is not good enough, is that it? Henry Tudor was good enough and what was he but some penniless outcast, and bastard blood at that? For God's sake, Harry, she's nobody.'

'She is the daughter of an earl and the sister of an earl.' Harry said stiffly. 'The King would never countenance it.'

'He would if you sanctioned it. It wouldn't be the first time a family has covered up its indiscretions by marrying them off respectably. Jesu, Harry. Do you expect him to couple with a tavern wench?'

'Why not?' Harry said cruelly. 'His father did.'

'So that's it!' Eleanor screamed. 'Spite. Pure spite. You'll not forgive either him or me. You want to keep him under your heel, don't you? You want to keep him in his place, grind him down, punish him, because you think you're punishing Thomas.'

'No.' For the first time in her life she heard him raise his voice. For the first time she saw him lose control and saw the look of longing and vulnerability that passed across his face before he could stop it.

'Oh Jesu,' she whispered. 'You want her for yourself, don't you, Harry?' She looked at him with sneering pity. 'Oh Harry, poor Harry. You are indeed your father's son.'

She began to laugh, and blindly Harry turned and went from the room, the wild sobbing laughter following him. He broke into a run, leaping down the stairs in twos and threes. At their foot he halted, his breath coming hot and fast, silvering the cold damp air. He straightened as a shadow darkened the doorway. He looked into eyes of bright unmistakeable blue — and they were smiling.

'Bastard,' he said softly. 'Filthy lowborn bastard.' His hand came up and struck the boy a blow that knocked him clean off his feet. 'Get out,' he whispered. 'Get back to the gutter where you belong. Don't ever let me see your face again.'

He left John crouched in the shadows, his burning face pressed against the wall. His eyes were wide and blank and stared at

nothing and for a long time he did not move, as if he were part of
the stones that surrounded him. Then his tongue felt tentatively
around his bruised and bleeding mouth. He licked a droplet of
blood from the corner and then pushed himself slowly to his feet.
Numbly, he turned and went back the way he had come, across
the deserted outer ward, through the middle gateway where the
guard stared at him curiously. He went first to his cramped and
airless little room and made a bundle of his clothes. He took a
hunting bow and a quiver of arrows and from the stables, where
he saddled his chestnut mare, a rough blanket and a bag of oats.

The guard did not halt him at the outer gate and straight-
backed and hard-eyed he rode across the bridge and out of
Alnwick.

Harry sat slumped in a chair cradling a half-empty flagon of
wine. The fire burned low. Rain darkened the windows, blown
by a light and vicious wind. He was mildly drunk, not enough to
heal the wound but enough to stop it bleeding. He closed his eyes.
He had not felt like this since he was fifteen years old, when he
had sobbed and sobbed but no tears would come. The pain was
lodged in a great iron ball, an unbearable weight pressing down
on his heart. Names, faces, voices came at him with wearying and
repetitive monotony. Maud, her perfection spoiled, her innocence marred by John's lusty image. He imagined those great ugly
hands upon her soft flesh. The vivid blue eyes mocked him —
Thomas's eyes — and it came to him that it was almost a repetition of Eleanor's sordid story. Harry's and Thomas's son, both
lusting after the same woman as their fathers had lusted after her.

Viciously he flung the pitcher away from him. It struck the
hearth and spilled its contents in a cloud of hissing steam. The
great dog leapt to its feet and snarled till Harry dropped a soothing hand on its neck and quietened it with his voice.

The wind was rising, sobbing and shrieking outside the walls,
an echo of Eleanor's laughter. That was the greatest anguish, to
have exposed himself to her and shown her a weakness that she
could, and would, use against him.

Suddenly Neill tore from his grasp and leapt towards the door.

He had not heard the cautious knocking.

He called out and the dog fell away and padded back to the fire.

Will Gascoigne advanced hesitantly into the room. 'My lord, forgive this intrusion. I would have waited till you came down to the hall. But the Countess insisted.'

Harry did not turn his head. 'What is it?' he said wearily.

'Young John, my lord. Young John is missing.'

'Missing?'

'Aye, my lord. He's not been seen since noon.'

Harry shrugged. 'I dare say he'll turn up when it's feeding time,' he remarked acidly. 'I have never known him miss his dinner.'

'I think not, my lord. He's nowhere within the castle grounds. We've searched everywhere: kennels, stables, mews — he's taken his horse and his clothes, my lord.'

Harry pushed himself slowly to his feet. 'I saw him myself about noon. Who saw him after that?'

'Only the barbican guard — and old Watt who lodges above the middle gate.'

'Not the countess?'

'No, my lord. It is she who instigated the search.'

Harry frowned. So John hadn't gone snivelling to Eleanor as he had thought he would. Why not? He must have known that their little scheme had foundered, but surely he would have wanted to hear it at first hand. For the first time uncertainty showed in his eyes. Could it be that he didn't even know?

Wordlessly he walked out into the lashing rain and for the second time that day climbed the stairs to his mother's apartments. This time Eleanor did not keep him waiting and turned eagerly towards him as soon as he entered.

'Well,' she snapped. 'is he found?'

It was his turn to keep her waiting. He smiled faintly, his eyes insultingly marking the change. She had abandoned the pose of martyr and saint and now looked more the ageing drunkard that she was. Limp grey hair framed a wine-red face. Her upper lip was filmed with sweat. She dabbed at it nervously with the sleeve of her robe. 'Well?' she demanded again.

'No. He is not found,' Harry said, still smiling. 'He is gone. Taken his horse and his clothes and gone.'

Eleanor paled. 'You drove him out, you mean,' she cried. 'What did you say to him? With what did you threaten him that made him take to his heels and run?'

Abruptly his hand shot out and dragged her to her feet. The dreadful eyes seared her face and he said softly, 'This marriage. Was it John's wish to marry Maud? Or yours? Careful now. The truth, madame. Your answer may depend on whether I stir myself to go and look for him or not.'

Briefly she stared him out. Then her shoulders slumped. 'It was mine,' she said defiantly. 'Someone has to look to his interests and you will not.'

He let her go. 'Did John know of your touching concern for his future?'

'He knew but he did not want the match.' Her lip curled. 'He did not find your little Welsh songbird so appealing.'

Harry forced himself to the last question. 'And Maud?'

'She does not know. Why should she? Women marry where they are told, not where they please.' She smiled at him. 'How else would I have married your father.'

He let her have the final word. It was enough to know even though the knowledge weighed him down with guilt. He had abused John cruelly. And he who knew Eleanor better than most should have known that the mischief was of her making. He couldn't blame John for not standing up to her bullying. There were very few who could.

Maud lay huddled on the low creaking bed. Rain lashed at the darkened window and streamed in cataracts from the sill. A man's voice, calling, disturbed the night. She sat up. Footsteps splashed in the courtyard below, lanterns flared on wet dark stones. They were still looking for John. This was the second time they had searched the inner ward. They wouldn't find him, she thought. Instinctively she knew he'd gone. He'd run as she herself longed to run from this evil and sickening place.

She lay down again and pulled the coverlet up under her chin. At the far end of the room whispers scurried in the darkness like mice. She heard Joan Eure's stifled laugh and her own name, smothered by a cautious hiss. She knew that it was her they spoke

137

of so furtively, that all the comings and goings to the countess's apartments had been in some vague unknown way connected with her. Harry had been one of those that had come. Hidden in the curve of the stairs she had seen him emerge from his mother's chamber; his dark face had been twisted with fury, the door behind had gaped like an open mouth and out of it had come Eleanor's demented laughter. She'd seen then the side of Eleanor that Harry knew; a shrieking foul-mouthed creature so convulsed with fury she could hardly stand. At the sight of her, Eleanor had screamed aloud and Maud shivered, remembering the high cracked voice, the jewelled claw lunging for her face. She would have struck her if her daughter Margaret had not pulled her back, but for what? How, suddenly, did she offend?

She turned her face into the pillow. Fear and misery welled up inside her. For the first time in her life she felt utterly alone.

She awoke the next morning heavy-eyed. The whispers began again, furtive, spiteful, intensified by the news that John was still not found. Margaret Gascoigne eyed her with joyful malice as she triumphantly resumed her place at her mother's side. Maud was pointedly excluded from the countess's chamber and the other women, sensing a fall, closed their ranks against her. She didn't care. She knew the whole sorry tale now, recounted with great relish by Joan Eure. And, she had added with blatant spite, it seemed the poor boy had taken himself off rather than take her to wife.

All morning she sat alone in the small airless solar whilst the other women fussed with gowns and jewels. After a while she rose and went toward the door. Margaret Gascoigne glared at her, for she had not bothered to bind up her hair. It hung wild and loose beyond her waist, a shout of defiance in the dim quiet room. As she passed Lady Eure sniffed loudly and muttered darkly on the godless Welsh.

Outside she breathed deeply, ridding her lungs of the smell of their perfumed flesh. In the walled courtyards the shadows leaned together. The windows watched her, dark glittering eyes beneath arched stone brows. She went quickly across the cobbles and through the archway that led to the outer ward. On the other side there was life and colour and movement: pages and grooms in bright livery; sober clerks in dusty black; a kitchen boy chased a squawking hen, laughing uproariously as it dived for cover beneath the robes of the earl's chaplain.

Listlessly she wandered among the buildings that clung to the curtain wall. Each had its own familiar and pungent scent: the hot clean smell of the laundry; the yeasty tang of the bakehouse that reminded her of home, when she and William had waited for the first loaves of the day and burnt fingers and mouth on hot crusty bread. She blinked and turned away, watching a carter load the weekly brewing of ale for Warkworth. A boy sat on the tail of the cart swinging bare brown legs. He stared at her curiously for a moment and then as the carter whipped up the horses and pulled away, he looked back at her and winked.

She smiled and it was like the opening of a wound. The pain rushed straight to her heart and the tears, so long withheld, broke from her with a loud cry.

Passers-by stopped and stared as she ran, sobbing, back the way she had come. She hid herself in the chapel, in the small dark room where the chaplain kept his plate and robes. Huddled in a corner, she wept and beat the stones with small clenched fists. And then, as suddenly as it had began, the storm of weeping was over. She felt quite calm now even though her breath still came in shuddering little gasps. She stared down at her trembling hands, pale and thin, childishly small. But she wasn't a child anymore, not inside; inside she was suddenly old and wise. From her isolation of disillusionment and injured pride she saw them all quite clearly. How sad they were, how greedy, as if all the world were a jewel or a new gown. She saw how joyless their laughter was, how empty their painted smiles. They never spoke but it was to wound or mock or carry tales. Their eyes were always hard and watchful, their faces intent, preoccupied with their own little corner of life. She saw Eleanor, poor Eleanor, who lived in a shadowy tormented world, consumed by past loves and hates. Even her own love for Harry could not blind her to what he was: a coward, afraid of life, afraid to step out of the cage of unfeeling indifference he had so painstakingly built for himself. She knew that there were men without passion and without feeling but Harry was not one of them. He thought he was, he tried to convince others that he was, but she knew it was not so. He was beginning to know it himself. Each day the pretence became a little harder to maintain, each day he moved a step nearer to the reality that no man could survive in the world alone, without love and friendship and commitment. One day he would know this, one day he would want these things as much as he now spurned them. And when he did he would come to her; reluctantly, grudging, but still he would come.

But not here, not now. There was only pain and misery for both of them here. Hatred and malice were all they knew; like cold or damp it pervaded the walls and chilled the heart and the spirit. She thought of John. He was the courageous one. He had run rather than become one of them. Instinctively she knew he would never come back; like her, he'd seen them for what they were. Like her, he pitied and depised them.

She rose stiffly and went slowly from the room. In Wales, music and love and kindness awaited her. It was there that she would wait for Harry.

It was not hard to pick up John's trail. At first it seemed he was following the coast. He'd been seen at Warkworth and Amble and the priest at Craster had given him food. Then he'd swung inland towards the Great North Road and called at every alehouse en route. At the last, a stinking hovel three miles from Morpeth, he'd started a brawl and been thrown out on his ear. Morpeth itself was the last place they had word of him, where he'd sold the clasp of his cloak for fifteen marks. By the time they reached Shotton they had lost him completely.

'He might be anywhere,' said Gascoigne gloomily, easing the wet cloak from his shoulders.

'I think he is making for Newcastle,' said Will Eure. 'He could lose himself well enough there.'

'Aye. In the taverns and cockpits,' Robert Plumpton sneered. 'That's about his mark.'

'But you need brass for that,' Eure argued. 'Fifteen marks won't last him long. The boy has no real skills to speak of. How's he going to live?'

Plumpton shrugged. 'Beg, scrounge, steal if need be. I reckon he could be skilled at that. The boy's got wits all right, of a certain kind.' He sipped distastefully at the lukewarm ale they had been served. 'After all, he's given us the slip right enough.'

Harry frowned at him through the tavern's steamy warmth. 'He's not a felon, Robert,' he said quietly. 'He was perfectly at liberty to go from Alnwick. He took nothing with him that was not his own.'

Plumpton raised his fair arrogant brows. 'Then from what, may I ask, is he running?'

'From me,' Harry said sharply. 'He is running from me, Robert. I did him a grave injustice.' He glanced meaningfully into their faces. 'Perhaps, in a way, we all have.'

Plumpton looked down thoughtfully at his square capable hands. 'Then why not let him go, my lord?' He said. 'It might be best in the end.'

'Best for whom, Robert?'

'Best for the boy himself, my lord,' Plumpton threw back. 'You know yourself he's never fitted in. He'd be better off among his own kind.'

Harry said nothing and glanced around the hot and hazy little room. A fire of sea coal belched thick yellow smoke into the faces of the men that crowded its warmth: pedlars and chapmen, carters bound for the Tyne, merchants in bright woollen cloaks worked with the arms of their guilds. There were a dozen soldiers playing noisily at cards, a pardoner hawking relics from a sack and here and there dusky faces of the men who burrowed for coal on Tyneside. Plumpton was right. This was John's world, where men laughed and spoke without restraint and were at ease in each other's company. In his heart he could not blame him for preferring it. Sometimes he almost preferred it himself. He rose abruptly to his feet. They must move on if they were to make Newcastle before nightfall.

By dusk they were less than five miles from the city but already the landscape was changing. Black ugly hollows pitted the soft hills, and all along the valley of the Tyne hillocks of earth and

141

shattered rock had sprung up as if the land were plagued by moles. Even the air was thicker and heavier. Coal had its own unmistakable smell.

Nearer to Newcastle the stench grew worse: dry sulphurous fumes blown from the iron works at Bywell and the salt pans at Shields, the furnaces of brewers and smiths within the walls. There were mines now at Elswick and Benwell and the burgesses of Newcastle were forever sinking shafts. Outside the town walls the castle moor was pitted with diggings, some no more than a few feet deep, abandoned as the sandstone had caved them in. Others had flooded and become dark stagnant wells; only one was a shaft of more than two fathoms deep. Above it a frail wattle cage housed a creaking windlass for hauling up the corves which barefoot children, dark as blackamoors, dragged to the carts on lengths of sacking.

They entered by the new gate, one of seven that pierced a high crenellated wall set with a score of strong fortified towers that had long ago rendered the old keep useless. Within the walls broad cobbled streets were linked by narrow alleys, all set with tall leaning houses. Churches arose like islands of piety: St Nicholas in the heart of the town, fixed by its soaring spire; St Andrews and St John in the west; All Hallows in the east; and on the bridge, St Thomas the Martyr whose chaplain also collected the tolls. Almshouses abounded, small and reproachful amid the gabled houses of ironmasters and wool merchants, a constant rebuke to their wealth. And if any man still feared for his soul there were always friars with their hands out: Black Friars from the great Dominican house by Westgate; Grey Frairs who begged barefoot in Pilgrim Street; Carmelites in austere white; Trinitarians banded with the Crusader's Cross; Austins from the Augustine house in Pandon; besides the convent of Benedictine nuns which occupied half of Newgate.

But it was the lower part of the town that was its true heart: the narrow tumbling streets that plunged headlong to the cluttered wharves and the shadows of tall warehouses crammed with fleeces. Every trade had its own quarter: fullers and dyers in Broad Chare; keelmen in Sandgate; brewers on the quay; butchers and poulterers in the steep Bank that climbed to the Side where the goldsmiths and mercers had their shops. Beyond the wall, huddled beneath it, were the dwellings of scavengers and thieves; dark stinking tunnels where pigs and whores rutted in doorways and no God-fearing body ventured after dark — roof-top piled upon roof-top, and shouldering above all, the ramparts of William Rufus's castle.

Harry glanced up at its crumbling walls as he passed. A fresh fall had scattered the mound with stones — almost half the east wall was down, the great drum towers of the barbican stood marooned in rubble, the drawbridge pit filled with slime and toads. Wind gnawed at the ancient stones, rats at the timbers, and all that were housed in the great square keep were felons and colonies of bats.

He moved on, past the shuttered and closed shops and the Merchant Adventurers' Hall. Hens foraged in the runnels for corn, dogs barked and snuffled ecstatically in the stinking ditch where the butchers cast their offal. Torches flared in the darkening street, the sweet drone of plainsong replaced the hucksters' cries.

He turned into the Close where his house squeezed itself between the river and the castle wall. His servant George Bird received him, a sharp fussy little man who lived up to his name, plucking and tutting as he reproached Harry mildly for not having sent ahead word of his arrival. Fires were hastily kindled, a boy sent out to the Cook Shop in Cowgate. Harry ate little and spoke less. All he could see was John's face, his lip split and bleeding from the vicious blow, his eyes blank from the worse hurts of the insults that Harry had hurled at him. He was plagued by conscience, and not just for this but for all the years before. What was John except what they had made him? Each of them had shaped him in a different way; each had used him as the whipping-boy for their own inadequacies. And he perhaps was the most guilty of all; to have punished the boy so rigorously for his lack of control in attacking Plumpton and then to have done the selfsame thing himself and with less excuse . . .

He went to his bed with a heavy heart. He knew he'd never be at peace with himself until he'd made his peace with John.

He awoke at dawn. The day was fine and clear and full of shy sunlight that came and went on the face of the hills like the blush on a maiden's cheek. Keels ploughed from the staiths laden with chauldrons of coal and smooth grey stones from Gateshead Fell; the wharves swarmed with men loading fleece and hides. A riot of scents filled the air: flax and dye and fulling earth; the raw bloody smell of fresh-killed meat; the delicious fragrance of new bread. He sent Plumpton and Gascoigne to search the lower town and wharves; he himself turned for the markets in Newgate. He held out little hope but was determined to try every chance, however small, and all morning he combed the narrow streets questioning merchants and 'prentices, friars and priests, innkeepers and toll-keepers and from all he received the same reply — none had laid eyes on John.

At noon he gave up, sick of the city stench and the futility of his search. He turned into Westgate, ill humour and frustration thinning his mouth. Two men in the Duke of Gloucester's livery lounged outside a tall stone house. He paused and glanced up to the painted shield set in the apex of the gable: Warwick's emblem of the bear and ragged staff — Gloucester had not had it taken down.

He walked his horse on a few paces then halted again. Abruptly he turned back, calling to one of the guards. 'Is his Grace of Gloucester within?'

The man knelt, seeing his face. 'Aye, my lord.'

Harry glanced up again at the painted shield. 'Ask his Grace if he will receive me.'

In the courtyard at the rear of the house he dismounted and flung the reins to a waiting groom. Another emerged from the stable doorway laden with a pile of harness. Harry checked his step and slowly turned. He found himself looking into the blue startled eyes of his quarry.

'And how was I supposed to know?' Gloucester snapped. 'He said his name was John Egremont. See here,' he stabbed his finger at the open ledger. 'My steward has entered it — John Egremont. Groom. Sixpence a day and livery. He said nothing about being committed elsewhere.'

144

'He's not in that sense,' said Harry evenly. 'I am not in the habit of demanding bonds of service from my kinsmen.'

'I was not to know that he was your kinsman. And it seems to me, my lord, he was at pains not to let me know. You must see, my lord, that this is a genuine error,' Gloucester said stiffly. 'I would never have taken him if I had known.'

'Would you not, your Grace?' said Harry stonily. 'How then do I see Gilbert Stokes in your livery as you have seen him often enough in mine? And I also hear that you were lately on my estates in Cumberland where you gave judgement on one of my villeins. And at Knaresborough, where you ordered my captain to relieve ten men of their duties for some personal errand of your own?'

Gloucester flushed. 'My purpose in requisitioning your men was quite legitimate,' he said. 'Besides, Knaresborough is a royal demesne.'

'But not within your jurisdiction unless the terms of my office have been changed. I thought I had made myself quite clear upon that point. I will tolerate no interference within my jurisdiction.'

Gloucester suddenly leapt to his feet. 'Yes, you made it clear, my lord, and just as clear that for all your talk of the weal of England, it's your personal pride that counts.' His dark eyes blazed with real anger. 'So I gave judgement upon a man who was a proven murderer, who would probably have escaped justice if I had not acted then. Does it matter which of us it was that condemned him? Do you think *he* cared? What matters is that the wrong was punished. Justice, by whosoever's word, was done.'

'So, your Grace, the end always justifies the means and as your ends are always so noble and righteous, it does not matter if the means are sometimes questionable. Well, it matters to me. Every man who acknowledges me as lord, free or bond, high or low, matters to me, and as no other man looks to their rights but me, I would have no other man judge their wrongs.' His eyes lingered for a moment on Gloucester's ashen face, then he turned away. 'And now, may I speak with my kinsman?'

John faced him manfully and only the trembling of his mouth showed that he was afraid.

'So, John Egremont. You've led us a fine dance,' Harry smiled

145

faintly. 'I must admit I had often thought to find you dead in the ditch but never in the Duke of Gloucester's livery.'

There was no answering smile on the boy's face. He stared at his feet, at Harry, at his feet again then he blurted out, 'And if it please you, my lord — so I would remain.'

Harry frowned, taken aback. 'Does it please *you*, John?'

John nodded mutely. Yes, it pleased him. He could never have said how much and even if he could, Harry would never have understood him. He knew now where he belonged; here, among the common men, the men at arms with their rough kindness and uncomplicated morals, among the simple soldier knights who had earned the distinction on the battlefield rather than had it handed to them by right. These men didn't know or care who his father had been. They expected nothing from him but basic honesty and hard work and the rewards for it were immediate and tangible. They didn't patronise or overawe him. They took him for what he was, they liked him for what he was. It was as near as he would ever get to the old life.

Then Harry said, his voice pitched halfway between surprise and regret. 'So you have no wish to return to Alnwick?'

'No, my lord.'

Harry dropped his eyes to the contemplation of a spider laboriously mounting the hillock of his boot. He could have left it at that and gone away knowing his duty done. But duty was not the reason he had come. He said, 'Do you know why it was that I struck you, John?'

'Does it matter, my lord?' John replied stonily.

Harry looked up into the young belligerent face and saw that it was too late to say all the things he had meant. 'No. I don't suppose it does now. There is nothing I could say that would justify it but for what it's worth to you, I offer you my apology for all that I said and did.'

John stared fixedly at a point above his head. 'Thank you, my lord,' was all he said.

The silence grew, drifting between them like a wall of fog. Harry stood abruptly. 'Well then, John. I wish you well. If you ever need' — he broke off awkwardly — 'you know there is always a place for you at Alnwick.'

He turned and went wordlessly from the room and John stood for a while listening to his footsteps on the hollow stairs. Only by keeping very still could he resist the urge to call him back. He blinked away the hot angry tears. He had almost weakened, he had almost been deceived again by that soft exquisite voice. Even now, the memory of it softened him. After all, he *had* come, he had cared enough to come. But there was still that other voice — as soft, as beautiful — hateful and cruel: *bastard. Get back to the gutter where you belong.* Resentment filled him, bitter as gall. It was not what he had said that hurt, he was used to that; but that Harry should have said it. For Harry, of all people, to have betrayed him so vilely; Harry whom he had trusted and even cared for in his strange grudging way. The perfect image was shattered and the illusion in too many pieces now ever to be whole again. He could never forgive him for it — never, as long as he lived.

For some reason John's decision to remain in his service seemed to please Gloucester inordinantly. He was in high spirits that night as they supped in the upper room of the house in Westgate Street. It was a small informal gathering. Gloucester and Harry; the Lords Dacre and Greystoke; the Mayor of Newcastle, William Blackett; the merchant adventurers Swinburne and Riddell; and Robert Rhodes, the lawyer. A sign of the changing times, Harry thought. Gloucester, like his brother the King cultivated the merchants assiduously; indeed Edward exported wool and hides himself through the Florentine Gerard de Carriziani.

'But your Grace,' Swinburne wagged his finger in gentle emphasis, 'the system is being much abused. As you know, the pelts of the northern hill sheep, being poor in quality, are shipped direct to the Netherlands free of duty rather than in the normal way to Calais through the merchants of the Staple. Only Berwick and Newcastle have this privilege. And what do we find?' The feather in his bonnet quivered indignantly. 'That merchants in both York and Lincoln are sending their fleeces up to the Tyne for shipment and therefore evading the tax.'

The merchants murmured warm agreement. Gloucester

looked grave. 'It will be seen to, Master Swinburne. Have no fear. It will be remedied.'

'I knew we could rely on your Grace's support,' said Mayor Blackett smoothly. 'Dare we claim a further indulgence, your Grace, in the matter of the alien merchants? Your advice would be greatly esteemed, as we were most distressed to hear that his grace the King had accorded the Hanse merchants special privileges, more favourable, it seems, than . . .'

Harry stared at the tapestry behind the mayor's pointed head and the cold grey eyes of King Henry at Agincourt looked back in mute disgust.

Lord Dacre leant close, and whispered disdainfully, 'I remember a time when merchants were content with selling cloth of gold but now it seems they're thinking of wearing it.' He threw a savage look at the grocer Riddell, who was complaining loudly about the state of the town ditch wherein, despite the mayor's ordinance, were cast all manner of filth and refuse.

'God's teeth,' Dacre muttered. 'Fish and coal and stinking sheep. Do they never talk of anything else?' He jerked his head towards the arras. 'Honourable days, eh, my lord?' He drew the flagon of wine towards him. 'And not gone forever, mayhap, if what I hear is true.' He met an enquiring glance. 'Have you not heard, my lord? The King seeks to renew the war with France. He's approached Parliament for a grant.'

Harry glanced at Gloucester. No, he hadn't heard and neither had the merchants whom Gloucester was obviously priming for a loan.

He leant forward and interrupted Mayor Blackett. 'Is it true, my lord,' he enquired smilingly of Gloucester, 'that the King is about to declare war on France.'

Gloucester glared at him ferociously, for he had meant to broach the subject more discreetly. The merchants looked aghast. War meant loss of trade and shipping, and worse, the King was bound come to them for money.

'Is it true, your Grace?' the grocer Swinburne ventured timidly.

'Nothing is definite,' Gloucester said evasively. 'There has been some little discord between his Grace the King and Louis of France. I dare say it will blow over well enough. Like yourselves, the King knows that England's interests lie in peace. He will not make war unless he is forced to it.'

The merchants smiled weakly, unconvinced. Gloucester attempted to sooth them as best he could but the damage had been done and the evening ground to a strained and abrupt halt. The merchants departed, feeling themselves already the poorer. Dacre and Greystoke followed swiftly seeing Gloucester's inhospitable face. Only when Harry made a move to take his leave did Richard attempt to detain him.

He poured wine into handsome silver cups. 'I shall leave for York in the morning.' He added casually as he handed Harry his cup, 'I should be glad if you would come with me.'

Harry laid the cup aside, untouched. 'Why?' He demanded bluntly.

Richard's smile grew increasingly strained. 'Because when we go our separate ways we always end up at odds. I thought we might do better together.'

'I really ought to return to Alnwick, your Grace,' Harry said evasively. 'My mother, the countess, will be waiting for news.' He smiled thinly. 'She is much attached to her nephew.'

Richard waved the excuse aside. 'Surely you can send one of your men with the news. I wouldn't have thought you could have spared the time, my lord. The King is shortly to hold a special council at Nottingham. You will be summoned to attend.'

'To persuade us to a war with France?'

'Among other things. And there's no question of persuasion, my lord. Most men are eager for it. Every Englishman feels the loss of our French possessions, dissipated through Lancastrian incompetence.'

Harry flung him a scathing look. 'Do you truly believe that, your Grace? I thought you had more respect for truth. You know full well that we lost our French lands simply because we could not hold them. There was neither money, nor heart, to continue to garrison a hostile country that could not even feed itself, let alone its conquerors. Do you not think it time to acknowledge the fact that a man cannot ride two horses at once, especially with the Channel between them? France is France. England is England. Better the King keep what he has sound and whole than go

149

chasing after a crown to which he has only the faintest right.'

'The King has a perfectly legitimate claim to France,' Gloucester said hotly. 'The mother of the third King Edward was Isabella of France . . .'

'Your Grace,' said Harry coldly, 'I am more than familiar with King Edward's descent and I wonder if it's wise to make so much of a blood claim through the female line? Often when a man spits into the wind it comes back and hits him in the face.'

'Meaning, my lord?'

'Meaning that by the simple law of logic, if King Edward has a better claim to France than King Louis, so then had Henry of Lancaster to England.'

Richard slammed his wine cup down. 'My God, Northumberland. If any other had said that I would have taken it as treason.'

'You may take it how you like, your Grace,' Harry said coolly. 'It's the truth. You cannot make out a case for one thing and then turn it about just when it suits you.'

'That was not my intention and you know it was not.' Richard flung himself away, struggling to contain his rising temper. 'For God's sake, my lord. What have you got against the war?'

'It's a waste: of time and money and life that could be better spent elsewhere. And for what? The raking up of some hundred-year-old claim that would not hold water in any just court.'

They had both raised their voices, and their eyes clashed with the same hot look. Gloucester was the first to look away. 'There's more to it than that,' he said grimly. 'Louis is meddling in our affairs, promising aid to known Lancastrian exiles, sending bribes to the Scots to break the truce. And there are still a few old scores to settle. Edward has never forgiven Louis for his support of Warwick. It's time that he learnt that he cannot mock England with impunity. Edward sees it as a matter of pride.'

'England should come before his pride.'

'As the north does before yours?' Richard suddenly rounded on him. 'How dare you complain of the King taking offence at Louis's interference when you have done just that over mine. You didn't take it so lightly when it was your rights that were threatened or is it only others who must turn the other cheek?'

'I have turned the other cheek, your Grace.' Harry said softly. 'Any other man who presumed so much would have paid a far higher price.'

Richard stiffened and his pale face grew paler with suppressed fury. 'I see,' he said. 'You think I presume do you, my lord? You think I exceed my powers as Warden?'

'Yes. I do,' Harry answered him quietly.

'Then perhaps we should refer the matter to council. Let us see then who presumes.'

Harry inclined his head courteously. 'As you wish, my lord. I shall be content to abide by their ruling.'

In the great hall at Nottingham, Chancellor Rotherham screeched for order over the tumult of an hundred voices. The King, resplendent in azure velvet, lounged in his chair, a wine cup dangling from his fingers. Clarence was sulking, viciously sleeking the plumage of the hawk on his wrist with a plump bejewelled hand. Richard of Gloucester sat between them, small and dark, like a crow between two peacocks.

The chancellor loudly cleared his throat and darted like an industrious bee among a honeycomb of rolled parchments. Richard raised his eyes obediently as he began to speak. The talk was all of war — or the lack of it, for despite all their careful preparations the prospect of a summer campaign was fading. Their foreign alliances were crumbling fast — Brittany had been the first to renege, intimidated by subtle threats from Louis and perhaps the thought that Edward's terms of treaty were rather too much in England's favour. Burgundy's reasons were quite different and as much as he had once nagged and chivvied for war with France now he shuffled and sidestepped and could not be brought to terms. It seemed that since the betrothal of his daughter to the son of the Holy Roman Emperor, Burgundy aspired to greater conquests than the mere partition of France. In flagrant breach of his sworn word to Edward, he had agreed a brief truce with Louis of France whilst his attentions were occupied elsewhere.

Richard glanced covertly round at the tense and preoccupied faces. At least now he did not feel that every eye was fixed upon

151

him. His humiliating little set-down of the previous day was forgotten. Thank God, since news of Burgundy's defection had come, a new fever seized them. But he hadn't forgotten. At the thought of it his cheeks burned with mortification. He had been so sure that he was in the right — he still was — yet the council had voted overwhelmingly in Northumberland's favour, and worse, had insisted that he give his word to make no further encroachments on Northumberland's rights. He could feel his face burning with the same hot colour as when he had stumbled and stuttered his way through the oath. Hastings and the Woodvilles had openly smirked, even Edward had looked amused. And Northumberland? His eyes had immediately gone to Northumberland's face, expecting to see the triumph he had been so sure was his. The dark impassive face had given nothing away. At least he'd had the grace not to gloat.

Afterwards Edward had privately taken him to task; a mild rebuke but nevertheless a rebuke. His handling of Northumberland had been unforgivably tactless, Edward had told him plainly. And then to be so rash as to insist that it be brought before council . . . Rash, arrogant, tactless, epithets that only those who knew him particularly well would ever have applied to him. But his brother Edward did know him particularly well. He knew the hot rash streak that lay beneath his reserve, that sudden and impulsive side of his nature that would sometimes break out and take them all by surprise. Once an idea was fixed in his mind he rushed at it headlong like a blinkered horse and never even saw that he trampled others down. Such tactics won battles but they didn't win friends. You couldn't affront a man as powerful as Northumberland and not come out of it without scathe.

He hadn't argued, though in his heart he had thought the criticism unjust. To alienate Northumberland had been the last thing in his mind. He had wanted Harry Percy to share his vision, he had even thought of friendship. Richard stared down miserably at his small thin hands. As always he had bungled it and more than ever he envied his brothers their easy charm. Edward only had to smile to have a man eating out of his hand; even George, loud, arrogant and overbearing George, could get his own way when he chose. Why not him? What was wrong with him that men always stood him off? Only at one thing did he truly excel. War inspired him as nothing else and he knew he was a better soldier than either of his brothers. Hadn't he proved it at Barnet and Tewkesbury? All of England had loved him then. His sensitive mouth drooped. Yet it seemed that he was to be cheated even of that. He heard the chancellor's dry impassive voice informing the council what he already knew. The war with France would have to be postponed. They could not proceed until they were sure of Burgundy. But postponed, not abandoned. There would be another time, another chance to prove himself. It was the only time he felt anything like equal, when he was on horseback and his lack of height did not strike men so forcibly, when his thin limbs were encased in shining steel. Men followed him then; common men perhaps, but still men who had life and limb to lose — Warwick had once told him that it was the greatest accolade a soldier could have, the trust and love of the common man. And, he thought savagely, worth twice as much as the empty friendships with which Edward seemed content. He turned his head to survey the men who kept themselves close to the King, and his austere and chilling gaze marked them down: Hastings, lecher and pervert, plump and sleek as a well-fed hound, replete with his recent appointment as Captain of Calais; John Morton, the holy hypocrite, with his foot poised and impatient upon the ladder. And there, the real nucleus of offence: the Queen's sons, Richard and Thomas Grey, shallow and frivolous wastrels; her brother, Anthony, poet, courtier and idler. There was the real heart of corruption, the leeches that fed upon Edward's love of ease and pleasure and drained away England's lifeblood . . . Richard swallowed hard. He could feel the storm of righteous fury rising up in his throat. His eyes fastened bleakly upon Northumberland's dark and sinister face. He sighed with heavy regret. He had thought that there was a man as aloof and incorruptible as himself. He had thought that together they would have made war on corruption and vice — as always he had been disappointed.

He rose, tardily, for the council had already broken up. Edward called loudly for wine. Hastings lounged familiarly against the King's chair and at his elbow Bishop Morton breathed heavily.

He walked swiftly toward the door. Men fell back and gave him passage. Some smiled tentatively, hoping for recognition, others made dour little faces behind his back. Outside the door he paused. Ahead of him he saw a tall familiar figure. He hesitated for a moment, then called out to him. 'My lord.'

Harry halted and slowly turned his head. 'Your Grace?'

Richard advanced towards him, noting with irritation that Harry made no move to come to him. Tread carefully, Edward had said. Cozen him a little and he'll soon come round. Richard gave a grim smile. That wouldn't work with Harry Percy any more than it would have with him.

He said, maintaining his grim amusement. 'I suppose I should congratulate you on your victory, my lord.'

Harry regarded him with his cold impassive stare. 'I was not aware that we were at war.'

'I think we are, my lord, whether we like it or not. Are not the battle lines already drawn? I shall not encroach upon the terms of your office nor recruit any man past or present who has ever worn your livery. The old war, my lord. The war that began all the other wars. Neville against Percy and every man so conscious of his rights and privileges and dignities that they cannot see beyond them to the injustice and misery they cause to others.'

His voice trembled with rare passion, rising shrilly so that the men about the door turned and looked at them. 'I am surprised you have so little taste for war, my Lord Northumberland.' Gloucester shouted. 'It is men like you who begin them.'

The bitter words rankled all through the long dreary banquet that marked the closing of the council, and far into the sleepless night that followed. He left Nottingham the next day and they stayed with him, biting deeper into his conscience with every mile. '*I am surprised that you have so little taste for war. . . . It is men like you who begin them.*' Was it true? He asked himself so many times that he knew that it was. He only had to look back — the old war, the old hatred, the old feud that had become the greater feud of Lancaster and York. And all begun so innocently, because

154

a Neville had dared to cast his eyes on a Percy's power — as Richard of Gloucester did upon his.

He passed a night at York, the best part of it spent by his father's grave. For the last ten miles he had been waylaid by ghosts: Bramham Moor where the old man had fallen; Towton, where his uncle Richard had been slain and where his father had been so mortally wounded before he had crawled back to this dim little church to die. In the Minster lay the handful of bones that was all that was left of Harry Hotspur; a few miles away at Beverley, his grandfather and three of his sons lay buried and not one old man amongst them: all dead, all martyrs to Lancaster and Neville ambition; four generations blinded by hatred — and he would be the fifth.

He raised his eyes to the bright unwavering flame that burned for his father's soul. Perhaps only in retrospect did it seem so futile. How was he the more content because Warwick was dead? Hatred bred only hatred, revenge bred revenge, and all that had ever come out of it was emptiness and loss. And he was on the verge of beginning it all again, the old feud, the old war, both sprung from the same bitter seed of unappeased hatred and envy. It didn't matter that Henry of Lancaster was dead. There was another Henry waiting quietly in Brittany, waiting for the small fatal spark to be struck. It wouldn't take much, a sudden quarrel such as the one that brewed between himself and Gloucester. One word from him could bring out the north, still simmering and aggrieved at its heart. Edward knew it and it was why he had given way to him at Nottingham. John Morton knew it and it was why he still furtively tried to wean him from York. Richard of Gloucester knew it — it was why he had challenged him.

He stared down unseeingly at the dim shape of his father's tomb. Was this the right that he had guarded so jealously, the means to plunge England back into war? Was the pattern of hatred burned so indelibly into him that it could not be changed? Was pride only another name for stubborness? Was ambition only a synonym for greed? The awful questions clouded his mind and if he had needed answer, it was here, beneath his hands, beneath the cold grey slab with its stench of death and decay. Had he so easily forgotten Towton? That day of nightmare and ruin, death and darkness that he had thought sealed up for ever in his father's tomb? He had watched him die, here, in this very place, slowly, the life draining out of him in a crimson flood. He had seen old men weeping and sniffling like raw boys; women growing suddenly old with grief. He remembered the blinding whiteness of the snow, the scarlet thaw, the limbless corpses littering the streets. And he thought he had forgotten; he had thought that he had made himself invulnerable, not knowing that the very need to be safe and protected was vulnerabilty in itself. He had made a virtue of solitude and believed it to be strength. Only now did he know it for weakness. The real strength was in acknowledging and overcoming grief and disappointment. Instead, he had cowered behind a wall of pretended indifference, shirking commitment, expecting of others what he could not give himself. He stared down bleakly at his father's grave. What else had he buried along with his dead? Heart and honour and conscience, all. Had he crushed his fear so ruthlessly that he killed all else? He leant and kissed the chill rough stone and wondered how much more alive he was than the man beneath the slab.

He rode on, pursued by his bleak and melancholy thoughts. Sometimes he glanced at the faces of his men and saw cautious respect and fear; but never liking, never affection. For the first time in his life he was aware that he needed it. He thought often of John, happier in a stable on sixpence a day than in all the splendour of Alnwick. He understood now why he hadn't wanted to come back. He had wanted to be free, to escape from himself and Eleanor and the bitter malignant hatred that was between them. Yes, he could well understand that. Didn't he long to be free of it himself?

At Warkworth he lingered, for no better reason than to eke out the time before he must return to Alnwick. He walked alone in the crimson dusk, part of the deep and intense stillness that was the prelude to night. The tall grasses whispered at his passing, the river breathed along the sandstone cliffs, a swallow skimmed the water in swift and noiseless flight. All was soft and shining silence.

He stared out into the quiet radiance. His grandmother Alianore had brought him here once and he had picked marguerites for her. The flowers still grew in profusion along the bank, long white lashes fringing round yellow eyes, nodding in perpetual remembrance of the Marguerite who lay buried in the hermitage beyond the curve of the river. She had been a Neville, when the Nevilles had been nobodys and thought it all the world to ally themselves to a Percy. Alianore had been a Neville too, another thread in the tangled skein of love and hate that had fettered and strangled them for nigh on a hundred years.

He halted abruptly and stared blankly down the pathway ahead of him. It led nowhere. To follow it would be futile and without purpose — like all of his life, blindly placing one foot in front of the other, deceiving himself that because he moved forward he had some destination or purpose. Sickness filled him, a hollow grinding emptiness that doubled him up as if a clenched fist had been driven hard into his body. *'You are cruel and bitter, and worse, you are empty — empty and cowardly.'* It was true. He was empty. He was afraid, but not of love. It was the thought of being without it that terrified him.

The sun drifted above the rim of the hills, suspended in vermilion clouds. Another day gone and still Harry had not come. Eleanor frowned and watched the edge of crimson light creep nearer to her chair. She had been so sure today. She could sense him, she could feel his nearness as a beast scented fear. But he would come; when he reached Alnwick and found her gone. Tomorrow, the next day, as long as it took for him to swallow his pride and come looking.

She stared out through the open shutters. Flies clung to the lattice drugged with the heat and beyond there was nothing to see but green meadows and grazing sheep. Nothing had changed in the four years since she had left except that the roof didn't leak anymore.

She still didn't know why she had come back to Leconfield: the need to run as John had run perhaps, except that there was no escape from what pursued her. Perhaps after all it was not so strange that she had been led back here. Alianore's gentle presence still clung to the walls and John, the child of her heart, had been born to her here. She had made her pilgrimage through all the silent empty rooms. In this cold and draughty chamber her son Harry had been born; in the great dark bed Alianore had died. Here, Warwick had strutted while he stripped the manor to the bone; here she had lost the last of her youth and beauty. Dark ugly memories, but there was a strange comfort in remembering them. They held no terror for her now, she had lived through them and survived. Despair and disappointment had become a habit with her. She could almost enjoy the sense of persecution. It justified her hatred, it soothed her guilt, it made the unbearable bearable. Besides, there were worse miseries. It had only been her body that had been cold and hungry then. This starvation of the spirit was infinitely worse.

She closed her eyes as the soft rosy light touched her face. At least she would be free from Harry here. He would only come this once, drawn by a love and concern that were not for her. Once would be enough, one last long look at that cold arrogant face stricken with the pain of rejection. Not that his pain would ever match hers. She could still see Plumpton's sneering face, his voice flat and uncaring as he had shattered her heart. 'Master John is not coming back. He has chosen, of his own free will, to stay with the Duke of Gloucester.'

Chosen! She hadn't believed that. *Of his own free will?* When he had no will but hers? She knew without doubt that Harry had forced him to it, as he had forced him to run in the first place. John would not have deserted her so cruelly; John loved her; without her he was nothing — or so she had told herself in the first few days. Her mind still clung to some part of that belief, but her heart, so battered and bruised by grief, knew the truth. John had forsaken her — as Thomas had, and her husband Harry had, not of their own will but by the will of One who was greater than them all. It was God's will that she should be alone and unloved and though she had tried to flout Him with every action of her life, it was only now that she knew herself beaten.

She opened her eyes and closed them quickly again. Her daughter Margaret had entered the room, treading stealthily for fear of waking her. Eleanor did not disillusion her. She often feigned sleep as a means of defence. She could remain still and silent for hours at a time, her mind going beyond her body to spend a brief hour with the dead. Lovingly they beckoned her and whispered into her tired mind of a world where love and forgiveness were all. There was only heaven beyond the grave. Hell was life itself, purgatory was here and now, day after day of hopeless despair. The only release was death. She almost longed for it now and would have hastened it if she dared. She had the means; in the elixir there was death, the slow lingering death of craving and dependence; or swiftly, the long dark sleep from which she would never awake. But she hadn't even the courage for that, such a flagrant defiance of God's will. She had only ever had the courage for small things.

Then Margaret solicitously touched her arm. The sharp acquisitive face leant close. A pendant of garnets and pearls swung from her neck, her gown was the finest Genoese velvet. Eleanor smiled. Dearest Margaret would never forsake her — at least, not until she had bled her dry.

Obediently she drank the posset Margaret had prepared; cinquefoil and yarrow and three drops of the precious elixir to quell her body's deadly appetite. The creature did not trouble her now. She kept him too well sated for that. She closed her eyes as the pleasurable warmth swept through her. After a while her body slumped, her mind grew blank. Sometimes she dreamed, strange brief apparitions that drifted into her empty mind and were gone before she could name them: a woman naked in an iron cage; a man with sad and melancholy eyes; a horseman riding . . . Her eyes flew open. A horseman riding — iron-shod hooves screaming to a halt — the soft belled sound of spurs . . . She smiled. She had been right after all. Harry had come at last.

She neither moved nor spoke till he stood before her, then slowly she raised her eyes and saw him breathless and dishevelled. That in itself was a revelation.

Harry stared at her in silent fury. 'And what new game is this, madame? Taking yourself off without so much as a by-your-leave.'

Eleanor returned his glance coolly. 'I was not aware that I needed your leave,' she said.

She saw him glance quickly around the room. His eyes lingered on her bedchamber door, straining his ears for a familiar voice so that he would not have to ask. He said stiffly, 'You intend to stay at Leconfield, then?'

'Yes. Why not? Do you not think it past time that we parted company?'

Again he was silent and Eleanor waited, her eyes intent upon his face. He came a step nearer and the fierce summer light burnished the sharp bones of his face and lit red angry fires in his eyes. At last he said wearily, as if he knew there was no help for it but to ask, 'Where is she?'

Rapturously she smiled. How strange to see tenderness softening that cruel mouth, to hear that honeyed voice roughened with longing. 'Gone,' she said happily. 'Back to Wales. And before you leap to the conclusion that I sent her away, let me tell you that I did not. She asked my permission to return to her family in Wales and I gave it. Her brother came to collect her two weeks ago.' She smiled maliciously. 'She went of her own free will, Harry — as John did.'

Her eyes had never left his face but even then she almost missed it. The anguished fire of his eyes was already dying, his mouth had resumed its cold inflexible line. But for a moment, for one brief joyous moment she had seen his naked misery.

'You see, Harry,' she said, 'you see how you drive people away from you. Your father was like that. People shunned him and neither he nor they ever really knew why. But I knew, Harry. Because underneath he was weak and timid and cowardly. You are your father's son, Harry. Does it not speak for itself? John has gone, Maud has gone and even I who bore you would rather spend my last days alone than bear you a moment's company.'

Then he looked at her and in the one brief measured glance there was all of his hatred and loathing. Suddenly he leant close and the dark sinister face filled all of her vision. The yellow pitiless eyes devoured her, the ruthless mouth smiled and he said, the ugly words intensified by his beautiful voice, 'And so you shall, madame. Indeed you shall, alone and sick and unloved, attended by only grief and misery and pain. And when you die — pray God you soon will — let it be slow and painful and lingering. I shall not look to see your face before then.'

She stared at him, her triumph allayed by the dreadful words.

160

Desperately she sought for words of her own but none came. Her mind was suddenly blank, her will passive as if her hatred had been defused and weakened by excess. He moved away from her but his image stayed fixed and constant before her eyes. She saw now that this indeed was her own true son, as cunning, as devious, with her own large capacity for love and hate and vengeance, with her own black unforgiving heart. However had she thought him even remotely like his father? However had she thought him weak? Suddenly she knew that it was never Harry she had seen, but only the man who had sired him. She had hated Harry in place of his father, as she had loved John in place of his, and somehow in the confusion of the dead and the living she had persecuted Harry because his father was beyond her reach. Tears of remorse and self-pity filled her eyes and for a brief moment she glimpsed something of what she had missed by not loving him. Slowly the shock of recognition passed. Now through the fading numbness she heard his footsteps leaving her.

'Harry,' she called wildly after him but he was already gone and she was alone, as she would be for the rest of her life. It was the last time she ever saw him.

The long hot summer burnt itself out into a chill wet autumn: days of drifting rain and leaves that clogged the runnels and made stagnant rivers of the Newcastle streets. There, in September, Harry met with the Scottish envoys to sign a prolongation of the eternal truce. The Scots, made bold by the rumour of the French war, were evasive, waiting to see whether the winds of advantage would blow from Paris or Westminister. At the end of a week Harry called the desultory talks to a halt with little or nothing achieved.

It was a bleak and dismal time for the north. In October the Aln and the Coquet burst their banks and for a week they were marooned in a turgid brown flood that lapped to the very walls of Alnwick. Eventually the water receded and left in its wake a sea of glistening mud littered with the wreckage of homes and lives. Forty men and a hundred beasts were drowned, whole villages were left without shelter. With the onset of winter the prospect worsened. In the waterlogged barns the harvest rotted and in

November there was a swift and killing outbreak of St Anthony's Fire from eating bread made from tainted grain. In the towns the price of corn rose to unheard-of heights. Those who could afford it grumbled and ate. Those who could not starved and died.

Christmas came, a few brief days of warmth and laughter, quickly stilled by the paralysis of winter. Inevitably snow fell and sealed them up from the world. Harry waited out the cheerless days at Alnwick, his own misery intensified by that of others. The bell of St Michael's tolled daily for the dead, and the poor starved corpses had to be packed in snow till the iron ground had yielded enough to bury them. Victuals grew scarcer, his men grew thinner and their tempers short. There was much brawling among the garrison.

Alone he paced the dark and shuttered room. He felt threatened and trapped by the blind white world that had slowly closed him in. He grew more withdrawn, his thoughts morose. He thought viciously of Eleanor, uneasily of John. Of Maud he never thought at all, except when he heard the sound of a woman's laughter; when the fire burned down to the dark crimson of her hair. The pain of wanting her had never left him, but he was easier with it now. He knew in his heart that it was not he that had driven her away. Knowing Eleanor he could think of a hundred reasons why, but not one good enough to overcome his pride and send him after her. Whichever way he thought of it, it came to the same thing. She had not cared enough to stay.

At last the thaw came, and spring hard on its heels, erupting in a froth of green buds and pale blossom. But its beauty did not touch him. In his heart it was perpetual winter.

In May, he moved with his household to Wressel. There at the end of the month word came from the King. The war was being pursued in earnest now. Fresh treaties had been signed with Portugal and Brittany and at last Burgundy had been brought to terms. And very favourable terms they were too — for Burgundy: all of Champagne and Nevers, Eu, Guise and Barr in exchange for ten thousand Burgundian troops to be maintained at English expense. Harry himself was charged with securing their rear from Scotland and King James drove an equally hard bargain: the betrothal of his infant son to the four-year-old Princess Cecily, plus a dowry of some twenty thousand crowns. It seemed for a moment that they had the French out-manoeuvred, but Louis, anxious as ever to keep the Lancastrian pot boiling, had furnished the exiled Earl of Oxford with money and ships for a diversionary raid upon England. In October Oxford and his brothers had descended on the Cornish coast and occupied St Michael's Mount. With only eighty men he was no very great threat; the danger lay in the raking up of old memories, the subtle reminder that a choice still existed. Henry Tudor was alive and well in Brittany and there were some still willing to remember it. Once more the talk was all of treason and plots; once more the Duke of Clarence's name was mentioned.

Then at the beginning of June, Richard of Gloucester came to Wressell.

It was a year since they had met, though a host of formal, carefully worded letters had passed between them. Gloucester had kept meticulously to the terms of the Nottingham agreement, consulting Harry in all matters that touched on his Wardenship, steering clear of disputes that might put them at odds. Only twice had they come close to a head-on clash, once when the men of Cockermouth caused an affray in Gloucester's township, once when one of the duke's reeves had been caught poaching deer on Harry's land. It seemed it was a like occurrence that had brought him now.

'There is no question of his guilt, my Lord Northumberland. The man was caught red-handed. The knife was still in his hand and the buck's throat cut as clean as you like.'

Harry regarded Gloucester suspiciously. 'A small matter to bring you so far out of your way, your Grace. Could not my bailiff have dealt with it?'

Gloucester flushed, swiftly on the defensive. 'I thought the affair at Knaresborough a small matter also, my lord. I thought to play safe this time.'

Harry smiled thinly, swallowing hard on the urge to provoke him and not quite succeeding. 'Well then, seeing as you have taken the trouble, your Grace. Who is the man?'

'No one of account, I am glad to say. A labourer, and verging on the feeble-minded from what I can see. He says his name is Tom Stoner.'

'You have him here?'

Gloucester nodded. 'Also a priest determined to speak in his defence. And your bailiff — Hockden, I think his name is.' He smiled. 'You see, I am determined to see fair play.'

Harry glanced away from the dark humorous eyes. 'Well,' he said stiffly, 'let's have him in then.'

The man had been badly knocked about and could hardly stand from weariness. Hockden the bailiff dragged him forward on a length of rope; a fat round priest puffed in his wake. The man regarded them with vacant bewildered half-closed eyes. His mouth too was crusted with dried blood and so swollen he could not even speak his name.

'Who beat him?' Harry demanded harshly.

'Not my men certainly,' Gloucester said quickly. 'He was sound and whole enough when I left him with your bailiff.'

Hockden cleared his throat. 'He became truculent, my lord, when we tried to chain him. I fear it became necessary to restrain him.'

'So much so that you've rendered him mute?'

'He *is* mute, my lord, or virtually so.' The little fat priest pushed himself forward. 'With your permission, my lord, I will speak for him. His name is Thomas Stoner, a stonecutter for fifteen years in your service before a blow on the head robbed him of his wits. I have known him since the day he was born; a good soul, my lord, a gentle soul who has never had a sinful thought in his head let alone committed any crime.'

'Yet he hunted and killed one of the Duke of Gloucester's deer,' Harry observed gently.

'Not true, my lord. Killed it, yes. But only out of mercy. Hunted it? How could he? He had no bow or lance with him, only a knife and home-made snare. You see, this is the way of it, my lord. Poor Tom was only out for rabbit, cutting through his Grace's wood bound for the common moor. He came upon the beast already fallen and crazed with pain. Its hindquarters were torn, its leg badly shattered. Tom only put it from its misery.'

'Well, we could all say that,' Hockden broke in. ' "Oh, my lord,

164

I fell over this wounded deer, my lord, and cut its throat to save it from suffering!" ' He laughed harshly. 'Ten to one if his Grace's men had caught him ten minutes later he would have been dragging it off home for his supper.'

'Is it true?' Harry looked at Gloucester. 'That the beast was wounded?'

'It's true that it was marked but not badly. I couldn't know if any limbs were broken.'

'Tom knows, though,' the priest said. 'Tom has a feeling for dumb creatures, being the next best thing himself. And I believe him, my lord. Every word. Tom's not got the wit for such a lie.'

'And how do you know all this?' Harry asked. 'I thought you said that the man was mute.'

'We have our own language, my lord. Signs and gestures mostly but Tom can write a few simple words.'

'The man's an idiot,' Hockden muttered. 'If you ask me it would be a kindness to hang him.'

The old priest glared at him. 'But good enough to hump stone twelve hours a day on half pay. Don't think I don't know how you rob him.'

Hockden flushed and threw a nervous glance at Harry. 'I pay him what he is worth,' he said sullenly. 'He's so slow he only does half a day's work.'

'With respect, my lord, that's a blatant lie,' the priest intervened. 'Tom works hard enough for two men. I have seen him myself, so weary he could hardly stand. And working long past curfew some days.'

Harry eyed the bailiff coldly. 'This man is employed on half pay only?'

Hockden's guilty flush deepened. 'Aye, my lord. When he is employed at all. He's not much good at anything except carting.'

'As I am sure your rolls and ledgers will show,' Harry said sharply. It was an old trick, the employing of rogues and simpletons who were glad enough to take half pay rather than nothing at all while the bailiffs presented their lords with bills for the full amount and pocketed the surplus. He turned to the man whose eyes were still fixed imploringly upon his face. How much did he understand? Harry thought. That he would be hung if he

165

was found guilty, or deprived of a hand at the very least? Yet he did not seem afraid. His eyes were full of a strange childish trust. It was not the look of a guilty man.

He said very gently, 'Do you understand me, Tom?' The man nodded. 'Did you kill the deer?'

A pause, a frantic glance at the priest, then again he nodded. 'For yourself? Did you kill the deer for gain, for your wife and children to eat?'

Tom frowned, as if the words were too many for him.

Gloucester said impatiently. 'Aren't we making too much of this, my lord? Strictly, according to the law, he is guilty.'

Harry turned to look at him. 'There are varying degrees of guilt, your Grace. He is, as you say, guilty of slaying the deer but not, I think, guilty in his intent.'

Gloucester pursed his lips, then shrugged. 'I fear I have not your enthusiasm for the finer points of law, my lord. But seeing that you are determined to play Solomon, I leave the judgement to you. After all he is your man.'

'But it was your buck.'

'Then I give you the buck as well. Do with both of them as you will.'

'Then let him go,' Harry ordered Hockden quietly, 'and see that he has the buck as well. I think he has more than earned it.'

The priest grabbed Harry's hand and kissed it fervently and ushered the still bewildered man from his presence. Hockden followed more slowly, studiously avoiding Harry's eyes. Gloucester stood stiff and silent till they were alone.

He said thoughtfully, 'Do you think that was altogether wise?'

'What would you have done then, your Grace?'

'Well, I would have thought a token punishment at least. After all he was guilty, whatever the extenuating reasons. When word gets about that you let him off it will be taken as licence to hunt your forest freely. As justice of the King's forests in the north I would not have thought you could have afforded a reputation for weakness.'

'Mercy is not necessarily weakness, my lord. And if I have any reputation at all, I would like to think it was for justice.'

Gloucester looked faintly aggrieved. 'Where is the justice in hanging one man for a crime and letting another go free? I notice that when my man was hauled up before your forest courts, you showed no great leaning to mercy then.'

'He deserved none,' Harry said coldly. 'Your reeve was a man in a trusted and well-paid position who abused it for his own profit and gain. And moreover, when he was caught he lied blatantly and would have shifted the blame onto an innocent man. I hung him because he deserved to be hung. To my mind Tom Stoner did not.' He glanced mockingly at Gloucester's stony face. 'Is that why you came, my lord — to even the score?'

Gloucester met his eyes steadily, refusing to be provoked. 'No, my lord, that is not why I came.' He smiled tentatively. 'You know quite well it was not.'

'Well, if it had been, I was going to offer you Hockden instead. Now there is a man I could hang with pleasure. It's obvious that he has been robbing both myself and poor Thomas Stoner. Do you not think that is the greater crime, your Grace? To deliberately exploit a simple-minded man?'

'Is that not the way of the world, my lord? The strong have always preyed upon the weak.'

'Then let us hope that we all remain strong men and the weak stay happy to be oppressed. Otherwise we might begin to prey upon each other.'

'Do we not already?' Gloucester said passionately. 'Oh, in our own noble and chivalrous way, of course; priding ourselves that we only pick quarrels with men of equal strength, not knowing that we do the more harm. When strong men fall out it is always the weak who suffer. Who was it said that when lions fight, it is the lamb who bleeds?'

Harry looked up and for a moment the two men surveyed each other gravely. Then Harry's eyes dropped to the cognizance that hung on Gloucester's breast. 'And when the lion and boar fight?'

Richard replied with sombre passion. 'Surely, my lord, in God's name we are charged to see that they do not.'

Gloucester stayed another five days at Wressell, effortlessly widening the breach he knew he had made in Harry's defences. In the mornings they rode out with hawks on their fists, coming home at night through the soft scented moorland air, laughing and squabbling like raw boys over who'd had the better kill. In the evenings they would sit in solemn discourse, Harry listening while Richard expounded his sometimes extravagant theories, then challenging, disputing till he'd whittled them down to a workable size. Only in one thing were they apart. Richard was totally committed to war with France and truly believed that conquest was possible. He saw a great crusading army shining with the virtue of England's right, he saw acclamation and glory and the vindication of all their wrongs. Harry saw other things: dysentery and colic, muddle and chaos, gargantuan sums expended on the winning and keeping of an alien aggressive land.

Richard laughed at him openly. 'My God, Harry. You're beginning to sound like a priest.'

Harry smiled, unoffended. 'Yes. I suppose I am. I'm afraid I was raised in a less aggressive school. I prefer to argue the point than drive it home with the hilt of my sword.'

Richard smiled. It was strange how vastly different they were yet in some things totally alike. 'I fear I am more at home with the sword than with words, Harry.'

'Words can be equally lethal.'

'But not fatal. There is no answer to the thrust of a sword.'

'Agreed. Therefore the question is still left begging for the next generation to answer. Remember, my lord. The old war, the old feud! I thought we had decided on a different reply.'

'And so we have,' Richard said earnestly. 'There's nothing I want more than peace.'

'You are inconsistent, my lord. With one voice you argue passionately for peace; with the other you cry war. A year ago you accused me of being a warmonger; now you call me a priest.'

'There are different issues,' Richard said doggedly. 'War with France is a just cause, war between ourselves is not.'

'A weathercock's philosophy if ever I heard one. You can veer it to the point that suits you best. There are no just wars any more than there are honourable deaths. Men bleed and die whatever side they are on. There is only one honourable reason for taking another man's life, to save yourself or to save others. To slaughter man just for gain or glory is a dishonour in itself, and that's what provokes most men to war, greed and glory, the lust for conquest, the need for more and more power.'

Richard stared at him in mounting irritation. 'Don't you think that's rather a cowardly point of view?'

'All men are cowards to some degree. The instinct for self-preservation is strong in all of us and there are only a few men who advance happily upon certain death: madmen or men blinded by an obsessive optimism that convinces them that they can always win. I am more aware of my capabilities, of what I can and cannot achieve. I would have said it was a practical point of view rather than cowardly. Do you not press for war with France because you think you can win? Do you not wish for peace with me because you know you cannot?'

Richard grew pale. 'Who says that I cannot?'

'I do, my lord,' Harry said. 'But then I am not sure I can win either.'

For a moment their warring glances held, then Richard dropped his eyes and his narrow shoulders slumped. 'For God's sake, Harry,' he said in a low voice. 'Can we never be done with it?'

Harry made no answer. He was not even sure that there was one. Always he came to the same impasse, his reluctant liking for this man stifled by suspicion and prejudice. The silence grew, dense and solid as a wall between them.

Then Richard said, his voice weary and strained, 'You know, I'm disappointed in you, Harry. I thought at least from you I should have truth and honest dealing, yet still you fob me off with half-truths and half measures.' He turned his head and fixed Harry with his dark intense stare. 'You're a hypocrite, my lord — mouthing platitudes about peace when your heart is full of war. You talk very grandly about England's weal. You mean your particular share of it, your own small part of it, all fenced in, boundaries set and God help any man who strays over them. But you'll not keep me out, you know. I love the north and I am determined that in the end it will love me. You can't deny that I have earned a place here. Why then do you grudge it me?'

'I do not. A place, yes. A part, but not all.' Harry smiled derisively. 'I do not see you as a man content with less than all.'

'You're wrong, Harry. You're wrong.' The pale intense face

grew paler. 'For God's sake, don't let us make the same mistake as our fathers did. They tore the north and England apart rather than yield place to the other. None of them saw the greater concept, the larger vision, the . . .' Richard shook his head and made a helpless gesture. Words failed him as they always did and usually men grew impatient with him and turned away, remaining for ever in ignorance of what he thought. But Harry was still listening, his eyes averted to the window where the stone tracery sprung darkly against the evening sky.

He began again, slowly, hesitantly, till the words flowed swiftly on the tide of his passionate belief. 'I have this dream, Harry — a vision — to see the north whole and prosperous.' He shrugged. 'Perhaps it's guilt, perhaps it's the need to make amends, to make reparation for some of the grief and misery for which I know that York is blamed. I've seen some of that grief, Harry: poverty, lawlessness, oppression. There is much abuse of the small man, either by intent or by neglect. And show me more than a half a dozen decently defensible towns — Carlisle's walls are practically in ruin and Newcastle's only fit for rats. Berwick has been in Scots hands these past twelve years — I have no mind to see that go on. Can't you see it, Harry? The north as prosperous and self-sufficient as once it was? I propose that we have our own council, just the leading men of course. There should be no need then to be for ever consulting Westminster, so that by the time we have asked and been answered the need has passed. I hope to persuade Edward to give me *carte blanche* in this. We would be virtually self-governing.'

Harry glanced at Gloucester's flushed and eager face and met the dark eyes with their fanatical glow. 'I see,' he said in his soft sneering voice. 'Your own little kingdom in the north.'

Richard coloured at the insinuation in his voice. 'No, Harry, nothing so grand as that. I just want to make the north whole again.'

Harry looked away. Something reluctantly stirred in him: excitement, fear, anger, he was not sure which. Perhaps all three, for was this not what he himself had dreamed of? Why then did he baulk at hearing it from another man? Was his dream so small that he could not share it? But with Richard of Gloucester? A man whose intense commitment to whatever he undertook would allow no half measures?

'I cannot do it alone, Harry,' Richard said bluntly. 'I cannot do it at all if you should hinder me. You already have what it will take me years to win: the implicit and unshakable trust of the people. You're a Percy and their hereditary lord. I'm the brother of the king they fought at Towton and they'll fight me too, unless they know that we are together in this. Separately we can only achieve second best. Together all is possible.'

'Together?'

'Yes. Together, in friendship and honour and loyalty.' Harry lifted his head and searched the thin eager face. The dark eyes met his full, neither evading him nor lessening their intent stare. 'That's all I ask, Harry,' Richard said. 'Your total commitment to what I hope to achieve, your complete support and loyalty.'

'You can have that and gladly,' Harry answered him gravely. 'No man could grudge you that.'

Richard held his look. It should have been enough. With any other man it would have been enough, but he knew the loyalty that Harry promised, the same loyalty that he gave to Edward, keeping his oath to the very letter but giving nothing of himself. He wanted more than that — no shades of grey but the blinding white of pure faith. As he gave of himself, he expected no less of others.

He said, his voice low and barely audible, 'Then will you swear it, Harry? Publicly, a formal oath of loyalty binding us?'

Harry froze. Caution flooded over him and he recoiled instinctively, his eyes suddenly hard and wary. His mouth turned in its familiar sardonic smile. 'Why, my lord,' he said with cold mockery, 'you sound like a woman. Are you not content with love that you must have marriage as well?'

'That's not an answer,' Richard persisted grimly. 'Don't sidle away from me as you do from other men. Will you swear or no?'

Harry was silent. He knew quite well what Richard asked of him. He would be bound to this man for the rest of his life. It would mean the sacrifice of the freedom of thought and action he had been at such pains to preserve, it would mean the loss of his independence and the abandonment of his ambition. But it would

171

also mean peace, it would mean the end of the long hatred, at least the surface healing of the deep wound that had bled and festered for the past fifty years. A faint smile pulled at the corners of his mouth. Had he so very much to lose anyway? Would it be such loss to yield up a fragment of his wonderful liberty and acknowledge this man as lord? All men bowed to some great authority: he to Richard, Richard to the King and all of them eventually to God. Richard offered him trust and friendship, emotions that he had treated as he would some leprous disease and shunned for fear of contagion. Yet it was he who had become the leper, for if there was safety in isolation, there was pain and emptiness too.

He sighed deeply and in the letting out of that long breath went all the fears and restraints of his life. He lifted his eyes to Richard's face. 'So be it,' he said quietly. 'But I should warn you, my lord, that if you ever break faith, I would not lift a hand to save you from all the fires of Hell.'

It was done. His long sprawling signature bore down on Gloucester's neat round hand, the loops and tails twined like loving arms, the words like chains binding him. He read it through for the third time, skimming the lofty phrases that bound him in love and fealty to Gloucester. On the last clause his eyes lingered. 'And also the said Duke shall not accept nor retain into his service any servant that was or at any time since hath been, with the said Earl retained of fee or promise. Neither shall he ask, challenge, claim any office or fee that the said Earl hath of the King's grant, according to the appointment taken betwixt the said Duke and Earl by the King's highness and the lords of his council at Nottingham, the thirteenth day of May in the thirteenth year of the King's grace.'

Strangely, that last had been included by the King's decree, a reaffirmation of Richard's oath at Nottingham and so obvious a safeguard of Harry's interests that for one brief moment he had hesitated. But it had only been for a moment. The indenture was a mere formality. He had been Richard of Gloucester's man long before that and willingly, gladly, he had surrendered the freedom that had been none at all and for the first time in his life found

172

himself truly free. In the beginning, instinct had told him to tread carefully for this was all alien ground to him. But his heart and mind had gone beyond restraint, neither did he know how to measure out his love and faith. Like Richard himself, he either gave all or nothing at all. Outwardly he was still the same. He still maintained that cold air of reserve that kept men in awe of him, but now they did not mark his words and actions so carefully or speculate on where his favour lay. He was committed now. For good or ill, he was Richard of Gloucester's sworn man.

He rose and stretched himself. His limbs were stiff from sitting so long; three days in all spent in close council with the King, sanctioning his strategy for the war. Once more Gloucester's hopes of a summer campaign had been disappointed. Although Burgundy had been pinned down to a formal treaty, he was still committed to an earlier truce with France that extended till June of the next year. Besides, money as always was lacking. The grant that Parliament had voted the previous year had dwindled down to nothing. Grudgingly another subsidy was raised but even that was not enough. Edward had been forced to tout his charm among the merchants. He smiled, wheedled, bribed, and when all else failed he asked point-blank. None refused. Even when it came to parting men from their money, Edward had lost none of his appeal. Harry crossed to the window to set the shutters wide and heaved out of his lungs the smoke and constriction of the last week. A stream of chattering magpie clerks passed beneath him on their way to the hall. Richard would already be there, the peacemaker, for Clarence was out of favour again, though for what reason they could only conjecture. He would be watching the door, between soothing his brother Clarence's splenetic little outbursts, and more often than not, when Harry entered, he would rise and come to meet him, laying his hands possessively on Harry's sleeve as if to emphasise their new alliance.

Not that any needed the subtle reminder. All week the council had buzzed with it and Harry had smiled to see the Bishop of Durham, pale with dismay, remembering his past castigation of Gloucester. John Morton had merely smiled at him with heavy regret and swiftly transferred his interest to the Duke of Clarence. Others had reacted more strongly and Harry had soon discovered that he had taken on more than the Duke of Gloucester's cognizance. Richard's enemies were now his: Will Hastings, whom Richard particularly disliked as the perpetrator of Edward's loose morals; all the Woodvilles, especially the Queen and her two sons Exeter and Richard Grey.

There were new allies too: Frances, Lord Lovell, Richard's boyhood friend who had been raised with him at Middleham; the two sharp lawyers Richard Ratcliffe and William Catesby; John, Lord Howard, a man of less account than he himself would have liked and who was determined to amend it; young Harry Buckingham who drifted in and out of Richard's circle as mood and fancy took him. But none it seemed was as favoured as he. He fingered the heavy gold collar that lay on his breast — Richard's gift to him, a chain of Yorkist suns and roses and, suspended from a jewelled clasp, a white enamelled boar with glittering ruby eyes. Its weight was irksome, its associations more so. He thought suddenly of his father, a Lancastrian to his very last breath. For some reason, Henry Tudor's long reproachful face came into his mind. He heard the high thin voice prattling of honour and heritage. *'But Harry, your very blood is Lancastrian.'* And how had he answered him? That he thought it no dishonour to give allegiance to a Yorkist if the man himself was worthy. And Richard was worthy, he told himself fiercely, more so than poor Daft Harry had been, more even than either of his golden brothers. It was Richard Plantagenet and England that he served, not the House of York. Nevertheless before he left the room he loosed the chain from his neck and laid it down. He was not ready for collar and leash yet.

The English host lay sprawled along the banks of the Somme, a miniature city of canvas and silk sprung up round the walls of Amiens, where ten thousand bored and disillusioned men lounged and scratched and swatted flies and slept out the worst of the fierce August day. At night they got drunk on free French wine. The war was over. Not a blow had been struck. King Edward, like Judas, had sold them.

In the King's scarlet tent, Edward and his council thrashed out the final terms of treaty. The King himself had done particularly well: 'An outright gift of seventy-five thousand gold crowns, a yearly pension of a further fifty thousand secured by Medici bond, besides a seven-year agreement for trade and the marriage of the Princess Elizabeth of York to the Dauphin Charles, with a jointure of sixty thousand crowns a year . . .' Chancellor Rotherham enumerated the benefits of peace with rare enthusiasm, for Louis' generosity embraced them all. Even the chancellor himself was to receive a thousand crowns.

Harry sighed with undisguised boredom and watched with interest two flies copulating on George of Clarence's sleeve. Beside him the King lounged in his chair of estate; Hastings yawned; Lord Stanley fanned himself with a sheaf of parchments; and Anthony Woodville built himself a house of cards. For all of them this was the culmination of weeks of frustration and wasted effort. Since their landing at Calais at the beginning of July, disappointment had followed disappointment. For the first ten days they had kicked their heels in port, awaiting the forces of the Duke of Burgundy — and thus they had lost their first tactical advantage, for the French had been expecting them to land farther west and accordingly had massed their army there. Eventually Burgundy had deigned to show his face but with only fifty men at his back. Of the promised army there was no sign, and not likely to be before the end of the month as they were still pressing siege to a German fortress some two hundred miles away. More promises had followed, more excuses, each weaker than the last and eventually they had no choice but to march on into Burgundy's county of Champagne where again he had promised to join them. Bad weather had set in, two weeks of driving torrential rain that had slowed their army to a crawling pace and allowed the French king time to change his tactics and their tentative allies to change their minds. The Count of St Pol had been the first, and they had approached St Quentin confident of entry only to find the gates shut in their face and his guns turned full upon them. They had fallen back on Peronne and waited two days. The wet stormy July had passed into a blazing August and still there was no sign of Burgundy. It soon became clear that if they were to fight the French they would have to do so alone. By the end of August Edward had had enough and when

Louis made a tentative move towards peace, his envoys were welcomed with open arms. There were only two dissenters: the English commander Louis de Bretaylle who advocated war on principle; and Richard of Gloucester.

'God's teeth!'

Bishop Rotherham broke off and looked aggrieved as Gloucester sprang furiously to his feet. 'I never thought to see the day when the English were bought off like so many cheapjack merchants.'

Harry groaned inwardly. It was one of the more disturbing facets of Richard's personality, this stubborn persistence when no hope remained, like a dog worrying a long dead rabbit. Besides he was not wholly convinced by the righteous flush that stained his cheeks, though he truly believed that Richard was. It was a year since their pact at Nottingham and he knew Richard a great deal better now, better than most men who would never have believed that beneath that plain drab exterior there was a man who harboured an almost inordinate love of display, a sense almost of the theatrical, that could have him playing to the crowd as convincingly as either of his brothers. Yet this time Richard had misjudged his audience. His passionate words fell on deaf and closed ears. In desperation he appealed to Edward.

'Your Grace.' His dark eyes fastened pleadingly on his brother's face. 'Your Grace, I cannot believe that you will see us so dishonoured.'

Edward shifted uncomfortably in his chair and his heavy face was flushed with something more than wine. 'How is it dishonour?' he demanded irritably. 'It is Louis who sues for peace, not I.'

Richard stared at him in miserable silence and saw a plump, red-faced and indolent man. Where was Edward? he thought in sudden anguish. What was left of his adored golden brother in this coarse drunken wreck of a man who thought more of his ease than his honour?

'It's defeat,' he shouted. 'Wrap it up in fine words if you like, but it is still defeat, shameful and ignominious defeat, without even a blow being struck.'

John Morton intervened, obedient to the King's prompting

176

look. 'Force of arms is not always necessary to prove a point, your Grace. What says Holy Church? "Blessed is the peacemaker".' He smiled his narrow guarded smile. 'Apart from which we have very little choice.'

'We have every choice,' Richard argued. 'We have an army out there. Ten thousand men we have hauled all the way from England and we brought them to fight, not to sit in the sun and guzzle free French wine. I beg you to let them prove their worth, my lord. Can none of you see that by this treaty you make cowards of us all?'

'Such valour, your Grace,' Morton said with heavy sarcasm. 'It truly puts us all to shame. It is well that there are some amongst us who are older and wiser, who have a greater respect for life.'

Richard glared at him. 'Are you sure it is not King Louis's bribe you are more concerned with losing? Two thousand crowns, is it not? Not very much for a man's honour, though for myself, I think you overpaid.'

Morton's eyes grew hard but he continued to smile. 'You speak much of honour, your Grace. Most praiseworthy, I am sure, but shall we instead consider a few practicalities? Item. Burgundy has failed us disastrously, Brittany also. Without the support of their troops, the French are numerically superior to ourselves. Item. Stores and money are dwindling fast — as is time. Soon we shall be faced with the prospect of a winter campaign. On what shall we feed our men then, your Grace? Perhaps this honour that you speak so much about. Can you eat it? Can you burn it to keep our men warm and dry? Behind us, the French have already burnt Picardy and Artois. Ahead of us lies Rheims, fortified and garrisoned to the hilt, and King Louis lies only a few miles away with a great army at Compiègne.' The full mouth curved into an open sneer. 'And against such odds you would still have us fight, your Grace? For honour's sake?'

The strong voice ending on that high derisive note gave way to a deep and uneasy silence. Then Richard said, knowing himself defeated but unable to yield. 'Do I take it, then, that *all* are content to be Louis's paid men?' He looked earnestly around the assembled faces, searching desperately for a crumb of support. Hastings and the Woodvilles he hardly spared a glance, knowing them well and truly in Louis's pocket; Lord Stanley too, if it came to that — the Stanleys always went to the highest bidder. Morton had already said his piece and Bishop Rotherham gently shook his head to show that he had decided against him. Norfolk and Suffolk both stared bleakly to their feet. Even William Herbert, the young Earl of Pembroke who had made warlike noises throughout the campaign, was silent with the King's eye fixed firmly upon him. That only left Harry. Between them they might persuade the rest. Their joined voices would be too great to overlook. Apart from the forces of himself and his brothers, Northumberland's was the greatest.

'Well, my lords,' he cried, his eyes on Harry, 'give me yea or nay. Are you all content?' Harry looked up into Richard's face, stark and sickly with the pallor of rage. For the first time in his life he felt the dragging weight of friendship. He knew what was expected of him. Whatever their differences of opinion in private, publicly Gloucester expected his support. That was what loyalty meant to Richard, turning a blind eye to an obvious fault, backing a man when you knew he was wrong. And Richard *was* wrong. At the heart of them they both knew it.

His silence was answer enough and Richard looked away. He said, rage and disappointment thinning his voice to a whisper. 'Very well then, my lords. Do as you think but I will have no part in it. When Parliament demands to know who set their names to this deed, mine, thank God, shall not be among them.'

John Morton watched him go and pursed his lips in admiration. He smiled cynically at Thomas, Lord Stanley. 'Magnificent,' he said. 'Truly magnificent. But the man's a fool for all that.'

Harry found Richard sulking alone in his tent. Gloucester glared at him in bitter accusation. 'I take it, then, that you have thrown in your lot with the peacemakers.'

'I have,' Harry answered him shortly and poured himself a generous measure of King Louis's superb wine.

'And how much was it that Louis offered you, Harry? I have forgotten. More than thirty pieces of silver, I trust.'

'Oh, much more,' Harry said, unoffended, for they had passed to that easy stage in their friendship where insult could be offered and no hurt taken. 'Is that what irks you, Richard? Did Louis not offer you enough?'

Richard leapt angrily to his feet. 'I wouldn't touch a groat of his filthy money and neither would you if you had an ounce of conscience. I had thought of all men I could depend on you.'

The smile faded from Harry's eyes. 'Depend on me for what?' he demanded bluntly. 'You knew very well my mind in this. Did you expect me to change it just to please you? This whole venture has been a travesty from start to finish. It should never have been begun and you know full well that to pursue it further would be madness. At least Morton was right in that. Better honour lost than countless lives.'

'All right then,' Richard yelled. 'If we are so outnumbered and outmanoeuvred, why is Louis so anxious to buy us off?'

'Because Louis is a practical man and for one thing it is cheaper to pay us to go home than to keep a standing army in the field. Louis has learned as we should have learned that there is no long-term profit in war.'

'Profit! Is that all that matters? What of honour and right? What of all those good people at home whose money we took? What of all those men out there who've been cheated?'

'Cheated!' Harry threw him a pitying glance. 'Cheated of what? Raping and plundering and whatever they could steal or scrounge? You speak as if profit were some obscenity. Why do you think all these men are here? Just for the joy of getting themselves cut to bits? They came because they were paid to, because they had to.' He smiled maliciously. 'I think it is you who feel cheated, Richard, my lord — of your little piece of glory, of being able to ride home with your name on every man's lips as you did after Tewkesbury.'

It was near enough the truth for Richard to flush. He did not deny it. He did feel cheated. His dreams of glorious conquest had become a nightmare of compromise, and worse, he had lost his pride in Edward. It was more the perfect illusion of his brother that he could not relinquish; to have to admit that his great golden idol had feet of clay was almost more than he could bear.

He turned away and struck his fist into his open palm. 'You

179

don't understand, Harry. None of you understand.' He began to pace the dirt floor with swift angry strides. 'None of you can see beyond the moment. This will lose us all credence in the eyes of the world. And how will we answer them at home when they question this betrayal? We gave them our word. We took their money and promised them victory and we're bringing them shame instead. We haven't even tried to win! De Bretraylle has the right of it. He said that of the nine victories Edward has won, this one defeat will outweigh them all. And it's true, Harry. People only ever remember the bad things.'

He had halted in his pacing and now looked at Harry in mute despair. Such a long and extravagant speech from one who was usually so sparing with his words. A faintly resentful look hardened his eyes. Sometimes he longed to break out of the dull reserved image that he showed to the world. He knew men sneered at him for it: his sincere piety, the rigid moral code that made him seem prudish, the slavish adherence to conscience that made him seem inflexible and stubborn. They thought him dull and mediocre and yet he was neither — only in comparison with his brothers did he seem so. The look of resentment deepened. All his life had been a comparison with his brothers. Once he had wanted desperately to be like them, till he had realised that, outwardly at least, he never could be. So he had never competed and any bitterness he had felt at being outdone and outgrown he had smothered with blind worship and loyalty. If he wore plain fustian when his heart yearned for cloth of gold, it was because he could not bear the comparison of his thin spare limbs with the formidable stature of his brothers. And because he fell so far short physically, morally and spiritually he had to be perfect. This capitulation was a stain on that perfection. However he tried to gloss it over it was still defeat, worse, it was craven and dishonourable surrender.

He shook his head blindly, 'You don't understand,' he said again.

'I understand your anger and disappointment, my lord,' Harry said, 'but I don't understand your refusal to accept what cannot be changed. It's all over. In two days we are to meet with King Louis and his envoys at Picquigny to sign the final peace.'

'Then you'll go without me,' Richard said sullenly. 'I'll not lend my presence to such a charade.'

Harry sighed. 'Richard, my lord. Whether you come or not, it will change nothing. Why in Heaven's name persist now?'

'Because I can't compromise,' Richard shouted furiously. 'I have more thought for honour.'

'And neither can I,' Harry answered him coldly. 'Not even for you will I perjure my conscience, and to pursue this war and sanction the needless sacrifice of even one life, just to appease your pride and the pockets of your merchant friends, would be an affront to *my* honour.'

Richard kept his eyes averted to the far wall of the tent. 'I'm sorry, Harry,' he said stiffly, 'but I'll not change my mind. I don't know whether it is a fault or a virtue, but once I have chosen my road I can't turn back.'

'Even if the road leads nowhere?'

'All roads lead somewhere, Harry — if only to Hell.'

'As this one surely does. And at the heart of it, you know it, Richard. You're too good a soldier not to know it.'

'And what would you know about strategy?' Richard snapped. 'You've never fought a man in earnest in all of your life.'

'Perhaps not,' Harry said quietly. 'But that is not to say I do not know how to defeat my enemies.'

'Oh yes. I know the way that you fight, Harry. A smile on your face and a knife in their back — the same kind of weapon that Louis would use.'

'But King Louis has never lost a fight,' Harry pointed out. He added in his soft threatening voice, 'And neither have I.'

Richard held the faintly intimidating look for a moment then turned away. He was bitterly disappointed, in Harry, in Edward. The world seemed to be full of men with easy and corrupt morals who swore their oaths and made their promises, and somehow still managed to go their own way. As always, it seemed he had expected too much.

'Sometimes, you know, Harry,' he said sulkily, 'it's hard to know where your true loyalty lies. I could on occasion, be forgiven for wondering whether you are for me or against me.'

'Sometimes, my lord, it is more necessary to protect you

against yourself than against other men.'

'As well I know, then, for no other man would.' Richard turned and glanced almost with hatred into Harry's faintly smiling eyes. He was suddenly consumed with a childish urge to hurt, to find fault. He said critically, 'The gold collar I gave you. You never wear it?'

'No, my lord. I never wear it.'

'Why not? Are you regretting our pact already? It's not as if you were averse to ornament, is it, my lord? That diamond in your collar would choke an ox.'

Harry walked away from him and stood for a moment staring out into the blazing day. 'Richard, my lord,' he said quietly, 'I am your man until the end of my life, but I am not a dog to be collared and leashed.'

'You think I treat you like one, then?'

Harry turned to look at him. 'No. But I think you require a like fidelity.'

'And why not? There are no degrees of love and loyalty, any more than there are of truth. There are no half loyalties or quarter loyalties. There is only complete and total loyalty, the kind that I give to my brother Edward and England, the kind that I give to you. Do you not think I am entitled to the same in return?'

'And you think by wearing the white boar around my neck it will make me the more loyal?'

'It will make me believe that you are.'

Harry smiled, a faint deprecating smile that brought a flush to Richard's ashen cheeks. 'Very well, my lord. If it pleases you, I will wear it.'

Harry stood with his arms raised as Gascoigne stripped him deftly of his armour. Beneath the heavy breast-plate and coat of mail his flesh boiled at furnace heat and within minutes of the soaked undershirt being peeled from his back, his skin was sheened again with sweat.

He swore viciously and flung the brass-knuckled gauntlets to the far end of the tent. This was all part of the continuing charade of war, that had had himself and nigh on eleven thousand men boiling their brains out in the midday sun. At noon the two kings had met at Picquigny — Edward resplendent in black velvet and diamonds, Louis gowned like a dowdy clerk — and as a sop to the pride of both English and French, the two armies had been drawn up in full battle array on either side of the river. Harry had stood on the bridge with Edward as proxy for the Duke of Gloucester. Richard had been as good as his word. Despite the pleading of both the King and council, from Picquigny he had stayed away.

Stripped to the waist Harry went out into the sun. Outside he paused, narrowing his eyes against the blinding glare. A man rode past him and Harry raised his hand to acknowledge the brief murmured greeting. That was the sum total of his acquaintance with John now, a nod, a brief salute exchanged in passing. He was content to have it so. John still made him feel uneasy, perhaps because only John ever recalled Eleanor to his mind and Eleanor in turn reminded him of Maud. To give the boy his due, he'd done well for himself, without Eleanor, without him. He was esquire of the body to Gloucester himself now and with dogged determination he pursued his knighthood. Never once had he even attempted to make capital out of their kinship. In fact, very few men even knew they were cousins. John kept his distance in that respect. He was always polite, always courteous — always there.

Harry moved away and entered the dusty labyrinth of tents and pavilions. Flies massed over islands of dung and rose in buzzing clouds beneath his feet. The stench of sour and rotting meat filled the air and all around, sleeping drunken men littered the ground, huddled beneath wagons and carts for shade.

He passed the great guns shrouded in canvas, the mountains of shot that would never be used. For a moment he felt much of Gloucester's anger and disgust. All that money and effort — for nothing.

Then he halted as a man emerged from a tent and called to him. William Herbert advanced shyly upon him, his pleasant vacuous face creased in an uncertain smile. Harry sighed. He had been unconsciously avoiding this encounter since the beginning of the campaign. Even now, two years on, he still flinched from so strong a reminder of Maud.

'Harry.' William fell in beside him as he turned and walked down to the river. 'It's hot, isn't it?' he said.

183

'Very.'

'They say you can boil water on the stones up by the town.'

'Do they?' Harry knelt by the water's edge and sluiced his face and neck. A fish emerged from a cloud of weed and regarded him with a pale cold eye.

'Well. It's all over, then.' William dropped on his haunches beside him and skimmed a stone toward the far bank. He glanced uneasily at Harry, who continued to pour water over himself. He never quite knew with Harry whether he was welcome or not. He found silence unnerving at the best of times, and Harry's silences especially so.

He began to speak in his high facile voice. 'A complete waste of time and money, if you ask me,' he pronounced gloomily. 'And mark me, there'll be trouble later on when Parliament wants to know what we have done with their money. The commons won't take too kindly to it either. Some of my men are turning quite nasty, thinking I'm going home a rich man.' He gave a shrill laugh. 'A thousand crowns sounds all very well but it's barely enough to cover expenses. I had a new set of armour made that cost almost the half of that.'

He flung another stone into the dark water. 'Besides, I could well have done with staying at home. My wife is near her time with child.' He looked up at Harry who sat with his hair steaming dry in the sun. 'She lost the last two, you know. Both boys.' He frowned, pondering silently on his own private grievance. In more ways than one his wife Mary had proved a disappointment. Being brother-in-law to the King should have counted for something, yet he was very much aware that there was a move afoot to oust him from his earldom of Pembroke and bestow it on the King's son, the Prince of Wales. He glanced again at Harry Percy's dark face, wondering if he could approach him as an ally.

Then Harry said, gratifyingly recalling their past connection, 'And how is your lady mother?'

'Oh well, quite well. Though she is given to an unhealthy amount of prayer and meditation of late. She still grieves over much for my father.'

Harry picked up a fallen shaft and inspected its perfectly set flight feathers. 'And your sisters?'

William grinned. 'Still outnumbering me,' he said. 'Only two wed so far, though Grey of Ruthin is to relieve me of another next year.'

The shaft snapped between Harry's clenched fingers. 'Which one?'

William glanced at him, surprised to hear his voice so harsh and strained. 'Anne. Do you remember Anne? Small and dark and pretty.'

'Yes. I remember Anne.' Harry flung the broken arrowhead away from him. He watched it float swiftly downstream, then he said, 'And the Lady Maud, your eldest sister?'

William glanced at him uneasily. He had never quite fathomed the reason for Maud's abrupt return home. 'No,' he said hesitantly. 'Maud is not wed yet, though she's had offers — Rhys ap Thomas, Lord of Ardudwy . . .'

Harry stared blankly downstream. They were already dismantling the makeshift bridge at Picquigny. And when the sun had cooled they would begin to fold the tents and load the wagons. Tonight they would eat and drink themselves sick at Louis's expense, tomorrow they would start for home; William for Wales and himself for the north . . .

'William,' he said slowly. 'Would you mind very much if I came with you to Wales?'

Pembroke

> The men who went to Catraeth were famous,
> wine and mead from gold was their drink
> for a year, according to honoured custom,
> three hundred and sixty-three gold-collared men.
> Of those who met over flowing drink
> only three escaped from the fury of battle,
> Aeron's two wardogs and Cynon came back,
> and I from my bleeding for my song's sake.

The young boy's voice filled all of the hall with the immortal words of Y Gododdin — like a raw March wind, the old bard thought, loud and harsh and gusty. Gwilym Ddu sighed and chewed on his beard. He was old and blind now, and like all old men his mind was fixed eternally in the past, when both he and the world had been young. And a better world it had been too, he thought fiercely, when upstart boys had known their place and poets had been venerated like gods. He scowled malevolently in the direction of the youth. This one now, no better than a *beirad yspyddied*; cheap rhymsters with reedy voices and vulgar songs and no respect for their art or their elders. He thought back longingly to the old lord's time. He'd known the hall crammed with over a thousand men, real men too who could hold their drink and their tongues and didn't fidget and chatter throughout the songs. Not that these young ones could have held a pig in thrall. They sang the words and played the notes and all they made was a noise. Yet when *he* played, when *he* sang, it was a woman weeping, a child laughing, an eagle soaring over the frozen wastes of Snowdon, a stream bubbling down from the Brecon hills . . . He winced as the boy's voice screeched to an impossible note.

'Soft, soft,' he screamed. 'Like a woman's flesh. You sound like a hen being slaughtered.'

Wearily he motioned for the boy to begin again. He would have this perfect for the young lord's homecoming. He doubted that the Lord William himself would care. But there would be men there that would: Rhys ap Thomas, Lord of Ardudwy and Evionydd, Richard ap Howell of Mostyn, true Welshmen who'd know a fumbled note if they heard one.

A feeling of elation stirred his tired blood. It would be almost like the old days: the men coming home, war-weary and calling for mead and the great intoxication of hearing their names and deeds exalted in song. Then his face fell. Only old men drank the blue mead now, and what was there to celebrate in this last pitiful campaign, unless it was who'd squeezed the most gold from King Louis? Again, he sighed loudly, an old man's sigh of regret and discontent. He remembered all the great halls he'd sung in: Harlech, Caer ny Arvon, and once, as a boy, before Prince Owain Glendwyr at Glyndyrrdwy. Men had listened then, revering the past. They'd seen as clearly as he the images born on his breast. The notes of the harp drawing the sharp definitive lines, his voice adding brilliance and colour. So Arthur had walked in this very hall and here, at least a hundred times, Culhwch had vanquished the giant Ysbaddaden. Tears pricked at his blind empty eyes. He could still hear the rapturous applause. He still cherished the princely gifts: from Glendwyr, a clasp of beryl and amethyst; from his old lord and patron Margoah Glas, a chalice set with pearls. And there could have been more, so very much more if he'd had the desire and ambition. Once he'd dreamt of being *pencerdd* to some princely house, even aspiring to the chair of Maelgwn Hir. But somehow the dream had always eluded him, like all the dreams of the Welsh. All the great houses were fallen, all the great voices stilled: Llywarch the old and Einiawn Wan, Aneirin, the ancient warrior bard whose stirring englyns now filled his ears:

> *Men went to Catraeth in a band, with a shout,*
> *with the power of horses and trappings and shields,*
> *with shafts held ready and pointed spears,*
> *with gleaming armour and with swords.*
> *He led, he cut through armies,*
> *five fifties fell before his blades:*
> *Rhufawn Hir gave gold to the altar*
> *and a reward and a fair gift to the singer.*

He squirmed as the boy's flat voice rendered the Gododdin's bloody sacrifice meaningless, and more, he hadn't even got it right. *Annwyl Crist*, but they couldn't even remember the words these days, whereas he had known all of the *Red Book of Hergest* before his eleventh year.

He rapped his staff sharply against the wall. The boy broke off and regarded him fearfully, awaiting the usual farrago of criticism. It never came. Instead the old man waved him wearily away. 'Go now. We will try again tomorrow.'

He sat alone in his world of sound. He heard the sigh of deep water against the walls, the whine of a dog fretting in the heat. All sound was music, music was life, from the first strident staccato notes of youth to the soft lingering chords of old age. To him, the only true silence was death and while there was still the smallest

187

whisper to be heard, the rhythm of his life would go on. He had never regretted even the loss of his eyes. The vision of the mind was infinite, the soul of the poet knew no earthly bounds. With the eye of long memory he could see all of Dyffed: the grey straggling village below Maenor Pyrr where he had been born, the soft sleepy grasslands and secret woods, the ragged sea coast torn by pockets of shining water — sea sheen and storm shadow, the grey shoreless cliffs haunted by the curlew's song. And at his back, the bluestone peaks of Mynedd Prescilli where the rivers of Dyffed sprung thickly as the hairs on a giant's head and the true Welsh waited for Arthur to come again. As he surely would. That most fervently he did believe. Had it not been foretold since earliest times? By the prophet and poet, the great Taliesin, by the prince magician Meryddin. Was he not *awenyddion* himself, and not one of those who conjured their visions from mead and mushroom? His was the true sight.

He struck a discord: '. . . And the Britons then shall have their land and their crown, and the stranger swarm shall vanish away . . .'

And nearer his own time: 'Jasper will build for us a dragon. Of the fortunate blood of Brutus he . . .' Only there did his voice lose its firm conviction: *the Tudor cub?* It was he that men spoke of now in fervent whispers, men perhaps who had not known him, Gwilym Ddu thought cynically. He had, and it was hard to reconcile that whey-faced skinny youth with the reincarnation of Arthur. He strained his mind for a better recollection of the boy. Close-faced and close-fisted as he remembered and he doubted that manhood would have much changed him. Still, he shrugged. *Ar Dduw y Gyd* — the best wine sometimes came in the strangest vessels.

He heaved himself up, shifting his chair to catch the last of the sun. Like an old blind hound he lifted his head and sniffed the air. The wind blew up from the salt marshes, sharp and clean and smelling of brine. The haven would be at full ebb now, draining the little creeks and inlets to hollows of shining mud. He heard the raucous calling of scavenging gulls and, faint and far, the bell of the saint's oratory on Mynacchlog Ddw.

Maud would be here soon. His little girl, his *Blodeuedd*. He smiled foolishly at his fanciful name for her. *Blodeuedd* — flower face, the woman that the magician Gwydyon had made from wild blossoms.

He stroked a sweet sad note from the harp: 'From primrose of the mountain, from broom, meadowsweet and cockle . . .'

Sometimes he fancied himself as another Gwydyon, in a symbolic and more earthly way. He felt he'd more than a hand in her making. Her peerless voice had been shaped by him. It was he who had bred in her the love of Wales. He had taught her the old ways, the old faith and the old songs and everything that was good and beautiful in him he had seen born again in her. She was the child of his spirit, unchanging, ageless, forever young, for his last sight of her had been as a child before she had left him and gone to the north and come back with that sadness upon her. He knew that sadness, that stillness of the heart — there had been a girl once in Aber . . .

His head drooped and for a while he dreamt of love, long past. Then he heard a light footfall at the door, the sigh of a woman's skirts upon the floor. He lifted his head. She was tired. He knew from her slow dragging step, and her voice when she spoke was weary.

'God greet you, *pencerdd*.' Maud set the pitcher of mead beside him and dropped a kiss on his withered cheek.

The old man smiled, loving her, knowing that she probably only came out of pity but grateful all the same. She had never failed him, except for that time when she had been in the north. Every evening she came to him, in the old days to listen and learn his skills, now just to please him.

He drank deeply of the strong metheglyn and licked the droplets of honey from his beard. 'Is it a fine evening?' he asked, more for the pleasure of hearing her voice than for any need to know.

'Yes.' She moved away from him and stood by the window. 'The swallows have gone,' she said sadly. 'The sky seems empty without them.'

'It is their time,' Gwilym Ddu said. 'They will return.'

Maud stared out into the sun-drenched stillness of the valley. Yes. They would come back — as Harry would one day.

189

Gwilym Ddu said, 'Is all ready for the lord's homecoming?'

She nodded and then remembered that he could not see the gesture. 'Yes. All is ready, *pencerdd*.' That morning alone the slaughterers had split a thousand carcasses and hacked the heads off twice as many fowl. Now they all hung from their heels in the great stone kitchen: boar and venison, mutton and beef; a monstrous flight of plucked and naked birds.

Gwilym Ddu nodded in approval. 'It will be a goodly feast, like in the old days. Your grandfather Margoah Glas feasted King Henry of Monmouth here and I remember . . .'

What it was that he remembered she did not hear. Her mind drifted away from him. She thought of mundane and trivial things, like the tear in her sister Cecily's best gown; the rancid stench that drifted up from the slaughterhouse — they would need more sweeteners for the hall.

From the chamber below she heard a child's faint cry; the weak and puny infant son that William's wife had brought forth. It would not live, she thought sadly. Its mother knew it too, and her life seemed to wane with the child. Perhaps the sight of William would cheer her. Only a week now and he would be home from France. She felt her own spirits lift a little. Entwined with the pleasure of seeing her brother again was the hope that he might bring word of Harry. It was two years since she had seen him — a long time, but not long enough. She still loved him, her love intensified by dreams, undiminished by his absence. He would come after her, she still believed that; when he had overcome his fear of loving, when his need for her became too great. The belief was part of her now, never questioned, never doubted. It was all that made life bearable. Sometimes the waiting was hard, when Rhys ap Thomas leant close and lovingly touched her hand, when she saw her sisters flushed and happy with their children and husbands. It always passed. She would think of Harry's eyes; she would remember the feel of his hands upon her flesh, his voice . . .

She turned. The old man was speaking, 'Rhys ap Thomas will be at the feast. This time he will expect answers.'

'And I shall give him answer,' Maud said calmly, 'as I did before. No. I will not marry him.'

She moved away from the window and came to sit at the old man's feet.

'There is still this other then? In the north?'

Unconsciously Maud glanced towards the little niche where the old bard's treasures were housed. Arawn smiled savagely at her out of the dark wood. Yes. There was still this other. She had never named him but sometimes she thought the old man knew, as he knew so many things.

'Rhys ap Thomas is a fine young man,' Gwilym Ddu said loudly. 'And Welsh.'

Maud smiled. 'Yes, I know. You've told me before — and so has he. But I'll still not marry him.'

The old man scowled. 'You're a fool, girl,' he said harshly. 'Waiting and wasting for some worthless *lloegyr*. You don't know gold when you see it, girl. What you're hankering for is only the dross.'

'*Pencerdd*, did you not once tell me that all our lives are written even before we are conceived? That we think we make choices but in truth the choosing is already done?'

'I did — and it's true, but . . .'

'Then what does it matter? What will come, will come and the two of us quarrelling will not alter it.'

'Yes, child.' The old man sighed and laid his hand gently upon her head. 'You are right. The pattern is already laid. The gods have already made up their minds which of us is to live or die.'

That night the sight came to him after long barren years. It came in the guise of nightmare, vivid, hideous, so that he awoke with a fearful scream. It was dark and quiet. He could hear nothing but his own whimpering breath. It was the silence that frightened him most, for even at night he had never known the world to be truly still. There was always noise — the sigh of wind and water, the calling of night birds . . . He sat up, truly blind, for only from the outside sounds could he tell whether it was day or night.

He breathed deeply to still the pounding of his heart. The vision was still strong upon him, a blur of half-forgotten colours and shapes; a strange cacophony of distorted sound, as if every song he had ever sung had given tongue at once. The confusion of

191

images came again into his mind, half-seen, half-understood: a riderless horse, a headless man, a harp with broken useless strings that he thought for some reason was himself. In recall the vision grew frighteningly clear. He saw the red dragon, y Ddraig Goch, embattled with the white boar, Ysgithyrwyn. There was blood, much blood, but strangely it was the blood of neither beast. He saw a man, a known yet unknown face. His eyes were closed, as if he slept or was blind and though the boar and the dragon raged at his back he did not turn his head. A woman came from the shadows; the man held out his hands. Gwilym Ddu's heart leapt. His girl, his little girl — but never as he had seen her. She was naked, her breasts heavy with milk, her belly swollen grotesquely with child. The man called to her and the old man wept to hear his voice, so achingly beautiful, like the Birds of Rhiannon, soft and sweet and deadly. Then the boar screamed, a sound like all the demons of Hell and at last the man opened his eyes. Ysgithyrwyn was slain, his blood a thin trickle that swelled suddenly to a dark ugly flood. The man did not move, even when the fierce torrent roared toward him, he did not move.

Gwilym Ddu cried out as the awful redness overwhelmed him. Horror distended the sockets of his eyes. He strained his mind beyond the red roaring mist. Where was his girl? Oh, *Annwyl Crist*, where was his dear girl?

The day was warm and still, luminous with water and reflected sun. Beside the mill pool, where the great keep flung its long perfect image, Maud lay, one hand supporting her chin, and watched the mirrored clouds.

She was waiting for Harry, with the same quiet certainty that she had waited out the last two years. He would come. He knew the place, the bower of reeds walled in by green willows. It was where she had always come with her secrets.

She smiled rapturously and relived for the hundredth time the few precious hours that had passed since last night. It had been almost dark when he had come. From the roof of the gatehouse she had seen the great cortège enter the town, men and horses and wagons, lanterns bobbing like the flies that danced on the marsh at night. She had run down to the courtyard, pleased and happy to see her brother home. William had swung her up to his saddle bow and kissed her — and when he had set her down, she had seen over his shoulder the face she had seen every night in her dreams since she was ten years old. Harry had come back as she had always known he would.

He had bent to kiss her, a brief formal kiss, his mouth barely brushing her cheek. But she had seen the sudden softening of his eyes, she had felt his hands tighten on her arm . . . Then William had thrust himself between them, dear sweet silly William, giggling and chattering like a schoolboy, dragging Harry off to see his hawks and hounds; sitting between them at table, kneeling between them at mass so that all that could pass between them were occasional smiles and glances. This morning he had taken Harry off to hunt in the woods above the Cleddau.

She sighed impatiently and smoothed the bodice of the green silk gown that had once belonged to her sister Margaret. A little breeze had sprung up and lifted the fall of crimson hair from her back. The river seethed against the high stone dam, the mill wheel threw up a rainbow arc. From an island of reeds a flight of plovers rose into the air. She watched their graceful soaring flight and then she saw him, leaning on the bridge that spanned the mill-race. Her heart quickened, echoing the slap and thunder of the great churning wheel.

As if she had called to him, he came towards her. She watched him, as she had watched him so many times before, unashamed of the pleasure that it gave her. The sun gleamed on the fierce bronzed bones of his face, the wind rustled his soft dark hair.

He stood looking down at her, grave and unsmiling. 'So,' he said at last. 'This is where you are hiding.'

The beautiful voice reached out and touched her, almost like a physical caress. She smiled. 'But not from you, Harry. Come.' She beckoned to him. 'Sit with me for a while. It is cool here.'

He stooped beneath the trailing willows and dropped down in the grass beside her. The sleeves of his tunic were splashed with mud and one hand was scratched and bloody. She reached out and touched him. 'You're hurt,' she said with quick concern.

'No. It's nothing.' He withdrew his hand quickly. Just the light

193

brushing of her fingertips against him and he was suddenly weak with longing.

She felt his sudden tenseness and looked away. 'Did you kill?' she asked lightly.

'No. We chased a stag as far as Slebech but lost him.'

She nodded and for a while they were quiet, watching a pair of swans flirt and preen on the far side of the river. Then suddenly Harry said, 'Why did you leave?'

She did not answer him at once. The cob swan plunged beneath the water and emerged in a shower of diamond drops. She said at last, 'Because I was unhappy and frightened. Because hatred is such an ugly contagious thing. I did not want to become infected.' She looked at him. 'I did not want to become like you, Harry.'

He flinched at her cruel honesty. 'Did you dislike me so much then?'

'I disliked what you were; what you thought you were.'

'And now?' He was appalled to hear the almost pleading note in his voice.

'You've changed, Harry.' She smiled at him tenderly. 'You would not be here if you had not.'

A fraught little silence fell between them, like the pause before a song reached its crescendo. She said, 'What happened to John? Did he ever come back?'

'No. He didn't come back. I think he rather despised us too. He serves the Duke of Gloucester now. He seems very content.'

'I'm glad.' She laughed softly. 'You know, I was beginning to think I was fated. All my intended husbands taking to their heels; first Henry and then John . . .'

'It doesn't look like Rhys ap Thomas is going to take to his heels though,' Harry commented grimly.

Maud looked out across the shining water, aware of his dark dishevelled head and his brilliant eyes upon her. 'You think I should marry Rhys then?'

'No.' There was only the slightest tremor in his voice. 'No. I don't.'

'William does.' She spoke lightly though her heart was beating fit to burst. 'He says I'll not get a better offer.'

'You might.'

She did not look at him but she thought that he was smiling. 'Who from, Harry?' she asked softly.

'Me.'

She turned to look at him then. How strange to see him unsure of himself. The light mocking smile clung to his mouth but his eyes were bleak and full of doubt. He looked very young, very vulnerable, like a child eying a longed-for treat that he expected to see snatched away.

'Harry.' She reached out and touched his mouth very softly with her fingertips.

He closed his eyes and beneath the thick dark lashes she saw the glint of tears. Then he pulled her down beside him. She felt the hard stretched agony of his body that stripped the smile from his mouth and twisted it in pain and longing. He bent his head and kissed her and the reality of him was even sweeter than the dream.

She clung to him with eagerness and passion, moving softly against him till the ache of his body for hers was more than he could bear.

'Say it, *cariad*,' she whispered. 'Or are you still afraid?'

He lifted his head and looked down at her. He felt strangely tired and breathless as if he had come some great distance, as if he had surmounted some gigantic obstacle that had stood for a long time in his way. 'No. I'm not afraid. As long as you are with me I am not afraid.' He stooped his head again to kiss her. 'My love,' he said. 'The very first and the very last.'

The old man's voice, still sweet and clear as a young boy's, held the long note without tremor, and long before its echo had died away, the applause broke, loud and tumultuous, beating up the proud colour into his withered cheeks.

He rose, an impressive and barbaric figure, his hair and beard combed to silver sleekness, a torque of red gold clasping his throat. He wore the sacred scarlet robe of his guild and on his hand, the ring of the Prince of Abberfraw. Regretfully he laid his harp aside in spite of the avid cries for more. Such could never be repeated. He was drained, his throat was hot and dry as sand, his heart still pounding like the sea wave, his spirit still riding with

195

Hywell ap Owain Gwynned along the shore of Aber Menai:

> *A white wave, splendid in attack, foams over me*
> *Coloured like hoar frost in the hour of its advance,*
> *I love the sea coast of Meirionnydd,*
> *Where a white arm was my pillow.*
> *I love the nightingale of the wood,*
> *Where two waters meet in that sweet valley. . . .*

The *menestr* knelt and offered him the cup of praise and he drank till his lips touched the hard edge of gold coin. He thought how once they had brushed the roundness of pearls; once it had been nothing to find a fair jewel in the cup. He felt his elation slipping away and called to his boy for mead. The honied fire sweetened him again and he smiled at the boy who had been his eyes for the night and told him the little that his ears could not. Thus he knew the name of every man in the hall, thus he knew every dish that had been served to the high table: a boar's head planted with lozenges of gold; great haunches of venison and roasts of beef; schools of pike and sturgeon swimming in pepper sauce; and a sugar subtlety of St Dewi confronting the heretic Pelagius — a most wonderful thing, the boy had said, with the saint's mitre and cope set with seed pearls.

He himself had eaten little, a brace of small and succulent fowl, a dish of wardens and figs. Prudently he had left the figs. All knew that figs bred lice and stirred up lust as well as playing havoc with the bowel. He sighed pleasurably. Yes, truly it was a goodly feast. He had not seen it surpassed in his time.

And his little girl was happy again. Once more he heard her joyous laughter ring out and his blank lofty gaze swept across the hall and fastened on the sound. Her joy was his sorrow for she was lost to him now. Soon she would be gone, with her *seisin* lord, the man who had come home with the young Lord William; this man Northumberland, he was the one. And no stranger as he once had thought. Harry Percy he had known and had known again the minute he had heard his voice, that unmistakable and enviable voice — and heard lately, though he could not remember where. The man himself was as hard to recall, a face that hovered in shadow on the threshold of his mind and refused to be drawn through the door.

He tapped the shoulder of the boy at his feet. 'This man Northumberland — show me his likeness. And all, mind,' he added, knowing the boy's tendency to skimp. 'Leave nothing out.'

The picture grew, building before his inner eye. Tall and dark, sharp featured and strong limbed. Yes, yes, he had him now. Quite clearly he remembered him, in the hall of the Yellow Tower at Raglan playing chess with Henry Tudor. He had sung the *marwnad* for Black William that day and he recalled with unabated fury how they had chattered all the way through. From the English he did not expect respect but young Tudor at least should have known better.

He frowned, drawing his thick white brows together. Yes, all was clearly seen now with his inner eye. He had seen Harry Percy only once more, in the company of the young Duke of Gloucester who had come to escort him home. He remembered him too: small and dark, looking sour and spent as a man of fifty though he could not have been a day older than seventeen. Rhys ap Thomas had mocked him, sniggering at his thin broomstraw limbs and narrow chest emblazoned with his cognizance of the white boar. They had laughed outright at that, such a fierce emblem for such a puny lord.

His hands tightened convulsively upon the arms of his chair. The boar, the white boar — Ysgithrwyn! The dream rushed in upon him and drove out his breath. The boar, the dragon, the sleepwalking man; he knew the man now, he knew his voice. His shoulders slumped as he saw past the darkness of his bleached sightless eyes. Yes. All was clear now. He had heard the man with the voice like the Birds of Rhiannon; he had seen the white boar Ysgithyrwyn.

1481—1482

The boar shall be extolled in the mouths of
the people and its deeds shall be meat and
drink to those who tell tales
                                        Prophecy of Merlin

It was nine years since they had met, nine years that had so changed and shaped them that they met now almost as strangers. Eleanor stared at him resentfully.

'So. John Egremont — *Sir* John Egremont. It's a fine knight you have made of yourself, then?'

It was said derisively and even after all these years he found her voice could wither his self-esteem. He fended her off in the only way he knew how. 'Yes,' he said, aggressivley thrusting out his jaw. 'It's a fine knight I've made of myself — without you, without Harry.'

'Then why have you come, John?' she said coolly. 'What is it that you want that you cannot do alone?'

She stared at him almost with dislike. He had coarsened, grown heavy and brutish and though the dark sleek beard aged him and narrowed his face, it could not conceal the massive jaw and the full sensual lips. She thought sadly that there was nothing left of the boy she had loved, there was nothing left of Thomas.

He came and sat beside her. He wore a doublet of gaudy yellow satin — there was a wine stain on the sleeve where he had wiped his mouth. His hands resting on his powerful silk-clad thighs were large and red, the nails broken and rimmed with dirt; a peasant's hands, she thought, for all that he was a knight.

She looked down at her own hands, pale and veined.

'Whatever it is, I fear you will go away empty-handed. As you can see, much has changed.'

Looking at him, she wondered exactly what he did see: an old woman, painfully thin, a papering of shrivelled yellow skin over sharp hungry bones. She fasted rigorously now; a dish of broth, a few crumbs of bread, a half cup of weak and watered wine, these were her staple diet now. Only on feast days did she ever eat meat. She had no servants except for her steward and his wife; her only companion was old Dame Widdrington. She gave generously in alms, two-thirds of her income, and all her furs and jewels she had given away. All she possessed now were two gowns of plain woollen cloth and beneath these she wore a coarse hempen shift that chafed constantly at her flesh. Yet she was stronger now than she had ever been. She had conquered all the demons. Those of her body she had starved into submission, those of her mind she had exorcised with prayer. Nearly ten years of her own company had brought her a certain kind of peace. She could not help but resent John for disturbing it.

She smiled faintly as she saw his cunning look. He didn't believe her. 'Truly, John,' she said. 'I have nothing now to offer you.'

He rose ponderously, his brow furrowed in confusion. This was not how he had seen their reconciliation. It had never occurred to him that Eleanor would be anything less than pleased to see him. Then he looked at her with the pensive charm with which as a boy he had always melted her. His smile too was wholly his father's.

'You think I have neglected you,' he said gravely. 'And I have — though it was for a reason. I needed to prove myself, to show that I could achieve something on my own. This is the first opportunity I've had to come. Since the Scottish war began I have been much with his Grace of Gloucester on the Border. All of last year I was garrisoned at Carlisle. Of course, you don't know, but the raids have been bad. Such burning and killing. I heard men say they've not seen the like since the third King Edward's time. Then just before Christmas the Earl of Angus laid waste to Bamburgh. They burnt the town to ashes; forty townspeople dead, burnt in their beds. . . . Mind you, we soon repaid that and with interest.

Burnt our way to the walls of Dumfries, we did. I killed seven men myself that time.'

He laughed savagely, remembering the fat little merchant in Lothian who had offered him and Tom Wernick twenty marks each not to cut his throat. They had roasted him alive instead; hung him by the heels from the rafters of his guild hall before they fired the roof. He fingered the glossy yellow satin. He had bought himself a new doublet with the twenty marks. Tom had spent his on ale.

He went on, his voice eager and articulate. War was something he did know about, the only thing he knew about now. 'Of course,' he said, 'we've not yet had the chance of a real fight. The trouble with the Scots is that you can't pin them down. Reiving is all they know about: night raids and burnings and back over the Border before you can blink. That will change soon. They know now that Gloucester prepares in earnest for war. Twenty thousand men he's raised, and cannon, bombards . . .' He launched into a description of a new gun that Gloucester had had brought from Flanders. 'I've heard say that it can blow a man to pieces at twenty yards.' He dwelt happily on the prospect for a moment. 'It's only the King we're waiting on now. He insists on leading the main army himself.' He scowled. It was the French campaign all over again; waiting, wasting, passing up opportunity after opportunity. They had struck a decisive blow only a month ago. Jack Howard had sailed up the Firth of Forth, burning Blackness and capturing a dozen enemy ships. If they could have followed it up with a simultaneous attack on land . . .

'You can't blame the Duke of Gloucester for growing impatient,' he said. 'He'd set his heart on a campaign this year. We've already begun to lay seige to Berwick. It's time the King faced facts. If he's in no state to lead the army, than he should relinquish command to Gloucester.'

Eleanor rounded on him sharply. 'Gloucester! Gloucester! What of Northumberland? Is he no longer Warden of the East and Middle Marches?'

John looked at her in surprise, to hear that caring and defensive note in her voice that had once been only for him. 'Well, yes of course,' he said in confusion. 'Harry commands the Border counties as he has always done, but naturally as the King's lieutenant in the north, Gloucester has overall command for the duration of the war. Besides,' his own voice sharpened, 'I do not serve the Earl of Northumberland, I serve the Duke of Gloucester.'

'And how is my son?'

Again the softness of her voice confused him. 'He is well, the last I saw of him.' That had been a week ago at Alnwick, when Harry and Gloucester had quarrelled openly in council. It was over a triviality, nothing more than the movement of troops. Yet Gloucester had backed off though he'd had the authority to override Harry and the whole council put together; but he hadn't and in the end Harry had had his way. Giving an order on Harry's home ground was one thing, getting it carried out was another. If they had been in York things would have been different. There, Gloucester could have passed for God. John thought with pride of the rapturous welcome they had received: all the aldermen turned out in their scarlet coats; little bands of fifes and drums all playing together; the crowds roaring Gloucester's name. Oh, it meant something to wear Gloucester's livery there, the White Boar opened doors to free ale and comely girls and his credit was always good in York. The merchants especially loved Gloucester and he'd heard some say that he'd bought that love with grants and remissions of taxes. Perhaps he had, but not in the sly ingratiating way that they meant. Gloucester had made the people of York his special concern. He loved them and they loved him in return. But there it ended; Lord of the North he might be, but once past the Tyne his brilliance dimmed. In the true north they still heard no voice but Northumberland's and though they obeyed Gloucester's orders readily enough it was never without a sideways glance to Harry. Gloucester knew, as did every man, that one word from Harry and his command would have been of little or no account. And all so effortless. That was the most galling thing — Harry didn't even have to try.

'Yes,' he said again jealously. 'He's very well. You know of course that he has wed Maud Herbert?'

'Yes, I know.' Eleanor looked up at him and saw his eyes burning with resentment. 'And he has sons now,' she said quietly.

201

'Three strong healthy boys.' It was said as a warning, to remind him that the dream that she had once had for him could now be no more than that.

John eyed her maliciously, hearing the soft longing of her voice. 'You never see Harry now, then?'

'No. I never see him.' And she never would. After all this time she had no real desire to. She could love and protect him as well from a distance. She knew all that she needed to know about him; that he was happy and content, that he was loved. He spent a great part of the year at Wressell now. Near enough for her to get word of him, far enough to restrain her from the rare impulses she had to see him. She had seen his eldest son, another Harry — a fair boisterous child, the image of Harry's father. The past was never truly dead, she thought. The years passed, the memories faded, then suddenly the wheel swung full circle and the past came round to confront you again.

She rose stiffly. 'Have you long, John?' she asked him lightly. 'Shall I tell the steward to prepare you a bed?'

'I have two days. Gloucester remains at York till the twenty-fifth of the month. We go then to Nottingham to consult with the King.' He added proudly, 'I have command of the escort whilst Lord Lovell remains in the north.'

Eleanor turned to face him. 'You have done better for yourself than I had thought, John, to have ingratiated yourself so well in Gloucester's favour in so short a time. I understand he is truly the man of the day now — the King ailing, his brother Clarence dead.' She sat again and folded her skeletal hands in her lap. 'Is it true that Clarence drank himself to death rather than face a public execution?'

John stared at her. *Ingratiated*! As if he had fawned and wheedled his way to a knighthood, as if he were not worthy. He thought of all the work, the effort, bringing himself up from nothing, fetching and carrying; the long hours of duty so that he should always be under Gloucester's eye, long hours spent perfecting his mediocre skills till he could hold his own with the best of them.

'Is it true?'

He stared at her vaguely. 'What?'

202

'That George of Clarence was drowned in a cask of wine?'

John shrugged. 'So they say. Anyway he's dead, and rightly too. He was a traitor.'

Eleanor was silent. These men were nothing to her — names without faces. Edward of York she had seen only once; his brothers Clarence and Gloucester never at all. Her world had never included them. When her ambition had been at its height, none of them had even been born.

'Tell me,' she said. 'What became of Queen Margaret? Is she still lodged in the Tower?'

'Not for five years now. Louis paid her ransom as part of the French treaty. Sixty thousand crowns I heard. Not that it actually cost Louis anything. The Queen was forced to sign over her rights in Anjou and Maine to him in return for his buying her free. I don't think she cared very much. I saw her when they brought her from the Tower. She looked very old from the little I could see. She kept her face covered. I heard it said that she had the Spanish disease.' He laughed crudely. 'I bet she didn't catch that from Daft Harry.'

Eleanor shivered. Poor Marguerite, poor tragic Marguerite. She could still remember the fair lovely girl who had come to England as King Henry's bride. How she had envied her, and who would have thought then how cruelly life would deal with her? Would deal with them both, for she sometimes thought that their lives had a curious parallel. Both had fallen victim to Warwick, both had married ineffectual men, both had known great loves and great hatreds, great hopes, great bitter disappointments and in the end both were left with only themselves. Two old women, waiting to die with nothing but memories to sustain them.

She rose and moved towards the window. It had begun to rain, blind heavy rain that rattled like flung stones against the casement. She glanced at John. His eyes looked very blue and somewhere at the back of her mind they lit a small dim flame. He was uneasy. Sweat filmed his upper lip. Repeatedly he rubbed the palms of his hands together — a gesture she knew well. Abruptly the flame died. 'John,' she said sharply. 'What do you want?'

He answered her without hesitation, as if he had only been

waiting to be asked. 'What I have always wanted. What I am entitled to: my father's lands.'

She grew still and sad. He had not forgotten. She had taught him better than she had thought. 'And you think I can help you to that?' she asked quietly.

'You said you could once.'

'That was a long time ago, John.'

'You've still got influence.'

'With Harry?' She laughed incredulously. 'You don't honestly believe that.'

'I didn't mean with Harry,' he snapped.

'Well, who else then? Who else can grant you Egremont?'

'And Wressell.'

'Wressell was granted to your father only for his lifetime,' she reminded him. 'You have no claim to Wressell.'

He smiled at her cunningly. 'Actually it was neither Egremont nor Wressell that I was thinking of. I haven't set my sights quite so high yet. There are some tenement lands in north Lambeth that once belonged to my father. They are of little value and at present they are leased to the Abbot of Westminster. The last time the grant came up for renewal it was signed by my father's only surviving brother, William, Bishop of Carlisle, as it was not known then that my father had left issue.' He raised his brilliant eyes to her face. 'I think it is time that it was known. I want to sign the release as Thomas, Lord Egremont's son and heir.'

Eleanor stared at him. 'And what would that give you?' she asked quietly. 'Apart from a pittance rent.'

'Acknowledgement. Legal recognition that I am his son and heir. Once a precedent has been established it follows that any future claim I might make has some standing at law.'

Eleanor eyed him scornfully. 'Whose words are those, John? Not yours. You've not the wit for anything so devious.'

He flushed angrily. 'You think not?'

'I know not. Now, whose words, John?'

He stared at her defiantly for a moment, then shrugged. 'There is a knight in Gloucester's retinue: Richard Ratcliffe. He's a lawyer, so he knows these things. He thinks I could lay a petition before the King. My father was never officially attainted. In law there is nothing to bar me from inheritance if I can prove my right.'

'Oh John, John,' Eleanor cried. 'I beg you not to set too much store by these rights. God forgive me for making you so sure of them, but in law, you have no actual title. In truth, you are only one of a dozen who could lay claim to being Egremont's son if they had a mind to. You see, Thomas never actually acknowledged you as his son. That counts for a great deal, you know.'

'But you acknowledged me,' he shouted at her. 'You told me I was Thomas's son. You said I was entitled to Egremont.'

'Yes. I did,' she answered wearily. 'I believed it myself then.'

He came and knelt beside her. 'And you still believe it,' he said urgently. 'Nothing has changed except our approach. We begin small and wax large. I know full well that Harry would never grant away Egremont, but a small parcel of land yielding less than ten pounds a year . . . And once my foot was in the door, well, then we could think of Egremont. I would need your support, though. My word wouldn't be good enough by itself, but if you spoke for me then others might. You're still the Dowager Countess of Northumberland. Your favour would carry much weight.' He touched her hand fleetingly and smiled. 'It would be what my father would have wanted.'

Eleanor avoided the intense blue gaze. Was it? Was it what Thomas would truly have wanted for the son he never knew he had? He'd had other sons, daughters too. The north abounded with Thomas's bastards. This one was different only because she had plucked him from the heap and tried to make of him something that he was not. Perhaps she owed him something for that, but not this much. Harry was strong now and getting stronger. He'd achieved more in fifteen years of peace than his father and grandfather had in twice as many years of war. If she supported John she could destroy that strength, perhaps even destroy Harry himself. She smiled faintly, thinking of all the years she would have given her heart's blood for such a weapon. And now she had it, it lay cold and blunted within her grasp. Once, once — the watchword of her life. Everything always came too late: the banquet spread after she had filled herself with crusts, the wine poured when her thirst was slaked with plain water.

She looked steadily into John's eyes — Thomas's eyes. 'Your father was not always a good man,' she said slowly. 'Not even always an honourable man. But he was an honest man. Except for once in his life, he deceived neither himself nor others. What he wanted he took, and the consequences with it. He needed none to speak for him, none to hide behind. If you want your father's lands then you must have something of his courage. I cannot and will not help you. I have no courage left.' She reached out her hand and touched his dark curls. 'Forgive me for letting you believe that I ever had.'

He recoiled from her touch, stumbling blindly to his feet. His legs felt quite weak, as they had after his first time on horseback. So Harry won again; effortlessly, without even a fight. All for Harry, nothing for him. The silent rage burned up into his throat and he swallowed it down as he always did. The taste of his own gall sickened him and twisted his mouth into a bitter smile. With an effort he made himself look at her. Whore, he thought; faithless whore! If there were dozens like him there must have been dozens like her. Loudly he drew the breath into his lungs, a wind to launch the torrent of abuse that throbbed and ached in his throat. But he never said them. She looked up at him then and the breath came out of him in a loud painful groan. He saw the naked suffering in her eyes. He saw then that he could not hurt her. He could say nothing that she had not already heard or thought. As always Harry had been there before him.

It rained all that night. Black rain falling from a thunderous sky, white rain glimpsed by lightning. Eleanor stood by the window alone. She saw her steward scurrying across the yard to fasten a flapping door. He ran, his body doubled over to shield the lantern. She saw his face all squeezed up like an old man's, his mouth open against the wind. So man looked in great anger or great pain, she thought. So John had looked tonight. He had gone now. Despite the rising storm he had departed, ridden back to York. Only a dozen more words had passed between them. There had been nothing left for either to say. Now, with the recollection of his face came a stab of fear. This wouldn't be the end of it. She'd bought Harry a breathing space but no more than that. If she had taught John one thing it was persistence. Her refusal to help him would not discourage him for long. There would be others, like this Richard Ratcliffe, men who saw in John a weapon to use against Harry. She knew that he was not without his enemies.

Then suddenly the fear left her. She could never retain any emotion for long. Harry knew well enough how to take care of himself. He'd survived this far without hurt — it occurred to her that he would be thirty-two this year. Was she so old? She had been only twenty-eight years old when she had borne him.

She turned back into the darkened room. It was cold and functional, like herself. Cultivated poverty, as she sometimes called it. The walls were bare. The bed narrow and hard, but from choice rather than necessity. A quiet room usually, a room for prayer and contemplation, a room for remembering, but always she had chosen her memories with care. They came at her bidding, a quiet orderly procession of thought. Now they came at her from all sides, whirling in confusion around the room as if when John had blundered in he had stirred up the dust of years. His presence still hung in the room, heavy and cloying. It would soon fade as all earthly things did. By the morning his visit would have taken on the semblance of a dream that had briefly disturbed her long sleep. And then would begin again the long sterile days; hours of solitary prayer punctuated by her spartan meals. In the evenings she sewed; altar cloths for the monks at Beverley, hoods of brown homespun for the poor men of York. But not tonight, her thoughts were far from pure and charitable tonight.

Slowly she unlaced the white linen coif and pulled down the two skinny braids. Her hair was quite white now, lank and thin, and her scalp showed through pink on the crown.

She knelt stiffly before the Virgin's jewelled image, the only thing of beauty in the room. She winced as her bones cracked against the iron floor and as the pain persisted, she smiled. For years now she had found a curious pleasure in the discomfort of her flesh: the shift that tortured her dry itching skin, the dull ache of an empty belly, the agony of her cramped fleshless limbs as she knelt for hours in prayer. There was only pain to remind her that she was still alive, that there was some reason and purpose in still being alive. Life itself she knew was her punishment; her penance for all those sinful years. God knew, perhaps only God knew, how she had suffered. He would know when she had suffered enough and let her die in peace. She had thought for a while now that the time might be near. As the needs of her body diminished, so surely did the days left to her. It became harder and harder to maintain the rigorous punishment of her flesh. She had become used to harshness, and pain like hunger was commonplace now. There was no purpose in self-denial unless she had something to reject. Fasting was so easy when there was nothing on the plate; to turn your back on a feast was the true test. Had today perhaps been that test? Like Christ on the Mount, had she been tempted?

She bowed her head. 'Holy Mother,' she whispered. 'Of your mercy protect my son.'

Smoke blew on a sullen wind, drifting like fog beneath the bridge. The river ran high, pulsing against its shallow banks. At the water's edge, Maud held her five-year-old son by the heels as he fished happily among the dross washed down from the hills. Triumphantly he held aloft the haft of a broken axe then passed it for inspection to his younger brother William who laid it reverently among their treasures; so far, a leather bottle and a feather; a gawdy strip torn from a plaid; and a buskin that Henry was certain had once belonged to a giant. There had been a sheep's head too but Maud had insisted that he throw that back. He was consoled for it by the find of a piece of wood that he fancied was shaped like a sword.

Maud smiled contentedly, listening to her children's happy laughter. Her third son Jocelyn slept in her sister Cecily's arms. Her daughters Alianore and Elizabeth sat at her feet and made bracelets of coltsfoot and celandine. She lifted her head. The wind had dropped. The smoke seemed to be denser. Reivers had broken the Border the night before, raiding down as far as

Bellingham; firing Rothbury and Eslington on their homeward run. Only the harvest fields had been spared; they had not been worth the burning. This was the first day for three weeks that it hadn't rained. And there was more to come, she thought, as she glanced at the sky. All morning the sun had struggled between great banks of grey cloud. Now the clouds piled darkly on the horizon. The air grew still, heavy with the smell of saturated earth and rotting corn. It would be a bad harvest; a bad year, for there were rumours of plague as close as Durham.

Even as she thought it, the first drops of rain spattered her gown. Scrambling quickly to her feet she called the children to her. Henry protested loudly and refused to relinquish one part of his haul. He pushed Alianore who screamed as she slipped in the mud and Elizabeth wailed loudly to be carried.

Clutching the buskin and two filthy children, Maud ran laughing up the slope. They were drenched long before they reached the postern gate. The guard craned from his tower and grinned as they plunged beneath the vaulted arch — and straight into the arms of the Duke of Gloucester.

Richard stared at them incredulously, his cold eyes sweeping from the hem of Maud's sodden skirts to her steadily reddening face. They lingered speculatively for a moment on the buskin clutched to her breast.

'Madame,' he said, 'have a care. I would not have thought this a time for frivolous excursions. Are you not aware that we are at war?'

Maud glared at him. And how could I not be aware? she thought furiously, with all of your household cluttering up mine and your sour face everywhere I look. She said, 'Your pardon, your Grace. I thought the children would benefit from a change of air.'

He looked at her bleakly. 'Would not we all, my lady? Would not we all?'

He moved on, leaving her feeling angry and foolish. She thrust the buskin savagely at her sister and marched off across the bailey, muttering in Welsh.

The castle wards seethed with unknown faces in Gloucester's livery; the white boar snarled at her from every sleeve. In the outer bailey there was hardly room to move; men and horses, carts of weaponry, rows of lances buttressed the curtain wall and from beneath an awning of oiled canvas the black snouts of cannon protruded.

She saw John coaxing a terrified horse between the traces of a cart. John Egremont he called himself, *Sir* John Egremont; a changed name, a changed man — a dangerous man she sometimes thought, seeing the way he fawned upon Gloucester and used him to influence Harry. It was Gloucester who had persuaded Harry to grant John title to some tenement lands of his father's. The property itself was of no great importance. What was more significant was the way he had styled himself — as the son and heir of Thomas, Lord Egremont. Now that could open a lot of doors, as she had pointed out to Harry. But Harry thought it a cheap price to pay. It soothed his conscience, he had said. After all, he thought they owed John something.

She moved on, pausing again to let Elizabeth down. At the same time she reprimanded Henry who had lunged at a passing groom with his makeshift sword and dealt him a hefty blow on the shins.

'My lady, my lady.' She turned and saw the chaplain bearing down upon her like a crow in full flight. 'My lady.' He halted, his plump cheeks quivering with indignation and exertion. 'Your pardon, but I must protest. I am informed by the constable that I am to be turfed from my lodging to make way for four of Gloucester's knights. Surely, my lady, this cannot be so. For the comfort and wellbeing of the Church to be seen as secondary to those of rough and ready fighting men! And not even our own men at that.' His eyes admonished her severely. 'I can tell you this, my lady. I will not sleep in hall with the riffraff.'

'I will speak to my lord,' Maud reassured him. 'I am sure there has been some mistake.'

In the hall another deputation awaited her. Her steward advanced, purple with outrage. 'My lady. Forgive me. But I can no longer countenance this constant filching of my stores. Another fourteen sacks of grain have been requisitioned by Gloucester's clerk — for Bamburgh this time. Last week I lost four barrels of salt fish to Norham. We'll be on short commons ourselves by the end of the month if this legalised pilfering continues. And I might add, my lady, that it's all very irregular. Half the time Gloucester's men have no proper authorisation. I can't be expected to grant away victuals purely on word of mouth.'

Maud sighed. 'Very well, I will speak to my lord. I am sure he will see the matter put right.'

She went purposefully towards the stairs. Oh yes, she would speak to my lord all right. If Harry didn't put his foot down with Gloucester then she certainly would.

Maud blew the bloom of fine dust from the harp. It had been Gwilym Ddu's gift to her before she had left Wales; his own harp, the pale sycamore wood rubbed to a dark glossy sheen from years of nestling against his breast. The strings were new, virgin strands of gilded wire. She had never played it. It would have been a kind of sacrilege, for she could never have matched the old man's skill or feeling. He had told her once that music was born of longing: passion and sadness, grief and pain, but mostly of longing. A song was merely the crying aloud of an aching and unfulfilled heart. Music was the endless search and struggle for perfection. And it was true in a way. Other loves filled her heart and mind now. She was content. She was happy. All her longings were fulfilled. But still she treasured the harp and the memory of the old man. On his saint's day she always sent him a gift. In return he sent her all his heart's love. He still remained at Pembroke, even though her brother William was no longer its lord. The King's infant son was Earl of Pembroke now and William had been placated for the loss by the less prestigious Earldom of Huntingdon. Except that William was not placated. Like Gwilym Ddu his heart was still in Wales.

She sighed and glanced wistfully to where Harry lay upon the bed reading a jewelled manuscript. She smiled lovingly. How solemn he looked with his eyes cast down like a schoolboy to his book. Now and then a fleeting smile touched his mouth as he came upon a passage that amused him. She had a childish impulse to call out to him, to see the fire as he raised his eyes, to see them soften and smile as he looked at her. She smiled herself. Six years!

It might have been six days. The flame between them had never cooled. She thought of that first year, the days of laughter and childish joy, the nights of almost frightening passion. He was gentler now, sometimes exquisitely tender. He had exorcised all his griefs and his guilts. There were no restraints between them now.

She sighed louder and went to sit on the window seat. The rain had stopped and dried in a burst of late evening sun. She wished she could rid herself of this feeling of disquiet. Why lately did she feel so ill at ease? It was more than the war; more than the irritation of Gloucester's continual presence. The feeling intensified as she saw Gloucester himself crossing the inner ward with Thomas, Lord Stanley — the weasel. She had names for them all: Stanley the weasel; Ratcliffe the rat; Morton was the toad, with his bulging eyes and the pouch of skin beneath his jaw which seemed to inflate whenever he was displeased. Gloucester himself, all skinny black legs and crouching mien, she had named the spider. Harry, rather unflatteringly he thought, she had christened the snail for his tendency to retreat into his shell if anything touched him too closely. And criticism of Gloucester surely would.

She went and lay beside him on the bed, pushing back a wayward lock of hair to kiss the tip of his ear.

'No,' he said without looking up. 'Whatever it is, no.'

She pulled a face. 'And what makes you think I was going to ask?'

He rolled up the manuscript and turned to face her. 'You have that look,' he said and smiled. 'For the past half hour I have watched you, fretting and fidgeting. What is it that troubles you, *cariad*?'

She looked up at him uneasily. 'I'm not sure. The war. The weather perhaps. John Widdrington says that all the harvest will be lost. And there is plague at Durham.' She looked at him fearfully. 'Twelve dead in the last week. I can't help fearing for the children.'

He kissed her lightly. 'Durham is a fair way off, *cariad*. Don't worry about things that might never happen.'

'Yes. I suppose it is foolish.' She slid her hand inside his open shirt. It checked on the gold enamelled boar he always wore on a

212

fine gold chain. Her smile faded. Ysgithyrwyn — white tusk, the beast of death.

'Harry,' she said suddenly. 'Do you not sometimes think that Gloucester grows too powerful?'

He glanced at her in surprise. She was the second person to have asked him that. The first had been John Morton, Bishop of Ely now, but anxious as ever to exploit a possible grievance. He gave her the same answer as he had given Bishop Morton. 'There's nothing wrong with power if it's used wisely and well. Richard does use it well, for the good of all, not just for himself.'

'You think so,' she said peevishly. Why did it irritate her so to hear Gloucester praised? 'You'd better tell your steward that, then. Gloucester has all but emptied his stores.'

'The Border garrisons must be maintained.'

'At the cost of our own?'

'If need be.' He gave her a cold and warning look. 'It's not a game, you know. It's war we're at, fought in fits and starts at the moment maybe, but nevertheless it's still war. You didn't see what they did to Bamburgh, did you?' He grasped her wrist as she tried to pull away. 'There was nothing left of the town, just a heap of ashes and a few charred bones. They threw babes like ours into the burning houses. The mothers they raped, then threw them in as well.'

'Stop it, Harry.' She flung herself away from him. 'All right. You have made your point but I should still like to make mine. For all you say, I cannot help but resent being ordered about like a kitchen wench in my own household. I took the children down to the river this morning for air and he as good as told me to my face that I was a fool.'

'Yes, I know,' Harry interrupted her quietly. 'He told me. He was concerned that you would take what he had said amiss. And more, he was concerned for your safety. He's right, you are a fool to put yourself and the children at risk. And besides, it was I who gave the order that none were to be allowed beyond the gates, not Gloucester.'

Maud was silent. It was always like this. Somehow Gloucester inevitably ended up being in the right. It was always the greater cause — the wider concept — she had heard him say that a man couldn't plough a straight furrow without crushing a few worms. She presumably had the status of a worm.

Then Harry said, 'Why do you dislike him?'

'I don't know,' she said. 'He's so joyless, Harry. There's no laughter in him. It's as if the very soul of him were dead.' She moved away from him and sprang down from the bed. 'Besides, I don't like to see any man treat you as his servant.'

'But I am his servant. I chose to be his servant. That makes a great deal of difference.' He came and put his arms around her. 'You're making too much of this, sweet. Nothing is done without my knowledge and consent. I am in entire accord with Richard over the conduct of the war.' He smiled at her. 'I had not thought you so small-minded, *cariad* — so conscious of your dignity.'

'I'm not. Oh Harry, you know I'm not.' She gave a bewildered little shake of her head. 'It's just that . . .'

'It's just that Richard has things on his mind. He would be greatly concerned to know that he had offended you.'

'Would he?' Maud sat down again on the edge of the bed. 'Yet I hear he is very tender to the feelings of the men of York. He gave them exemption from the Parliamentary tax and reduced the contingent of men that they must supply for the war to a mere one hundred and twenty archers. No wonder they love him, Harry. Didn't they even prefer to serve under his banner rather than yours when you both summoned the York levies to attend you?'

Harry laughed at her softly. 'Is that what grieves you? That the men of York prefer Gloucester to me?'

Maud coloured hotly. She had said far more than she had meant to. Harry did not care for her meddling in politics. It reminded him too forcibly of Eleanor. 'I don't know what I am suggesting,' she said miserably. 'I'm just afraid, Harry. I'm just tired of hearing Gloucester's name.'

He sat down beside her. 'It's not like you to condemn a man without a hearing. It's very easy to misjudge him, you know. Sometimes he seems harsh and overbearing because he doesn't know how to flatter and charm.' He tilted her face up towards him. 'This war means a great deal to him. He's determined to win. He needs to win, and not just for himself but for England's sake. God knows we will need something to lift our hearts these next few months. It's going to be a long hard winter.' And he deserved to win, Harry thought. For a year they had held the Border between them with no more than their usual resources. He couldn't deny that the greater effort had been on Richard's part. He'd run himself ragged after the burning of Bamburgh: night raids, parleys, offensives by both land and sea, and in between times he trailed back and forth to Westminster, trying to coax Edward from his pleasures and money from Parliament. So far he'd had little success with either. Harry had heard that Edward was now so gross that he couldn't even mount a horse unaided. But still he refused to relinquish command and give Richard charge of the campaign. Next year, he promised; in the spring he would come north and lead the affray. Yet Harry reckoned it was more than failing health that kept Edward in the south. Since the war with France his golden image had tarnished. Though they hadn't known it then, they had lost more than face that day at Picquigny and Louis had struck the greatest bargain of his life. The following year, Charles of Burgundy had been slain at Nancy and left his daughter Mary as sole heiress. Her marriage to the Holy Roman Emperor's son had not staved off Louis's pretentions. Within a year he had overrun all of Burgundy and now threatened Flanders and Artois. Edward had hedged and shuffled, one eye on Louis's much-needed pension and the French marriage which he was equally loath to lose. To their shame they had done nothing, despite the Burgundians' repeated plea for aid. Louis's pension had kept Edward tame. For a miserable fifty thousand crowns a year he had abandoned Burgundy to the mercy of France. It was a false economy, for with Burgundy firmly under his heel and past all help, the payment from Louis had ceased. It was also Louis who had provoked James of Scotland to make war on England, while he pursued his own ambition in France.

He went on heavily, 'If you think I am getting pushed into second place it's because I want it that way. It's easier for me. For the most part I've had everything that I have ever wanted. Richard has only achieved the half of his desires. Edward and Clarence were always first in line.'

He smoothed back the hair from her face. 'Where is all that

wonderful passion that you used to lavish upon the world? Is there not a morsel to spare for Richard of Gloucester? He has much to bear, *cariad*. His wife, the Duchess Anne, is ailing and he fears his son Edward may have the contagion. His brother Clarence's death hit him hard.' Harder perhaps than any of them knew. Richard was much changed since that time. 'Try to think of him more kindly, my love. His is not a happy life.'

He lent forward to kiss her and Ysgithyrwyn swung on his long gold chain, his tusks needling her throat.

She swallowed hard and closed her eyes. Yes. She would try to think more kindly of him. Harry loved him. So must she.

Winter came, crueller and harsher than any had feared. There was famine throughout all of England, and on the Border it was only by the grace of the Duke of Gloucester that hundreds instead of thousands starved. Before Christmas he'd obtained licence from the King to purchase victuals where and when he could. At all costs the Border garrisons must be fed even if it was only on half rations. Maud was not impressed. There were others in the north besides Gloucester's army — ordinary folk who starved because once Gloucester's men had been to market there was hardly any food to be had. And what there was, was far beyond their price. No wonder the merchants sang Gloucester's praises. Why sell grain for six shillings the bushel when they could get twice that from the Duke of Gloucester? There were riots on Tyneside; a wool merchant and his wife were bludgeoned to death for half a sack of mouldy corn and two small loaves. In Newcastle a miller was hung by the mob for grinding flour in short measure. And in the wake of all this, as if they had not suffered enough, came a fresh outbreak of plague. In a month it had swept the length of England. The Queen lost an infant son — ironically, so Harry had thought, named George. At the convent in Whitby twelve nuns died all in a night. It was a priest from Whitby who brought it to Alnwick. It claimed five lives in as many days: the priest, two of Gloucester's men-at-arms, the constable's young and pretty wife and Maud's youngest daughter, Elizabeth. If Harry had been with her she might have borne it. She would have wept and washed away the worst of the

216

pain. But Harry wasn't there. He was with Gloucester at Norham, appointing the commissioners of array. So the grief hardened and grew brittle and crystalline like the slivers of ice that hung from the walls. When he had come, he found her subtly changed. Some of the laughter had gone from her.

He stayed two nights, long enough to get her again with child. Then he rode south with Gloucester to meet with the King at Nottingham. It was as far north as Edward would ever come, and in the spring he reluctantly relinquished command and gave sole charge of the campaign to his brother Gloucester. He also gave him a new and unlooked-for ally. Alexander Stewart, Duke of Albany, the younger brother of James of Scotland. Another Clarence, Harry had thought, driven by spleen and thwarted ambition into alliance with the English and willing to betray kin and country in a bid for his brother's crown. At Fotheringay, in June, he swore himself King Edward's man and promised to yield Annandale, Lochmaben and the town of Berwick in exchange for English aid in usurping James's throne. It was an uneasy alliance, for Gloucester could hardly bring himself to be civil to the man, let alone treat him as an ally. Such men were treacherous, he said, easily suborned. He'd rather put his faith in a fifty pound cannon than in a hundred such as Albany. Yet Harry thought they might have a more powerful weapon in the renegade Scotsman. They had learned this much from him at least, that James of Scotland was not a well-loved man: aesthetic, effeminate, with a penchant for jewels and baseborn young men. His latest favourite, an upstart named Cochrane, had alienated all but the major lords. It was common knowledge that enthusiasm for war with the English was steadily on the wane. The Douglas himself had told James to his face that he should think about putting his own house in order first before they turned their eyes south. It was a weakness that Harry had thought to exploit. Traitor or not, the presence of Albany in the English army was bound to affect Scots morale; it was bound to affect James's judgement, to know that he marched against his own brother. Of all men, Gloucester should have known that.

By the middle of July the army was massed and ready for an all-out offensive. Gloucester made them a solemn vow: there would

be no compromise this time, no retreat, no last-minute concessions to peace. Berwick, he said, would be theirs again by
Christmas.

They moved slowly north toward Berwick, and the town,
worn out by six months of relentless siege, capitulated without a
fight. Only the great fortress above the Tweed held out and they
left Lord Stanley to press the siege, while they moved north-east
into Lauderdale to intercept King James who was advancing
toward them at the head of a vast army. They had not gone more
than twenty miles across the border when the astounding news
came that the Scots had abandoned their march and had turned
north again for Edinburgh. It was as Albany had predicted; the
Scots lords had risen against James and after hanging his
favourites from Lauder Bridge had barred their king up at
Edinburgh.

Savage with disappointment at being cheated of his battle,
Gloucester gave chase, burning every town and village en route,
in the hope of provoking an engagement. By the last day of July
they had reached the city without encounter. On the first of
August, Gloucester accepted its unconditional surrender. Of the
Scots army there was no sign and an obsequious mayor informed
them that they had withdrawn to Haddington, eighteen
miles along the Dunbar road, taking their captive king with
them.

Gloucester recieved the news grim-faced. Only Harry knew
how desperate he was to bring the Scots to battle. The army were
growing bored and restless. There were stores enough for only
another few days, even assuming they could live by forage on the
hundred and ten mile homeward march. In the event, none of
these thoughts mattered. The next day the Chancellor of
Scotland rode into the town suing for peace.

There was nothing else to be done. Even Albany gave in grace-
fully and made his peace in exchange for a full pardon and the
restoration of his lands. Gloucester held out as best he could;
nothing could be binding, he said, whilst James was captive and
the lords in anarchy — and he added the proviso that whatever
the terms eventually agreed, Berwick must be left to its fate.
Berwick was his last hope, his last chance to salvage something.

And this time he was not disappointed. Berwick fell to the Duke of Gloucester on the twenty-fourth of August, after twenty-one years in Scottish hands.

It was winter again, pale chill February, the hills and fields still marbled with snow, the hollows of the streams still darkened by ice. In the upper solar of the house at York, Maud stared dejectedly at the row of clumsy stitches with which she had punctuated the hem of her daughter's gown. She sighed and laid the offending garment aside and leaned to pluck an apple from the dish. It was sour, the pale flesh speckled with blight, but manfully she ate it. Food was not so plentiful yet that she could afford to waste it.

On the other side of the hearth a small dark woman sat stitching at a square of linen. She plied her needle as she did her tongue, in quick malicious stabs. 'Of course,' Margaret Beaufort, Countess of Richmond, said, 'it was not the out-and-out victory that his Grace had hoped for.'

'No,' said Maud, and wondered where Harry was now. The last word she'd had from him had been at Northampton, but that was four days ago. He should be at Westminster by now.

'Having marched as far as Edinburgh unopposed, one might have supposed Gloucester would have come back with something more substantial than the promise of a few Scottish burghers to repay the Princess Cecily's dowry. If I remember rightly, Gloucester made a great noise when his brother the King came home from France without giving battle. I can't see that he has come out of this with a great deal more credit.'

'He regained Berwick,' Maud said, more for Harry than for Gloucester.

'*He* regained Berwick?' the countess said archly. 'You speak as if he took the town single-handed. Although I dare say that's how it's been told. All will have forgotten that my husband Stanley had the town under siege for nigh on a year while Gloucester played the general.'

She looked across at Maud and smiled knowingly. 'But then I don't suppose that either your husband or mine will receive the recognition that is due to them.' She dropped her eyes and

thought grimly of the lavish praise that both Stanley and Northumberland had received for their part in the campaign; but what
was praise compared to the riches that had been heaped on
Gloucester's head? Permanent possession of the Wardenship of
the West March to him and his heirs; the castle and profits of the
city of Carlisle; all the royal lands in Cumberland — fifty lush
manors, fee farms by the hundred. She smiled. No matter.
Discontent was ever her friend. This would wean Stanley from
his Yorkist ways more surely than love or money could.

Maud stared listlessly into the fire. She shouldn't have eaten
the apple, she thought. It was now lodged in an indigestible ball
in close proximity to her heart. She winced as the child lashed out
furiously. She was near her time, too near Harry had said for her
to accompany him to Westminster. Her mouth drooped in discontent. It hadn't ever bothered him before. Their children had
been born all over the north; she'd almost given birth to William
in the middle of Cloughton moor. No, it wasn't that. He didn't
want her to go to court. He never had. Did he think it would turn
her into another Eleanor?

She sighed and eased herself upright in the chair. The apple
burned in her breast and no matter which way she lay she was
never comfortable. She had always carried her children so well,
none of the sickness and vapours with which her sister-in-law
was cursed. For comfort she tried to envisage the tiny mite curled
within her. Another daughter perhaps, to replace her darling
Elizabeth. It still hurt, the thought of her beautiful child pussed
and stinking with plague. She had been so young, barely three
years old. Firmly she put the thought from her. There were a
thousand happinesses to outweigh that single grief. All her other
children were healthy and strong, too strong sometimes, for that
very morning Henry had bloodied William's nose as they had
wrestled playfully for possession of a ball.

She glanced with sudden compassion at Margaret Beaufort,
suddenly remembering another Henry. How long, she wondered, since the countess had seen *her* son. It must be ten years at
least since he had taken flight from Pembroke — a long time for a
woman to be without her only child. How cruel it must be,
thinking of him growing to manhood so far out of her reach,

never to be able to smile or touch, always wondering, waiting for news.

She leant back and watched the woman through half-closed eyes. How old was Margaret Beaufort now? At least forty, yet she hadn't changed so very much from the days at Pembroke. Still smiling, still stitching, still calling herself Countess of Richmond though she hadn't a vestige of right to do so. They said she was holy and abhorred the flesh. It was well known that both Stanley and Henry Stafford before him had been wedded to her in name only.

Maud said, very gently, 'And how is your son, Countess?'

Margaret looked up. Soft colour tinged her pallid cheeks. 'He is well,' she answered shortly. Speaking of Henry was a luxury she could rarely indulge.

Maud smiled encouragingly. 'I don't suppose I should know him now. He must be a grown man.'

'Yes. He was twenty-six this January gone — on St Agnes's Day.'

'And he is still in Brittany with his Uncle Jasper?'

'Yes.' Margaret picked up her needle again. Yes. He was still in Brittany, despite Edward's efforts to buy him home. He had nearly succeeded once, five years ago, when Louis was casting speculative eyes on Brittany and Duke Francis had been desperate for English support. Edward had been especially persuasive, promising Henry an honourable place at court and marriage to one of his daughters. She'd almost been tempted herself. To have him home, to have him near — what mattered a crown? But destiny would not be cheated. It had been divine intervention that had struck Henry with fever so that Edward's envoys were forced to halt at St Malo. It had been the hand of God that had roused Francis to his senses and sent Pierre Landoris to bring Henry back. Her heart swelled with love and pride. Did that not show that he was destiny's child, that God was with him?

She raised her eyes to the woman who but for the quirk of fate would have been his wife. That hair! Really, it was quite barbaric. Her eyes dropped distastefully to the prominent swell beneath her gown. There was something almost obscene about a woman who was so constantly *enceinte*. Though, of course, that

221

would be an advantage in the wife of a king. The bride that Henry chose must be as fruitful, the stock from which to breed their dynasty. Praise God, that she herself was done with all that. Dominance of her lands she granted to her husbands and welcome, but her body was her own — a shrine to Edmund Tudor and the seed of greatness he had planted.

'And will Henry ever come home?'

The countess answered without looking up. 'Perhaps. One day.' She smiled enigmatically. 'When the time is right.'

Soon. Soon. Her needle flew, ploughing through the froth of white lawn like a silver fish. Slowly but surely events were shaping themselves to that end. The Yorkist flame was nigh on spent. Clarence was dead, Edward ailing — Bishop Morton had it from Master Hobbes himself — a disorder of the bowel and stomach, the physician had told them, continually aggravated by the King's rich and excessive diet. So Edward was digging his grave with his teeth, and the Queen — she recalled Elizabeth as she had seen her last, alone and friendless, growing pliant and in need of council, for her mother the witch Jacquetta was long dead. Even now, she struggled to maintain her influence both in the King's bed and in council against the encroachments of Edward's mistress, Jane Shore. Fierce factions split the court: the parvenu Woodvilles against the old nobility. If Edward died within the next few years he'd leave a young untutored boy as his heir — and Richard Gloucester. She frowned. Perhaps she had been mistaken in Gloucester. He had kept himself aloof from the court and so remained uncorrupt. Stanley said that he was politically naïve; Morton, that he was a man of conscience — an unhappy combination, she thought. He wouldn't survive long in the world of power. And yet . . . She recalled his face when he had returned triumphant from Berwick; again, when he had made his entry into York. It hadn't been the face of a man who disdained power; he liked power, and thinking on it, he had pursued it very thoroughly in the north these last few years, mostly at Harry Percy's expense. She paused, a thoughtful frown drawing her dark brows together. She had always regretted the lack of Northumberland's support. The consent of the north was essential to any change of power and though she knew that in the

222

past Morton's overtures had met with rebuff, might not Northumberland be feeling a little threatened now, with Gloucester's stock so high in the north?

From beneath her heavy milk-white lids she eyed Northumberland's wife and saw a new avenue of approach. Many man of iron will were susceptible to womanly persuasion.

She slipped the needle into the edge of her work and folded it, once, twice, smaller and smaller till it fitted in the pouch at her waist. She looked up at Maud. 'Child,' she said, 'you look chilled to the bone. Shall I have Lady Scrope warm you some wine?'

Maud nodded gratefully. Yes. She did feel cold, as if the ice of winter was fixed in her bones.

The countess laid a fur across her knees. 'And when do you expect your lord home?'

'Not for a while. The Duke of Gloucester has much business in council. I don't really look to see Harry before the end of March. I dare say he will pass a few days at Middleham . . .' Maud's voice trailed off dejectedly.

'He is much with Gloucester then?' the countess murmured.

'Yes.' Maud's voice told the older woman that it was more than she liked.

The countess patted Maud's shoulder. 'Yes. Northumberland is loyal, despite everything — I know that Stanley admires him for it.'

Maud glanced up, frowning. 'Why shouldn't Harry be loyal?'

'It must be hard for him. The Percys have always been supreme in the north. Yet now . . .' She shrugged. 'The King has virtually granted his brother palatine status in Cumberland — a small but very effective concentration of power. Oh, I know that as yet Gloucester has no sway in Northumberland itself, but in Yorkshire he seems to have made great inroads into Northumberland's sphere of influence.'

Maud stared unhappily into the fire. Gloucester, Gloucester, at every turn of her life. She felt an overwhelming and childish urge to weep. She remembered when she had been very small, she had made a chaplet of flowers and her brother William had stamped on it because she wouldn't give him half of her apple. She had that same feeling now, as if something beautiful and irreplaceable had been wantonly destroyed.

Then Elizabeth came with the posset of wine. It was sweet and potent. She felt her mind slacken and looked up smilingly into Margaret Beaufort's narrow face.

The countess knelt. 'Are you eased now, my lady? I fear I distressed you, speaking of Gloucester.' She patted Maud's knee. 'It was meant for the best. Forewarned is forearmed. I fear your lord has much to fear from this man.'

Suddenly the cup slipped from Maud's hand and streamed like blood over her skirts. She cried out as the first of the pains engulfed her.

The child was born that same night, five weeks before it's time; another daughter, small and frail. As Harry had wished, she named it Anne, in honour of Gloucester's duchess.

1483—1485

*The Boar shall stand waiting for its
brethren. As soon as they come it will kill
them and then have itself crowned with a
Lion's head.'*

                              Prophecy of Merlin

•

Middleham
Richard Plantagenet, Duke of Gloucester, stared bleakly into the
cup of untouched wine. He saw himself, mirrored darkly: his
eyes great bruises in a chalk-white face, his mouth a wound, his
narrow jaw shadowed with stubble though he had been freshly
shaved that very morning. Sometimes he saw other faces: the
strong dark features of his beloved Warwick; the milky countenance of saintly King Harry; and lately, bobbing like a putrid
apple beneath the wine's glassy surface, the plump, bitter face of
his brother George.

Clarence! He closed his eyes. Vain, treacherous, greedy
Clarence; dead Clarence, murdered Clarence; drowned, Edward
had said, at his own request, in a vat of his favourite malmsey. A
bitter smile contorted his mouth. That would have been like
George. He could not even die like other men.

He swallowed hard to ease the constriction of his throat. The
guilt still weighed heavily upon him. He'd tried to absolve himself
with fasting and prayer. Not *his* guilt, he had told himself a thousand times. The deed had been wholly Edward's. But when had
Edward's shame not been his? When had he not lived through his
beloved brother?

He opened his eyes. The wine shimmered darkly. It was
burgundy, rich and red as a balas jewel. Burgundy was dead

225

now; six years his perjured soul had rotted in Hell. It had been Burgundy's death that had sparked off Clarence's madness. Such a trivial thing, and hardly the first time that Clarence had over-reached himself. Neither he nor Edward had been truly surprised when George had offered for the hand of Burgundy's heiress, less than three months after he had been widowed himself. Edward had swiftly quashed that idea. Indulgent as he had ever been to George's delusions of grandeur, he could never have trusted him with so much power. Predictably, George had sulked and complained volubly, and there it might have ended if it had not been for the Queen. Richard's face darkened. He knew very well that it was Elizabeth Woodville who had cajoled Edward into proposing her brother Anthony as a husband for the Duchess Mary. As far as George had been concerned it was the final humiliation. It was one thing to be passed over for a man of his own standing, but for an upstart like Anthony Woodville . . .

So it had begun. George had plunged himself into an orgy of retribution. Deliberately, he had flouted Edward's authority; deliberately, he had insulted the Queen. Every day the Woodville spies had brought Edward news of some fresh madness; that his Grace of Clarence had accused a woman called Twynhoe of poisoning his duchess and hanged her out of hand; that his Grace of Clarence had arrested, and hanged, one John Thursby, charged with murdering his infant son. The implication behind all this being that they had been paid to do so by the Woodvilles.

By midsummer, George was openly inciting rebellion. To their mother's grief, he spread the tale that Edward was no true son of York but the bastard whelp of a Flemish archer. He accused the Queen of sorcery, witchcraft. He said that she was not the King's lawful wife. It had been enough. His brother's arrest and trial on a charge of high treason were a foregone conclusion, as was the verdict of guilty. But death? And such a death; furtive and secret, hidden behind the Tower walls. George must have known, he must have suffered. Sweat broke out on his long upper lip. How long did it take a man to drown? How much could be swallow before his lungs burst?

On his knees to Edward, he had pleaded for George's life. He was their brother, their flesh and blood. Surely a spell in the

226

Tower would be penalty enough? He had almost swayed him. Edward had hesitated, for so long that the Speaker of the Commons had demanded of the lords what was to be done. Then suddenly it was over. Clarence was dead and his brother Edward stood his murderer.

But why? Crazed with grief and shock, Richard had burst into Edward's apartments. The Queen had been with him, smiling with quiet triumph as she discreetly withdrew. Edward had stared at him; half-drunk already, he had called for more wine. *Sweet golden malmsey*, Richard had yelled. *To drown your sorrow as you drowned poor George?*

Edward had wept. 'I had to, Dickon. There was no other way.' He had averted his bloodshot eyes from Richard's face. 'You don't understand,' he had whispered piteously. 'You don't know.'

And he still didn't. It was something that he had not as yet fathomed. What was it that George had known or said that he had to be silenced so quickly? But he knew the true culprit; that royal whore who used her body to promote her upstart family. The tally against her grew in his mind: Warwick, Montagu, Tom Desmond and his two little knaves. And most grievous of all, Clarence. All done cleverly, mind, with soft smiles and whisperings; careful that no taint could be attached to her. But *he* knew. He, too, had his spies and he had no doubt that his brother Clarence had been sacrificed to the whim of Elizabeth Woodville.

He rose at last and went toward the bed. The new clothes that had come that morning from York lay spread upon the coverlet. They were costly, and for him, inordinately fine: a shirt of soft tussore silk; a doublet of Spanish blackwork with discreetly padded shoulders and wide belled sleeves, lined and faced in cloth of gold and clarry velvet. He began to dress himself; slowly, with ceremony, like a priest robing himself for the Mass. He thought of the King the last time he had seen him: the great powerful body run entirely to fat, the sharp astute mind rotted with debauchery. Glutton and drunkard, lecher and pervert, Edward was no more his glorious golden king.

A wave of misery and despair overwhelmed him. He saw their greatness slipping away. Remorse over Clarence had driven

227

Edward to greater and greater excesses. He had seen him spew up a thirty-course dinner and then sit down within the hour to dine again. He still had his women, pushing the wreck of his splendid body to its limits, as if he were a lusty young boy. He was rarely sober, even in council. His grip upon the government had slackened. And as Edward weakened, Louis of France grew stronger. In January of this year he'd shown them the full measure of his contempt, when he'd signed the treaty of Arras with Maximilian of Burgundy and betrothed his son, the Dauphin Charles, to Maximilian's infant daughter. Blatantly, Louis had reneged on the treaty of Picquigny, spurning the Princess Elizabeth of York, and through her, Edward and England. In one fell swoop they had lost Burgundy as an ally, the marriage on which Edward had counted so much, as well as his filthy pension. And added to that was the threat to Calais, now within Louis's newly acquired province of Artois.

His thin body twitched in a spasm of rage. Perhaps they would see now that he had been right. They should never have conceded to Louis at Picquigny. It was too late now for Edward to start muttering about renewing the war with France. He had lost all credibility with Parliament, and the merchants would bear no heavier taxes. The London guilds had made that quite plain, and it was only by virtue of his own success in regaining Berwick that they had been persuaded to press the Scots war.

He smiled fleetingly. He would not disappoint them. His offensive against the Scots was just beginning. James was back on his unsteady throne, whining for renewal of truce and the marriage of his son Rothesay to the English princess, Cecily. His smile hardened and became thin and brittle, remembering how Edward had milked his triumph at Berwick for all it was worth, trying to recapture his lost popularity. It had made a change for Edward to be basking in his glory, instead of the other way round. Not that he thought any had been decieved. They'd cheered Edward but they had cheered him the louder. It had been his name on every man's lips. He'd noticed too a subtle shift in men's attitudes. Once it had been to Edward they had looked for glory. Now, it was him.

He shivered pleasurably. This feeling of power was a new kind of exhilaration; for so long he'd been subordinate to his brothers. But now with Clarence gone and Edward relying upon him more and more . . . At last he felt he was reaping the reward for all those loyal years: all of Cumberland and Westmorland under his sway; all of the Neville lordships in Yorshire. A little of his jubilation faded, remembering that Middleham, Sheriff Hutton and Penrith were only his while Montagu's son lived and bore heirs. Time passed. He must get young George wed, for he had acquired the boy's wardship and marriage two years ago. He gnawed at his lip. Easier said than done, for even that solution was fraught with dangers. Who could he trust not to exploit the situation and make a bid for the Neville lands? Harry perhaps? He had daughters.

He laughed out loud, a brief barsh sound, quickly bitten off as if the sound of it surprised him. Now there would be a real measure of Northumberland's love and trust. Did he really believe that Harry would not be tempted? Strangely enough, he did. If Harry was going to turn on him, he would have done so long before now. He had given him cause enough these last few years. Not conciously or deliberately. He'd always been very careful not to challenge Harry's power openly or push his own beyond acceptable limits. But he had no scruples about enlarging the sphere of his influence in Yorkshire, even if sometimes it was at Harry's expense. In York especially, he had supplanted Harry in their favour. He still remembered that day, years ago, when he and Edward had crept through the streets like thieves. It gave him an immeasurable feeling of satisfaction to think that now it was to him that York looked for judgement; that there, his was the only voice they heard. Did Harry care, he wondered, and knew with irritation that he did not. Harry had never cared who loved him.

He moved leisurely to the window. The April sun was warm and pleasant and brought a faint colour to his face. He leant forward at the sound of childish laughter. Two small boys staggered across the pleasaunce pursued by a woman laughing like a child herself.

His thin lips pursed in mild disapproval. For some reason he rather disliked Harry's wife. Her hair disturbed him, the colour of blood; also, the fact that she wore it loose. He would have

229

thought it more seemly for her to have kept it covered, as was the custom for matrons. And she was up from childbed with almost indecent haste. Was that the fourth or the fifth she had borne Harry?

He thought unhappily of his own dear, sweet Edward, with his mother's eyes and hollow cough. And so frail that they could not let him out into the air, unless the weather was especially clement. Anne herself was not in much better health. She had spat blood again that morning.

He turned away. The sight of that woman threatened his good humour. There was no justice, he thought savagely. Some men were born with all, whereas others strived for all their lives and only achieved half as much. His shoulders sagged. For months now he had struggled against acknowledgement of this truth, for it struck at all his most cherished beliefs: that right was right; that honour and decency brought their own rewards. But in his heart, he hadn't believed that, not since Clarence had died. He knew now that only an absolute devotion to self brought a man power and recognition. And what a mockery that made of a life that had always denied self for love of others. He'd sacrificed himself for the glory of York, for the greatness he had thought could only belong to his brothers. But Clarence was dead now; Edward a decaying unrecognisable hulk. Only he was left, the last pure son of York. Dear God, surely now he had earned his freedom.

With hands that suddenly trembled he loaded his fingers with gems. Around his narrow shoulders he laid a golden collar embellished with pearls. He looked long and hard into the burnished glass. For the first time in his life he saw only himself and not the reflection of his golden brothers.

Richard pursed his lips in irritation as for the second time Harry interrupted him.

'I'm sorry, Richard, but I can't for the life of me see the sense of it. We have regained Berwick; King James is all but on his knees for peace. What will be gained by pursuing the war further?'

'English prestige, for one thing; at a very low ebb, you must admit, since Louis signed the treaty of Arras.'

'Prestige buys no bread,' said Harry shortly. 'Have you

thought of the cost of raising another army? Who will pay? Not your wonderful merchant friends, that's certain; and the subsidy from Parliament won't be enough.'

Richard glared at him. 'By God, Harry, you try my patience sometimes. This is more of your mealy talk.

'I have never been an advocate of war purely for the sake of it. I see nothing mealy about weighing up the gains and losses and arriving at a balanced judgement.'

'We have nothing to lose,' Richard cried. 'The Scots are on the defensive, their government in turmoil, their lords forever at each others throats . . .'

'What then have we to gain?' Harry smiled obliquely. 'It sounds as if we shall loose a lion to quell a mangy dog.'

'In the end we shall have peace to gain; an ordered, settled long-term peace. For all that James snivels for truce, the border is flouted daily.'

'But not by James's men,' Harry argued. 'Reivers. And there will always be reivers, both English and Scots. As long as there are hungry men and greedy men there will always be reivers.'

'What do you suggest then?' Richard demanded acidly. 'That we do nothing?'

'No. I don't suggest that. I merely have my doubts about raising an army the size and magnitude of the last. Such an army has to be paid and fed and harnessed and equipped and our present situation does not justify the cost. It would only be a repetition of the last campaign where we took twenty thousand men across the Border and found no enemy to fight.'

'That was through circumstance,' Richard countered defensively. 'When we marched, the Scots were moving toward us with an equally powerful force.'

'But could they raise such a force now? On your own admission, they could not: their military is in disorder and chaos. Surely a defensive strategy would be best, till we see what King Louis is up to. To concentrate all our fighting power in the north, when the French are openly raiding the Channel ports . . .'

Richard smiled and threw up his hands. '*Absit*, my lord. I take your point.' He was silent for a while, thoughtfully pulling at his lower lip. 'How many men could be raised from the East and

Middle Marches at, say, half a day's notice?'

'Three thousand, perhaps more. Berwick has a standing garrison of five hundred men; Alnwick and Bamburgh not much less. Two thousand from my own Northumberland estates; six or seven hundred from Durham and Yorkshire, but not within half a day. Enough certainly, to deal with anything that James can send against us.'

'So. How many men at Berwick? Five hundred you say . . .' Richard broke off and frowned as his secretary John Kendall abruptly entered the room.

'A courier, your Grace — from the Chamberlain, Lord Hastings.'

The man knelt, his head bowed. Richard saw that his sleeve was bound in black silk. He proffered a small sealed roll.

'My heart's blood not to be the bearer of such news, your Grace.' The courier looked up. 'Your brother King Edward is dead.'

Richard stared numbly into his face; an unknown face, burnt red by the wind, like a summer apple. He saw too that the man was sweating, little beads of moisture gathered upon his upper lip. He licked them away. 'Your Grace,' he said hoarsely and again held up the roll. 'The letter from my lord Hastings.'

With trembling fingers Richard broke the seal. Silently he read the brief scrawled message . . . 'The King has left the governance of the realm to you. Secure the person of our sovereign lord, King Edward, and get you to London with all speed.'

Then Richard spoke quietly, 'When and of what did my brother the King die?'

'A week ago, your Grace. The ninth day of April. As to the cause, no man I think truly knows. Master Hobbs, the King's physician, holds that it was the flux; others say his Grace took a chill. He had been ailing for nigh on a week but not grievously so. Then suddenly, in the night, he sickened and died.'

Richard shook his head in a blind, helpless gesture. A shaft of sunlight pierced the lattice: pale, translucent, like the sun that had gilded Edward's head on the morning of his crowning; that had shone in triumph through the mist on Barnet field. Hot summer sun on their backs at Tewkesbury, blinding white on the sea

232

at Calais . . . Edward laughing, weeping, shouting for joy . . .
The Sun in Splendour forever quenched.

Then Harry reached out a hand and touched him. 'My lord,' he
said softly. 'What now?'

'We wait,' Richard said, and his voice was very thin and faint.
'There will be more, Harry. Believe me, there will be much more.'

And while they waited, Richard despatched a formal letter to
Earl Rivers at Ludlow, enquiring as to when and by what route he
would be bringing his nephew, the King, to London. Another, of
brief condolence, he sent to the Queen; he had begun a third,
directed at the council, when two days later a second messenger
arrived. This man he knew: William Catesby, the chamberlain's
man-at-law.

'The worst news, your Grace,' Catesby began without preamble. 'The Queen has taken control of the council; her son,
Thomas Dorset, is Constable of the Tower, her brother, Sir
Edward, commands the fleet. She is set on a speedy coronation
for her son, your Grace — less than three weeks hence, on the
fourth of May. The young King comes from Ludlow with an
escort of some two thousand men; it would have been more, had
not my Lord Hastings intervened. As commander of the garrison
at Calais, he threatened to withdraw across the Channel if the
numbers were not drastically reduced.'

He smiled his dry, mirthless lawyer's smile. 'Apparently, your
Grace, the Queen is enough of a strategist to appreciate the threat
of a hostile Lord Hastings entrenched at Calais.'

Richard looked grave. It wasn't hard to follow the Queen's
reasoning. Edward had named him Lord Protector — but legally,
his position was only valid until the new king had been crowned.
And then Elizabeth Woodville would rule England — through
her son, through her brothers, who would be translated to every
high office in the land. Dorset already had control of the Tower
and, therefore, of Edward's arsenal and treasure. It was almost a
fait accompli. Almost — they didn't yet have possession of the
King.

'The council?' he asked thoughtfully. 'How are they disposed?'

'Divided, your Grace. Praise God, the more moderate men
have started to fall away from the Queen and her party. She

seems to have Cardinal Bourchier at her beck and call but Bishop
Russell stands firm against her more extreme demands. Bishop
Morton, as usual, is sitting on the fence. Lord Stanley also seems
to be uncommitted, though his wife, the Countess Margaret, is
close with the Queen.'

Richard nodded and beckoned to Kendall to bring quills and
ink. A fourth letter was begun, to Anthony, Earl Rivers, directing
that he and his party should await the Lord Protector at Northampton. The Duke of Gloucester also wished to enter London at
the side of his king.

'All is in your hands then, Harry.' Richard leant from the saddle
and clasped his arm.

Harry nodded. 'Richard, my lord. Are you sure?'

'Yes. I'm sure.' Richard smiled at him. 'The north cannot spare
both of us and Harry Buckingham has said that he will join me at
Northampton.'

That had been another surprise; another messenger, hard on
William Catesby's heels. Buckingham's man had brought his
lord's duty and service, and the offer of himself and an escort
of a thousand men to join Richard on the road to London.
Richard had demurred at the size of the escort but otherwise he
had welcomed Buckingham's support. If the rumours emenating
from the south were true, he would need all the help he could
get.

He glanced across at the party of men who waited in the warm
April sun. He was anxious to be gone. It showed in the restless
twitching of his mouth, the way he plucked at his reins. He
looked again at Harry.

'God willing, I shall be in London by the end of the month. I
shall send word as soon as I can.'

Again Harry nodded. For some reason he was reluctant to see
him go, for some reason he wanted to prolong this last moment.

He said quietly, 'Farewell then, my lord. God speed.'

Richard turned his horse toward his waiting men, a small
diminutive figure in his mourning black. He was smiling, a faint
nervous smile that pulled spasmodically at the corners of his
mouth. He felt more alive than he had done for years. For the first

time in his life he was on his own; for the first time there was no Edward.

It was nearly two weeks before Harry had news and even then it wasn't from Richard. His steward wrote to him from his manor at Dagenham, a brief letter that offered no explanations or excuses. Gloucester had reached Northampton on 29 April, only to find that the young King and his party had gone on ahead to Stony Stratford. Only Earl Rivers had been there to greet the Lord Protector, full of some weak tale that there had not been sufficient lodging in the town to accommodate the retinues of both the young King and Gloucester. The Duke of Buckingham had arrived the same night. What had passed between them his steward did not know, but at dawn the next morning Earl Rivers had been arrested. The two dukes had then ridden to Stony Stratford to take possession of the King. Also arrested were the Queen's son, Sir Richard Grey, and two of the young King's attendants. He had heard that they were being sent to imprisonment in the north. He had also heard, that on receipt of the news the Queen had taken her daughters and the young Duke of York and fled to Westminster sanctuary.

It was the middle of June before he heard from Richard himself:

My lord Northumberland and well beloved cousin;

I recommend me to you as heartily as I can; and as ever you love me and your own weal and security, and this realm, come to me, defensibly arrayed in all the haste that is possible, and that you give credence to Richard Ratcliffe, the bearer of this letter, whom I send to you instructed with all my mind and intent.

And my Lord, do me now, good service as you have always done before, and I trust now so to remember you as shall be the making of you and yours.

God send you good fortune.

Uneasily, Harry read it through again. It had an almost hysterical note. And that last, *I trust now so to remember you as shall be the making of you and yours.*

He looked up into Richard Ratcliffe's long face. Not only had he brought Richard's letter but also the death warrants of Earl Rivers and Richard Grey.

'I was not aware that they had as yet been brought to trial, let alone found guilty,' he said.

Ratcliffe stared at him coldly. 'Trial is hardly necessary in such a *prima facie* case.'

'Nevertheless, it is the right of every free-born man.'

'Their guilt is obvious. On their own admission they attempted to set aside the late king's ordinance which named his brother, the Duke of Gloucester, as Lord Protector of the Realm and guardian of the young King's person. Also they seditiously plotted to encompass the deaths of both his Grace and the Duke of Buckingham.'

'In what way?'

'My lord,' said Ratcliffe archly, 'are you not aware that great cartloads of weaponry were found among their train, and other munitions stored in various places — for what other purpose than armed rebellion? The Lord Protector had them paraded through the streets so that none should be in doubt of the villiany of the plot against him.'

'You surprise me, Sir Richard,' said Harry mildly. 'I can envisage the Woodvilles as manipulators of events but not as the leaders of armed rebellion.'

'Nevertheless, my lord, it is so,' pronounced Ratcliffe gravely. 'The Lord Protector is continually at risk. Plots abound, fomented by the Queen and her family, who still flout his Grace's authority from behind sanctuary walls. Constant vigilance is necessary.' He paused and brushed an imaginary speck of dust from his hose. 'It was only through such vigilance that the treachery of Lord Hastings was discovered.'

'Hastings? Lord Hastings?' Harry put his cup aside with a trembling hand. 'You jest, Sir Richard. Hastings's loyalty is unquestionable.'

'One might have thought so. The Lord Protector was likewise deceived. But there is no doubt that messages were passed between Lord Hastings and the Queen. She employed the harlot Jane Shore as her courier. It is well know that since King Edward's

236

death, both the Marquis of Dorset and Lord Hastings have often frequented her bed.'

'Fornication if hardly high treason, Sir Richard,' Harry commented dryly.

Ratcliffe threw him an ugly look. 'Perhaps not, my lord. But conspiring with the Woodvilles to suborn and hinder the Protector in the execution of his office, is. Lord Hastings was not alone in his treachery. Lord Stanley, Chancellor Rotherham and Bishop Morton were also concerned and consequently placed under arrest.' The lawyer smiled thinly. 'The Protector, in his mercy, spared their lives. Only Lord Hastings was executed.'

Harry caught his breath. He felt an icy coldness seeping into his limbs. 'Lord Hastings is dead?' he said hoarsely.

'Aye, my lord. Three days ago, on the thirteenth.'

'After he was given trial by his peers and presumably found guilty?'

For the first time Ratcliffe looked uneasy. 'It was thought better to make a swift end,' he said abruptly. 'The prolongation of the chamberlain's life would also have prolonged the unrest. These things are better quickly nipped in the bud.'

Harry's heart lurched sickeningly but he pressed him. 'But there was irrefutable proof of his guilt?'

'Such proof as the Lord Protector thought necessary,' Ratcliffe answered coldly. 'Forgive me, my lord, but are you questioning his Grace's judgement?'

'No.' Harry held the lawyer's cold eye. 'I am merely confused, Sir Richard. I was there at Middleham when news of King Edward's death came. It was Will Hastings who sent that news when the Queen and the Woodvilles would have withheld it. Again, it was Hastings who sent warning of their attempt to seize power. If it had not been for the chamberlain's swift action, the King would have been in London and crowned and the Duke of Gloucester none the wiser.' He smiled quizzically. 'I am just wondering what made him change his mind.'

Ratcliffe shrugged. 'Who knows the minds of men, my lord?' He rose. 'With respect, my lord, I must take my leave. I have other calls to make as well as being charged with mustering the levies for York.'

He pulled on a pair of heavily embroidered gloves. 'We shall meet, then, at Pontefract on the eighteenth, my lord. And with as many able-bodied men as you can raise. Even draw upon your garrisons if necessary.' He smiled unpleasantly. 'The Protector intends that there shall be no further obstruction to his will.'

When he had gone, Harry drew Richard's letter toward him again. Why, in God's name, should Richard feel himself so threatened as to need such a formidable army at his back? All this against a woman and two small boys?

He felt sick with doubt and premonition; a confusion of uneasy thoughts filled his head. It was only two months since Edward had died but already one man was dead, another four were about to die. Had Richard thought of the consequences of what he did? The execution of her brother and son would alienate the Queen forever and turn the young King against him. Like it or not, he was half a Woodville and he had known and loved Earl Rivers well. He was only a boy now, but boys grow into men and how then would he see the man who with scant justification had killed his uncle and stepbrother?

And Hastings! That was the greatest blow; the hardest thing to reconcile. No man had loved King Edward more, no man would have felt more bound to protect and honour his son. How then had be and Richard come into conflict? How had Hastings overcome the loathing of twenty years and brought himself to conspire with the Queen? Only one thing would have driven Hastings into the Woodville camp — the certain knowledge that Richard of Gloucester no longer served the interests of his dead master's son.

Anthony Woodville, Earl Rivers, paced out the confines of a small dark room high in Pontefract's keep. The walls were damp; silverfish swarmed among the cracks, black slugs clung limpet-like to the stones. There was a small window set high above his head. It let in the wind and the rain but it also let in the light. Light was the last thing a man should willingly relinquish.

He seated himself again at the table, moving his chair so that the last of the daylight fell upon his face. It was a handsome face: smooth, bland, introverted, a somewhat characterless chin. His

eyes were rather fine — clear and blue, with the glazed myopic
stare of the dreamer. It was the face of a man content to drift, to
accept whatever life and luck brought him.

He sighed and drew the unfinished poem toward him.

> Methinks only
> Bounden am I,
> And that greatly
> To be content.
> Seeing plainly
> Fortune doth wry
> All contrary
> From mine intent.

He smiled ruefully; not his best but certainly his last — he was
to be executed at noon the next day. Strangely, he didn't resent
it as much as he would have thought. At the heart of him he
was still a gambler and he'd been on a winning streak for so long
now that he couldn't believe that at last his luck was changed.
And even if in the end the dice fell out against him, he couldn't
complain. He'd had the most incredible run; twenty years of
following his heart's desire, of easy living and pleasure. He'd
indulged every whim and passion of his life. His name was
renowned in the tourney and not unknown among scholars. His
poems and translations bore witness to his learning, his religious
foundations to his love of God. He sighed again. Twenty years,
half of his life, swept away as if they had never been. He thought
of Elizabeth, who had brought him all this, whose greed and
ruthlessness were to take it away. Even now the thought
of his sister cheered him; whilst there was Elizabeth, there was
hope.

He turned his head. In the lock of his cell a key had turned. A
little wind blew in and lifted the parchments from the desk. He
stared for a moment without recognition at the man who had
entered. Then as the dark saturnine face came at last into the light
he knew him: Northumberland, another of Gloucester's
henchmen.

'My lord.' He rose and sketched a mocking bow. 'I take it you
are not come with my reprieve?'

Harry regarded the tall elegant figure gravely. 'No, my lord. I fear I am not.'

Rivers' brave smile did not waver. 'Is there news of my sister, the Queen?'

'As far as I know she remains in Westminster sanctuary.'

The smile faded then. 'So my nephew Edward is not yet crowned?'

'Not as far as I know. I fear, my lord, I have no more certain news of the happenings in London than you do yourself.

'There has been no word at all then? We are all to die — even poor old Tom.' He laughed harshly. 'His Grace pursues vengeance to extremes. What harm has Sir Thomas Vaughan ever done him? He's an old man. He's had charge of Edward ever since he was a babe in arms. Tom Vaughan has never done a dishonourable thing in his life, and he's committed no crime unless love and duty to his King is such.'

'You do not deny your own guilt, then?'

Rivers smiled. 'I would not have thought hastening my lawful king to his crowning constituted treason. And believe me, my lord, that's all it was. I admit to being guilty of a little sharp practice but no more than that.' He shrugged. 'Besides, I am past the stage of hot and passionate denials now, my lord. There are none who care to listen.'

'I am listening.'

Rivers looked at him. He smiled. 'Well then, seeing there is no other, I shall let common sense be my advocate and you my judge.'

He paced out a little square of the cramped and stinking room. 'I received a letter from my sister, the Queen, urging that I bring young Ned to London with all speed. The council had agreed for him to be crowned at the earliest opportunity — mark that, my lord: *the council agreed*. Nothing was done without their consent, and when Gloucester accuses us of not sending him word of King Edward's death, he should remember that neither did they. Does that make them culpable also?'

He paced out another, smaller square. 'Gloucester's order that we delay at Northampton did not reach me till we were en route. I saw nothing particularly heinous in taking the King on to Stony

240

Stratford, a mere fourteen miles away. I myself rode back to Northampton to greet Gloucester with an escort of less than a hundred men!' He glanced up at Harry. 'His Grace accuses me of trying to put the King out of his reach but he was only a short distance away and he was *still* there at noon the next day when Gloucester and Buckingham rode in. There had been a day and a half to get clear away, if evading Gloucester was the plan.

'Gloucester says that you attempted his life, and the assembly at Stony Stratford was an ambush.'

'Yes, well, he would, wouldn't he?' Rivers frowned. 'You know, I rather resent that. I think I'd rather be known as a traitor than as a fool — and that, my lord, is what I would have been if with an escort of nearly two thousand men I couldn't have routed Gloucester and Buckingham. Between them they didn't have half of that. Apart from which,' he smiled archly, 'you may or may not know it, but I am not unskilled in combat.'

'And the carts? The armour and the weaponry?'

'Ah, yes, the carts — his Grace has made much of those, has he not? And indeed, there were cartloads of armour, all bearing the Woodville arms — and smothered in goosegrease and packed in straw for the most part. God's eyes, we had just dismantled the household at Ludlow. If an armed attack on Gloucester had been our purpose, would it not have been more to the point if we had had them on our backs?' His voice grew hoarse. He shook his head in a blind helpless gesture. 'My lord, are you all so besotted with Gloucester that you cannot see? This is his revenge: payment for crimes past, for what he thinks we did to his brother Edward, for Warwick, for Clarence.' He shrugged his broad elegant shoulders. 'And perhaps I should not complain too loudly at it, my lord, but as God will be my judge tomorrow, of the thing that I stand accused, I am innocent. We are all innocent.'

He smiled his quiet charming smile. 'Think on it, my lord. It would comfort me to know that at least one man believed me.'

From the steps of the keep, Harry watched as Anthony Woodville came out into the sunlight for the last time. He had made himself fine for death; the hot June sun gilded his fair hair, he wore a doublet of sky-blue silk powdered all over with tiny diamonds. He walked with a swift, long stride, outpacing the priest who scurried behind muttering unheard prayers and exhortations.

They had set a scaffold up so that the watchers who crowded the ward were afforded a better view. He paused at the foot of the short flight of steps, smiling resolutely at the other three men who were already there. Haute and Tom Vaughan he separately embraced. To his nephew Richard Grey, who was quietly weeping, he said, 'Courage, Richard. Let us give these carrion their taste of flesh. Tonight you and I shall dine upon ambrosia.'

He had elected to go first, to give the others heart. He mounted the steps unflinchingly and knelt, bowing his head compliantly for the collar of his doublet to be ripped away.

The axe rose. The sun fastened greedily on its crescent blade. Harry recalled the earl's last words to him: *Think on it, my lord. It would comfort me to know that at least one man believed me.*'

The axe fell. 'Be comforted, my lord,' Harry whispered.

Harry contemplated the vast tapestry which adorned the wall of Thomas Stanley's London house. Very appropriate, he thought: Christ banishing the moneylenders from the Temple.

He glanced again around the quietly opulent room. He did not even know why he was here: the need to know perhaps, the need to quell the dreadful doubts that had filled his mind ever since he had left Pontefract. He had been only three days upon the road before a courier had come: on the 25th June, the very day of Anthony Woodville's execution, Richard of Gloucester had been proclaimed king.

'It was Stillington who let the cat out of the bag.' Lord Stanley turned from the table where he had been pouring wine for them both.

'Stillington?'

'Robert Stillington, Bishop of Bath and Wells — the priest who is supposed to have performed the marriage ceremony between Eleanor Butler and the late king.'

Harry took the wine from him. 'Why do you say supposed?'

Stanley shrugged. 'He seems such a small insignificant little man to have harboured so great a secret.' He smiled acquisitively.

'If I'd have been in Stillington's shoes, I'd have been Archbishop of Canterbury, at least, by now.'

He sipped his wine, rolling it appreciatively around his mouth. 'And to be truthful, my lord, it's all rather unsatisfactory. It is a matter of trothplight rather than actual marriage, which I know in the eyes of the church amounts to the same thing. But then there's the other side of the coin. A good lawyer could argue a case for the Queen. She has *been* queen for more than twenty years. I don't dispute the truth of what Stillington says, but it *is* only Stillington that says it. There is no actual proof, except the granting of a few manors to the lady Eleanor, which could mean anything. Also, Eleanor Butler was dead by the time the Queen's sons were born, which again could cast doubts upon Gloucester's claim that they are bastard.' He grinned. 'I dare say a hefty bribe to a cardinal or two in Rome would set the matter to rights. I have no doubt that if Edward had been married to the daughter of the King of France, instead of to Elizabeth Woodville, some means would have been found to accommodate her.'

Harry stared at Stanley, disliking him, distrusting him even more. 'And when were you yourself released, my lord?' he asked pointedly.

Stanley answered him easily enough. 'Two days ago, together with Chancellor Rotherham. John Morton is the only one who has not been freed. The Protector has packed him off with an armed guard to Wales. I hear he's held prisoner in Buckingham's castle, at Brecon.'

Harry gestured toward the barely healed wound on Stanley's head. 'You had a lucky escape, my lord.'

'Oh, I don't think I was ever in any real danger,' Stanley said airily. 'Hastings was the main target, and perhaps Morton to a lesser degree, except that it's not quite so easy to part a consecrated bishop from his head. Rotherham and I were just there to make up the numbers.'

'And of course, my lord,' said Harry with heavy sarcasm, 'you had no part in the plot.'

Stanley looked amused. 'You surprise me, my lord. I had not thought you so naïve. There was no plot, not on our part anyway.'

'How did it happen, my lord?' asked Harry quietly.

Stanley grinned wolfishly. 'Swiftly, my lord. Swiftly and suddenly. We were all of us unprepared. The storm broke out of a seemingly clear sky. We were assembled in the council chamber of the Tower, summoned by Gloucester to finalise arrangements for young Edward's coronation, then set for the 25th June. Gloucester arrived late — about nine of the clock. Suddenly and quite irrelevantly, he asks Morton for strawberries from his garden at Ely Place. A messenger is sent. We resume. Again, Gloucester interrupts, excuses himself and withdraws. Within the hour he is back, all but foaming at the mouth; ranting on about treason and plots, accusing the Queen of sorcery, and of compassing and imagining his death. There are those, he said, within this very chamber, who conspire with her to that end. Then he demands of Hastings what such treachery deserves. Death, your Grace, says Hastings like a fool, at which Gloucester bangs his fist on the table and cries "Treason". Suddenly the chamber is swarming with guards. I was knocked down in the scuffle. Poor Rotherham almost swooned with fright. Then he, myself and Morton were hustled out under guard. Hastings was hauled out onto Tower Green and without more ado, parted from his head.'

He laughed harshly. 'It was a nasty moment, I can tell you, Northumberland. We've been very tame men since.'

'But in God's name, why?' Harry cried. 'Gloucester must have had some justification.'

'Oh, he had. Hastings was becoming obstructive. He was reluctant to broaden the scope of the Protector's power. Gloucester was formulating a demand for the term of his protectorate to be extended past the King's crowning until he came of age. Hastings made it clear that he would block such a move, and also he refused to sanction the removal of the young Duke of York from sanctuary by force.' He shrugged. 'Gloucester could well have construed these things to mean that Hastings was in sympathy with the Queen.'

'Was there force?'

'Yes and no. Two days after Hastings' execution, Gloucester ordered his troops to surround Westminster sanctuary. He stationed himself in the Star Chamber, Buckingham in Westminster

Hall. Then he sent Cardinal Bourchier in to plead with the Queen to give the boy up peaceably which, after much hysterical wrangling, she did. There was no actual force but there was the threat of force. Gloucester made it very clear that one way or the other he would have the boy out. He said it was an affront to both himself and the young King, for him to go to his coronation whilst his brother cowered in sanctuary.'

'But there was to be no coronation.'

'No, not of Edward's son, anyway.' Stanley threw him a significant look. 'Perhaps Hastings also knew that.'

'And then of course the Stillington affair broke,' Stanley went on. 'On the Sunday following, the mayor's brother, Ralph Sha, preached a mighty sermon from St Paul's Cross, having been well primed as to his text by the Duke of Buckingham — 'bastard slips shall not take root,' and all that. Except that poor old Sha got a mite carried away and raked up that unfortunate myth about King Edward himself being the spawn of a Flemish archer. The Londoners weren't very impressed with that — proud, pious old Cis, an adulteress. Gloucester was there, making a very spectacular appearance as Sha's sermon reached its climax. I think it was hoped that the crowd, swayed by Sha's marvellous eloquence, would instantly acclaim him as king. But for the most part they just stood, open-mouthed. They had expected to see young Ned crowned within the week and were merely stunned by this sudden *volte face*. Then two days later, Buckingham himself harangued the citizens in the Guildhall and provoked even less response. In the end, he had to resort to the shameful expedient of having his own men throw their caps in the air with ecstatic cries of 'King Richard'. In the end it was Parliament and the council who decided the issue; myself and the majority taking the line that anything was better than a child for king dominated by Woodville counsellors. The rest were soon persuaded by the reminder of Hastings, and the knowledge that a great northern army was en route.'

Harry was silent, rigid with shock and disbelief. He reminded himself that this was only Stanley's version, and Stanley was not the most impartial of men, expecially where Richard was concerned. It was the death of Will Hastings that stuck in his throat.

Whether Hastings was guilty or not, didn't really matter. What did matter was that Richard had taken a man's life without trial, without a prayer.

'My lord,' he said at last. 'Hastings' death — his Grace must have had some sort of proof.'

'He had the word of the lawyer Catesby, who said that he suspected Lord Hastings of contact with the Queen through the medium of Jane Shore.' Stanley threw him a frowning look. 'Have you seen his Grace as yet, my lord?'

'No. I only arrived this morning and have been overseeing the quartering of my men in Moor Fields. I received word from his Grace there. I am to sup with him tonight at Barnard's Castle.'

'I think you will find him quite changed, my lord; quite magnificent, since he has put off his mourning and now rides through the streets in purple velvet, with a thousand armed men at his back. That apart, he has acquired a very strong taste for power that has given a few men pause for thought; Hastings was one of them.' His voice rose on a warning note. 'Don't question it, my lord. It's better not. The thing is done, however it was done. A week hence Richard of Gloucester will be crowned King of England, and I, my lord, will be first in line to pay my homage. From the moment that crown sits on his head, he shall have no more loyal subject than Thomas Stanley. I shall follow the example of good Harry Buckingham. Have you heard how his Grace has rewarded him? Constable of the Tower, Chief Justice and Chancellor for all of Wales, constable and steward of all the royal demesne, besides the restoration of the de Bohun lands, which were absorbed into the Crown on the accession of Henry Bolingbroke.'

He smiled enviously and furiously, for Buckingham's ascendancy in Wales touched very closely upon his own province of Cheshire and the Marches. 'Oh yes, my lord. Buckingham's star is the one we lesser satellites must follow. If his Grace is so grateful to those who put him on the throne, will he not be more so to those who keep him there? Take my advice, my lord, and get in line for your share, whilst there are still honours to be had. His Grace has already stripped his nephew, the Duke of York, of two of his possessions and bestowed them elsewhere: Berkely has the

earldom of Nottingham; Jack Howard is Duke of Norfolk.'
Stanley threw a grim look at Harry's set face. 'And if your con-
science troubles you that much, my lord, console yourself with
the thought that England will be no worse off under Richard of
Gloucester than she would be under a boy of twelve, ruled by his
Woodville mother.'

Richard Gloucester, king elect, read through the draft of the
council's decree: 'that Edwardus Quartus, late reigning over us,
had unlawfully taken in wedlock, one, Dame Elizabeth Grey . . .'
He smiled. *Dame Grey*. That was perhaps the sweetest revenge;
plain Dame Elizabeth Grey, plunging her back into the obscurity
from which she had come.

He stroked the skin of vellum with a small jewelled hand — the
Titulus Regis: the instrument of Elizabeth Woodville's damna-
tion, the salvation of the House of York. He read it through
again; the words soothed him, stifled those last few pangs of
uncertainty and conscience. *Edward! Edward!* His heart cried out
— not three months dead and already he had usurped his son. But
for England, not for himself. The boys were bastards, fruit of
Edward's illicit union, the whelps of his harlot and concubine.

He rose and paced the edge of the silken carpet, treading a
forest of vine leaves and exotic-coloured blooms. He was only a
little less exotic himself, in his long gown of blue cloth of gold,
powdered all over with the Yorkist rose. At the heart of every
flower a tiny diamond gleamed, their petals were clusters of seed
pearls, their stems and leaves twists of beryl and jasper.

He turned and began to retrace his steps, carefully placing one
brocaded foot in front of the other, as if beyond the edge of the
carpet a precipice yawned. So! The Woodvilles had thought him
of no account, that he could be overpassed and set aside as a non-
entity. They had thought that he would stand aside, while they
corrupted the son, Edward, as they had his father, while they
brought England to anarchy and ruin with their greedy schemes.
Well, they didn't think so now. Thus he had purged England of
their poison: Anthony, that false, corrupt knight; Richard Grey,
the son of the harlot. '*I am innocent, I am innocent, as God is my
judge*': so he had wept upon the scaffold. Innocent of that crime,

mayhap, but guilty of a hundred others more heinous. The real culprit had still to be brought to justice: Dame Grey and her whoremongering son, Thomas Dorset. His face darkened. Despite the vigilance of a heavy guard, Dorset had escaped from sanctuary. In vain he had had him hunted across London with dogs, smiling scornfully when Cardinal Bourchier had protested. Why not? Was that not how vermin were brought down?

His mind raced on, leaping from one inconsequential thought to another. He knew it would be madness to stop and think. Events had happened at such a pace, sweeping him along on a sweet heady tide like the first glorious charge of a battle. In the beginning he had viewed it as such: his right pitted against the Woodville might; a holy cause against the Devil's machinations. Only later had other adversaries swept into the field: Hastings, Morton, that turncoat Stanley. Oh yes, he'd seen what was in their minds. They had thought to use him to stave off the Woodville menace, only to gain control of the young King themselves. He'd seen how, when it came to implementing *his* will, they had begun to fall away from him. Hastings would have thwarted him, limited his power. Fornicator, adulterer, coupling nightly with that cackling bawd Jane Shore, while she was still warm from Dorset's bed. As low as she was, he'd brought her lower. On his instruction, the Bishop of London had ordered her public penance: walking barefoot through the streets of London in naught but her shift, a lighted taper in her hand.

And Morton, that holy hypocrite, there was another long score. Stanley's wife was the catalyst there; that proud clever dame with her airs and graces and bastard taint. Margaret Beaufort worked the Queen's will through Morton, subtly undermining his policies, fencing him in with caution and restraint, weaning men from love of him to love of the young King Edward. Suddenly he'd seen the whole pattern of his life repeated. He'd heard them: how handsome the young King was; how like his father; how wise and gracious for one of his years. He'd known then that the decline of his own power was inevitable. He could not keep Edward in tutelage for ever. As soon as he was crowned, his mother would have emerged triumphant from sanctuary, and even if he could have got the term of his protectorate extended, to ward off the worst, it was only a matter of time before his power would end. He hadn't wanted it to end. He'd been in the light too long ever to live in another man's shadow again. And then at the beginning of June, the shattering news had come of young George Neville's death, and the last of his restraint had been swept away. On his own death, the Neville lordships would revert to Richard Latimer, but long before that loyalties would start to fall away with an eye to a change of master. It would have been the end of his hopes of supremacy in the north. The Neville lands were at the heart of his dominance of Yorkshire. If he lost them . . . But he wouldn't lose them. As King of England, all of the Warwick inheritance would be his.

That was when the idea had first taken root, or perhaps it had always been there. In the beginning he'd fought against it with all his heart and soul. For weeks he'd closed his ears to Buckingham's wild schemes and prayed daily for deliverance from his own longings. Then a letter had come from the Bishop of Bath and Wells asking for a private audience . . . God's messenger with the answer to his prayer — and the answer to a years'-old question. He knew now, why Clarence had had to die. Bishop Stillington had told George the same thing.

He stared down at the parchment beneath his hand, 'Clarence, my brother,' he whispered, 'you are avenged.'

Abruptly he stood again and resumed his quiet pacing. He must not rest, he dared not, until the crown was actually on his head. At the moment they were still in awe of him. Hastings' death had silenced not a few lordly tongues; armed men filling the streets had achieved a deathly sterile quiet. And now Harry was here with the northern men. He smiled. They should stand guard upon London whilst he was crowned. The Londoners would see then how he was loved.

He turned his head and saw his mother enter the room. The rustle of her skirts seemed loud to his ears; silk on silk, whispering against her flesh. The sound recalled another time: in the Tower, years ago — the night they had sent Daft Harry to God.

The duchess came and stood beside him, resting her hand lightly upon his shoulder. 'So, my son. In a week you will be crowned.' She nodded. 'It is well. The glory of York goes on.'

She moved away from him and he seated himself once more at the desk. She watched him as he broke the seal on another roll. He bent his head to the parchment, thoughtfully stroking the quill along his cheek. She still marvelled at the change in him. He had surprised even her. More ruthless than Edward had ever been; as devious and calculating as Clarence. She must guard him well. He was the last of her sons, the last, the very last of that sweet glorious vintage. How strange that out of all her great strong sons, only Richard the weakling had survived. God was good, she thought piously. He could have taken all. He could have allowed York to be vanquished by the Woodville pestilence. But Richard would be king, as his brother had been king, and after him his son, sweet, gentle Edward. No Woodville taint there, she thought with satisfaction. Edward's blood was purely Neville. She smiled, almost sadly. How she wished that Warwick could have seen this day; his great ambition achieved at last. His daughter would be Queen of England, as he had once envisaged. He would have been grandfather to kings after all.

She looked again at her son and saw how the last few weeks had marked him: the twitching mouth, the nervous hands that were never still. Was he still troubled over the death of Will Hastings? Did he have a conscience still? This, she knew, was his one weakness. If he ever stopped and allowed himself to think, only then would his courage fail him. She knew his faults. Only she could protect him. She knew that at the heart of him he still felt himself unworthy. He would attempt to buy men's favour, to win their approval, not knowing that there was no need. Some men would exploit that. Buckingham was one. He saw himself as another Warwick. He had been heard to say that at Richard's crowning there would be more Stafford knots than there had ever been ragged staves. Already she saw how he would weaken Richard. Already he had persuaded him to deplete his own crown holdings by granting him the de Bohun estates.

She moved toward him, suddenly fiercely protective of this, the last and youngest of her sons. There were greater threats than Harry Buckingham.

'Richard,' she said, soft and caring. 'Shall Anne bring your son Edward with her to London?'

'Yes. Why not?' He laid down the quill and looked up at her. 'Of course Edward will attend my coronation.'

Cecily lowered slack and wrinkled lids. 'Is that wise, my son, in view of the times? Have you thought that your own son is of a like age to Richard of York? Might not such a reminder be a little unfortunate at this time? In the same way, I wonder if Edward's boys should be allowed quite so much freedom. Bishop Russell tells me they are seen frequently playing in the gardens of the Tower. It might be wise, my son, if they were seen less frequently for a while.' She paused. 'And in the end, perhaps, not at all.'

She saw how pale he had grown but he said nothing. She smiled. It was better so.

'What is to be done with them then, my son?' She came and stood close to him and saw the film of sweat that beaded his long lip. 'Do we keep them in hold for the rest of their lives, the rallying point for every malcontent? Or do we free them, treat them with honour, let them marry into some lordly house, have sons . . .'

'They are bastards,' Richard cried out suddenly. 'In law they are debarred from the crown.'

'Some men make their own laws. Besides which, it has never been put to the test. Legitimate or not, they are still Edward's sons. Alive they can never be anything but a source of unrest, a focus for anarchy and bloodshed. Jesu, Richard, but we have lived through such times. We lost your father and your brother, sweet Rutland, in such times. Would you have them come again?'

Still he did not answer and she moved away, her voice coming softly across the space between them. 'Once before a life was sacrificed for the good of the realm, a life more saintly and blameless than either of those boys. Thirteen years of peace and prosperity for England have been our vindication — one life in exchange for thousands.'

'No.' He wrenched his head away from her. 'I will not think of it.'

'You must think of it, if you wish to remain king.' She came and knelt by him, taking his hands between her own. 'For England's sake, for York, for your own son Edward. If anything happened to you before Edward was grown, how would he fare against your nephews, against the Woodvilles?' She saw that she had him now. Not for himself, not even for England, but for his son Edward.

'Let it be quietly done,' she said. 'Use the small men, men who still have a long way to climb; the lawyer Catesby would be such a man; Ratcliffe perhaps.'

He looked down wearily into her face. 'Madame my mother,' he said. 'Pray for me.'

'I shall, my son,' She kissed his small pale hands. 'Devoutly.'

Then they turned together as a discreet knocking sounded at the door. Richard Ratcliffe entered, bent almost double in an exaggerated bow. 'Your Grace,' he said. 'The Earl of Northumberland.'

Richard almost ran across the room, his hands outstretched. 'Harry! Dear God, but I am pleased to see you.' And he was. Harry brought the familiar and well-loved with him. Richard could almost smell the north upon his breath. And this was the last and most stringent test; the one man who *would* question, who would not be deceived.

And yet he was. Harry looked into Richard's face and saw only the man he had loved and honoured for the last ten years. He knelt and kissed Richard's hand. 'My liege. My King,' he said softly.

Across the room the Duchess of York watched him approach. Strangely, it was the first time she had ever seen him. As he drew near and she saw his face, her feeling of elation and well-being vanished. She thought suddenly of Alianore, that poor pathetic starved little corpse, that filthy priest: 'Madame, if you had been kinder, God might have spared you the grief that's to come.'

He heard Westminster clock strike ten; the deep notes ponderous and long-drawn-out. He had been King for exactly twelve hours. After the roar and thunder of the day, the silence of night was almost frightening — a bruised throbbing against his ears, like the echo of a violently struck bell. It was not quite dark. The sun had set long ago but the sky still glowed with reflected light, and the spires and sloping roofs of the distant city stood out sharply, as if

252

they had been drawn with a fine quill upon parchment. The golden day was over but in his mind every hour of it still burned clear, not one molten detail had cooled or dimmed.

Again he heard the clamour and roar of the crowd as he had ridden out from the Tower. In the city the crowds had stood twelve deep, pressing so closely about him that he could smell their hot unwashed flesh. Had they also smelt his fear? Down Lombard Street into the Chepe, where the narrow shopfronts had shut out the light. He had quickened his pace. Lately he had grown to dislike the darkness and if he was alone at night, he kept the candles burning late.

And then Westminster Hall; the coolness of the marble bench beneath his sweating palms as the lords spiritual and temporal had acclaimed him as king. Then the short walk to the abbey that had seemed like miles: the prick of scarlet cloth beneath his bare feet, the dragging weight of four yards of purple velvet and miniver, and the sun so hot upon his back, shining with a brilliance that hurt his eyes; the sun in splendour, the sun of York. An omen, he had thought, a blessed omen. He had been terrified that it would rain.

Ahead of him, the Kings of Arms in their gilded crowns cried a way before him: Garter Writhe, Clarenceux and John Norroy Blore; the pursuivants Blue Mantle and Rouge Croix, his own Blanc Sanglier. Behind him, walking with slow and measured steps, came the lords and bishops. Stanley had borne the mace, his man now, soothed with grants and this show of favour. Harry, aptly, had borne Curtana, the blunted sword of mercy; Jack Howard, weeping with pride and emotion, had held the crown between his capable hands; and Harry Buckingham, more resplendent than all of them in blue velvet with gold cartwheels, had carried his train and the white wand of the Earl Marshal. And behind them, so great a concourse of knights and ladies that by the time he had reached the abbey doors the last of them had not left Westminster Hall.

Within the dark portals the light had withdrawn from him, shrinking and diminishing, absorbed by the stone. On either side of him, marble pillars had strained and soared toward God and the light. He had paused and looked up to where the ribs sprang from the piers of the nave and cupped the radiance like praying hands. He also had prayed.

He walked on, alone within himself in spite of the glittering throng that trod at his heels and the ministering hands of the bishops. He looked straight ahead of him, past the choir and the outflung arms of the transepts. The sanctuary steps were wide and white; and beyond, the jewels embedded in the Confessor's shrine glittered like watching eyes. Then the light broke again upon his face, streaming down from the high clerestory windows, diffused by intricate traceries of wood and stone to alight like gilded birds at his feet.

He knelt upon the jewelled mosaic of tiles and bowed his head. He saw the swaying hems of the bishop's pontificals; a long procession of silk-shod feet. He raised his eyes fractionally and saw Anne, breathless and trembling as she was led to her place. Then unseen hands raised him up; more hands lifted his mantle clear. He heard his own voice — was it his own voice, so thin and strained? 'I, Richard, by the Grace of God . . .' He shivered. The white linen of the colobium had been like ice on his burning flesh. Then he had been swathed in the tunica of cloth of gold. Rotherham's pious and uneasy face leaned close. He felt Bourchier's hands, warm, oily, smearing the chrism on his brow and hands. Then the archbishop had stood before him, the great cross on his breast level with his eyes. He had closed them and heard the sighing of the primate's vestments as he had raised his arms; the little grunt of effort as he had held the crown aloft; the long exhalation as he had lowered it onto his head. He felt only a coldness at first as Bourchier continued to bear the weight. Then it was there: St Edward's Crown, seven pounds' weight of gold and gems. He was King.

And so, he told himself now, he would remain. He dabbed at the sweat which moistened his lip. There was still much to be done, still a few dissenting voices to be silenced. As yet they were still afraid, unsure, as at the heart of him, he was himself. He must keep them content for a while longer. It needed only one wolf to leave the pack, one small spark of real opposition . . . He swallowed down the ever present unease. In a year he would have proved himself. He would have justified what had been done.

254

Already his mind was bursting with innovation: he would decree that all serfs on the royal estates should be enfranchised; he would ease the lot of the common man. Peace and justice would be his paramount concerns; jurors would be chosen from men of substance, who would be the less easily bribed, and he meant to establish a court of requests for hearing the pleas of the poor. He envisaged an England rich and prosperous, feared and respected throughout the world. An England renowned for her justice and unbreakable laws where even the meanest scullion had rights and redress. The dream, like a flung parchment, unrolled before his hungry eyes: perfect, unblemished, without stain or flaw — except for the shadow of two small boys.

Maud's soft infectious laughter soothed his aching uncertainty. Harry watched, laughing himself, as she sat in the middle of their chamber floor, surrounded by opened parcels and children.

'Oh, Cecily, will you look?' She held up a length of green silk brocade; there was another of blue for her sister. For Alianore there was a tiny pair of cordovan shoes and a necklace of pink coral. William had a book of hours, which he had taken to a corner to read quietly. Henry strutted, brandishing an ineffectual but showy dagger which he continually thrust beneath his small brother Jocelyn's nose. Maud rebuked him smilingly but firmly and opened the last parcel: Harry's special gift, a gold pendant made up with tiny emeralds into the shape of her emblem, the green dragon.

'Oh, Harry!' Ecstatically she flung herself at him and fastened her arms around his neck. For a moment he was reminded of a little girl, a long time ago, but this time she was laughing instead of weeping.

She kissed him, gently but provocatively and he felt his body grow hot. Then aware of Henry watching them avidly he pulled her arms from around his neck. 'Wanton,' he whispered softly.

Maud laughed and slid away from him and he let her go smilingly. There would be time later — but not much. The King awaited him impatiently at York.

He smiled as his daughter Alianore came and thanked him

prettily for his gift and with great solemnity he fastened the coral beads around her neck. She kissed him shyly and went back to her task of rocking her baby sister's cradle with a firm and maternal hand. She was a pretty child, Harry thought. Soon she would be of marriageable age. The King had suggested Buckingham's son. The uneasiness returned: great marriages, great gifts and the realisation of a lifelong ambition. For at the next sitting of Parliament all the attainders against the Percys were to be reversed. 'All attainders and confiscations of land enacted against the House of Percy, since the days of Henry Fourth, late in deed, but not of right, king of England, are henceforth to be annulled . . .' Innocuous-sounding words, but in one fell swoop all the lost lands that had eluded his father and grandfather were swept back into his grasp. No more than his due, he told himself. Why then did he feel he was being bribed? And not just him. Harry Buckingham groaned beneath a wealth of fees and offices; Stanley was replete with honours and grants. And apart from bestowing the dukedom of Norfolk upon Jack Howard, Richard had created his son Earl of Surrey. Since they had left London at the end of July, every major town they had passed through had received concessions and financial relief; Bishop Russell was aghast at the King's lavish generosity. Even so, Richard had not been able to buy off the threat that had hung over him from the moment he had assumed the crown. By the beginning of September there were murmurs of unrest; there was talk of rescuing Edward's sons from the Tower. The names of the known conspirators had filled Richard with dread: Sir John Fogge, William Stoner, William Norris and John Cheyney — not Woodville names, but solid respectable Yorkist knights who had served King Edward faithfully. This overt rebellion was spreading rapidly now. The men of Kent were in open revolt. And this last week another two names had been added to the list: Richard's own brother-in-law, Thomas St Leger, and Peter Courtenay, Bishop of Exeter.

So they had reached York only to have to turn south again. Norfolk was adequately holding the Kentish men at bay, Buckingham had charge of the defence of the west, but the situation desperately needed the King's presence and he had granted Harry only this one day of respite. They were leaving for London in the morning.

He glanced again at Maud. Jesu, how he loved her. She was so clean, so uncomplicated, so pure. He thanked God that he had never taken her to court. He'd always had a ridiculous fear of her becoming like Eleanor. He frowned. He rarely thought of his mother, except to marvel that she was still alive. But think of her he must now, for the recovered lands included part of her vast inheritance, the barony of Bryan and FitzPayne. It occurred to him that her dowry lands were not entailed. She could dispose of them where she would.

It was nightfall before they reached Lincoln. All day it had rained; light, vicious scuds blown by a chill October wind. In the council chamber of the Bishop of Lincoln's palace, the King flung off his wet cloak and gloves and went to stand by the fire.

'For God's sake, Harry, warm me some wine. I'm chilled through to the bone.'

Yet when it came he did not drink it. He sat, turning the cup between his hands. He looked up as Thomas Stanley entered the room.

'All's quiet, my liege,' Stanley said, smiling. 'This night we can sleep in peace.'

Richard gave a twisted smile. 'There is no news then?'

'No. But then that's all to the good. If the situation in the south had worsened in any way, we should have heard. There are couriers posted all along the road from London.' Stanley glanced at Harry. 'Am I not right, my lord?'

'Yes. Lord Stanley is right. No news is good news, sire.' Harry eyed Richard's pallor uneasily. This was all part of his duty now. Constant reassurance, constant attendance — the King did not like to be alone.

Richard nodded dully. Yes. He could rely on Norfolk. He had the rebels blocked in at Gravesend. At all costs they must be kept from entering London. His eyelids drooped. Perhaps tonight he would sleep. He felt so unutterably tired.

Then his head jerked up. They all heard: blown horses

257

stamping in the courtyard below, the sound of running feet upon the cobbles.

Stanley was at the window first. He thrust open the steamy lattice and a mist of rain blew in and silvered his dark beard. 'The knight John Egremont.' He glanced at Harry. 'Your kinsman, I believe.'

Harry was at the door in three long strides and came face to face with John upon the threshold. He pulled him quickly into the room. Water streamed from his cloak and hair. He fell on his knees and stayed there, too weary to rise.

'Your Grace,' he said hoarsely. 'The gravest news. The men of Wales are in open revolt and are marching to join the rebels.'

He looked away from the King's grey face and threw a wild glance at Harry. 'Your Grace, God's mercy that I should be the one to tell you, but they are led by the Duke of Buckingham.'

There was silence, broken only by John's laboured breathing and the dripping of water upon the floor. Harry glanced at Richard. He looked like a dead man, his bloodless hands gripping the edge of the table as if it were all that held him to the earth. Then out of the stricken silence Stanley's voice came, shrill as a maid's. 'Buckingham? Harry Buckingham?'

'Aye, my lord,' John said, eyes lowered for he dared not look at the King. 'Also, he has broadcast abroad that your Grace is usurper. And in concert with the southern rebels he has come out in support of the Lancastrian pretender, the Welshman, Henry Tudor.'

It was an even greater shock than Buckingham's defection. Harry looked at John in disbelief. Proud, haughty Buckingham to risk life and lands for a penniless Welsh exile he had never even seen? Morton was the obvious link there, but however had he persuaded Buckingham to abandon Richard? At the very height of his fame and power and with the promise of more to come? For Henry Tudor, who had less of a claim to the crown than Buckingham himself? And how had hundreds of die-hard Yorkists been suddenly persuaded to the Lancastrian cause? What had turned them from support of Edward's sons?

He questioned John sharply. 'Are you sure there is no error in what you say? I thought that it was given out by the Kentish men that they rose in support of the late king's son.'

'So it was, my lord,' John said quickly. 'But that cause, for some reason, seems to have been abandoned. Both the Duke of Buckingham and all the rebel captains have declared for Henry Tudor. It seems that Bishop Morton was involved, for he accompanies Buckingham's force. And also' — he stole an apprehensive glance at Lord Stanley — 'and also the lady Margaret Beaufort, who it appears has privily agreed with the Queen — with Dame Grey — to the betrothal of her son, Henry Tudor, to the Lady Elizabeth of York.'

Then Richard spoke, his voice calm and steady. He had sustained the blow and rallied. Letters were despatched to Bishop Russell and the council; summonses to arms sent out to all the lords. He worked far into the night; untiring, unapproachable, untouched by the fearful speculation of his men. Out of all of them, only he did not question why Buckingham had deserted him. He knew why.

'Your move, my lord.' Stanley smirked at him from the far side of the board, having just put Harry's king in check.

Harry frowned and advanced his bishop and suddenly heard Henry Tudor's thin voice: *I fear your king is in great jeopardy, my lord. I think my bishop has him by the throat.* He smiled grimly. Not now, he hadn't. Bishop Morton was fled to France. Harry Buckingham was dead. It was all over. In the two short weeks that had passed since they had departed from Lincoln, Harry Buckingham had been taken, sold by one of his own men as he had fled on the heels of Bishop Morton after the dismal collapse of their revolt. The news had been brought to the King as he had brought his army south from Leicester, planning to drive a wedge between Buckingham and the rebels advancing from the south. It had been raining; black, unholy rain falling heavy as a man in chains from a thunderous and overcast sky. The same rain had kept Buckingham pinned to the far side of the Severn and reduced his army to a sodden rabble. After five days his men had begun to desert, following the example of the wily Morton. Then Buckingham himself had made a run for it and three days ago he had been brought captive to Salisbury. Yesterday he had been summarily tried by Sir Ralph Ashton; today, despite the bishop's protests that it was a Sunday, he had been beheaded in Salisbury's market square.

'Your move again, my lord,' said Stanley impatiently, having recklessly advanced his king.

'I'm sorry,' Harry murmured, countering with his rook. 'I was thinking of the last time I saw your stepson, Henry Tudor. We were playing at chess then.'

Stanley smiled drily. 'Did he win?'

'Yes. As a matter of fact he did. But only because I let him.'

'He wouldn't have cared,' observed Stanley. 'As long as he won.'

'Have you ever met him?'

'Not in the flesh. But needless to say, I have heard much about him.' He tried another tactic and brought his queen into play. He threw Harry an amused look. 'I know what you're getting at, Northumberland. And I won't say that I am unaware of my lady wife's ambition for her offspring. But then so are you, my lord. That does not make you a party to it.' He gave a short cackle of laughter as he captured Harry's knight. 'No, I'm too cautious a man to put my money on anything less than a certainty. Possession, my lord, is all of the law as far as I am concerned. Richard *is* King. My stepson only thinks he should be. There is a world of difference, you know.' He smiled ruefully as Harry took his bishop. 'That's why I can't understand Buckingham.'

No, Harry thought. None of them could understand him. Of all men, none had more to gain by putting his own stepson upon the throne than Thomas Stanley. Yet he hadn't risked it, whereas Buckingham, who had all the more to lose and only half as much to gain, had.

'He wasn't very forthcoming at his trial, I understand,' Stanley remarked casually.

'No.' Neither of them had been present by the King's wish. Neither had Richard himself. 'But he didn't deny any of the charges brought against him,' Harry added.

'He didn't offer any reason either. I find that strange, considering that his life was at stake. Harry Buckingham was not the stuff that martyrs are made of, yet his only plea was for an

260

audience with the King. I gathered from what Ashton told me, that perhaps he had some last card up his sleeve which he was willing to show only to Richard.'

'Perhaps,' said Harry, swearing softly as he made a clumsy move. None of this was news to him. All knew of Buckingham's frantic and impassioned appeals to the King, every one of which had been refused. Right up until the very end, Richard had stead-fastly refused to see him. But Harry had seen him briefly, for less than a minute, as he had emerged under guard from his cell. Hope had flared in the condemned man's eyes, but only for a moment. He had known from Harry's face that there was no reprieve. He would have passed on with nothing said but at the last minute, Harry caught his arm.

'Why, your Grace?' he had whispered fiercely. 'In God's name, why?'

Buckingham had shaken off his hand with a flash of his old arrogance. 'Ask *him*, my lord,' he had answered bitterly. 'Ask our gracious King.'

He turned away and was moved on by his guards. Then just as he reached the head of the stairs, he turned and called back to Harry. '*Souvent me souvene*,' he cried the words of his own raison. 'Think of me often, my lord. God have mercy upon us all.'

Harry looked up as Stanley snorted with triumph. 'Check and mate, I think, my lord.' And with a short blunt finger, he toppled Harry's king from the board.

'*Souvent me souvene*.' And he did, all through the last dreary months of that year. They lingered in the west country till mid-November. There were a spate of confiscations and executions; Thomas St Leger, Richard's brother-in-law, was one of those that lost their head. Stanley, as always, came out of it well: Garter knight and Lord High Constable in Buckingham's stead and though his wife, the countess, was stripped of her titles and lands, the King awarded them to Stanley. Buckingham's lands were given away piecemeal, bribes for the waverers, rewards for the faithful. Harry himself received the lordship of Holderness; his kinsman, John Egremont, the rich manor of Kempston. In all, over a hundred men were attainted, only a third less than in all the twenty-three years of his brother Edward's reign. And so the voices of protest were stilled, but the whispers went on, and by the time they had reached London, in mid-December, they had swelled to a roar of accusation. It was commonly believed by the citizens of London that both King Edward's sons were dead.

'Lies. Vicious lies and slanders put out by the Woodvilles,' the King said, when the voices were so loud that they could no longer be ignored. 'You must know that this evil was conceived in Bishop Morton's brain. Thus was he able to win Buckingham to his cause, thus he suborned the men of York to Lancaster.'

The Bishop of Hereford rose. 'Your Grace, forgive me,' he licked at his lips. 'But it is being said by the people that the Queen Dowager . . . that is to say, Dame Grey . . . that for Dame Grey to have sanctioned the marriage of her daughter to Henry Tudor, she . . . er . . . she must have an inclination that all is not well with her sons . . .'

Richard stared at him coldly. 'Dame Grey,' he said, 'is a drowning woman clutching at dross. Her sons are bastard. She cannot look for the resurrection of her power there. So she looks to the Welshman Tudor for her salvation, who thinks that marriage to a daughter of York, legitimate or not, will give credence to his puny claim.'

'We know this, sire,' Bishop Russell said. 'Every man here knows that these rumours are baseless — as you say, vile calumnies put out by your enemies to undermine the people's love. Nevertheless, my liege, if a thing is said often enough sometimes it comes to be believed. Would it not be wiser to still these evil tongues once and for all? If the people could be reassured that the children were . . .'

'No, my lord Bishop,' Richard interrupted him. 'Has it not occurred to you that this is exactly what the Woodvilles want? This is the purpose of these slanders: to force my hand, to bring the Lords Bastard out from the Tower, out into the open and place them at risk of abduction. No, my lords. It shall not be so. Whilst the realm is in disquiet they must remain in ward. Let the gossipmongers say what they please. I am King of England. I do not have to defend myself against such obvious lies.'

The bishops and lords glanced at each other. It could be so. And it was said in such a calm and reasonable voice that the majority were soothed and reassured. The few that were not thought their own thoughts and said nothing. These were fearful times. It was not wise these days to think too deeply or question too closely. Hastings' swift and untimely end was not so long ago that it had been forgotten.

Harry kept Christmas with the King at Westminster; a lavish glittering affair, paid for with five hundred pounds' worth of King Edward's plate that Richard had sold to the mayor, Edmund Sha. Men laughed loud and ate hearty and drowned their uncertainties in rich burgundy wine.

The King watched them and saw in their faces the tension of awe and fear. It filled him with a sweet excitement. Ah, yes, they were loyal; some out of love, some out of fear, some out of pure greed and avarice, but nevertheless they were loyal. It was enough.

Harry looked on, silent and withdrawn. He saw the King's dark and unquiet mien, the white glittering pallor, the hot febrile eyes. *Souvent me souvene*. Ask him, Buckingham had said. But he could not. In his heart he already knew the answer.

And then on the last day of the year, news came that dimmed a little of the brilliance. On Christmas Day, in the cathedral at Rennes, Henry Tudor had sworn a solemn oath to take in marriage Elizabeth of York as soon as he was king. And all the lords present had knelt to him as if he were already crowned.

The fire burned low in the cavernous hearth, without flame or smoke, a brittle, amorphous skeletal shape cooling slowly to dead white ash. Eleanor opened her eyes, faintly surprised that she still could. On the periphery of her vision, she was aware of a woman and a man: Dame Joan, weeping silently, and a priest, a black crow, wings folded and sleek, waiting.

She sighed faintly. Dame Joan crept to throw a handful of twigs on the fire. The priest muttered on incoherently. Painfully she turned her head toward the fire, the only warmth in this cold sterile room, and the dead came out to court her. She saw Alianore, her face drawn in a dust of fine ash; Thomas and her husband Harry, ghostly and insubstantial in the writhing smoke, together at last in love and forgiveness. And at the fire's heart, smiling and beckoning, a woman with hair like a coronal of flame — Elizabeth. Soon, she promised them. Very soon. She must wait a while longer for Harry.

She sighed again. Would he come? Would her message reach him in time? Would it reach him at all? She did not know for certain where he was. She'd heard that he was on the Border fighting the Scots, but then she'd heard many things and only believed the half of them: that Richard of Gloucester was king now; that he had usurped the crown of his nephew; that he had murdered his nephew . . . Harry was right. What did it matter who was king as long as he held the land in peace? There was no profit in war. All her life had been blighted by it, all those she had loved had been consumed by it; all that had come out of it was loss, of life, of land, each new generation fighting to regain what the last had lost and they, in their turn, adding to the toll. And now Harry had won it all back, bloodlessly, effortlessly, and from a Yorkist at that. Painfully, she smiled. So in the end he had proved her wrong. Even from a distance he could intrude upon her life and deprive her of her worthy death. He still mocked and thwarted her.

She could see now that it had all been for nothing; twelve years of privation to atone for her greedy and sinful life, all rendered meaningless now. She had thought she was nothing, that she had nothing and then a month ago the lawyer Middleton had come and laid at her feet a hundred times more than she had ever renounced. All of the great inheritance she had brought to Northumberland; more, for now she had her dead sister's share. Now, when it was too late, when she no longer wanted or needed it, she had her heart's desire.

The thin blue lids drooped over her tired eyes. Oh, how blissful was the darkness on eyes that had seen so much, how peaceful was the silence. She longed for sleep, the deep black velvet sleep of death; so close, so familiar now that she could not be afraid of it. The shadows had been gathering for a long time; silent and loving they filled all the corners of the room. She had but to call them out, for it was only her stubborn will that held them at bay.

But not so stubborn tonight. The long fight was drawing to a close. She could not wait much longer.

She slept for a while, a light troubled sleep plagued by dreams. When she awoke it was dark. A single candle lit the chamber and she called to Dame Joan for more light. The priest was still there, silent, impatient, fidgeting with his breviary, resentful that she kept him from his supper. Twice he came and peered down upon her sickly, fading countenance. Twice he sighed and resumed his place. She wondered vaguely herself, why she was still alive. She knew that Harry would not come now. There was nothing to keep her. All her dispositions had been made. Her lands she had bequeathed to Harry, and there was little else: a silver and ebony rosary and fifty pounds a year for Dame Joan; an annuity for her steward. But there were other legacies of the less material kind. *John!* Her old heart leapt. Sly, greedy, ruthless John; her creation, the mirror of all her old hatreds. John also she would leave to Harry. She could not will him away.

She whimpered faintly and the priest came, pressing the crucifix against her trembling lips. She smiled and contentedly closed her eyes. The shadows advanced and this time she did not send them away. They bent their cold dead lips to her shining face and in their strong loving arms bore her away.

In the north it was easy for Harry to forget. Among the soft hills and shadowed valleys the deeds of kings seemed far distant. And didn't he have everything that he had ever wanted? Was he not greater than his father and grandfather had ever been? More powerful even than the first Northumberland; more wealthy, more dominant . . . Yet still he turned his mind to other things, anything that could keep his thoughts from reckoning the cost of his supremacy to two small boys lodged in the Tower.

In January the Scots broke the Border and burned Coldstream. That roused him, the rape and plunder of his beloved land, and for once he welcomed the chance of aggression. The fighting was brief, the outcome decisive and by the spring, King James was suing again for peace.

It was June before he saw the King again; a quieter, more subdued Richard since the death of his only son Edward in April.

It had been a killing blow that had struck not only at his heart but at his whole future. He had no heir now, and was not likely to have from his sickly Queen. In desperation he named the son of his sister, the nineteen-year-old John de la Pole, Earl of Lincoln.

They had met at Pontefract, to greet the Breton envoys whom Richard hoped to persuade to relinquish Henry Tudor. His hopes were high, for Duke Francis was ailing and the French had recovered enough from the death of King Louis to pursue their usual policy of aggression. The King tried a subtle combination of bribery and threats, and after three days of wrangling the Breton treasurer, Pierre Landios, agreed to hand over his hostage before the end of the year.

They met twice more; at Scarborough in July and in September at Nottingham to sign a three-year truce with the Scots. And each time they met, they knew that something was gone between them. Both had changed but neither would acknowledge the change and both clung desperately to the remnants of their old loyalty and friendship. Neither dared look beneath the surface of each other's mind and salved their consciences with the thought that what was done was done, and what had been done, had been done for England. It had seemed for a while that they were justified in their belief. The rumours died down, stifled for lack of air, and the people had seen that Richard's laws were just and for the common good. But that had merely been the lull before the storm. The rumours were no longer rumours. In the minds of men they had become hard fact and in January, Guillaume de Rochfort, Chancellor of France had publicly denounced King Richard before the Estates General as the murderer of his nephews.

It was April now; two years since Edward had died, a little less since Richard had been crowned, less still since Edward's sons had been shut up in the Tower. On the smooth grassy knoll of Tower Hill, Harry sat his horse in the light teasing wind. Below him the Tower sprawled in shadow and sun, a Labyrinth of dark walls and squat turrets. His eyes swept along the solid line of the outer walls that rose sheer from the scarp of the ditch: twenty feet high and six feet thick, and higher still by some three or four feet the sweep of weathered stone that ringed the inner ward, where no man could pass but he held the King's writ. This wall was set with twelve tall towers, so smooth and round that even a raven could not have gained a foothold. And towering above all, the great square keep with its four projecting turrets: the White Tower, where two small boys lived out their lives in fear and shadow. Or did they? It was the first time he had asked himself the direct question and still his heart shied away from the answer. For the last year and a half the boys had been hidden behind a wall of silence and secrecy as impenetrable as those of the Tower itself. He knew of no man that had seen them in all that time. They had no formal attendants. Two of the warders were supposed to see to their needs. There had been a doctor, an Austrian named Argentine, who had once attended the elder boy Edward. He had been the last man outside the Tower to see them; a long time ago now, before Richard had been crowned. Was it possible that they were still there, still alive? He told himself that it was. The Tower was full of forgotten men. Hadn't he been one himself? He knew the Tower. He knew the darkness and the silence, the massive walls that smothered all sound. He knew the damp dingy passageways, the dark secret rooms and the forest of towers where you could have lost a whole army, let alone two small boys. They could still be alive. They must be alive, for surely Elizabeth Woodville would not have given herself and her daughters up into Richard's protection if she thought he had murdered her sons. But conversely, would she have given up at all if she had thought them still alive? Survival and self-preservation were all of her creed and she was not the kind of woman of settle for half, while there remained the faintest chance that she could have all. She had emerged from sanctuary after a year of harassment and privation and only then on condition that Richard swore a public oath to harm neither herself or her daughters. Harry frowned, remembering Richard's promise given before the lords and bishops and the leading citizens of London, 'that if the daughters of Elizabeth Grey, late calling herself Queen of England, will come to me out of the Sanctuary of Westminster and be guided, ruled and demeaned by me, I shall see that they be in surety of their lives . . . nor any of them imprison in the Tower of London or other prison . . .' The

267

words jarred uncomfortably in his mind. Whatever Elizabeth Woodville believed was the fate of her sons, she had certainly felt both herself and her daughters threatened. No man could know for sure, none wanted to know. All dreaded to turn the stone, for fear of what might crawl out from beneath. And he was one of them, he thought bitterly. With the rest of them he had kept silent and maintained the pretence of ignorance. Out of love or fear? He didn't know. Better, men said, to let sleeping dogs alone. Will Hastings' swift and untimely death was no longer necessary as a warning. There had been others since, to remind them.

He turned away and rode down the green slope, past the raised scaffold and the squat ugly block. Here, this December just past, he had watched another man die, slowly, agonisingly. It had taken almost an hour to reduce William Collynbourne to a jerking, mangled horror, even longer for him to die.

Harry spurred his horse, remembering the white, jerking, blood-spattered limbs, the stench of the ruptured bowel, the animal scream torn from the man's throat as the executioner had plunged his arm into Collynbourne's body and ripped the live heart out of him. He remembered, too, the ominous silence of the crowd. There had been none of the usual catcalls and jeering, none of the usual bestial excitement. William Collynbourne had been a small man, a minor servant of the Duchess of York. All knew his crime — the scurrilous rhyme that he had nailed to the door of St Paul's:

> The Cat, the Rat and Lovell, our Dog,
> Ruleth all England under the Hog.

There was another charge of which the King made much: that Collynbourne had offered one William Cate eight pounds to bear a message to Henry Tudor. It was the crime with which he had been formally charged, but all men knew why he had died. Then a week later, Collynbourne's treason had paled into insignificance beside that of Sir John Blount, the governor of Hammes Castle. He had released his prisoner of ten years, the Lancastrian Earl of Oxford, and fled with him to France and Henry Tudor's burgeoning court of exiles. It had been a bitter blow to Richard, not just the loss of Oxford but the defection of a lifelong Yorkist like Blount, which caused men to examine their consciences. Henry Tudor was more than a vague threat. He was a very real and potent danger. And the worst of it was, that he was now even further out of their reach. Warned by Morton, watching affairs from Flanders, Henry had fled from Brittany to France, to the protection of the young King Charles and his council, who now cossetted him as the future King of England, to the extent that they had lent him three thousand pounds with which to equip a fleet. Invasion was imminent. King Richard full expected Henry Tudor to land before the end of the summer.

He turned into Fenchurch Street. A group of merchants emerged from the Ironmongers' Hall and drew aside to let him pass. He was aware of their hostile eyes upon his back and the sudden silence that marked his passing. The silence hurt more than anything they could have said; not because of who he was, but because of what he was — a northerner, one of the hated breed with which the King surrounded himself and thrust into every vacant high office. It was here in the City that disaffection for Richard was worst. Here the damning whispers had their source; in the inns and alehouses, in the merchants' great halls. The silence of the common people was not so easily bought and soothe them as Richard might, with grants and remissions, they still doubted and questioned and in the absence of clear answers made their own judgements.

In March, to Richard's terrible grief, his wife Queen Anne had died. Even then they could not leave him alone. There was talk of poison, talk of murder, talk that Richard meant to make Elizabeth of York his queen to forestall any union with Henry Tudor. Some had believed it, at least that he meant to marry his niece, and to that end had assembled twelve doctors of canon law to condemn such a marriage as incest.

Two days before Easter, Richard had stood in the Hall of the Knights of St John at Clerkenwell, and before the lords and bishops of his council, he had publicly disclaimed any intention of marrying his niece, Elizabeth of York. He had repeated it a second time before the citizens and aldermen in the Guildhall, and finally he had written a letter in his own hand to the council at York to assure them that the rumours were without foundation. Few were deceived, though they paid him the lip service of appearing to be. It had been said. The damage was done. Men whispered, amongst themselves, that there was never smoke without a fire. Yet the accusation that Richard had murdered his nephews had raised enough smoke to choke all Christendom and still Richard did nothing. The awful doubt filled Harry again. Were the boys dead and did Richard stand their murderer? Only silence answered him, the deep impenetrable silence engendered by fear. Was he more afraid of knowing the truth than of the truth itself? The cold hard logical core of his mind knew it, yet his heart constantly argued against it. But he had to know. And there was only one man who could tell him.

King Richard lowered his eyes from the messenger's blank face and slowly laid down his quill. So it was come, the moment he had dreaded since Northumberland's abrupt and unannounced return to court. He knew without doubt why he was here, and asking for audience privily. *Privily* — the messenger had emphasised the word — because what was to be said between them could never be overheard. His shoulders sagged wearily. Any other man he could have fobbed off. Any other man would not even have wanted to know. And would he tell him? Dared he tell him? Yet he knew before the question was formed in his mind, that he would not. There were few enough as it was that he could depend on, even fewer that he could wholly trust: Ratcliffe, Brackenbury, Catesby and Tyrell, bound to him by more than mere loyalty. Use the small men, his mother had said. And he had; men of small mind and conscience, men of small honour. But not men of small ambition. They continued to expect reward for their silence and loyalty. Outside that select inner circle stood Norfolk and Stanley and Harry, the props which supported his unsteady throne. If he lost one of them the whole edifice could come crashing down. He shivered. It might not even take so much. Men had seen that he was fallible and were less in awe of him now, and his justification for taking the crown was wearing thin in their minds. There were no more gifts of land and office; Edward's vast treasure was gone. He had pawned the last of it three months ago to Stephen Gardener; the twelve apostles of silver and gilt, a gold salt encrusted with rubies. His debts were colossal. He owed twelve hundred pounds for gowns alone, besides what he'd had to borrow to cover the cost of the coming war. Shamefully, he'd had to resort to the benevolences that he had once so vociferously condemned, and even more frightening was the reluctance with which the money was coming in. Of the twenty thousand pounds that he had asked for, only four thousand had so far been received.

He gnawed agitatedly at his lower lip. Dear God in Heaven, who would have thought it would have come to this: that some faceless, landless Welshman could thus have thrown his plans into turmoil. He had promised England peace, and yet within two years he had brought her to the brink of war. But in a way he welcomed that. Better an all-out fight to the death than this never-ending battle against suspicion and rumour. He wished he had a clearer idea of the man. It would have helped to have had some tangible focus for his hatred. All of his torment he could lay at this man's door. He had sacrificed honour and conscience to eliminate one threat, only to have this other rise in its place. Because of Henry Tudor, he had been driven to ever more desperate and despicable measures; it had been only to thwart Tudor that he had ever thought of marrying Elizabeth of York, though in truth, it had been the Woodville bitch who had thought of it first, part of the bribe that had brought her out of sanctuary. Still, he *had* thought of it, in desperation, not knowing the storm of protest that he would raise, never dreaming of the vicious and unbearable accusation that would come out of it.

He had heard Ratcliffe's panic-stricken words in disbelief: 'Your Grace, you must make immediate public refutation. Apart from the fact that such a marriage would be an offence to both God and man, it would strike directly at your support in the north. Queen Anne, of blessed memory, was Earl Warwick's daughter, and the love the Yorkshiremen bear unto you is grounded in the love they once bore to Earl Warwick. If this gains credence in the north, if only half believed, as is being said, that you hastened the death of Queen Anne to marry the Lady Elizabeth . . .'

He had screamed him to silence. 'Do not soil your tongue with such a foulness. The very suggestion is infamous.'

'Quite so, your Grace,' Catesby had said smoothly. 'But the one follows the other. Any move to make the Lady Elizabeth your wife would give substance to this slander. It is known that you are desperate for an heir. It is also known that you could not look for further issue from the Queen . . .' He had spread his long hands expressively. 'I would advise, your Grace, that you make no marriage at all as yet, least of all one bound to raise such an outcry. Such a marriage could not be, politically as well as morally. The Lady Elizabeth is, by your own decree, bastard. The union would cast grave doubts upon the validity of the statute of *Titulus Regis* and therefore,' again those thin hands had fluttered, 'it could give rise to all kinds of unpleasant speculation. I must insist, your Grace, that for all our sakes, you put all thought of this marriage from your mind and make immediate denial, before the council, to that effect.'

Richard ground his teeth together in remembered chagrin. Another public oath, another public humiliation, as if he were some errant schoolboy caught in an immoral act instead of the King of England. And that was not the worst of what they said against him. How long before he was called to account for that other monstrous act? Not yet, not yet, he reassured himself. No man yet had the courage to face him with that; no man was yet sure enough to loose the whirlwind. There was a world of difference between what a man knew and what a man believed he knew. Belief and knowledge were not the same thing and as long as there was a shadow of doubt, as long as no man knew for sure . . .

He drew a long deep breath and made a gesture of dismissal to the men at his back. To the messenger who still waited he said, 'Tell the Earl of Northumberland that I will see him.'

He watched him advance; the long confident stride, purposeful and unhurried. Edward had always walked like that, so sure of himself. Tall men always were.

Harry knelt and laid his mouth against the outstretched hand. Smilingly the King bade him rise. 'Harry,' he said, forcing a lightness into his voice. 'I am glad you have come. I have just received the census returns for Durham. Only a hundred men, Harry? I

272

would have thought the bishop could have raised more than that?'

'He could,' said Harry carefully. 'If he had a mind to.'

Richard laid down the parchment. 'And he doesn't have a mind to?'

'No. It seems he has little taste for the war.'

'For the war or for me?'

Harry looked full into the dark shadowed eyes. 'For either,' he answered bluntly.

Richard moved away and Harry's eyes followed him as he crossed the room. He looked so small and thin and the rings hanging slackly on his pale hands rattled like chains upon his fingers.

In silence he poured wine. He raised his cup. 'The old salute, Harry. Remember? *Esperance en Dieu.*'

Harry smiled faintly. '*Loyaulte me lie,*' he answered softly and for a moment the old warmth flared between them and a little of the tension eased from the King's face.

Wearily Richard flung back his head. 'God, Harry. I can't believe it has come to this, that some anonymous Welshman could have caused all this havoc. Christ's wounds, I've never even seen the man.'

'You have — once. When you came to Raglan to escort me to Westminster. Henry Tudor was there.' Harry smiled wryly. 'I don't suppose you would have noticed him. There is something very unremarkable about Henry.'

'Of course, you know him.' Richard turned to him eagerly.

'I *knew* him. I dare say he is much changed.' But not that much, he thought afterwards. Henry's personality had been stamped upon him long before his time at Raglan. He recalled the pale, repressed face, that unshakeable belief in his own glorious destiny. He had laughed at him then. It had been laughable then, that scrawny youth putting forward his flawed blood-right, bolstered by vague prophecies. And yet whilst he and all the world had been laughing, Henry had been quietly pursuing that destiny. He had said that there was nothing remarkable about him, yet to have come so far against such odds was quite remarkable in itself.

'What is he like, Harry? What kind of man is he?' Richard

273

laughed shakily. 'It's a grave disadvantage, plotting a strategy against a man you don't know.'

'You know his mother. You know Bishop Morton. That is the kind of man he is.'

'You do not comfort me, Harry.' Suddenly Richard struck his fist against his open palm. 'It's the waiting that is so killing, not knowing where or when.'

'There is no fresh news then?'

The King shook his head. 'The Tudor fleet still lies off Harfleur, some fifteen ships and two thousand men; mercenaries mostly, I gather.' He threw a desperate look at Harry. 'That's not enough. If he's the kind of man you say he is then he would not attempt conquest with so small a force. He must be assured of massive support in England.' He turned a pale and haggard face toward him. 'Will he get it, Harry?'

'He'll get some. The Welsh in all probability will come out for him. I should think it would be on the Pembrokeshire coast that he will land.'

'I've already anticipated that. Your own brother-in-law, William Herbert, guards all of South Wales; James Tyrell watches from Builth and Llandovery; and the Stanleys will block his passage into Cheshire and Lancashire.'

He smiled as he saw the uncertain flicker of Harry's eyes. 'Oh, I know about the Stanleys,' he said bitterly. 'I have never deceived myself that it is anything but greed that keeps them loyal. But at least they're consistent. Both Lord Stanley and his brother Sir William will stick with the man that brings them the most advantage. I intend to see that it is myself.'

He moved away toward the window. 'But there are others, Harry, not so consistent, not so predictable. I know some of them; men that bring their smiles and homage to court, then plot with my enemies behind my back — traitors, turncoats. But they're careful, cunning, they won't show their hands yet awhile. They're waiting and watching to see which way the wind will blow.' He broke off, hearing the high hysterical note creep into his voice. He was silent for a while, plucking at his lip. Then he said, 'I am surrounded by treachery, Harry. You are one of the few I know I can trust — you and Jack Norfolk and Lovell.

You've stood by me through all; loyal, steadfast. You've thought the best when others have thought the worst. I'm grateful for that, Harry.'

Harry looked away from the pale intense face. Richard had led him to it almost by design. He knew he must speak now or the moment would be lost, yet even now, he was tempted to leave it alone, to be loyal as Norfolk and Lovell were loyal; blind, unseeing and as Richard himself had said, thinking the best when all others thought the worst. That was the kind of loyalty that Richard had always wanted from him, the kind that he could never give.

He said, low-voiced, 'Richard, my lord . . .' There his voice broke and the King, listening, knew by the very inflection of that soft and expressive voice that they had reached the thing he had come here to say. He knew he should speak, say something to divert him, to prolong the peace between them for as long as he could. But he said nothing and the inexorable voice began again.

'My liege, you must be aware of the accusation against you, that the Chancellor of France has publically denounced you as the murderer of your nephews.'

'I am aware of it.'

'Are you also aware of the damage to your reputation that such a statement can cause?'

'Of course I am aware of it. That is why these calumnies are spread abroad, that is why I am constantly maligned, so that men will turn against me. The French are supporting the Welshman's cause, so naturally they will say anything that could gain him support.' He smiled contemptuously. 'Have you not also heard that I murdered my wife, and Clarence, my brother, and that I bludgeoned poor Daft Harry to death whilst he knelt at his prayers?'

'No. I had not heard, my lord, though as you say, it is common practice to accuse the enemy of past crimes, crimes beyond proof one way or the other. But the crime of which Guillaume de Rochfort accused you is not beyond proof.' Harry sought Richard's gaze and held it. 'For your own sake and that of England, my lord, would it not be wiser to prove him wrong?'

'In what way?'

'Bring King Edward's sons out of the Tower or wherever they are kept. Let the people see that they are alive.'

The King looked away from his burning gaze. 'I have told you before, Harry. I cannot risk the Lords Bastard falling into the hands of my enemies. The Tower is the only place where they are safe from the machinations of the Woodvilles.'

'Then at least allow the council to enter the Tower and see for themselves. It need not be more than a half dozen men: Cardinal Bourchier, Bishop Russell . . .'

'And you yourself, of course, Harry?'

'No. Not necessarily. I would be quite prepared to take Bourchier's word for it.'

'But not mine?'

Adroitly Harry evaded the challenge. 'My lord,' he said with heavy patience, 'we are on the brink of invasion and war. You need the loyalty and support of every man you can get.' He snatched up the parchment that Richard had discarded. 'You send out demands to know how many men each lord can bring to battle. Well, I can tell you. Those that do not desert to Henry Tudor will sit at home doing nothing. It doesn't matter whether what is said against you is true or false. If it is believed by enough, it becomes truth. And it is believed, not just by your enemies but by men who loved you and have denied their own consciences to make you king.'

'Like you, Harry.' Richard smiled bleakly. 'Do you believe it?'

'I believe, Richard, that you are a sensible man, that you would not knowingly jeopardise your crown and England out of pride and stubborness, that you would not see men fall away from you, if there was any help for it.'

'You think not?' said Richard stiffly. 'Then you are wrong. I refuse to demean myself by even refuting such obvious lies.'

Harry stared at him coldly. 'Yet you didn't mind demeaning and defending yourself against the accusation that you had murdered your wife. You were quick enough to stop their mouths then when you thought the men of the north would turn against you. Well, it's not just the support of a few thousand you're in danger of losing now, it's all of England. It's not just your reputation that will be lost, it's England. I beg you, my lord, listen to

276

me. If you want to remain King of England you must show that those boys are alive.'

Richard turned a white and furious face toward him. 'I will not.'

'You will not or you cannot?'

They stared at each other with such savage intensity that the very air between them was bruised and hurt. Then the King bowed his head and shadow obscured his face. For one moment, for one brief aching moment, the longing to unburden himself was almost too much. If Harry had put out a hand, if he had spoken one tender word, it would have been enough to loose the flood. But Harry neither moved nor spoke, and the moment passed and he was walled up in his prison of silence again. Silence was both his advocate and his shield, his best and only defence. He wanted to smile. He wondered if Harry remembered that it had been he who had taught him that.

Harry felt the dreadful coldness creep insidiously into his heart. He knew now. As surely as if Richard had cried his guilt aloud, he knew. And the truth sickened and weakened him as if a great fist had been driven hard into his body. He hadn't even the breath for words and it was the King who spoke first, calmly, easily, as if nothing had passed between them more than the commonplace.

'I intend to remove to Nottingham at the end of the month, Harry. I shall be well placed there to hear of the Tudor's landing from whichever direction it comes.'

He rose and crossed the room to seat himself again at his desk. 'No doubt you will wish to return north as speedily as possible. There is still much to be done.' His eyes fastened with cold regality upon Harry's face. 'I have your word, my lord, that you will attend upon me in full strength within two days of my summons?'

He held his breath. This was the testing time, for if Harry was going to desert him, it would be now. Once his word was given he would not break it, and once it was given he would be compromised, his fellow-conspirator and accomplice. He felt sure enough of himself to take the gamble, for as always he had left himself a bolt hole of escape. He had said nothing. Harry had

277

heard nothing and what had passed between them could never be put into words.

'Your word, my lord,' he said again and his heart thundered in his narrow chest as Harry raised his eyes. He was surprised and exultant to see their cowed and beaten look, to see so clearly the pain of his shattered faith. He heard Harry's voice, very faint and thin, as if he spoke from a great distance.

'You have my word,' he said dully.

The King smiled with the sickly sweet excitement of power. 'It is well, my lord.' His eyes hardened. 'And tell his Grace the Bishop of Durham, that a hundred men will not suffice. He will send the full quota or suffer for it.'

He picked up his quill again in a gesture of dismissal. 'And also, my lord; you may tell all those that are solicitous enough to enquire, that my nephews are still kept safe within the Tower.' And they were, buried beneath a heap of stones at the foot of the tower stair.

'Oh, dear God have mercy,' Maud said faintly. 'Those two innocent little knaves.' She sank down upon the edge of the bed. 'You are sure?'

Harry did not look at her. 'As sure as I can be without seeing their bodies.'

Maud swallowed hard and her hand instinctively moved to her belly where her own child writhed in protest. 'There is no possibility that they are other than within the Tower? Was there not some rumour that they had been sent into the north?'

'And where in the north could he hide them that I would not know? Where in all England could he hide them but that some man wouldn't know? And it doesn't answer why he would not show them. God, Maud. I know the man. He's not a fool. He knows full well why men are turning against him and he's desperate enough to keep his crown that he'd bring those boys from the ends of the earth if he thought that it could save him.' Harry covered his face with trembling hands. 'I know, Maud. I asked him outright and he could not answer me. I saw his face. God help us, but those boys are dead.'

She went to him and cradled his head against her breast. She

278

felt the awful shuddering anguish of his body and wept herself to see the tears that seeped through his closed and rigid fingers.

'But why, Harry?' she whispered. 'What threat were two little bastard boys?'

He looked up, dragging his fingers over his face. 'They wouldn't always have been little boys,' he answered her bleakly. 'They might not always have been bastard. The act of *Titulus Regis* was tenuous at best. It might not have stood up in law, if it were ever challenged. Men might not have stirred themselves overmuch for the rights of a child dominated by the Woodvilles, but for a grown man, able to speak for himself . . .'

She listened in silence. She knew it eased him to talk, yet the passionate vindication did not touch her. She could have told him long ago that the Boar when cornered was treacherous. She too had known Richard of Gloucester; the paragon, the pillar of moral virtue, the man of conscience and honour. She had seen from a distance that which Harry could not see, though it was before his very eyes. A man who lived by such high ideals was broken even by the smallest compromise of his principles. They had held out to him power and dominance and he had not been able to resist, yet at the heart of him he had known that he didn't have the right. From the very beginning he had been weighed down by guilt. He had sold his honour for the price of a crown and once honour was gone his life could only be a ruthless justification for its loss. Harry should have known: there was none more iniquitous than a fallen angel.

She looked up at Harry and saw the anguished workings of his face. Pain and disillusion devoured him. He was bitterly hurt, the betrayal had cut him to the heart. Yet he was not repelled, he was not outraged in the sense that she was.

He said quietly, as if he spoke to himself, 'For the sake of peace, men set aside the rights of Edward's son. For peace, they consented to Richard's assumption of the crown, not knowing that they gave him an impossible task, for there could be no peace while Edward's sons lived. Their very existence was a constant challenge to peace.'

'My God, Harry,' she said in a shocked whisper. 'Even now you're defending him.'

279

'No.' He dragged his fingers wearily over his face. 'No, I'm not.'

'Justifying him then. It's the same thing.'

'Not him. Myself perhaps. For none of us can be absolved from this.' He looked at her, his eyes full of self-disgust. 'For God's sake, Maud, we all knew. But none of us wanted to admit that we'd made the wrong choice. None of us wanted to risk the lands and honours that had bought our silence. From the very beginning we connived at those boys' deaths, albeit unknowingly. We did not question Hastings' murder, for that's what it was, nor the execution without trial of Rivers and Grey. We doubted, but we did not voice those doubts. And our silent assent to those first outrages paved the way for others. What Richard took by force he could only keep by force, and none of us did anything to stop him.'

'You can't blame yourself, Harry. No man could have foreseen this.'

'I could have,' he said quietly. 'If I'd thought about it deeply enough. But because I loved him, I didn't want to think about it. I couldn't.'

He broke off and she knew from the brittle sound of his voice that he was again close to tears. She said, reaching out to him, 'What will you do?'

'What can I do? Richard is still king and whilst he is, no man can force his hand.'

Her own hand, soft and caring, pulled away from him and her voice assumed a hardness and sharpness he had never heard. 'So all will be as it was before? You are content to bend the knee and continue to give your loyalty to the cold-blooded murderer of innocent children?'

He looked at her savagely. 'Do I have a choice?'

She was silent, suddenly fearful of the growing hostility between them. She saw now how it must have been. She understood his fear now, not of Richard himself, but fear that the illusion would be destroyed, that his faith and trust would be irrevocably shattered. She felt the same temptation herself now, to say nothing, to maintain at all costs the love and trust that had never once been questioned in nearly eight years and to push away this ugly hideous thing that was suddenly between them. But she had never deceived him. It was too late to start now.

She looked up searchingly into his face. 'Yes,' she said calmly and clearly. 'You do have a choice — Henry Tudor.'

She had expected anger, fury even, but she was unprepared for the dreadful shrinking pallor that suddenly invaded his face. Even his voice was bloodless. 'And what do you know of Henry Tudor?' he said.

Quickly she answered him before her courage faded. 'I had a letter . . .' Her throat closed convulsively. Her lips moved but no sound would come. She licked them nervously with the tip of her tongue. His eyes were still frozen upon her. He was so still, so silent, yet rage and violence emanated from him in thick heavy waves that bore down upon her so terrifyingly that she swayed as if she had been struck.

'Harry,' she whispered. 'Harry, my lord.'

He sat at last, his voice like the bludgeoning of a sharp stone. 'And what did this letter say?'

She lifted her chin bravely. 'It asked that I use my influence to persuade you to the worthiness of his cause. He spoke of a marriage, perhaps with my sister Katherine, if his proposal to wed Elizabeth of York was frustrated.'

Harry smiled, an ugly twisting of his mouth that held no vestige of humour. 'He is persistent, I'll give him that.' He moved away from her. 'And no doubt he reminded you of past affections, past ties, reminded you, perhaps, that if it had not been for the unkindness of fate you might have been Queen of England?'

Maud moved her head in a blind futile gesture and the child leapt within her as if it sensed her despair.

'And what makes you think that dear Henry would make a better king than the one we've already got?'

Anger penetrated the dull misery at last. She lifted her head. 'Because his hands are clean,' she cried. 'Because all his actions will not be governed by the need to alleviate his awful guilt.'

'And you think it is as easy as that? That kings are replaced as easily as a displeasing gown? That I can turn my back on Richard, just like that?' His voice was rising, beating about her ears like a shrieking wind. She saw his face change: ugly, cruel, the veins knotting and straining in his throat. 'Christ, woman,' he shouted. 'I loved the man.'

'I know, Harry,' she said quietly. 'But I thought you loved honour more.'

She watched him ride back through the dark and shadowy gateway. He was unshaven, dishevelled, his cloak patched and stiff with mud and as he leapt from his horse she saw his knees buckle and sag. He had been gone for three whole days.

Maud turned away from the window and sat herself listlessly before the burnished glass. She stared at herself. She looked older; lines of strain had appeared around her mouth and her eyes seemed to shrink back into their sockets. They were all marked with it: herself, Harry, all that knew. The very knowledge was tiring and depleting. Harry was right, they were all the King's silent accomplices, murderers themselves of truth, giving assent and concurrence to the awful deed because they were too cowardly to speak. Only the common people had the courage to question. Fear had stilled the tongues of the lords and they drew inward upon themselves. They had grown blind and deaf, concerning themselves with the familiar and trivial and ironically the silence that Richard had so carefully nurtured was now turned upon him. He beat the war drum but no man heard. He sent out letters and summonses — pleading, threatening, now frantic, now desperate — and received only silence in reply. And she was glad. She exulted in the thought of his miserable isolation, the thought of him wretched and friendless and alone. She bit at her lip. How cruel and vengeful they had all become. She thought back to the night of that terrible quarrel with Harry: she had accused him of cowardice for his refusal to denounce Richard; he had accused her of being Henry Tudor's spy. He had ridden away from Wressell that very night. She'd had neither sight nor sound of him for three days and nights. But now he was back. She could hear his slow footfall upon the stair.

She did not turn her head. She saw him advance, spectral and distorted in the shimmering glass. He had the look of death about him, bloodless, skeletal, the sharp attenuated bones thrusting from ashen skin. She turned to look at him then. 'Oh, my love,' she said softly. 'Oh, my dearest love.'

He halted, swaying and the sweet sound of her voice broke him more surely than three days and nights of bitter anguish and cold. He fell on his knees and she ran to him wordlessly.

He clung to her, grinding his face into her soft flesh. He could not speak, he could not move. He dared not lose her, for he had the strangest feeling that if he did he would float away like a speck of dust and be nothing.

Then slowly, as if he were an old and feeble man, she helped him to his feet. She was weeping silently. Tears ran down her face and trembled in the corners of her mouth. He looked so old, so beaten, his great strong body diminished and shrunk. Silently she fetched him wine and knelt by him while he drank it. Slowly a faint colour flushed beneath his sallow skin. 'Oh, Harry,' she said in quiet despair. 'Where in God's name have you been?'

He lifted his eyes to her face, red and raw through lack of sleep. 'Nowhere. Anywhere. Just riding.' To Hell and back, he thought to himself. Trying to exorcise the demon of love from his heart.

She did not press him, for she knew just from the look of him that he was still not free of his love and loyalty but neither could he shake off the horror of his betrayal. Yet he must. He must turn his back on one or the other, or be destroyed himself. But she said nothing and sat leaning against him. The silence wrapped itself lovingly around them and he drew her close against his heart.

She awoke in the night and found him gone. She stretched out her hand. The silken pillow held no warmth. Panic seized her, foolish and irrelevant, and she flung herself from the bed and across the room.

Then she heard him call out to her, the silken thread of his voice frayed and knotted with pain. She turned. Moonlight pooled the floor but he sat in a small island of shadow thrown by the great tester bed. Between his hands he held a parchment; the seal, the Great Seal of the King of England was unbroken.

She touched it, withdrawing her hand quickly as if it burned. 'When did this come? I heard no messenger.'

'Four days ago,' he said.

She sat beside him. The moonlight shone whitely on her flesh

283

and sapped the vibrant colour from her hair. He too had a ghostly look and though he shrank from the edge of the light she could see the sharp edge of jaw and brow and the dark empty hollows that were his eyes. So we are, she thought, ghostly and insubstantial. Will we ever be whole and alive again?

She looked down at the cylinder of parchment. 'You have not opened it?'

'There is no need. I know its contents well enough. Every lord in England has received one. It is the King's summons to attend upon him at Leicester. Henry Tudor is expected to land before the end of the month, at least by the beginning of August.'

It was the most she had heard him say since his return and the effort seemed to have exhausted him. She heard his quick uneven breathing. 'Will you go,' she asked him.

'Yes,' he said quietly. 'Yes, I shall go. I gave my word. I cannot break it.'

She turned her head in a little gesture of despair. Then she heard his voice, low and level out of the darkness. 'And I also gave him my word, a long time ago, that if he ever broke faith, I would not lift a hand to save him from all the fires of Hell.'

The pain began as a slow dull ache at the base of her spine. It grew slowly and insidiously, almost imperceptibly. All through the day she felt its advance, like a child piling one counter upon another, till the weight and pressure were unbearable and she screamed aloud. The pain opened out, burst from her. She felt the warm rush of blood against her thighs. She stood transfixed. Elizabeth came and took her arm, 'My lady?'

'The child,' she gasped. 'Too soon! Too soon!'

Elizabeth's yelping cry summoned the rest of her women. Anxious faces filled her vision; hands, fluttering, tentative, raised her up. They stripped the bed; they stripped her of the heavy stained gown. She saw her shift smeared scarlet. Fear rose in her. There should not be blood. Not yet.

She lay down and the pain receded. Elizabeth fed her capers in honey. Cicely came and smoothed her brow and said repeatedly and infuriatingly that all would be well. She closed her eyes. The pain was transient, hardly perceptible, not even true pain, more a discomforting sensation, like a rough hand being drawn across her belly. Involuntarily her rigid muscles eased. She felt drowsy, weightless, perhaps she would sleep . . . Then she felt it, a small hot flashing pain as if a spark had been struck in the darkness. She tensed, grew rigid, expectant but nothing could have prepared her for that terrible onslaught of fiery agony. Her face contorted into a soundless scream. She gasped, drawing great gulps of air into her lungs. She had suffered before but not like this, not this dreadful devouring intensity of pain, this sensation of being torn apart. And there was no respite as there had been the other times, no draining away, no blessed moment of relief for her to gather her strength. Even before the last contraction had fully died away another had slammed into her body. She moaned feebly, her strength draining. Once she lifted her head and stared down at her body. She saw the hard rhythmic thrusting movements beneath her pale stretched skin. Then Master Benedict leaned over her and she turned her face from his wine-tainted breath. He laid his hands on the hard swell of her belly, sucking his cheeks in and out with little explosions of sound. Then a face, grim with anguish, distant, shifting and fluid, seen through a haze of pain.

'Harry,' His name emerged as a deep growling in her throat. She flung out a hand, slippery with sweat. He clasped it, pressing his mouth against her fingers to stifle the sound of his own agony.

She clung to him as if he were all that held her anchored to the earth. Dimly she heard his whispered words of love and comfort, a faint constant murmur above the screaming of her own tortured flesh. The pain intensified, as if her body were pounded by some murderous fist. Gradually she grew away from it, her senses numbed, her mind shocked and paralysed and unfeeling. She heard nothing but Harry's soft and loving voice. She felt nothing but the warm strength of his hand.

The child was born at midnight, bursting from her body with a sickening rip of muscle and sinew and dying without uttering a single cry. Seeing its large malformed head the women crossed themselves and bore it quietly away. Master Benedict fell to his knees and prayed loudly.

Harry still knelt by the edge of the bed, clutching her hand so tightly that long ago the blood had been driven from it and it lay numb and inert in his grasp. He stared down at her face, pale as wax, her sweat-soaked hair streaming across the pillow. Her breathing was shallow as if she slept. A slow intermittent pulse throbbed in her neck.

He turned his head. 'My lord,' Master Benedict touched his shoulder and beckoned him away.

'My lord.' The physician's face was grey and wretched. Again he said, 'My lord,' and hesitated. He wiped his face on the sleeve of his robe. 'All is not well, I fear, my lord.' He fluttered his hands delicately, 'The countess is badly torn due to the excessive size of the child. There is much bleeding, and worse, I fear all has not come cleanly away.'

Harry stared at him blankly. He could not even summon his wits to make answer. Instinct told him to look away from the physician's eyes, never to see what was there; most of all, never to understand it.

Maud woke to the cool impersonal touch of Master Benedict's hands and the dulled murmur of voices. She lay inert, her eyes tightly closed, whilst the unseen hands prodded and probed. She felt him draw the coverlet up under her chin. The hands transferred themselves from her breasts to her brow.

'No fever yet,' she heard him mutter.

Still she did not move. She felt her body grow tense and fearful. But there was no pain, only a dull ache, a yawning emptiness, a strange slow draining of her strength.

She opened her eyes. The chamber was full of dull reflected light. She glimpsed the soft-footed retreating shadow of Master Benedict. Harry stood alone by the window, the harsh planes of his face flushed and gilded by the light.

She called to him and was surprised to hear her voice so weak and thin.

She looked up into his face as he came to sit by her. He still had that dreadful underlying pallor but the haunted look in his eyes was gone. In its place was a quiet intense despair that was somehow infinitely worse.

She said faintly, 'Harry, the child . . .'

'Dead,' he answered her harshly, so harshly that she understood

286

and did not question him further.

He lifted her small cold hand to his mouth. 'Sleep, my love,' he whispered. 'Master Benedict says you must rest. You'll soon be strong and well again.'

She felt his mouth moving against the back of her hand, murmuring words of strength and courage. Grief and pain trembled beneath the tranquil voice and with sudden premonition she turned her head.

'Harry,' she asked quietly. 'Am I going to die?'

She had her answer in the look in his eyes. The flame was doused. They glowed a dull smoking red like the ashes of a dying fire.

She closed her eyes and smiled weakly. 'If I do, Harry —' She was not so brave that she could exclude all hope. 'If I do, don't lay me in the dark, will you, Harry? I want to be near the light, near the sun . . .' Her voice faded away to a faint inaudible sigh. She was so very, very tired.

Harry watched her, his face blank, without expression. He was protected from the worst of the pain by a blessed coldness which had settled upon his heart and frozen all feeling and thought. He was even afraid to move, lest it set the blood flowing in his limbs again and he would be overwhelmed by terrible and abysmal grief, by fury and rage at having to watch helplessly whilst the lifeblood drained out of her.

Slowly he turned his head. He heard his son Henry's voice, shrill with childish fear.

'I *will* see her. I *will*. You shall not keep me out.'

Small angry fists pounded at the door, threatening Harry's strenuously acquired calm. Then Master Benedict entered, hissing with outrage.

'My lord, I must protest . . .'

Harry made a feeble gesture. 'Let him come,' he said wearily.

He could not look at him. He could not bear to see his own pain and misery written so clearly upon that small face. Visibly he flinched as an insistent hand tugged at his sleeve.

'Father,' Henry said in his clear high voice. 'Is it true that my lady mother is like to die?'

'We are all like to die some day,' he said. Tentatively he laid his

287

hand upon his son's red-gold head. 'Only God knows when and how.'

She woke for the last time to sombre golden light. Harry was still there, an effigy of despair, his shoulders bowed, his head sunk upon his breast. Other images came close but never quite touched her. Reality itself assumed a dreamlike quality. She was quite free from pain now. She felt light, weightless, as if she had drunk of some sweet heady wine. She stirred tentatively and knew that they had put fresh linen upon the bed. It felt crisp and cool against her flesh.

With an effort she turned her head. It was so quiet, so dim. Blue shadows encroached on the periphery of her vision. She sensed rather than saw Harry lean toward her. She could not see his face clearly, just the thin stark edge of bone where the fading light touched it, like the reflection from the facets of a stone.

'Harry,' she whispered. 'Harry, my love.'

He bent to kiss her, his mouth like ice upon her burning flesh. She strained to see him. Why did they not light the lamps? It was growing so cold and dark. She shivered. She hated the dark, and soon she would be plunged into its depths.

She cried out fearfully, and knew that Harry spoke to her but she could not hear what he said. There was a rushing sound in her ears as if she were falling, and all around her it was growing so dark. Then quite clearly she heard the strong tender voice, not Harry's voice, but a known and loved voice; sharp and lucid, a bright clear flame in the darkness. She could see his face now, sad and wise, the blind white eyes turned toward her.

He laid down a sweet sharp fall of notes, sparks of shining perfect sound. The beautiful voice reached out, calling her home. He sang the sweet measure she had loved as a child:

> Slowly the white hemlock weakly leans,
> Coloured like bright dawn even at resting time.
> Shining, frail, fair and pensive . . .

She closed her eyes and went unafraid into the darkness.

The great dark hall was full of men, men who moved with soft furtive footsteps, whose speech was restrained and subdued. More than a hundred, Gwilym Ddu gauged by the level of noise. And there were more outside the wall; foreigners, men who were neither English nor Welsh, whose rough speech he could not decipher.

He sat unnoticed in his dim corner, incongruous with his flowing hair and robes among these steel-clad men. His harp lay across his knees, the strings broken and useless. He had only played once in the in the last few years, since the Lord William had gone and strangers had come to Pembroke. *Lleogyr*. Filling the hall with their harsh arrogant voices. He had stayed because he was too old to move on and no one really had wanted him. Here he had been born and here he would die. None had troubled him. They fed him and housed him as they would a stray dog. His needs were few. He had a straw pallet on which to sleep, though they had chivvied him from his warm place by the hearth. He ate little and drank less. They brewed no mead now and he had to content himself with watery ale.

Regretfully and tenderly he touched the useless harp. The last time he had played had been for his little girl, on the very night she had died. Not so long ago, little more than a week, though to him it seemed like years. All the music had died in him then; he had given her his last. All his heart and love and comfort had been in that brief and final song. He had been alone in the hall, alone in silence and darkness, sunk in reverie. He had been thinking of the old days, when the hall had rung to the sound of his voice, when he'd had eyes to see. He had seen his little girl, he had heard her voice. At first he had thought it part of the reverie. Then he had felt her fear, so strong, so overpowering, as tangible as cold steel piercing his bowels. He had done the only thing he could to soothe her. He had sung, that foolish little *awdl*, the first thing he had ever taught her. But long before the song was ended the rotten harp strings had crumbled beneath his fingers and he had known that her life was ended. He did not grieve. She was closer to him now than she had ever been. And he had the comfort of knowing that when his time came there would be a voice to guide him through the darkness.

He tilted his head. A silence had fallen, full of expectation, full of awe. A man had entered — two men. The first, slender and of medium build to judge by the length and weight of his stride; the second, heavier, older, slower but deliberately slow as if he thought it politic to lag behind. Instinctively, Gwilym Ddu knew it was the first man that was important.

They were kneeling to him. He felt the sudden downsurge of movement, the dull impact of steel-clad knees upon stone. He waited, impatient to hear the man speak. He heard a voice, not his, though. This voice he knew; Rhys ap Thomas, Lord of Ardudwy and Evionydd. He addressed the stranger as 'sire'.

Then, acutely, he was aware that the stranger was coming toward him. Taller perhaps than he had at first thought. It was caution that inhibited his stride. He lifted his head, sniffing the air like a dog. A dozen different smells clung to the man; sea-salt and wind, a strange medicinal smell; sweat and tears and penury, and overlying all, strong and pervasive, the acrid stench of fear.

'*Pencerdd*?' The man spoke to him in Welsh. Only the one word but he knew him.

The bard sighed. So. The Tudor Cub. He was come then, at last.

'You know me, *pencerdd*?'

'Yes, I know you. *Y Ddraig Goch.*'

Henry Tudor's face did not change in expression but something stirred in his eyes. The bold epithet pleased him and soothed a little of his mounting fear. He restrained the urge to look behind him and count his small following yet again. Not so many as he had hoped, less than he had been promised . . . Terror filled him, yet he had schooled himself so well that no tremor of movement showed on his face and his eyes remained clear and steady. It was early days yet, he told himself. Rhys ap Thomas had spoken of mighty support: the men of Monmouth and Flintshire, the Salisburies of Ystrad Clewydd. There were many, he had said, who were for him. And how many against? He closed his mind to the rumour that John Savage and Walter Herbert had thrown in their lot with the Usurper. William Herbert, without doubt, had declared for the Boar. A disappointment but not a surprise, considering that Herbert had recently wed the Usurper's bastard daughter. He thought, too, that William Herbert would not have cared to bend the knee to one who had once been his prisoner.

He looked with reverence into the bard's ancient face. It comforted him mightily to see him here. The old man reminded him of how far he had come, how much he had achieved since he had fled like a frightened rabbit from this very place. Only now could he see the pattern of it all, the purpose of all the years of exile and misery. All had been predestined, nothing had happened purely by chance. Every knock and blow had hardened and shaped him into the man he was: cautious but not cowardly, hesitant but not slow. He never speculated or overreached himself and he knew precisely his own limitations, as well as those of his fellow men. In that was he was rarely disappointed. Avarice was his only weakness, the worship of wealth and of power, a weakness, as yet, he had had no opportunity to indulge. He smiled. Was that not why he was here?

'*Pencerdd*.' He knelt, a humble gesture that filled the old man with pride. 'Will you give me your blessing, *pencerdd*?'

Gwilym Ddu raised him up and clasped his hands, soft and smooth and ringless, like a girl's, yet he felt their latent power. He knew now that this was the one, the fulfillment of all prophecy, the hope of Wales. Here was the flame that would rekindle their fire. Here was the seed from which would spring a mighty tree that in time would overshadow all the world.

He flung back his head and once more his mighty voice filled the hall with the words of the immortal prophecy.

'Brutus, beyond the setting of the sun, past the realms of Gaul lies an island in the sea. A race of kings will be born there descended from your stock, and the round circle of the earth will be subject to them.'

Then solemnly he raised Henry Tudor to his feet. 'Lord,' he said, 'you have the blessing of the gods. What need have you of man's?'

He knelt on the hard stones of the cool dim church, his lips moving soundlessly in the ritual of prayer. His eyes were cast down, devout, worshipful, masking the swift inexorable flow of his thoughts. Repeatedly he reassessed and analysed his position. It was tempting to become complacent, to indulge his belief that all was preordained and thus he could not be thwarted. In truth, it was hard not to believe that some protective hand was not held over him, that his triumphant progress through Wales was not blessed by God: Cardigan had welcomed him and the first of the Welsh chieftains had come to him there; Richard Gryffys and Evan Morgan had rallied wholeheartedly to his banner. No hand had been raised against him as he had moved north-east, through Aberayron and Aberystwyth, Machynlleth and Llwyn Dafydd. Cautiously at Llanbadarn he had divided his force, one part moving up the Severn Valley, the other swinging northward to Llanvylin. At Cevn Digoll, near Welshpool, they had joined forces again and here he had received a massive influx of men. Rhys ap Thomas had brought in the men of Ardudwy and Evionydd, Lleyn and Arvon, the men of Monmouth and of Flint. Still unopposed, they had marched for Shrewsbury, which had flung open its gates at the news of his coming. Here the first of the English lords had joined him: Sir Gilbert Talbot with five hundred men and the tidings that the Usurper still tarried at Nottingham, apparently unaware that he had even landed. He had moved on to Stafford, then Lichfield where the great cathedral had pealed in welcome and the guns had fired in majestic salute. They came in their droves then: Walter Herbert and John Savage despite the rumours; the knights, Hungerford and Bourchier, Digby and Sandford, so many that he had lost count. His army resounded with paeans of praise. They called out at his passing, 'Richmond, sprung from British race, from out this land the Boar will chase . . .'

From Lichfield they had moved along Watling Street to Tamworth. It was from there that he had ridden secretly, at night, to meet with the Stanleys in a dingy upper room at the Three Tuns Inn. The meeting had been brief and inconclusive. Lord Stanley, as always, was full of yeas and nays, and although privately he had sworn himself and his brother to Henry's cause, publicly he must still hold his hand since the Usurper held his son, Lord Strange, as hostage for his loyalty. Henry had had to be content with the vague promise that the Stanleys would join him as soon as they could. Henry smirked. Did the Stanleys rate their loyalty as a woman did her virtue and think it the more prized for being hard won?

He looked up and momentarily caught his Uncle Jasper's eyes fixed upon him in pride and jubilation. He dropped his own and resumed his prayers. Bishop Courtney's voice rolled over him like a mighty wave, exhorting the Trinity to bless their cause, invoking God and all his saints to confound their enemies and reward the pursuit of righteousness with victory. Again, that acrid little smile touched his mouth. He had no doubt that the men gathered here would expect their rewards to be of a more earthly kind. Most would be disappointed, for he had promised himself that there would be no favourites or hangers-on. He would buy no man's loyalty — no woman's either, if it came to that. He thought briefly of the woman he had promised to marry if God gave him the victory. He had never met Elizabeth of York, though he had heard that she was comely. It wasn't important. Love and passion were nigh-on extinct in him now. Only once had he ever truly loved: a frivolous little Welsh girl with crimson hair. How ironic that she had married Harry Percy. The long mouth twitched, remembering that he had had no answer to his appeal for help. Still, he had much else to thank Northumberland for; that pitying condescension, that silent mockery, that had been worse than an open sneer. All these had spurred him on. He had kept Harry Percy's face before him for years; when his resolve had flagged, when he had been almost overborne by hopelessness and despair, then he would remember that deprecating smile . . . Henry wondered, as he rose to his feet, if Harry Percy was smiling now.

He came out of the church into the summer dusk. The hot flushed day had cooled and paled. Toward the east, the sky was white and luminous, shot like a bloodstone with reflected light. In the west, long drifts of fiery cloud burned on the horizon like tongues of flame; the dragon's breath, he thought exultantly. Indeed, the sky itself was a revelation, a gaudy banner flaunting his colours. He saw it as a certain omen: the white sky, the green earth, torn across by crimson cloud . . . Impulsively he knelt. He felt God's presence here more surely than he had in the dim

293

church. There was no wind; the air was still, expectant, held like a long-pent breath. A vast silence lay over the land, a momentous calm, perfect, unbroken. Not even the call of a bird disturbed the luminous peace.

He bowed his head, moved by the poignant tension of the moment. God was here, in the red eye of the fallen sun, in the breathless hush that seemed to have stilled even the beating of his heart; as if all his life and destiny were seen and judged in this one brief moment. The very earth sweated and was still.

He felt himself suddenly in shadow and knew that God looked into his heart. A flood of love and humility broke over him in a great shining wave and he was again in the light, his face suffused with the rapturous glow of righteousness.

He rose to his feet, smiling, jubilant, unafraid. He heard again the old bard's voice. 'You have the blessing of the gods. What need have you of man's?'

Three miles away in silence and shadow the King of England knelt — but he did not pray. His thoughts were dark and stagnant, plunged fathoms deep in an agony of remorse and painful recrimination.

Outside his tent there was movement and sound: the muffled tread of feet upon dry hardened ground, the murmuring of subdued but urgent voices. He could not hear clearly what they said but he heard the underlying note of panic. They were afraid, yet they didn't know why. Strangely, he was not; of all the exhausted emotions that wrung his heart, fear was the least of them. He would have welcomed that. Fear might have made him feel alive, it might have penetrated this dreadful apathy. Even when he was at his most despairing, even when he imagined the worst, there was nothing. He felt only a numbness, as if the coldness that had settled on his heart so long ago had spread to his mind and his body. If he felt anything, it was anger, a dull rage against himself that he had so dismally failed to estimate and anticipate the outcome of his own actions. He saw now how he had not taken the full measure of the common man. He had not seen how they had loved his brother Edward, despite his faults, how they had loved his fair angelic sons. They had loved him too, once — but

294

as the Duke of Gloucester, not as King of England.

He looked around him. All was greyness, shadow, shifting ghostly shapes that advanced upon him and closed him in. He knew now the full extent of the treachery against him. He knew, now, how he was spurned and despised, how he was accursed of God and men. Of all the lords he had summoned to attend upon him only five had come — and Northumberland was not one of them. He stirred then, a sharp jerking backward movement as if a knife had been thrust in his bowels. That had been the ultimate despair, that Harry would rather have been forsworn than be with him. He believed in nothing now, he trusted none. He had no hope, no faith, either in himself or the men who shared this moment with him; cowards, fainthearts, quivering like maids and seeing themselves cursed because he would allow no priests in the camp, because he would not add hypocrisy to his crimes. If the cause was God's, they had no need of priests; if it was not, then to invoke His aid was blasphemous.

Abruptly he turned his head, flinching as a light fell full into his eyes.

Norfolk set the lamp on the table between them. The shadows retreated and lingered only in the King's eyes.

'Is there news?' he asked harshly.

Norfolk raised a pale and sweating face. 'No fresh news, sire. The enemy are camped for the night on Redmore Plain, less than three miles distant.'

'So. The Tudor intends to force the issue, then?'

'It seems so, my liege.' Norfolk hesitated. 'Sire, would it not be wiser to delay? The men of York are on the road and Northumberland . . .'

'Northumberland will not come,' the King said bitterly. 'If he could not stir himself to send out the summons to the men of York, how will he stir himself to march to battle? He has betrayed me like all the rest.' His voice rose shrilly. 'Even Suffolk, my own brother-in-law. . .'

'Your Grace,' Norfolk intervened swiftly. The King was lately prone to fits of hysteria. 'There might be extenuating circumstances in Northumberland's case,' he said placatingly. 'His wife, the countess, was buried in Beverley Minster only three days ago.

295

It could well be that the death of his wife . . . You know yourself, sire . . .'

Richard shuddered. Yes, he knew the terrible numbing grief. Hope stirred, tentative, painful. He crushed it ruthlessly. Better to have no hope at all than see all come to nothing.

'The Stanleys?' he said hoarsely. 'What of them?'

'Ours, I think, sire. If only by the virtue of the fact that you hold Lord Strange as hostage. They are camped a mile away, roughly halfway between the two main armies. Neither Lord Stanley nor his brother Sir William has made any move to join the Tudor camp.'

'And no move to join ours either,' Richard observed grimly.

'Your Grace,' Norfolk said, reading his mind. 'I beg you to wait just one more day.'

'No,' Richard cried. 'No more waiting, Jack.' He shook his head. 'A day, two days, it will make little difference. If it is to come, let it come now.'

Wordlessly Norfolk withdrew and Richard sat wearily. The shadows drew in again and fastened darkly in the gaunt hollows of his face. It was fully dark now; imperceptibly the day had slipped away, the very last he might spend upon this earth. He could view the prospect quite calmly. Death was the only alternative to victory. As with all his life, there could be no compromise, no half measures. It must be all or nothing at all.

His eyes wandered dully around the silk-hung walls. In a corner, disembodied and skeletal, his armour hung upon a pole; perfect, unblemished, damascened with gold. A gold circlet emblazoned his helm, studded with gems, the symbol of his kingship — the symbol of his guilt and shame and sorrow. He breathed deeply. And not lightly won. He had not been fool enough to think that there would not be a price to pay, but such a price — honour, conscience, the lives of the two he had loved more than life itself. And all for nothing, all the great good he had done overborne by that one evil; all his statutes and reforms, his just laws, forgotten and set aside. It was true. Men only remembered the bad things.

Again his eyes strayed to the glittering circlet. Something deep and powerful stirred inside him, an irresistible and overwhelming urge, a frenzied compulsion that drove him beyond himself, beyond conscience and honour, beyond fear except the fear of losing. It had made him a murderer and a liar, a tyrant and a cheat, and yet still he could not relinquish it. It drew him with an awful fascination. It was all he had left, all, apart from his life, of which they could deprive him.

Then he lifted his head. A small insistent noise beat upon his ears; distant, as yet unrecognisable, but known and familiar. He rose slowly and clumsily to his feet. Horsemen! And not one but thousands, advancing at a slow and steady pace with a sound like muted thunder. He could not move. Hope and fear had him transfixed, a terror of anticipation that held him paralysed and inert. Then slowly, painfully, relief thawed his frozen mind. He heard Norfolk's joyful shout. 'Northumberland!'

They faced each other without hypocrisy, without deception, each seeing the other quite clearly.

Richard stared at Harry for a long time before he spoke. He was thinner, the bronzed skin stretched tautly over sharp attenuated bones. As always, a faint bitter and astringent smile turned his mouth but his eyes were quite dead, burnt out, lifeless, as if the light had been quenched in a lantern.

'You came then,' Richard said quietly.

'Yes. I came. I gave my word, did I not? To attend upon you with all the men I could muster? And I have. Three thousand and forty men to be precise.' Harry smiled at him almost tenderly. 'You know I never break my word.'

The hair lifted on the King's scalp. There was warning to be read in the quiet innocuous words, a threat, an echo of another time, another oath . . . But his tired mind could not reach beyond the surface meaning, beyond the fact that Harry was here and with three thousand odd men at his back. If he had been wrong about Harry, he could be wrong about other things. Perhaps after all he was not wholly damned. Perhaps God, having visited upon him this awful penance, was now appeased.

He turned to Norfolk who now entered the tent. 'Prepare the men,' he said, almost with jubilation. 'Tomorrow we do battle with our enemies.'

The sun beat down upon Redmore Plain; the Sun in Splendour, the Sun of York — an omen, the King thought, a glorious omen that God after all had not forsaken him.

He rode the low crest of Ambien Hill, a stiff steel-clad glittering figure upon his great white horse; a king, perhaps only for these next few hours, but nevertheless a king. He felt strangely and quietly elated, drunk with the heat and noise of the day. He looked up again into the brilliant sky. A faint colour tinged the flat grey planes of his face, the ghost of a smile curved his tired mouth. He had slept badly, a light fitful sleep haunted by phantoms, so real that he had cried aloud. He had woken plagued by dark and morbid thoughts, weighed down by a hopeless and nameless despair. Not until he had walked out into the clear and sanguine day had hope risen in him, urgent and clamorous. Again he had wondered if it could be that he was absolved, that God, in His mercy, had forgiven him. All else was with him: the day, the terrain, even the elements. He had the advantage of the higher ground, positioned so that the sun blinded the enemy. He had more guns, he had more men . . . He paused: unless the Stanleys decided to desert him.

His eyes swept down to the field and fastened in turn upon the separate forces of the two brothers; both still standing aloof, both maintaining an overt neutrality. Yet Lord Stanley had in part showed his hand. Only minutes before, he had given the order for Stanley to move up, under threat of his son's immediate execution. Stanley had sent back word that he had other sons and that under no circumstances would he alter his position. The King ground his teeth together in remembered fury. Madness had almost prevailed, to the extent of making block and headsman ready and dragging Lord Strange from his tent. Norfolk had calmed him. Better to keep Stanley quiescent and neutral than to have him join with the Tudor. The King swallowed hard. Compromise. Compromise, all was compromise.

His sharp long-sighted gaze moved on toward the enemy host. He saw the banners floating like gaudy sunset clouds: the Red Dragon upon its green and white field, the Black Raven of the Welshman, Rhys ap Thomas. Oxford's emblem of stars and streamers he knew well. Had he not fought and beaten him at

Barnet? In all, the enemy forces numbered no more than seven thousand, and most of those were French and Breton mercenaries, the scum scavenged from prisons and gutters. But not all. Savagely he marked down the men that had deserted him . . . and for a man that few had even seen, a Lancastrian milksop who had never fought an encounter in his life, as if to emphasise that they'd rather have the Devil himself for king, if the only other choice was Richard Gloucester.

He turned away, closing his mind to the dark and depressing thoughts. For the twentieth time he checked his own dispositions: archers to the fore under Jack of Norfolk, backed by foot and flanked on either side by horsemen; then cavalry again, the knights and men-at-arms under his own command; Northumberland's solid ranks making up the rear.

He raised himself up in his stirrups and peered through the mist of heat. He could see Harry only distantly; a still, motionless figure beneath his blue and gold lion banner. Too still, he thought suddenly, inanimate almost. A vague sensation of panic brought a cold sweat to his hands. He felt his danger. He could almost smell it, as pungent and acrid as his own sweat. Yet he could not name it, he dared not name it.

He turned back as the discordant shrilling of trumpets split the still and sweating air. The enemy was advancing, suicidally it seemed, moving directly across his own front line.

So, he thought with wild jubilation. Oxford meant to assault his position head-on. He signalled to his own trumpeters to stand ready.

The enemy were strung out beneath him now, manoeuvring through streams and patches of bog to the more solid ground below his own left flank. He saw Oxford's strategy, to put the sun at his back and turn the royalist front line so that they would be at the same disadvantage.

He lifted his hand and two short blasts were given. 'Archers advance.' A third was drowned by Norfolk's bellow of 'Loose!'

Then under cover of the arrow fire, the front line under Norfolk charged, gaining such savage momentum on the downward slope that the very air shuddered and screamed upon impact.

Richard saw now that the enemy's strength lay with Oxford's men, a solid wedge of mounted horse that bore down effortlessly upon Norfolk's foot. He saw his front line buckle and heave and knew that he had spread his men too thinly. The centre was falling back under pressure from Oxford, the whole line bending into a crescent. Swiftly, the King sent reinforcements to both centre and rear, seeing a chance to close Oxford in between the horns of the crescent. But the enemy commander had anticipated him and sounded a retreat. The enemy were falling back toward their own standards.

Then Richard stared in incredulous and furious disbelief. A quiet had fallen over the field. His men were standing still, hesitating, holding off while the enemy regrouped at their ease. Dear God, what was Norfolk about? His eyes frantically scoured the disordered ranks. He heard the dismal shout go up. Norfolk was down. The King felt his heart plunge within him. His good Jack Howard was slain.

He trembled, shivering and sweating. His calm and control shattered. He threw a desperate look at the Stanleys, still holding off, still biding their time . . .

He called to a courier, his voice high and shrill. 'Tell my lord Northumberland to advance.'

Grimly he looked back toward the field. The fighting had resumed under Norfolk's son, Surrey; a writhing formless mass of horses and men . . . He turned his head. The courier had returned and was on his knees in a fearful abject posture.

'Well?' said the King, suddenly aware that the man's stillness and silence had spread to the men behind him. 'Did you tell Northumberland to advance?'

The courier looked up at him, his eyes wide and blank. 'I did, your Grace. He said that he would not.'

The man's face exploded into a thousand fragments of sharp red light and came together, distorted, ugly, like a hideous demonic gargoyle.

The King turned his horse, riding past his ashen-faced household, toward the rigid close-packed lines of men that stretched across the entire summit of the hill.

The man at their head rode forward to meet him, gently pacing his mount, unhurried, uncaring. His face was expressionless, cold and dead except for a faint spark deep in his eyes. Yet the King looking into it knew it for the face of his open and deadly enemy.

'Advance, my lord,' he said hoarsely. 'Or be in forfeit of both your honour and your life.'

Harry smiled at him, wearily, contemptuously. 'My honour, sire, is already lost. My life you may have, and gladly.'

Richard stared at him, his eyes opaque and filmed with tears. 'Advance, my lord,' he said again. 'You are forsworn and perjured. You have broken your sworn and solemn word.'

The spark burned up in Harry's eyes, vivid and dangerous. 'You are mistaken, sire,' he said coldly. 'I have kept my word to the very letter: to attend upon you in full strength — you said nothing about putting my men in the field. I always keep my word. Every promise I have ever made to you, every one I shall keep.'

The King knew then. He remembered. *'If you should ever break faith, I will not lift a hand to save you from all the fires of Hell.'*

A wild sobbing noise arose in his throat. 'Traitor,' he screamed. 'False ingrate, traitor . . .'

Harry raised up his cold torpid eyes. 'Murderer,' he answered softly.

The King swayed in the saddle, as if from a blow. He wrenched his eyes away from that implacable face and looked past him to the men at his back; the men of the north, the men he had loved and honoured and cherished above all others. But they didn't see him and he knew that despite his mercy and justice and generosity nothing had changed. They would not side with him against Northumberland.

He turned his horse, savagely driving his spurs into the smooth white flanks. His head was full of fearful sound, an agonised screaming and wailing that came from inside himself. He stared out blindly. The battle still raged, desultorily, half-hearted, unreal as if it were some badly-staged drama played out before bored and restless spectators. They had no spirit, no courage or conviction left. They knew that both he and they were accursed.

301

Tears of rage and bitterness filled his eyes. He could not see for tears. He could not hear for the drumming of fierce hot blood against his brow.

Then suddenly, quite clearly, through the tears and the dust and the heat, across the wide and bloody field, he saw, on a little rise of green earth, vivid, undulating, monstrous and real, his enemy, the Red Dragon.

A harsh animal sound arose in his throat. The raw crimson burned his eyes, its raking claws gouged blood, its gaping jaws breathed fire into his brain. His own breath came loudly. He panted like a cornered beast. Blood swelled and suffused his face, blazing redly from the dark pits of his eyes.

He turned to his men, his face primeval and savage, his lips drawn back from ferociously bared teeth. 'Let all true knights attend me,' he roared. 'And if none will follow me, I will try the cause alone.'

He crouched down, his head lowered, drawn down between his slender shoulders. He couched his lance, laying himself along the shaft so that it became an extension of his body, protruding like a sharp white tusk. Then he charged, wildly, irrationally, without thought or care. Dimly he was aware of men at his back, a hundred at most — Lovell, Zouche, Ratcliffe, Brackenbury, the young knight John Egremont — but only dimly. He knew himself alone in this. This was between himself and Henry Tudor.

Head down, he saw the ground a green blur beneath his pounding hooves. With short jerky movements he flung himself in and out of the fray, skirting the writhing body of men, driving across Sir William Stanley's immobile front of scarlet-coated men. His pace barely slackened as he struck the base of the little knoll; up, up, toward the monstrous blood red beast. He could see it now; hard steely scales glittering as it moved. He saw it writhe away from him. It was afraid, flinging out scaly limbs to protect itself. He fended them off and saw the traitor John Cheyney fall, felled like a massive oak. The body drew in upon itself, hard, shining. He gored its flanks and saw the spurting of its blood. Again and again he plunged with lance and axe, hacking his way to its heart. He could feel its palpitating terror as he drew close. It rose up on its hind legs in fear, clawing at the air. He struck, a murderous

302

blow. He saw it jerk and slope to its fall. Then he looked into a face so mild and passionless that for a moment he checked in uncertainty. He hesitated, stayed by some unseen and unknown hand. The cold dead eyes bore him down so that he was only dimly aware of the shout at his back. Redness engulfed him, hundreds upon thousands of red-coated men, fresh new blood flooding the Dragon's heart. Stanley at last had made his choice, but it had not been for him.

Then he was falling, being drawn down into darkness and pain. He screamed, a high animal sound that held all of the pain and agony of his short life. His body twitched in a last convulsion and then it was still.

On the ridge of Ambien Hill, Harry sat his horse, unmoving, as he had since early dawn. The light, grown bloody, diffused in long level rays across Redmore Plain, gleaming dully on the battered crown that Lord Stanley had ripped from King Richard's helm and set hastily upon Henry Tudor's head. It was all over, finished, and behind the tumultuous and victorious procession, in shadow, despised and forgotten, they brought Richard Plantagenet home.

They had stripped him naked and flung his broken body across the back of a horse. His head hung down, the dark hair stiff and matted with blood, and here and there a froth of spittle bloomed where men had spat upon his corpse.

Harry raised his eyes as the grim little cortège approached. He saw the blotched and naked limbs. He saw the contused and beaten head. He saw the body of the man he had loved dishonoured and reviled, and the tears ran unashamedly down his face.

Snow fell, soft, translucent, surging in pale nacreous drifts against the Tower's walls. The room in the Lantern Tower was cold and dim, despite the brazier of coals that pulsed a faint and grudging heat. Ice still sheathed the scarred walls and his breath hung in chill vaporous clouds, yet he was as unaware of cold or heat as he was of pain or hunger or the passing of time. He had lost count of the days. They passed, cold and static, days of grey desolation; grey walls, grey sky, bound with the grey thread of the river outside. It had been September when they had brought him here, golden, glorious September, the last of that brave fierce summer. Vaguely, he remembered October — wet earth and rotting leaves, days of soft weeping rain and on the last but one, Henry Tudor had been crowned King of England. It was January now, bright, sharp, clean; a new year, a new beginning, a new peace — three days ago, Henry, the last scion of Lancaster, had married Elizabeth of York.

But no peace for him. His mind and heart were locked in the past as surely as his body was locked in this small cold room. The dead were his sole companions; a young girl with hair like crimson fire, a man with dark melancholy eyes. He heard their voices sometimes, whispering, urgent, but never raised in condemnation. They spoke softly, with sorrow and regret.

He flexed his numb fingers toward the brazier, glancing up as the dull footsteps sounded above his head. Surrey was pacing again; five strides to the far wall, five back again. During the day the steps were quick and purposeful, at night they grew weary and slow.

Harry smiled with fleeting compassion. Thomas Howard would not take to confinement easily. The months that to him seemed like days would seem like years to a man like Surrey. It was easy for him. Familiarity always made a thing less fearful and besides, he had no real wish to be free. Outside these walls the guilt would be the harder to bear. He no longer had any desires or longings, no real belief. He existed, rather than lived, and was imprisoned and shut in by more than stone walls. Even if he was loosed tomorrow, he knew he would never be free again.

He looked up. Surrey had abruptly halted in his pacing. He would be standing before the small barred window, staring out as he sometimes did for hours. Harry wondered what he expected to see. The view must be familiar by now; stone walls and battlements, fragments of sky, a glimpse of the cluttered roofs of Southwark. He rose, out of a sudden and inexplicable curiosity. There had been something about the way Surrey's footsteps had ceased . . .

The day had an unusual brilliance, hard, scintillating, the sun falling in clear definite shafts between the crowded turrets. The air was cold, static, as if it waited, suspended and motionless. He saw then what had caught Surrey's attention, gilded lions upon a scarlet field, and suddenly he was wrenched back seventeen years. Seventeen years ago he had stood at this very window, watching and waiting for a king. Distantly he heard voices, so distantly that he did not know whether they were real and here and now, or imagined from that time long ago. Again he heard the hollow footsteps upon the stairs, the harsh grating of keys and bolts, and he knew that when the door opened it would be the King of England who would enter — but not Edward of York. This king looked more like a pilfering clerk in spite of his rich apparel.

Henry advanced into the room, grave and unsmiling. He wore a long gown of purple velvet lined and edged with miniver. A black silk bonnet was clamped severely upon his fine reddish hair. A cascade of pearls spilled along the brim. There were more pearls fastening his doublet.

They looked at each other, through air as clear and brittle as glass, across a void of seventeen years. Nothing was said between them that any man could have heard. The exchange was wordless, tacit, the years falling away, dwindling down to a small shared and vividly remembered moment: a man and a boy playing at chess, Gwilym Ddu's tenor bell of a voice falling between them. Then Henry smiled, brilliantly, exultantly. This moment he would treasure above all others. This was triumph, greater than when Stanley had set the Usurper's crown upon his head, even greater than the solemn splendour of his coronation. This was the ache and longing of years, to look into this man's cold and arrogant face and say, 'I am Henry, the King.' No dream, no vague prophecy or the mutterings of dead men, but fact, solid, accomplished fact. He *was* Henry, the King.

Harry looked back at him, acknowledging the victory with a grim and bitter smile. He saw now what he had failed to see seventeen years before, that what made this man so formidable was his stubborn and unshakeable belief in himself, that neither scorn, nor ridicule, nor exile had ever diminished. He was king because he believed it was his unassailable right to be king, because God and destiny so willed it. And he did not grudge Henry the victory now. It had been hard won, not in the field, but by years of patient endurance that would have broken stronger men.

Henry moved away from him, pleasurably aware of the weight and warmth of his robes, the hardness and brilliance of his jewels. He was also aware of Harry Percy's eyes upon his back, mildly derisive and no doubt smiling in that faintly supercilious way he had. He smiled himself. Still they underestimated him, even this man who should know better. He knew they thought him pompous and small-minded, avaricious and mean. They scoffed at his rigid insistence on being addressed as 'majesty', rather than the old form of 'your Grace.' They looked askance at his innovation of a personal guard. He knew that behind his back his Yeoman Warders were ridiculed. Yet to him, both these were weighty and solemn matters. He did not put himself upon a par with bishops and earls, and surely the protection of his sovereign person was his most sacred and foremost charge. Furthermore, he was appalled at the lack of reverence for his kingship. The image of the king had been soiled and cheapened by years of wrangling and warfare. It was his duty to drag the royal dignity up out of the mire. There was too much familiarity, too little respect. But that would change. He would have no court of drunkards and lechers; he would give no succour to harlots and pimps. Ostentation and extravagance would be things of the past. Not that he was averse to regal display. It had a place and a purpose. Like children, the populace now and then needed to be dazzled. His own coronation had been such an event. He thought grudgingly of the enormous cost: over a thousand pounds spent on garments alone, plus the wages of twenty-one tailors and fifteen skinners, who had worked day and night for three weeks (locked in their rooms — he had thought it prudent to order it, to prevent pilferage of the costly stuffs).

Oh no, he was not against spectacle and display, but not to excess. He abhorred excess, almost as much as he did waste, of time, of effort, of money, especially of money. Wealth was the bedrock upon which his dynasty would be founded, not the shifting sand of ambitious men's favour. He gnawed fretfully at his lip, thinking of the paucity of his exchequer. Parliament had granted him a loan of fourteen thousand pounds and the tunnage and poundage on all imported wine. But already that sum was heavily depleted: the cost of his marriage (his mercenary soul cringed — fifty-three pounds, four shillings and eightpence for velvet alone), and pensions and annuities — a thousand marks to Harry Buckingham's widow, a further hundred livres and the revenues of six lush manors to soothe his mother-in-law, the queen dowager. These had been of necessity, rewards of lands and honours. His Uncle Jasper he had raised to the dukedom of Bedford, Lord Stanley was now Earl of Derby, and Edward Courtney had Devon, his brother the bishop, the rich see of Winchester. His long mouth turned in a wry grimace. None could say that he didn't pay his debts — and promptly too, before too much interest accrued. But he raised men up, only with an eye to plucking them down again. He trusted none, not even those of his own blood. He needed none, he needed only to order and dominate, and this he knew he could only do through the constant and steady accumulation of wealth. Money was power, independence, the wherewithal to buy both peace and war, as his interests and those of England dictated. There would have to be taxes, fines, forfeits — already he had marked down those most able to pay, already Morton's fertile brain fermented subtle extortions. But first, he must still the quaking foundations of his house. First, he must make himself secure.

There was no real threat to his overall supremacy. There were none left to offer a serious challenge. Edward, Earl of Warwick, Clarence's son, was sickly and known to be half-witted. And he had him here, kept close in hold. So, Henry vowed, he would remain. In time he would be forgotten. There was the Earl of Lincoln, the Usurper's other nephew and designated by him as his heir, an amiable, unambitious young man; weak, Henry thought, and therefore liable perhaps to become prey to the strong. Nevertheless, there were obvious benefits in leaving him free. If nothing else, he would serve as a focus for any who still had Yorkist leanings. He would draw his enemies out into the open.

He moved closer to the window, leaning so that he could see

the scarlet tabards of his Yeoman Warders who crowded the ward below. The knowledge of their presence soothed him; fifty hand-picked men to attend upon him night and day. Two of them this very moment stood without the door. Ah, yes, he was secure. He was safe from all but the Devil's assault.

Unconsciously, his fingers stroked the fur of his robe. The feel of its richness he found especially comforting, sensual almost, like a woman's flesh. He thought of his Queen, his Yorkist Queen. Pray God that she already carried his seed, the embryo of his dynasty. A son, he longed for a son, a legitimate son of unflawed descent, for he had revoked the *Titulus Regis* that had declared his queen bastard.

Swiftly he stifled a pang of unease. He had nothing to fear. The boys were dead. He knew it. All men knew it. Yet still the sensation persisted, a feeling of something not quite finished, a ghost that was not yet laid.

His eyes raked gloomily over the embattled towers; walls ten and fifteen feet thick, a maze of passages and stairwells, under-vaults and cellars. They were here somewhere. Instinct, and the little news that his spies had been able to glean, told him that. Yet where? It offended against his orderly mind not to know, not to be able to parade their corpses, to show indisputably that the Yorkist rose was crushed. But no matter. He could wait. All things were revealed with time and patience. Someone knew. Somewhere there were men who trembled with the burden of their fearful knowledge. Men grew careless with time, and in time the burden would become too great to be borne alone, in time it would have to be shared.

Then he said in his low and strangely accented voice, 'My lord, what did he do with his brother's sons? Where did he lay their bodies?'

He had expected silence, the wordless denial he had had from other men. He was surprised to hear Harry answer him clearly.

'I don't know. I don't know what he did with them. And I would not tell you if I did.'

Harry looked away, regretting that he had spoken. He did not see the King's smile grow thin and strained. He did not see his eyes narrow with dislike.

308

Henry lowered them quickly, careful that he should not see. It still rankled that he owed some part of his triumph to this cold and strangely forbidding man. Cling as he would to his belief in his invincibility, he could not help but be aware that if Northumberland had not witheld his hand . . . But he had withheld it, though Henry was reminded now that he had not actually surrendered, he had not actually submitted and acknowledged him openly as king.

He worked his mouth in irritation. It would have pleased him inordinately to have done without him, to have left him to rot and moulder within these walls. But the north eluded him, defied him still. His appointment of the Lords Strange and Fitzhugh to Northumberland's duties had proved an abysmal failure. There had been riots, disaffections; the Usurper's henchmen, Lovell and the Stafford brothers, were still at large, fermenting anarchy and rebellion. The city of York especially was not weaned from love of the Boar, and it was only by Northumberland's command that they had grudgingly recognised him as king.

He said artlessly, 'I understand that you received a letter, from the Council of York, asking your good lordship and advice, as to what might be to their profit and safeguard in the matter of recognising myself as king?' Henry's face darkened fractionally, for he had read the letter before Northumberland ever had: 'since King Richard, late reigning over us, was piteously slain and murdered, to the great heaviness of this city.'

He had also read Northumberland's brief and stilted reply. 'I was glad to see, my lord, that you gave them good advice,' he said with an amicable smile.

Harry moved his head to look at the King but he made no reply.

'I take it that you intend to follow it yourself?' Henry persisted, smiling manfully over his mounting irritation.

'In what way?'

'Submit peaceably for the profit and peace of the realm. I think that was how you put it.'

Harry's eyes dwelt thoughtfully upon the King's long face, aware that in some subtle unknown way the mastery had passed to him. Henry had come for something more than just to gloat.

He waited. Henry moved toward him. His face had assumed a

309

secretive look, as if they were fellow conspirators in some dark plot. 'My lord,' he said softly. 'I can be generous if I am sure of a return. And I have borne in mind that although you appeared in arms against me, you took no active part in the conflict. I owe you some small thanks for that.'

'You owe me nothing,' interrupted Harry quietly. 'It was not done for you.'

'Nevertheless, it was done.' Henry said, and added cruelly, 'Who knows, my lord? But for you, the day might have had a different end.'

Henry looked close and hard into Harry's face, disappointed not to have struck a spark. He saw now that this man was empty and hollow, nothing more than a rattling shell. He had no pride left that could be humbled, no vanity or conceit that could be brought low. He went on, nailing Harry more surely to his cross, 'Because of that, and for the love and affection I bore your lady . . . For her sake, I am prepared to grant you your freedom and full restitution of your honours and your lands.'

Harry looked up at him, smiling. 'And what makes you think I even want them?'

The King blanched, taken aback. What then? His eyes narrowed. What manner of deceit and trickery was this? Then he saw: Jesu, but looking into his eyes was like looking into the fires of Hell. He saw fear, naked, ugly, a great tremulous quaking fear that reached out and touched him with its intensity. Northumberland was afraid: of himself, of life, of walking out from behind these walls, afraid of what he might find waiting.

Henry looked away, uneasy, fearful himself. He knew such men to be dangerous, for it must follow that a man so afraid of life would be reckless and uncaring of death. Such a man would not be driven as other men were, by greed and self-preservation. He pursed his lips, thinking of the hostile north, a hotbed of rebels and insurgents, but better perhaps, as Morton had said, the yapping of a thousand small dogs than the roar of a mighty lion.

He looked again, straining his powers of perception to see behind the bland facade. And what he saw reassured him. He knew suddenly that this particular lion was tamed.

He said in a gentle and persuasive voice, 'You have sons, my lord. Have you no care for them?'

Harry stirred. Yes, he had sons, daughters too, small perfect reminders of his loss. He had not seen them in nearly half a year. He had not even thought of them. But he thought of them now: Henry and William, Jocelyn and Alan, the two little maids, Alianore and Anne.

He looked across at the King. 'And in exchange for your magnanimity, sire, what would you expect of me?'

'Only your duty, my lord,' Henry said gravely. 'Your solemn and bounden duty to your king. I would ask for nothing more.'

1489

*And a man shall wrestle with a wounded
Lion, and the gleam of gold shall blind the
eyes of the onlookers.*

Prophecy of Merlin.

As he had promised, he had not laid her in the dark. Sunlight fell
through the high trefoil windows and endowed the effigy with
fleeting transient life. It seemed for a moment that the alabaster
lips smiled, that a heartbeat stirred the marble curve of her breast.
All around her there was light, threading through the coloured
leads of the east window, spilling like jewels at her feet. Slender
arches roofed her in. Leaning together like protective hands, and
out of the flushed and radiant stone, starry flowers bloomed in
shining profusion, angels soared heavenward with spread glittering wings. In the dim corners of the chapel where shadows still
dared to lurk, tall white candles burned, twenty-eight in all, one
for every year of her life.

Harry lay prostrate before the tomb, his body flecked and
mottled with rainbow light. Hers lay beside him, beneath the
stone, shrouded in bright cloth of gold, her head pillowed on the
quenched fire of her hair. On her feet were gold-embroidered
slippers. Beside her lay a little gilded lamp and a candle in a silver
sconce. As he had promised, he had not left her in the darkness.

He pressed his cheek closer against the stone as if it would bring
him nearer. Nearly four years on, and the pain had never
lessened, his sense of loss had never diminished. He had found no
consolation, even in their children. They were apart from him,
held back by an awareness of his awful silent grief, that was terrifying to them in its intensity. They loved and honoured him, but

fearfully, from a distance. He accepted that without too much regret. He was easier living within himself. Except for those few brief happy years with Maud, he had done so all his life. But it was not fear that held him confined now. He was as immune to that as he was to pain. Pain was all he knew and understood; the agony of merely being alive, of thinking and feeling and remembering, of enduring this anguish of regret and remorse that he knew would never end this side of death. There was almost pleasure in it, a masochistic thrill in accepting so thoroughly whatever life and King Henry thrust upon him. He had found a kind of peace in the constant subjugation of his pride, a sense of absolution in self-loathing. Of all of the hatreds that he bore to the world, none was greater than that which he bore to himself.

Stiffly, he rose to his feet and went out into the main body of the minster. At the west door a man waited, impatient, irreverent, scuffing the toe of his boot against the base of a pillar. John, dear John, as abrasive and chastening as a hair shirt and cherished, especially, for that purpose. John was the keeper of his conscience, a constant reminder of that evil August day when honour and friendship had died. John had been there, a witness to his cruel treachery, and a hundred times Harry had heard him recount King Richard's last glorious charge. With every telling the dead king's valour grew and that of Henry diminished, but all this privily, of course, for outwardly John was very much King Henry's man, as lavish grants from the attainted Lord Lovell's estates bore witness. With grim amusement Harry tolerated his wonderful hypocrisy, his veiled insolence and paltry slights. John was part of his long penance. He kept him by him, lest he should forget.

'My lord.' John came to meet him as he heard his step. Briefly their eyes met, vaguely hostile, like the dull clash and sliding away of blunted swords. 'My lord.' John fell in beside him. 'There is word from the King. A letter awaits you at York.'

He did not open the letter at once. Intuitively, he knew its contents; yet another refusal of his plea that the citizens of York, on account of their poverty, be exempted from Henry's latest and

313

most extortionate demand for tax. He should have known better than even to try again. In the matter of money, the King was rarely swayed.

Harry's mouth grew hard, thinking of the King's insatiable greed. He had returned to court only twice in the three years since his release. The first, to attend the belated coronation of Henry's Queen, the second, three months ago, to beg the King's indulgence for the city of York.

Henry had received him at Shene, called Richmond now, in honour of himself, and refurbished with a heavy sombre richness that was more telling of wealth than all the glittering splendour of his predecessors. Morton, as always, had been at his side — Cardinal-Archbishop Morton now, since the death of old Thomas Bourchier,

Both men had greeted him with suspicion and restraint. The King especially had looked upon him coldly. Henry could never see Northumberland without remembering his debts: Bosworth, and that first year, when Northumberland had smoothed his progress through the north, so well that even the citizens of York had welcomed him joyously and with lavish feasting. Henry had seen the error of setting him free then. In the north, it was not he who was king but this enigma of a man, Northumberland.

And then, more galling still, two months later, Lovell and the Stafford brothers had come out of hiding, to stir the north to rebellion. Infuriatingly, it had been Northumberland who had quelled them and all but snatched him from the assassin's path as he had sat at his dinner on the feast of St George. The need to be grateful again had deepened Henry's resentment.

Again the next year, when rumours had abounded that he had had the young Earl of Warwick done to death in the Tower. Some had believed it, enough to bring the Yorkist faction out of hiding to make a last desperate bid for power. Lincoln, as he had predicted, had at last shown his true colours and in concert with Lovell and other Yorkists had produced, miraculously, out of Ireland, a boy who claimed to be the Earl of Warwick, not murdered as men had thought, but delivered at the last minute by the mysterious hand of Providence. In Ireland, seeing the boy, so fair and guileless, they had believed it. In Burgundy, out of hatred and spleen, the Duchess Margaret had been persuaded to believe it. In England, in desperation, the Yorkists had believed, not so much that the boy was who he said he was, but that he could oust the Tudor from power.

And Henry, hearing all this as he heard all things, had merely smiled and brought the Earl of Warwick out from the Tower, parading him through the London streets, ensuring that many men of account and standing saw and spoke with him, so that it could be noised abroad that he was safe and well and that, as Morton had since discovered, the boy who purported to be Clarence's son was in fact the son of a common blacksmith. His name, it seemed, was Lambert Simnel.

It convinced all but the most heavily committed. The men who were set on war at any price clung stubbornly to their belief and in May, the boy who said he was Clarence's son was crowned King Edward the Sixth in Dublin. In June, he landed on the Lancashire coast with a vast army led by the Earl of Lincoln.

Only then had Henry known a moment's disquiet. Lincoln and the rebels were moving north, where disaffection for him was strongest. The rebel force, too, was greater than he had supposed: two thousand well-armed Flemings, supplied by Margaret of Burgundy; the rest, admittedly, were ragged Irish scum under the command of Earl FitzGerald. Nevertheless, the army was as large as the one with which he himself had invaded, and more, Lincoln was working on the same premise, that once in England they would gather support. To this end they had moved upon York.

Calmly he had advanced toward Nottingham where the royal army was to muster, little cheered by the news that Northumberland's kinsmen, Lord Scrope and his son, had declared for the rebels and that the city of York had secretly pledged its support. Fear had touched him then and he had remembered Bosworth. What Northumberland could do once, he could do again; the north was still his to command. Harry rode at the head of a massive army, twice the number he had brought to Bosworth field. What if he had them stand idle again, or worse, what if he turned them against him? God knew, he had given him cause. Covering his panic, he had written a brief and urgent letter, bidding Northumberland keep vigil over the city of York to see that they gave no succour to the rebels. If Northumberland had any thoughts of disloyalty, he would join them outright. At least then Henry would know where he stood.

Amazingly, Northumberland had obeyed his command to the letter and eventually, disheartened, the rebels had turned away and headed south toward Lincoln. Henry had waited, drawing them on, knowing their minds as well as they did themselves, for he had paid men within their ranks, so that he was as good as in the Earl of Lincoln's bosom and knew every hour what he did. As always, foresight paid dividends, cunning brought reward and it was Lincoln and the rebels who paid the toll. At Stoke, he had brought his enemies to battle and inflicted upon them a glorious bloody defeat, using only the half of his army. Lincoln and the rebel leaders had been slain, the traitor Lord Scrope languished in Windsor. His rival, the blacksmith's son, he had vanquished with ridicule and scorn. Lambert Simnel should not join the ranks of Yorkist martyrs. As befitted his birth, he now washed pots in the royal kitchens.

He had smiled slyly. Thus did the gods maintain their divine protection. Thus were his enemies put down. Then his eye fell upon Northumberland — except this enemy, for he was not deceived into thinking this man no longer a threat. It was not what Northumberland had done that made him a danger. It was what he could have done.

His smile broadened. It pleased him mightily to see Northumberland here, to hear him pleading so hard for indulgence. If the Yorkshiremen had known it they could not have sent a worse advocate. They would be refused merely because it was Northumberland who asked.

Still smiling, he pointed out curtly that he had already once before made an exception with York. Had he not, three years ago, halved his receipts and granted them exemption from their yearly payment? And had he not already granted relief to the Border counties? Indeed, he was becoming weary of these constant demands for relief. Was the north always to be the beggar of the kingdom, whining like a vagrant for alms?

His smile faded. There would be no further concessions. He

would have all. Not one penny should be abated.

He had laughed suddenly, a dry crackling sound like the snapping of twigs. 'I have always found, my lord, that those best able to pay are those that whine the loudest.'

Deep inside Harry something had stirred, a brief murderous hatred, quickly spent in the drawing of a breath. He had thought of Richard and his foolish reckless generosity, who would have beggared himself rather than see men in need. Richard had cared, but he had cared too much. This man did not care at all.

But he had said nothing. He had bowed and smiled and said nothing, reminding himself that this man was king because of him; that he was still king because of him, for he could easily have allowed the rebels to take him that time at York. He had smiled because the small ironies of life still amused him. He had saved the life of a man he hated; he had wantonly destroyed that of one he had loved — and still loved. Richard he had forgiven a long time ago. Himself, he never would.

Harry sighed wearily. And neither would the men of York. Behind their open defiance of King Henry was defiance of him. In their hearts they blamed him: for Richard's death and defeat; for Henry's harsh and crushing demands.

He leant forward suddenly and took the King's letter up. Swiftly his eyes scanned the blunt and brutal words. The King reiterated 'that not one penny of the demand should be abated for it would encourage others to pray the like release and mitigation and furthermore, I will not endure that the base multitude shall frustrate the authority of the king and parliament.'

He flung the letter away from him in anger and disgust. Now to see how the *base multitude* answered him.

They were waiting for him, aggressive, belligerent, primed like dry tinder awaiting a spark.

Harry walked through the silence he had made, remembering suddenly another day, another time, when he had persuaded the city to admit Edward of York. It was a sensation he experienced quite frequently now, as if all his actions were mere repetitions of something that had gone before, as if he were moving backwards in time instead of forward.

317

He looked out over the sea of hostile faces. Some he knew: Thomas Bullock and Eli Casse; the alderman, Thomas Wrangwish; all close partisans of King Richard. He saw John, standing by a man on whom Harry's eyes lingered with speculation, a familiar face only of late, a Welshman who went by the unlikely name of John a Chambre.

Alderman Wrangwish rose and cleared his throat. 'My lord, I trust you bring good news.'

'I fear not,' Harry answered him, more harshly than he had meant. 'The King is adamant. He will allow York no further concession.'

There was silence, menacing and cold. Eli Casse sprang furiously to his feet. 'We will not pay,' he cried. 'We cannot.'

'Have you any choice?' Harry demanded. 'The King's will is law. If you do not obey freely, then he will enforce it.'

'But my lord.' Alderman Wrangwish wrung his hands. 'Did you not explain to the King, did you not tell him of the hardship of the people?'

'I told him all. I pressed your case as strongly as I could.'

'But not strongly enough, it seems, for still we are refused.'

Harry turned his head. The man, John a Chambre, had risen to his feet — a King's man, Harry saw the royal insignia upon his sleeve.

'And you could have done better?' Harry asked coldly.

'I could have done no worse.'

Harry looked away from the provocative eyes and addressed the body of the council. 'I shall read to you the King's letter,' he said slowly, 'word for word, as I have it here. And if any of you think you can make better supplication than I already have, then you are all very welcome to try.'

He read the letter aloud, his dry, uncaring voice intensifying the harshness of the King's words. When he came to the last there was an outcry of rage. Voices, thick with fury, burst upon the air.

'Base multitude! Is that what we are?' Eli Casse roared. 'Good enough to pay his taxes and fight his wars but not to be named as men.'

'King Richard would never have treated us thus,' cried Thomas Bullock. 'Like worthless scum, like dogs.'

318

'King Richard loved us, God rest his soul.'

'King Richard is dead,' cried Harry above the noise. 'It is King Henry that we have to deal with.'

'Aye. King Richard is dead right enough. And it was you, God damn you, that murdered him.'

The voice came from the rear of the hall: young, roughly-accented, uncouth and unknown, yet all others fell silent before it. Harry lifted his head, aware of his danger in that dreadful quiet. Their faces seemed to crowd in upon him, silent, deadly, terrifying in their hatred. He knew that he should defend himself, yet he could not speak. The breath sighed emptily in his throat.

Then he flung the letter down and walked wordlessly from the hall. What was there to say, anyway? Of all men, he knew it for the truth.

'Who is this man, this John a Chambre?' asked Harry casually.

John looked up from the list of accounts. He shrugged. 'A man. No one of account. He is the King's forester for Richmond.'

'The King's man, then,' Harry observed thoughtfully. 'Yet he brews sedition.'

John laid down the sheaf of papers. 'But against you, my lord,' he said bluntly. 'Not against the King.'

'I am the King's servant, am I not? His deputy in the north. If against me, then surely against the King.'

Again John shrugged. 'As I said, my lord. He is no one of account. He is much favoured by the common men, but with the merchants and aldermen he holds no sway.'

Harry smiled faintly. 'I shall take your word for it, John. I suppose that you should know.' He turned his head and fixed John with his malicious and amused glance. 'I see that you also are in close council with the men of York, especially with this John a Chambre.'

John's heavy face coloured faintly. 'It is my duty to know what is going on, my lord,' he answered stiffly. 'How else can I protect your interests?'

Harry smiled and nodded. 'How else indeed, John? How else indeed?'

John bent his head again to his accounts: twelve shillings for

319

ale, for my lord's grooms of the chamber; four pounds for Gascony wine for his household at Wressell. He frowned. This was one of his own small perquisites, a mutual arrangement he had with the steward at Wressell that kept them both in free wine at Harry's expense. But to indent for so much was asking for trouble. He must speak to Master Hotham. He grew too bold.

But didn't they all? he thought, each in their own way. Even the men who had served Harry faithfully for all of their lives were falling away, looking for change, chilled by the cold wind of hostility that blew from Westminster. His heart leapt with wild excitement. And some were even looking to him, seeing how Harry relied upon him more and more and that he was favoured by the King above their master. Past thirty now, he was not the raw boy they had once despised, he was not just Thomas Percy's bastard. He was more confident now, surer of himself. He had friends and acquaintances in high places. Already he was a man of property and modest wealth, for apart from the income he filched from Harry's revenues, the King paid handsomely to be kept informed; small discreet gifts for the most part though last year he had had a more substantial show of favour. The King had granted him an annuity of forty marks. And there was the promise of more, so very much more, if only he had the courage. But he'd only ever had the courage for small things, small treacheries and disloyalties, small loves and hates. The enormity of the thing he considered was overwhelming and terrifying. For years he had dreamt of it, but no more than that. Now the dream was tinged with reality. He knew now that he was not alone in his longing. In Cardinal Morton he had a staunch ally.

He gnawed at a fingernail, remembering his first meeting with Morton, recalling that sympathetic ear inclined to hear how Harry had deprived him of his patrimony, how he still grudged him his due. The cardinal had been aghast to know him so ill used, but not surprised. He had said that he could well imagine Northumberland greedy and covetous of power. In fact he had added, strictly between the two of them of course, that the King himself was much concerned. It boded ill for the realm for one man to hold so much land and power. Nothing would have pleased His Majesty more than to indulge John's obvious moral

320

right — but in law, of course, there was little to be done. While Northumberland lived, while nothing more heinous than arrogance and apathy could be laid at his door. But if John ever heard of aught, as well he might being so close to the earl, if ever he heard anything, however small. . .

But he never had. Harry never veered from the straight and narrow. He was almost obsessive in his duty. The cardinal, too, had been disappointed. But he had smiled and patted John's shoulder in consolation. God was good, he had said, and worked His will in mysterious ways. They must hope that Providence would rid them of the earl, for if God so willed it that Northumberland met his demise before his son came of age, then naturally, the wardship would fall to the King. It would be in his power to grant Egremont and Wressell where he would. In the meantime. . . The cardinal had sighed heavily. While Northumberland lived, there was little to be done.

John glanced covertly to where Harry sat, staring, it seemed, at nothing. It would be so easy to take him unawares, to fasten his great hands round that arrogant throat. He wiped his clammy palms furtively upon his hose. No. Not alone. He could not do it alone. He was not even sure that he could do it at all, though he knew he had a ready-made accomplice in John a Chambre, paid by the King to foster discontent.

He licked his lips. This thing needed more than daring and courage. It needed cunning, a careful plan. He must be sure that no blame could be attached to him, for King Henry would have no time for compromised men. He must be clean. He must be sure.

He looked down, startled. The papers had slid from his knees and were scattered on the floor in confusion. When he raised his eyes again, Harry's were upon him, dull and quenched like the eyes of the blind.

Calmly he retrieved the papers and set them in order upon the desk. He said casually, to cover his unease, 'Do you intend to remain at York, my lord?'

'No,' Harry answered him listlessly. 'I had thought to move on to my house at Topcliffe. I have matters to attend to there.'

'I think that wise, my lord,' John said with grave concern. 'I foresee trouble if you remain in York. The commons are greatly incensed at the King's refusal of their petition. It might well be that as the King is beyond their reach they would vent their wrath upon you. Besides, my lord,' he added cruelly, 'it seems certain that they still bear you a grudge over the matter of King Richard's death.'

He smiled as he saw Harry turn away. How he loved to see that blank and rigid look settle on his features, at the mention of that name, to see the wound open and bleeding, to see his body contort with the pang of sharp suffering that he tried so hard to conceal. But not from him. He couldn't hide it from him. He didn't even seem to want to.

Then Harry said, his voice soft and steady, 'And you, John? What are your plans? Shall you accompany me to Topcliffe?'

'I think not, my lord,' John said, throwing another log upon the fire, for it had grown chill with the coming of night. 'It might be as well to watch events for a few days. Besides which, I have the Lenten rents to collect. If you have no objection, my lord, I will follow in two or three days.'

Harry nodded and threw him a softly smiling look. 'As you please, John,' he said mildly.

Harry stared out across the shadowed valley. There was a mist rising from the river and it gave the morning a curious floating quality in which the trees and hills were vague shimmering islands, caught midway between the sky and the earth. Again he had that strange feeling of premonition; something to come out of something that was past, like the day Henry Tudor had come to him in the Tower. He had the same feeling of time suspended, waiting, as if it had slowed deliberately so that he could see the moment more clearly. More than ever he felt the retrograde motion of his life. Every day took him further into the past. Like Eleanor, his thoughts were always with the dead.

He smiled, thinking of his mother with belated compassion. Poor Eleanor. He understood her now. He understood himself and knew, too late, that they had hated each other not because they had been different as he had once thought but because they were so alike. Both weak, thinking themselves strong. Both

322

desperate for love and warmth, both warped and twisted by their hatred of life. Eleanor's had been born of the blows that life had dealt her but he had come into the world full of his contempt, as if he had been infected within her womb. Briefly it had been warmed out of him, by Maud, by Richard. . .

Abruptly he turned his head aside. It seemed that today he was besieged by the past. He could not think for the memories crowding his head: himself and Richard hunting the slopes of the soft Yorkshire hills, laughing together over a shared cup of wine. Richard smiling and triumphant at Berwick's fall, weeping like a child at the death of his son, dead and dishonoured on Bosworth field, a felon's halter around his neck. He closed his eyes, not cringing from the memory as once he would have done. Strangely, now he felt no guilt, no more than if he had put a maimed and crippled hound from its pain; remorse perhaps, sorrow that he had been the one to do it, grief at the loss of a loved companion and friend. But not guilt. Today, for some reason, he felt truly absolved. He felt that at last he was forgiven.

He rose and moved to the casement. The court below was full of men, his men, if only for the moment, for he knew now that none were totally loyal. They had never loved him. Feared him perhaps and still feared him, out of habit, out of instinct, yet he thought that now that fear of him was overwhelmed by fear for themselves, to see him so wantonly inviting his fall. He had noticed that some about him had turned very thoughtful at the news that he was out of favour with the King. He had seen them casting speculative glances out of the corner of their eyes, wondering whether he could sustain the King's spleen and if he fell, would they fall with him. He did not blame them. He had shut them out when he had shut out the world. To them he was as remote and inaccessable as God in his Heaven and had not he himself turned his back on his friend and king? Could he expect any more of them?

He turned his head and called in answer to a frantic knocking upon his door.

An esquire fell into the room and straightway onto his knees. 'My lord,' the boy was panting hard as if he had been running. 'My lord. A mob, armed and in a fighting mood — about two miles away, at Asenby.'

Harry looked down into the boy's flushed face. 'How many and who are their leaders?'

'A hundred, perhaps more. I did not see them myself. Their leader is one John a Chambre.'

Harry smiled faintly. He was not surprised. In a way it had been almost predictable. Yet he was surprised that John had not sent him word or come as he had promised.

'Have Plumpton and Gascoigne been informed?' he demanded with a great deal more calmness than he was feeling.

'Aye, my lord. They arm themselves now.'

Harry nodded. 'Have Sir William come to me when he is ready.'

The boy rose and made for the door. His hand was already on the latch but he paused and looked back, his face flushed and uneasy.

'My lord,' he suddenly blurted out, 'there are some about you not so loyal as they should be.'

'I know it, child,' Harry said calmly. 'Treachery has a mortal stench and it has been strong in my nostrils this past week.'

He smiled gently, seeing the boy's obvious distress. 'Don't look so shamefaced, boy, unless you are one of their number.'

'No, my lord. As God is my judge . . .'

Harry stopped him with a gesture of his hand. 'Aye, child. I know that too and I shall not burden you further by asking you to name them. I dare say they will tell me themselves, when they think the time is ready. Go now,' he said. 'And thank you for telling me.'

Again he went and stared out over the quiet landscape. His thoughts were calm, precise, orderly, compact. Only one thing disturbed him and filled him with doubt. Where in heaven's name was John?

He did not deign even to arm himself, not against ragged vermin and scum. And that, for the most part, is what they were; beggars and thieves, filth dragged from the gutters of York. There were a few honest and simple men with them, labourers and 'prentices, men inflamed by grievance and mob hysteria; men who, if they

324

had stood alone, would not have dared to raise their eyes to his face, let alone stand against him in arms.

He came down into the hall, freshly shaven and attired in black velvet and diamonds, as if he went out to meet the King himself, instead of a ragged mob.

'My lord.' His chaplain, William Rowkshaw, followed hard on his heels. 'This is folly, sheer folly. I beg you, reconsider, my lord. There is no need even to meet them. They will soon disperse, left to their own devices. They are a wild unruly crew. They will not hang together for long.'

'My lord.' Will Eure caught at his arm. 'I mislike this whole thing. It stinks of something not quite right.'

'I smell it too,' Harry answered mildly. 'But I fancy the stink comes from within these walls rather than without.'

He strode out into the courtyard where his men waited. He paused, eying their faces with gleeful malice. One or two he marked especially: his brother-in-law Gascoigne, looking as if he had swallowed a stone; and Robert Plumpton, returning his look with such smiling innocence that even his cynical heart was appalled.

He rode in the lead, a dozen of his household close at his back, and saw how the rest lagged behind. He could see the mob now, not so many as he had thought, a hundred yelling undisciplined men beneath a tattered crudely-daubed banner.

He halted at a distance of about a hundred yards. One of the few mounted men came forward to meet him. It was the King's forester, John a Chambre.

'Have you come to parley, my lord?' he shouted, grinning.

'No.' Harry eyed him with open contempt. 'I have come to tell you to disperse and go back peaceably the way you came.' He added softly, 'I do not parley with rabble.'

'Oh no, my lord. You think yourself too high and mighty for that, but what are you but King Henry's tallyman?'

'And you are naught but a false and scurvy knave and men that listen to you hearken to dangerous counsel.'

Suddenly Chambre wheeled his horse. 'You hear that, my friends?' he yelled at the mob. 'He calls us rabble, scum, false and scurvy knaves. Is it the King who is our oppressor or

325

Northumberland himself? It is only from him that I hear these slanders.'

He rode towards the enraged press of men. 'Rabble, are we? False and scurvy knaves? Come, my friends. What shall we give him for answer?'

Suddenly the mob surged forward, yelling, screaming, lashing out with clubs and staves. Harry's horse reared. A man fell, his head crushed to a pulp by the flailing hooves. Like dogs turned vicious at the smell of blood they surrounded him. He breathed in the stench of their filthy bodies, the foulness of sweat and urine. He drew his sword and laid about him, fighting with a joy and abandon he had never known. From the corner of his eye, he saw his men ride into the fray. But not all: Plumpton, Gascoigne, even Will Eure, sat their horses and did nothing.

He would have laughed if he'd had the breath. He could see the perfect irony of it. They stood off from him as he'd stood off from Richard. Even to him, it seemed right and just that he should suffer the same ignominious end. And this, he knew quite calmly, was the end. For all his wealth and power, for all his vast and princely household, he was to be butchered by a nameless rabble.

No. Not nameless, now he thought of it. There was a name that could be put to this. These men were the weapon that would bring him down, but the hand that wielded it was the King's. He should have known, he should have remembered. Had he not used the same devious means himself? Was it not thus he had vanquished Earl Warwick?

Suddenly he saw himself truly revealed in the actions of other men. He smiled grimly. Only fools and heroes spat into the wind. There was always retribution.

Then he was down, clawing at earth and blood. Painfully he raised himself, dragging himself up on the housings of his mount. He felt a steadying hand at his elbow and looked up into eyes of vivid and unmistakeable blue. His smile grew weary. John, his fate, his Nemesis.

Tears filled his own eyes, like blood pricked from the very depths of his soul. He felt the cold plunge of the knife between his ribs, its sharp point piercing his heart.

Then he was falling. Cold damp earth pillowed his cheek. He

326

strained blindly to see but there was only darkness and a dull roaring in his ears. Then quite clearly he saw him, a bright steady light advancing through the gloom.

He flung out a hand and felt it firmly and lovingly grasped. 'Richard,' he whispered. 'Richard, my lord.'

The king ran a long ridged fingernail down the roll of accounts. With raised brows he read:

> For the Earl's interrment in the Minster of Beverley, £200
> For meat and drink, £266 13s 4d
> For thirty priests, at 12d each, 36s
> For 13,340 poor men who visited the grave a
> dole of twopence . . .

Pursing his lips, he calculated the staggering cost. Over a thousand pounds, almost as much as had been spent on his own crowning.

Thoughtfully he laid the roll aside. These men of the north were indeed a strange breed, to murder him like a villain, then bury him like a king.

He turned his head. The poet Skelton knelt and offered a parchment. The King nodded. Yes, let it be read. The world should see how he mourned Northumberland.

> *I wail, I weep, I sob, I sigh full sore,*
> *The deadly fate, the doleful destiny*
> *Of him that is gone, alas! without restore,*
> *Of the blood royal descended nobly;*
> *Whose lordship doubtless was slain lamentably,*
> *Through treason against him compassed and wrought;*
> *True to his Prince, in word, deed and thought.*

Henry sighed and drew fresh parchment toward him. Skelton's elegy promised to be lengthy and there was still the matter of the treaty with Spain . . .

By the fifth verse, he was resolved that an alliance with Spain was all his heart's desire; a marriage perhaps with the Infanta Catherine? His fair Bessy had already given him a sweet son, named Arthur in fulfilment of the prophecy. He glanced up at the dragon banners, that swung softly above his head. The first stone in the foundation of his dynasty was laid. Destiny was appeased.

At the sixth verse he looked up, smiling faintly:

> *But there was false packing, else I am beguiled:*
> *Howbeit the matter was evident and plain.*
> *For if they had occupied their spear and their shield,*
> *This noble man doubtless had not been slain,*
> *But men say they were linked with a double chain,*
> *And held with the commons under a cloak,*
> *Which kindled the fire that made all this smoke.*

Henry's smile broadened into silent laughter. *Men said they were linked with a double chain.* Yes. He liked that. Ambiguous enough to extricate all but the blatantly guilty. He could afford a little complacency now, though all had nearly gone disastrously awry. He picked feverishly at a spot upon his chin. Chambre, the fool, had exceeded himself and roused the commons to such a pitch that in panic, after the slaying of Northumberland, they had attempted to take York by storm. Still, even that could be turned to good account. It should be given out that the insurgents were Yorkists and partisans of the Boar. Thus he would emerge blameless and without scathe and in truth what had he done but scatter the seed? It was other men who had caused it to grow. Furthermore, here he saw opportunity to swell his coffers. The citizens of York especially would feel his wrath. The cruel murder of his good and faithful servant should not go unpunished. In consequence, their taxes would be doubled instead of halved. His complacency increased, seeing the whole affair soon forgotten for none would dare to remember that Chambre had been the King's man. He frowned then, with genuine regret. A pity. He had fought manfully for him at Bosworth.

Grudgingly he gave his attention to Skelton's posturings. They had now reached the twenty-fourth verse.

> *Oh, young Lion, but tender yet of age,*
> *Grow and increase, remember thine estate,*
> *God help thee unto thy heritage,*

And give thee grace to be more fortunate,
Against rebellions arm to make debate,
And as the Lion which is the beast of Kings,
Unto thy subjects be courteous and benign.

Henry pursed his lips. He did not care for that so much. It endowed Northumberland's son almost with an air of regality. He assuaged his irritation with visions of the lucrative wardships and marriages that now fell to his use. Northumberland's son was a mere eleven-years-old. It would be ten years before he was fully of age. He smiled happily: ten years of manipulating his revenues, ten years of controlling his estates. He closed his eyes ecstatically, calculating the worth of all those rich lordships, those fee farms by the hundred, those manors by the score. And he would see to it that the boy was schooled in reverence and obedience, married into a family of the King's choice. His thin body quivered pleasurably. The north would not see the like of Northumberland again.

He opened his eyes, knowing by the soft and stealthy tread that Morton had entered the chamber.

Testily he waved Skelton away and when the poet protested that there were still seven verses yet to be heard, he fixed him with a cold, watery eye and said, 'It took only minutes to slay him, hours to bury him. Why so long, Master Skelton, to lay him to rest?'

He turned to the cardinal, waiting until he knew they were quite alone. 'What news then?' he asked, smiling.

'The best, Majesty.' Morton showed his yellow teeth in reply. 'The rising has been speedily put down by our good Surrey and the leaders executed with the full rigour of the law.'

The King licked his lips. 'Chambre?'

'Hung, Majesty, and his bowels ripped, as befits a rebel and a traitor.'

Henry winced. 'And the other?'

'Fled to Flanders, to the court of Burgundy. Let him earn his keep till the storm has died down. It will be useful to have our own viper in the Yorkist bosom.'

'And will he be content to bide betimes?' the King murmured. 'I had thought this Egremont an impatient young man.'

'Impatient, but sensible,' the cardinal replied. 'He knows that it will be some time before you can receive him openly into favour. Naturally, he will expect reward. Nothing, Majesty, that we cannot afford: a small manor or two from his dead kinsman's estates — Judas money, as it were, Your Majesty.'

Henry smiled mirthlessly. 'Most fitting, my lord cardinal, most fitting.'

Then he rose and went swiftly from the chamber, his costly mantle billowing at his back. In the outer room, the courtiers who waited bent like bright flowers before a chill wind. Meekly they followed in his wake, bishops and knights, sages and clerks, a bevy of praise-singers and poets, the inevitable scarlet-clad Yeomen.

He emerged into the sunlight and paused, squinting out over the shimmering city. It was a fair land, he thought, a rich land and he would make it richer, fairer, the envy of Christendom, of all the world. Distantly he heard the echo of an old man's voice.

'Brutus, beyond the setting of the sun, past the realms of Gaul, lies an island in the sea . . .'